THE
SHOW

Tilly Bagshawe is the internationally bestselling author of thirteen previous novels.

A single mother at seventeen, Tilly won a place at Cambridge University and took her baby daughter with her. Now married to an American and a mother of four, Tilly and her family divide their time between the bright lights of Los Angeles and the peace and tranquillity of a sleepy Cotswold village.

Before her first book, *Adored*, became an international smash hit, Tilly had a successful career in the City. Later, as a journalist, she contributed regularly to the *Sunday Times*, *Daily Mail* and *Evening Standard* before turning her hand to novels, following in the footsteps of her sister Louise. These days, whenever she's not writing or on a plane, Tilly's life mostly revolves around the school run, boy scouts and Peppa Pig.

To find out more about Tilly Bagshawe and her books, log on to www.tillybagshawe.co.uk

Also by Tilly Bagshawe

Adored
Showdown
Do Not Disturb
Flawless
Fame
Scandalous
Friends & Rivals

The Swell Valley Series
One Summer's Afternoon (Short Story)
One Christmas Morning (Short Story)
The Inheritance

Sidney Sheldon's Mistress of the Game
Sidney Sheldon's After the Darkness
Sidney Sheldon's Angel of the Dark
Sidney Sheldon's The Tides of Memory
Sidney Sheldon's Chasing Tomorrow

To find out more about Tilly Bagshawe and her books,
log on to www.tillybagshawe.co.uk

Tilly Bagshawe

THE
SHOW

HARPER

HarperCollins*Publishers*
The News Building
1 London Bridge Street,
London SE1 9GF

www.harpercollins.co.uk

A paperback original 2015

1

A catalogue record for this book
is available from the British Library

ISBN: 9780007523023

Set in Meridien by Palimpsest Book Production Limited,
Falkirk, Stirlingshire

Printed and bound in Great Britain by
Clays Ltd, St Ives plc

MIX
Paper from
responsible sources
FSC
www.fsc.org   **FSC™ C007454**

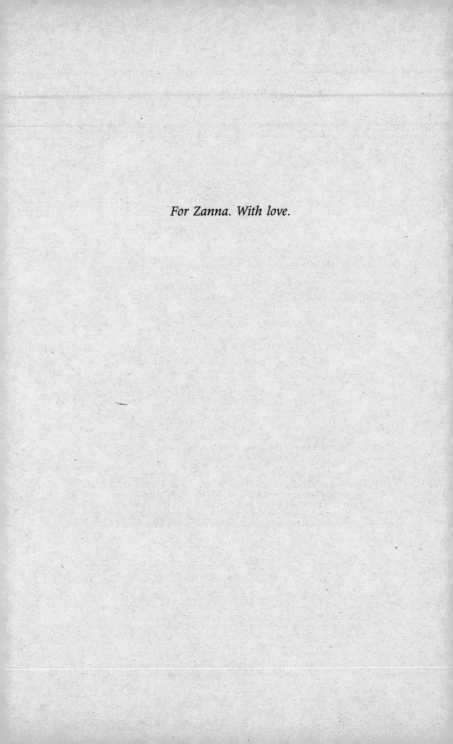

For Zanna. With love.

Acknowledgements

My thanks are due, as always, to everyone at HarperCollins for all their support, hard work and talent; and especially to my editorial team, Kimberley Young and Claire Palmer. *The Show* has been a huge team effort and I am immensely grateful for all your help, advice and input. There would be no book without you. Thanks also to my fabulous agents, Luke Janklow and Hellie Ogden, and to everyone at Janklow & Nesbit. And of course to my family, for their love and support, especially to my darling daughter Sefi and my husband Robin. It is ridiculous how much I love being your wife.

The Show is dedicated to my life-long friend Zanna Hooper. Zans, thank you for all your hospitality, generosity and kindness over all these years. I am so incredibly glad I met you.

TB. 2015.

Welcome to Swell Valley

The Cast of Characters

Wraggsbottom Farm

Laura Baxter née Tiverton a successful screenwriter and producer, wife to Gabe and mum to toddlers Hugh and Luca.

Gabe Baxter local Fittlescombe heart-throb. A family farmer with big ambitions.

Jennifer Lee young local vet with girl-next-door looks and a mischievous streak.

Brockhurst

Sir Edward Wellesley Eton educated 'Fast Eddie',
the most popular and charismatic MP ever
seen in Westminster, even after a stint at
Her Majesty's Pleasure for tax avoidance.

Lady Annabel Wellesley his beautiful but glacial wife.

Milo Wellesley their affable son. Booted out of Harrow,
and devoted to charming the female population of
Swell Valley, rather than acquiring any A-levels.

Magda Bartosz the housekeeper at Riverside Hall,
the Wellesley's new home.

Wilf Eddie's beloved border terrier.

David Carlyle media mogul and owner of the UK's top
tabloid, the *Echo*. Arch nemesis of Eddie Wellesley.

Louise Carlyle his long-suffering wife.
They live in a carbuncular McMansion on the
edge of Hinton golf course that Louise adores.

Fittlescombe

Santiago de la Cruz preposterously handsome cricket star. Plays for England, Sussex and now Fittlescombe. Completely smitten with his wife, Penny.

Penny de la Cruz artist. Her first husband, Paul, left her for another man on their twentieth wedding anniversary. Lives at Woodside Hall.

Seb Harwich Penny's son from her first marriage. Seb loves cricket, beer and girls (in that order), and has graciously forgiven Santiago for playing for Brockhurst before he married Penny.

Emma Harwich Seb's sister. Fittlescombe's first home-grown supermodel and all-round diva.

Delilah Penny's frisky wire-haired dachshund.

Angela Cranley ex-wife of Brett, mother to Logan and Jason. Angela lives at Furlings, the former ancestral home of Tatiana Flint-Hamilton.

Max Bingley the headmaster at St Hilda's and Angela's long-term partner.

Brett Cranley millionaire Australian property developer.

Tatiana Flint-Hamilton wild-child heiress of Furlings turned international business phenomenon. Ex-wife of Jason Cranley, and now Brett's long-term partner, but everyone knows that Furlings is the real love of her life.

Gringo a portly basset hound of advanced years, with a voracious appetite for all life's pleasures.

Bill Clempson Fittlescombe's hapless new vicar.

London

James Craven Santiago's friend
and England's cricketing hero.

John Bingham Head of ITV Programming and
Laura's married ex-lover.

Charles & Sarah French Eddie's literary agent and
his journalist wife.

Kevin Unger Eddie Wellesley's political agent,
married to Lisa.

Los Angeles

Macy Johanssen stunningly beautiful and single-
mindedly ambitious American TV presenter.

Paul Meyer Macy's savvy agent.

Austin Jamet partner at a top LA law firm.

Downs

To Chichester

ombe

Post Office

Willow Cottage
Max Bingley

Street

River Swell

Wragsbottom Farm
Gabe & Laura
Baxter

Brockhurst Wood

Woodside Hall
Penny & Santiago
de la Cruz

Foxhole Lane
Pub

To Brockhurst

Riverside Hall
Sir Edward & Lady
Wellesley

Swell Valley

PART ONE

CHAPTER ONE

Gabe Baxter leaned over and whispered in his wife's ear.

'This is *awful*.'

'Shhhh,' Laura Baxter giggled.

'I can't shhh. I can't stand it,' said Gabe, running a hand through his thick blond hair. 'Do you think if I offered to pay for the whole roof, she'd stop singing?'

'Be *quiet*,' Laura hissed at him. 'You can't even pay for your beer, never mind the school roof. So you're just going to have to let it go!'

Gabe groaned. The Baxters were in the snug bar at The Fox on Fittlescombe Green, along with the rest of the village on this wet January evening, watching the talent show. Danny Jenner, The Fox's landlord and village gossip, had organized the event to raise funds for a new school roof. The current performer, Claire Leaman, a dumpy twelve-year-old girl with boss eyes and a wildly misplaced confidence in her own abilities, had spent the last three minutes belting out the *Frozen* theme tune as if she were on stage at the Oscars, tossing her hair about and warbling like an opera

3

singer on helium. After 'Mike Malloy's Marvellous Magic' (a single, lame handkerchief trick) and Juggling Jack Willoughby, the half-blind church warden from Brockhurst, Gabe had dared to hope that they'd seen the worst of the night's performers. Apparently he was wrong.

'*HERE I stand! And HERE I'll staaaaa-aaaay!*' Claire screeched.

'She can bloody well stay on her own,' Gabe whispered back to Laura. 'I'm going out for a smoke.'

'Gabe. You can't.'

'Why not?'

'Because she's Gavin Leaman's daughter, for one thing.'

'All the more reason to get out of here,' Gabe said with feeling.

Gavin Leaman was one of a group of ramblers – 'The Swell Valley Right-to-Roamers' they called themselves – who had had the audacity to tramp through Gabe's orchard last weekend, and who had even wandered into his garden. Gabe had been enjoying *Match of the Day* in his living room when, as he put it, 'some sanctimonious cagouled muppet with an Ordnance Survey map' waved at him cheerfully, as if Gabe and Laura's land was some sort of public park. Gabe had marched outside to have words with the intruders, and had ended up getting into an unfortunate row with Fittlescombe's new vicar, Bill Clempson. It turned out the vicar was leading the charge on behalf of the ramblers, armed with a sensible padded nylon bum bag and a whistle.

'You put them up to this, didn't you, Vicar?' Gabe said accusingly.

Bill Clempson pursed his lips. 'I didn't put anyone up to anything. These people have a perfect right to ramble here.'

'First of all, they're not "rambling",' Gabe said with feeling. 'They're not fucking Wombles. They're trespassing.'

'There's no need to resort to bad language,' chided the vicar.

'If you'd taken the time to read the Countryside and Rights of Way Act 2000,' one of the walkers piped up, an overweight woman in much-too-tight breeches, whom Gabe recognized from his son's nursery, 'you would know that the British countryside belongs to all of us.'

Gabe stepped forward menacingly. 'Not this bit, sweetheart. You have precisely sixty seconds to get off my land or I'll set the dogs on you. You too, Bill.' Gabe growled at the vicar. *Fucking interloper.* Who did Clempson think he was?

This being Fittlescombe, exaggerated versions of this showdown were soon flying around the village, with Gabe Baxter either painted as the heroic defender of property rights (an Englishman's home is his castle, after all) or an elitist snob who begrudged ordinary villagers, and even the parish vicar, a harmless stroll through his fields.

Laura had tried to keep out of it as much as possible. Gabe was right, in her view, but as usual he'd lost his temper and been horribly rude to people that they ran into in the village every single day, which didn't help their cause, or make Laura's life any easier. Still, these sorts of spats were part of village life. Not the first time, Laura felt as if her life was morphing into one long episode of *The Archers.*

Claire Leaman, the rambler's daughter, was still caterwauling.

'Sorry,' said Gabe. 'That's it.' With a mortifying clattering of bar stools, Fittlescombe's best-looking farmer made his way noisily to the door, earning himself a furious look from Claire's father and envious ones from just about everybody else.

'I'm so sorry,' Laura whispered to her neighbours as she followed him, blushing furiously. 'He's got a migraine.'

'Haven't we all?' grumbled the old man near the door.

Outside, Laura found Gabe huddled beneath a willow tree, trying unsuccessfully to light a damp roll-up.

'That was rude,' she chastised him. 'Poor girl.'

'Poor girl?' Gabe's eyes widened. 'What about the rest of us? Good grief. She's got no more business singing in public than I have stripping naked and streaking through the House of Lords. Or going for a Sunday walk in somebody else's garden. It's just . . . wrong.'

He pulled an indignant face that made Laura burst out laughing.

'*You're* just wrong! Selfish arse.'

'I'm so wrong, I'm right.' Gabe grinned, lifting up an arm so that Laura could slip beneath it. 'Right?'

Even after nearly ten years of marriage, Laura Baxter found it almost impossible to be close to her husband without touching him. Leaning into his broad chest, she breathed in his familiar, musky smell. Gabe was so handsome, it was almost offensive – blond and brawny and with the sort of smile that could light up even a dreary, drizzly January night like this one. Laura had moved to the Swell Valley to be with him, despite a very rocky courtship, and they were now the parents of two small boys. The Baxters were often broke and always exhausted, but Laura wouldn't have traded their life for anything.

'Traitors.'

Santiago de la Cruz – cricket star, valley local and Gabe's close friend – slipped out a few moments later, nursing a glass of Laphroaig. Santiago was also gorgeous, although in

6

a very different way from Gabe. Tall, dark and quintessentially Latin, he was always perfectly groomed, a thoroughbred racehorse to Gabe's mud-splattered mustang.

'How could you leave me in there?' He rubbed the side of his head ruefully. 'I think my ears have started to melt.'

He was followed by his wife, Penny. Widely agreed to be both the kindest woman in Fittlescombe and the worst dressed, Penny de la Cruz was almost invisible tonight beneath about six layers of sweaters, her wild, Pre-Raphaelite hair spilling out at the top like a fountain. Penny, bravely, had been on the side of the ramblers in the great 'right-to-roam' debacle. Santiago felt strongly that they should all be shot.

'Honestly.' Penny looked at Gabe, Laura and Santiago disapprovingly. 'The three of you look like naughty school-children, smoking behind the bike sheds. Come back inside before you catch hypothermia.'

'Has she stopped?' Gabe asked.

'She's stopped.'

'Do you promise?'

'Yes,' said Penny. '*And* . . . I have gossip.'

That was all it took. Two minutes later the four of them were seated round a corner table, ignoring the next act while Penny spilled the beans.

'Riverside Hall at Brockhurst has finally sold,' she whispered importantly.

'That's it?' said Santiago. 'That's the gossip?'

'Nooooo.' Penny shushed him. 'The gossip is the new owners.'

She smiled cryptically.

'Well, go on then,' said Laura. 'Who is it?'

'Guess.'

'We can't *guess*. How are we supposed to guess?'

'Simon Cowell,' said Gabe.

Santiago gave him a look. '*Simon Cowell?* Why would Simon Cowell move to Brockhurst?'

Gabe shrugged. 'Why not? You did. All right then. Madonna.'

'Now you're just being ridiculous.'

'What? She loves the English countryside,' said Gabe. 'She wears flat caps and drinks pints, remember?'

'That was in her Guy Ritchie stage. Now she dates Brazilian teenagers and photographs her armpit hair,' Laura reminded him. 'Do keep up, darling.'

Never let it be said that she was behind on her celebrity gossip.

'I'll put you out of your misery,' said Penny. 'It's Sir Edward Wellesley.'

There was a stunned silence. Gabe broke it first.

'Isn't he in prison?'

'He gets out next week.'

'Blimey. That wasn't long. I might avoid my own taxes next year if that's all you get.'

'You have to have income to pay taxes,' Laura reminded him sweetly.

'Good point.' Gabe squeezed his wife's thigh.

'Are you sure about this?' Santiago asked Penny. For some reason he found it hard to imagine England's most notoriously flamboyant, disgraced politician settling down to the quiet life in the Swell Valley. Especially in Riverside Hall, a grand but isolated old building that had stood empty for well over a year.

'Positive. Angela Cranley saw Lady Wellesley with the estate agent last week. They completed ten days ago, apparently.'

'Isn't she supposed to be a nightmare?' Gabe asked. 'The wife?'

'God yes. She's a horror, a terrible snob. Do you remember how "Let them eat cake" she was at his trial?' said Santiago.

'I'm sure she was under immense pressure,' Penny said kindly. 'We must all give them a chance.'

Laura sipped her gin and tonic and felt a rush of pure happiness. She loved Penny and Santiago. She loved this pub, and village life, and the tight, gossipy world of the valley, a world where a new arrival with a scandalous past was 'big news'. But most of all she loved Gabe and their boys.

I'm so lucky, she thought, reaching for her husband's hand under the table. *Life really doesn't get any better than this.*

Sir Edward Wellesley looked around the room that had been his home for the last year. As odd as it sounded, he'd grown fond of it.

Pictures of his wife and son, Milo, hung on the walls, along with countless shots of his beloved border terrier, Wilf, and of Eddie himself, shaking hands with world leaders or speaking at the Tory Party conference. In the corner was a small desk where Eddie had spent many fruitful hours working on his memoirs.

It was a 'room' rather than a cell. Not like the awful hole he'd been shut up in for the first three months of his sentence at HMP Kennet. Some chippy pleb in the SFO had decided to make an example of the former Work and Pensions minister, packing Eddie off to the most overcrowded prison in Britain. It was a huge relief to be transferred to Farndale Open Prison, a rambling former stately home set deep in the Hampshire countryside. Compared to Kennet, it was the Ritz-Carlton. Eddie had gone from sharing a squalid cell with five men to sharing a comfortable room with one: a perfectly charming stockbroker named William Rees who'd been had up for insider trading. Will had been released a month ago. Since then Eddie had had the room to himself.

Not that Kennet was all bad. Eddie had made some good friends there too. The truth was, he made friends everywhere. Sir Edward Wellesley was an easy man to like.

In his early forties, with thick black hair greying slightly at the temples and a faint fan of laughter lines around his wickedly intelligent brown eyes, Eddie radiated charisma in a manner that had always drawn others in. Unashamedly posh, he somehow managed to carry off his Eton accent without making people want to punch him. Although not what one would call fit, exactly, at six foot four he carried his weight well, and projected a masculinity and youthful vigour not at all common in politicians. It was widely thought that Fast Eddie looked more like a handsome actor playing a minister than an actual minister. Women had always adored him and men admired him, perhaps because he never took anything too seriously, least of all himself.

'Ready, Eddie?'

Bob Squires, one of the prison officers, stuck his head around Eddie's door. A charming old boy in his sixties, Bob was a fanatical cricket buff. He and Eddie had bonded over their love of the game.

'Not quite,' said Eddie. 'I'm still packing up, I'm afraid. Never do today what you can leave till the absolute last minute, that's my motto.' He grinned, placing a neatly folded Turnbull & Asser shirt into his suitcase. 'Besides, chucking-out time's in an hour, isn't it?'

'It is.' Bob Squires held out an envelope awkwardly. 'I only stopped in early 'cause me and some of the boys wanted to give you this.'

Eddie opened it. Inside was a photograph of all the Farndale warders and staff, raising their glasses to the camera. On the back someone had written: 'Good Luck Eddie – We'll Miss You! – From all at Farndale'. Everyone had signed it.

'My goodness.' Eddie felt quite choked. 'That's terribly kind of you. I shall hang it up in my new house the moment I find a hammer.'

'I'm not sure I'd do that if I were you. You might not want to be reminded of . . . all this . . . once you're home.'

'Nonsense,' Eddie said robustly. 'It's been an experience! I shall hang it in pride of place in the downstairs loo. That's the only place one ever really *looks* at pictures.'

'Well, if I don't see you, I wish you all the best,' Bob said gruffly. 'And I hope you stick it to that bastard Carlyle.'

Eddie laughed. 'Thank you, Bob. I appreciate that.'

Zipping up his case, he took a last look around. Then he made a tour of Farndale's common room and cafeteria, saying his farewells to inmates and staff alike and promising to keep in touch. Eddie had learned a lot in prison, but the main lesson he had taken away had been that those inside Her Majesty's Prison walls were no different, intrinsically, from those outside. There, but for the grace of God, went all of us.

At ten fifteen, only a few minutes late, Eddie Wellesley walked out of Farndale to freedom. It wasn't exactly a Nelson Mandela moment – there weren't any gates to unlock for one thing – but it was still a strange and satisfying feeling. Last week's dreary weather had given way to crisp, bright blue winter skies. A glorious frost blanketed the Hampshire

11

countryside like glitter on a Christmas card. One couldn't help but feel hopeful and happy on a day like today.

Eddie recognized his old friend Mark Porter, the *Telegraph*'s political editor, amongst the scrum of press that had surrounded his car, a chauffeur-driven Bentley Mulsanne.

'Bit cold for you, isn't it, Mark?'

'I wouldn't have missed this for the world, Sir Edward. How do you feel?'

'Pretty good, thanks for asking,' Eddie beamed.

'Nice motor.' Luke Heaton from the BBC, a weaselly, chinless little leftie in Eddie's opinion, raised an eyebrow archly. 'It doesn't exactly scream "contrition", though, does it? Given that you were convicted of fraud whilst in high office, do you not feel such an ostentatious show of wealth might be considered in bad taste?'

Eddie's smile didn't waver. 'No.'

Eddie's driver, dressed in full livery, stepped forward to take his case.

'Ah, Haddon. Good to see you.'

'And you, sir. Welcome back.'

He opened the rear door and Eddie stepped inside. Scores of cameras flashed.

A girl from the *Daily Mail* called out from the crowd: 'What are you most looking forward to?'

'Seeing my dog,' Eddie answered without equivocation. 'And my wife, of course,' he added as an afterthought, to ripples of laughter.

'What about David Carlyle?' A lone voice Eddie couldn't place drifted across the melee. 'Do you have anything you'd like to say to him this morning?'

'Nothing that you can print,' Eddie said succinctly.

'Do you blame Carlyle for your incarceration?'

Eddie smiled, pulling the door closed behind him.

It wasn't until they reached open countryside, crossing the border from Hampshire into Sussex, that he started to relax. He was excited to see his wife again. Whatever outsiders might think about the Wellesley marriage, Eddie loved Annabel deeply. But it was an excitement tinged with nerves. He'd put his wife through hell. He knew that. Annabel loved their life at Westminster and the kudos she'd enjoyed as a senior minister's wife. When it had all come crashing down, she'd been devastated. It wasn't just Eddie's fall from grace and two-year sentence for tax evasion. It was the horrendous publicity of the trial, the humiliation of seeing Eddie's mistresses crawl out of the woodwork one by one, like so many maggots. David Carlyle and his newspaper, the *Echo*, had seen to it that every skeleton in Eddie's closet was dragged out and rattled loudly before the British public. Including Eddie's devastated wife.

They hadn't really talked about any of it during Annabel's prison visits. Not properly. Now they would have to. Despite having had a year and a half to work on his apology, Eddie still didn't fully know what he was going to say. 'Sorry' seemed so feeble. Annabel wasn't keen on feeble. He wanted to thank her for standing by him, but that just sounded patronizing.

As for the new house, their 'fresh start' far from London, Eddie had mixed feelings about it. It looked nice enough in the photos. But now that he was actually on his way there it felt surreal.

What if we're not happy there?

What if we hate living in the country?

Annabel had demanded a move, and he was hardly in a position to refuse her. But when she settled on the Swell

Valley, Eddie's heart had tightened. David Carlyle had a place there, a ghastly, overgrown Wimpey home on the edge of the golf course at Hinton. They wouldn't be close neighbours. But the thought of living within even a ten-mile radius of the man who had single-handedly wiped out his career and demolished his reputation did not fill Eddie with joy.

'Can't we try somewhere else?' he asked Annabel. 'The country's full of pretty villages.'

But it was no good. This was the house she wanted. The deal was done.

It's up to me to make us happy, he told himself firmly. *To make things up to her. The house will be fine. We will be fine.*

'Would you like to listen to the Test Match, sir?' The driver's voice drifted into the back seat. 'Coverage is on Five Live, if you're interested.'

'Haddon, that is an inspired suggestion.'

Eddie closed his eyes and sighed contentedly.

He was a free man in a free world, listening to the cricket.

Everything was going to be all right.

CHAPTER TWO

'Wilf! God help me, if you don't stop that racket this instant I will have you put down!'

Annabel Wellesley looked daggers at the scruffy border terrier with his snout pressed against the window halfway up the stairs. He'd been howling, interspersed with the occasional growl, for the last hour straight. Perhaps it was the presence of all the television crews at the end of the drive that had so discombobulated him. Or perhaps the little dog had a sixth sense and somehow *knew* that his master was coming home today. Either way, the constant noise was threatening to stretch Annabel's already strained nerves to breaking point.

She'd have liked to go out for a walk. To get some air and clear her head. But there was no way on earth she was going to run the gauntlet of all those vile reporters. Besides which, there was still such a vast amount to do in the house, to make things perfect for Eddie's arrival.

Moving in to Riverside Hall with no help, not even a cleaner, had been one of the most stressful experiences of

Annabel's life. A naturally gifted homemaker with a flair for interior design, Lady Wellesley was also a perfectionist and a woman who was used to delegating. In London, she and Eddie had had a full-time staff of three, including a cook and a butler, as well as a veritable fleet of 'dailies'. Here, once the awful, gawping removal men had driven away, she had nobody but herself to turn to. Every surface to be polished, crate to be unpacked and drawer to be filled, Annabel had polished, unpacked and filled herself. Part of her had welcomed the distraction. But another part resented – with every fibre of her tiny, perfectly honed body – being reduced to such menial tasks.

She could perfectly well have afforded servants. It was an issue of trust. After the humiliation, the *shame*, of Eddie's trial and incarceration, Annabel trusted nobody. Convinced people were laughing at her behind her back; or worse, that journalists posing as potential chefs or housemaids might weasel their way into the house under the pretext of coming to interview for the jobs, she had put off hiring anybody until Eddie was home and things were 'settled'. Whatever that might mean.

Walking into the drawing room – anything to get away from the bloody dog – she looked at the two remaining unpacked crates with despair. How was it that every time she unpacked one box another seemed to pop up out of thin air to demand her attention?

In reality, Annabel was being far too hard on herself. It was less than two months since she'd first seen the house. Back then it had been as cold and unwelcoming as a grave. As its name suggested, Riverside Hall sat right on the River Swell. Scenic and inviting in summer, after a long, wet winter the river was swollen, grey and ugly, a fat, wet snake encircling the house. Damp, or a sense of damp, had pervaded everything. The flagstone floors had been as cold as ice, and every window draped with cobwebs.

Today, the house looked like something out of *Homes & Gardens*. Understated antiques and Wellesley family heir-looms – mostly simple Jacobean oak pieces with the odd Georgian bow-fronted chest of drawers thrown in for good measure – combined effortlessly with classic modern designs like the B&B Italia sofa in pale pink linen or the upholstered coffee table from Designers Guild shaped like a slightly off-kilter kidney bean. Huge vases of flowers plonked everywhere gave the house a casual, inviting air. Annabel had made sure that all the chimneys had been swept and the fires lit, transforming the gloomy rooms she'd visited back in November into welcoming havens of warmth and light. Faded Persian carpets covered all the floors, and an old pine dresser full of cheerful mismatched crockery made the kitchen look as if the family had lived there for years.

But Annabel didn't see any of that. All she saw were the unpacked boxes. Combined with Wilf's incessant howling, the fact that she was effectively a prisoner in her own home, and her mounting nerves about facing Eddie again (what was she going to *say* when he walked in the door, for God's sake?), she felt close to tears.

The grandfather clock behind her struck twelve.

Noon. He'll be home soon, surely?

Grimly she cut open another crate of books and set to work.

*   *   *

Penny de la Cruz trudged across the sodden fields, her wellies squelching into the mud with every step. Today was dry and bright, a glorious change from the relentless rain of previous weeks. But the once-green pastures between Woodside Hall – Penny's idyllic medieval manor on the outskirts of the village – and Riverside Hall remained a slick, brown quagmire.

Not that Penny minded. It was lovely to be outside, although she felt guilty and strange going for a walk without the dog. Delilah, the de la Cruzes' wire-haired dachshund bitch, had given her a thoroughly reproachful look as she set off with a basket of home-baked goodies under her arm, a welcome present for the Wellesleys. Everybody knew that Delilah was the naughtiest, randiest dog in Brockhurst. If Sir Eddie and Lady Wellesey had a dog, she would be bound to start dry-humping it embarrassingly the minute she got in the door. Best to make this a solo mission.

Like everybody else in England, Penny knew the sordid tale of Fast Eddie Wellesley's fall from grace. Unlike everybody else, however, she didn't rush to judgement, either of Eddie or of his wife, a woman the British public loved to hate.

'She's so stuck up, she needs surgery,' Santiago commented over breakfast this morning.

'How can you say that?' Penny asked indignantly. 'You've never even met her!'

'I've seen her, though. On TV at Eddie's trial, looking down her nose at everyone. She's like Victoria Beckham, that one. She never smiles.'

'I'm sure she smiles as much as the next person,' said Penny. 'Just not at the press. After the way they treated her, can you blame her? Anyone would have thought it was her on trial, not him. And can you imagine, coming face to face with all his girlfriends?'

Santiago slathered marmalade on a third slice of toast. 'With a wife like that, I'm not surprised he played away. She looks about as much fun as a bag of nails.'

'Has it ever occurred to you that having a lying, philandering husband might not make a person feel full of the joys of spring?' Penny said crossly, clearing away Santiago's plate before he'd finished. 'Eddie's the one who behaved badly, but Lady Wellesley gets the blame. It's sexist and it's awful. I'm sure she's a lovely person.'

'You're a lovely person.' Grabbing his wife around the waist, Santiago pulled her down onto his lap, kissing her neck and deftly retrieving his plate of toast at the same time. 'You always see the good in everyone. It's one of the many things I adore about you.'

Penny smiled to herself as Riverside Hall loomed into view, thinking for the millionth time how ridiculously gorgeous her husband was and how lucky she was to be married to him. Women half her age and with much flatter stomachs and perkier boobs still fell over themselves to try to get Santiago into bed. But for some unfathomable reason, he wasn't interested. *He loves me.* Idly she wondered whether Fast Eddie Wellesley loved *his* wife, and what had really gone on in that marriage. *Perhaps we'll all become friends and I'll find out?* The Swell Valley was a small community. It was hard to imagine a family as high profile as the Wellesleys not becoming an integral part of it.

Seeing the scrum of press gathered around the gates, Penny slipped down to the river. Hopping across the stepping stones at the back of the house, she found it easy enough to worm her way through the thinning hedge and emerge into the kitchen garden. She knocked cheerfully on the back door.

'Hello? Anybody home?'

When there was no answer she tried the latch. It was open. Stepping into the kitchen, she immediately felt a pang of envy. The room was gorgeous, bright and colourful and *tidy*, with pretty cushions and china scattered around in that effortless way that Penny herself could never quite get right at Woodside. A real fire crackled in a wood-burner in the corner. Everything smelled of something amazing. Cloves or cinnamon or . . . something.

'Who the *hell* are you?'

Lady Wellesley had appeared in the doorway with a face like fury. In a black polo-neck sweater and chic cigarette trousers, with her blonde hair pulled back in a severe bun, she looked elegant, thin and utterly terrifying.

'I'm so sorry to startle you.' Penny proffered her basket of biscuits and cakes nervously, like a peace offering. 'I'm Penny.'

'You're trespassing.'

'Oh, no no no.' Penny blushed. 'My husband, Santiago, and I live over at Woodside Hall. We're your neighbours.'

Clearly this explanation did nothing to ease Lady Wellesley's fury.

'The door was open,' Penny continued sheepishly. 'I didn't want to come round the front in case those reporters . . . I brought you some goodies. A sort of "Welcome to Brockhurst".'

'You came to snoop, more like,' Annabel said rudely. 'Report back to the village gossips. Or to the press, I dare say.'

Penny looked horrified. 'I would never do that! I just thought . . .'

The words trailed off lamely. Looking down at her boots, she realized belatedly that she'd made a line of muddy footprints all over the beautiful flagstone floor.

'I'm so sorry.'

'You should be. We moved here for a bit of privacy. Walking into someone's property uninvited! It's outrageous. I've a good mind to call the police.'

'Please don't.' Penny sounded close to tears. 'I truly didn't mean . . . I'll go.'

She turned and fled, slamming the kitchen door shut with a clatter behind her.

A momentary frown flickered across Max Bingley's face as Angela Cranley handed him a magazine.

'*Hello!*? Really, darling. Must you?'

'I'm afraid I must.' Angela smiled sweetly as Max slipped the offending gossip rag underneath his armful of newspapers. 'Man cannot live by the *Financial Times* alone. Or, at least, woman can't. Don't you agree, Mrs Preedy?'

'I do indeed.' The proprietress of Fittlescombe Village Stores smiled broadly. Partly because she liked Mrs Cranley – everybody liked Mrs Cranley, and Max Bingley, headmaster of the village school and Mrs C's husband in all but name. And partly because today had been quite marvellous for business. What with the sun coming out, and the disgraced Eddie Wellesley on his way home from prison to his new house in Brockhurst, it seemed the entire Swell Valley had made a collective decision to go forth and gossip. Everybody knew that the Preedys' store was the epicentre of Swell Valley gossip. And so here they came, buying their papers and magazines and Bounty bars and home-made coffee and walnut cakes while they were about it. 'That'll be seven pounds and eight pence in total, please, Mr Bingley.'

Max handed over a twenty. At the back of the store there was an almighty crash as a shelf-ful of baked-bean cans clattered onto the floor.

'For fuck's sake!' Gabe Baxter's voice rose above the din. 'Hugh! How many times have I told you to look where you're going?'

Max and Angela walked over to where a frazzled Gabe had started picking up the mess. Next to him a dirty-faced toddler babbled happily in his stroller, while his four-year-old brother clutched a die-cast Thomas the Tank Engine toy and surveyed the chaos he had created in a nonchalant manner.

'I did look where I was going,' said the four-year-old. 'I was going over there.' He pointed to the sweetie aisle. 'The cans were in the way.'

'Yes, but you can't just knock them over, Hugh.' Gabe sounded exasperated.

The little boy sighed and said sweetly, 'For fuck's sake.'

Angela giggled. 'Hello Gabe.'

He looked up at her ruefully. 'Tell your husband he's not allowed to exclude children from St Hilda's just because they've got bloody awful language.'

'If I did that we'd have no kids left,' Max grinned. 'They've all got mouths like French truck drivers.'

'I blame the mothers,' said Gabe.

'Where *is* Laura?' asked Angela, deftly removing a glass bottle of Coca-Cola from Hugh's greasy little hands and placing it out of reach.

'Working.' Gabe put the last of the tins back and stood up. 'Unfortunately we need the money, but I'm going out of my mind with these two.' He looked at his sons with a mixture of affection and despair. Changing the subject, he asked Angela, 'Has he arrived yet, then?'

'Fast Eddie, you mean?'

'Who else?'

Max Bingley looked disapproving. 'Honestly, listen to yourselves. Like a couple of gossiping fishwives.'

'Not yet,' Angela told Gabe, ignoring her other half. 'Apparently there are scores of reporters lying in wait for him. They're practically lining the High Street at Brockhurst. It's like the royal wedding.'

The shop door burst open and Penny de la Cruz walked in, looking like she'd been dragged through a hedge backwards. Her hair swirled behind her in one giant, windswept tangle, her gypsy skirt was more mud splatters than fabric and her various layers of mismatched cardigans hung off her slim frame at a dizzying array of angles. She was also out of breath, and had clearly been running, quite some distance and for quite some time.

'Are you all right?' Angela Cranley looked concerned. 'Has something happened?'

'No. Not really,' Penny panted. 'I've just made a fool of myself, that's all. Not for the first time.'

Slowly, she recounted her earlier excruciating encounter with Annabel Wellesley.

'I should have gone straight home I suppose,' she said, pulling a chilled bottle of fresh-pressed apple juice out of Mrs Preedy's fridge and swigging from it thirstily. 'But I couldn't face Santiago's smugness. He warned me not to go over there. He thinks Lady Wellesley's a bit of a harridan.'

23

'She sounds worse than that,' said Gabe, furiously. Being mean to Penny was like kicking a puppy. Totally unacceptable. 'She sounds like a complete bitch.'

'Colm-peat bitch,' Hugh repeated emphatically.

'Sorry,' Gabe shrugged. 'I'm starting to think he was fathered by a parrot.'

'I wouldn't say that,' said Penny. 'I surprised her. And she must be so stressed out, with those vultures circling at the end of her drive. You can't blame her for being distrustful of outsiders.'

'No, you can't,' agreed Max. 'Although it sounds like she was awfully rude to you.'

'Someone should send her to the new vicar to confess her sins,' said Gabe.

Dragging his boys up to the counter he began unloading his basket: another TV dinner for tonight, four cans of lager and a packet of chicken nuggets for the kids. Laura was many things: loving mother, sex goddess and, recently, since going back to work in television, breadwinner. But Nigella Lawson she wasn't.

'Call-me-Bill's door is always open,' he added with a grin.

The new vicar of St Hilda's, the Reverend Clempson, had already become the butt of numerous jokes down at The Fox, even before the Great Ramblers' Showdown. In his mid-twenties, with a boyish face and an unfortunately earnest manner, Reverend Clempson had been transferred to the Swell Valley from a trendy North London parish. His invitation to the largely elderly, dyed-in-the-wool-conservative population of Fittlescombe to 'Call me Bill' had gone down like the proverbial turd in a swimming pool. Used to the equally elderly, equally conservative

Reverend Slaughter, many in the congregation were still getting over the shock of a new vicar who voted Labour, openly supported gay marriage, and wore T-shirts around the vicarage emblazoned with slogans, reportedly including the unforgivable: 'I roll with God' next to a picture of a suspicious-looking leaf. Call-me-Bill's arrival, and subsequent set-to at Wraggsbottom Farm, had been *the* talk of the valley, until the Wellesleys came along and trumped him.

'Why don't you come back to Furlings for tea?' Angela offered Penny. 'No offence but you do look a bit of a fright. Something hot and sweet would do you good.'

'Thanks,' said Penny. 'I'd love to.' She turned to say goodbye to Gabe but he was already wrestling his children out of the door, his shopping jutting out precariously from underneath Luca's stroller.

Max, Angela and Penny followed him towards the exit. Mrs Preedy called after them: 'Mrs de la Cruz? That'll be one pound sixty for the apple juice. I expect you forgot to pay in all the excitement.'

'I'm so sorry!' Penny blushed again, scrambling in her purse for the change.

'All the excitement, indeed,' muttered Max Bingley. 'A libidinous old tax dodger just moves in down the road. Does anybody really care?'

Sadly, he already knew the answer to that.

'This is a bloody joke. D'you think he's done a bunk and 'opped on a plane to the Seychelles with one of his mistresses?'

Harry Trent rubbed his hands together to keep out the cold. A veteran from the *Sun*, Harry had been shivering at the bottom of Riverside Hall drive since eight o'clock this morning. His back ached, he was starving, and if Fast Eddie didn't put in an appearance soon, he was going to miss the start of the Arsenal game.

'I doubt it.' Sasha McNally from Sky News was equally fed up with the long wait. 'He wants to get back into politics, apparently, so I'm sure he'll be on his best behaviour. They probably got a flat tyre or something. Shit!' She grabbed her microphone. 'Here he comes!'

A black BMW with darkened windows approached the gates at a stately pace.

'Wasn't he picked up in a Bentley?' Harry asked.

'Told you. Flat tyre,' said Sasha. 'If he had to change motors, that explains the delay.'

The gates swung inwards. As the car drove forward, the press pack surged behind it, like a swarm of bees around its queen, shouting questions before the door had even opened.

'Sir Edward!'

'Eddie!'

'How does it feel to be back?'

Then the door opened. A boy of about seventeen stepped out, smiling broadly.

'All this fuss for me?' he asked, pulling a suitcase out of the boot. 'I'm honoured, but it's really not necessary.'

With his mop of blond hair and piercing blue eyes, Milo Wellesley looked a lot more like his mother than his father. But the cheeky smile and easy confident manner were Eddie to a T.

Milo zeroed in on Sasha. She was old, thirty at least, but she had a pretty face and amazing knockers. 'You look freezing,' he said gallantly. 'Would you like to come inside and warm up? I'm sure Mummy would be happy to offer you a cup of tea.'

'Milo!' Annabel's voice rang out through the cold air like a bell. 'What are you *doing* here?'

It was the first time the front door had opened all day. Immediately the reporters surged forwards, their cameras *click-click-click*ing as they ran.

'Get inside! Now!'

Reluctantly, Milo turned away from Sasha.

'You don't happen to have a hundred quid on you, do you?' he asked his mother sheepishly. 'For the taxi? I seem to be a bit short.'

A ripple of laughter ran through the assembled press.

'Like father like son, eh?'

Mortified, Annabel darted back inside for her handbag, then came out to pay the driver. *Click, click, click.* In all the commotion, few people noticed Fast Eddie's Bentley pulling up behind them. By the time they'd turned their various cameras and boom mikes back round, their long-awaited quarry was already halfway up the steps to the front door.

'Hello, Milo.' Eddie clapped his son warmly on the back. 'I wasn't expecting you here. Shouldn't you be at school?'

'Oh, that. Sort of. I'll explain later.'

Milo slipped inside, leaving Annabel frozen on the door-step like an ice sculpture.

'Hello, darling. Sorry I'm late.'

Eddie leaned forward to kiss her. She hugged him stiffly, her arms opening and closing like a puppet's as the cameras clicked away. This was exactly what she hadn't wanted: a public reunion. She could cheerfully have strangled Milo.

Eddie turned to face the media while the chauffeur brought in his case.

'It's good to see you all and great to be home,' he announced. 'I'm looking forward to the next chapter in my life and to getting back to work.'

The questions came like bullets.

'What sort of work?'

'Are you planning a return to politics?'

'Has the prime minister been in touch?'

Eddie smiled graciously. 'I'm sure you'll understand this is a private family moment. All I want right now is a cup of tea with my wife. Thank you.'

Ushering Annabel inside, he closed the door behind them.

'I've missed you.' He pulled her to him.

Annabel said nothing.

'The house looks beautiful.'

'Thank you. Where have you been? I expected you hours ago.'

'Oh, we stopped off for lunch in Winchester,' Eddie said nonchalantly. 'You'll never guess who I ran into afterwards?'

Annabel wasn't in the mood for guessing games. She was still trying to get over the 'stopped for lunch' part.

'Charles French!' Eddie beamed, apparently oblivious to his wife's displeasure. 'You remember Charles, my literary agent? Anyway, I invited him and his wife for dinner.'

What little colour Annabel had left drained from her face. 'You invited him for dinner?'

'Yes.'

'Here? Tonight?'

'Yes.'

'Eddie, you've just got out of prison.'

28

'Exactly. So I thought it might be quite jolly to have some friends round. And we can talk about the book. You know, the prison memoirs.'

Annabel forced herself to count to five before speaking.

'You should have asked me, Eddie. I don't have a cook. I've nothing prepared.'

'Charles won't mind. As long as there's wine. Milo can go and pick us up something in Chichester.'

Annabel could barely speak.

'Milo!' Eddie yelled up the stairs. 'Make yourself useful and go and do the shopping for your mother. We're having guests for dinner tonight.'

Milo appeared on the landing. 'Great. Am I invited?'

'No. It's business. You can walk down to the pub for supper. Oh, and FYI, if you've been chucked out of Harrow it's the end of the line. I mean it. No more school fees. You can get a bloody job.'

'Oh, *Dad*.'

'Don't "Oh, Dad" me. I mean it. *Have* you been expelled?'

'Let's talk about it later.' Grabbing his mother's car keys and purse, Milo wisely slipped out of the door.

'We need food for four,' Eddie shouted after him. 'And when you get to the supermarket, ask them if they're hiring.'

'This is delicious.' Sarah French, Charles's journalist wife, took another bite of fish pie. 'And the house is spectacular. Truly, Lady Wellesley, you've done an amazing job.'

'Thank you,' Annabel said stiffly. Sarah was still waiting for a smile, or at least a 'Please, call me Annabel'. So far she'd received neither, but she wasn't giving up.

'It's terribly kind of you to have us over. Especially on

Eddie's first night back. If it were me I wouldn't dream of entertaining.'

'Yes, well. It was Eddie's idea.'

Clearly Annabel only bothered to turn on the charm for people whom she believed could help her and Eddie politically. *And I don't fit into that category*, thought Sarah. She was so rude, it was hard to feel sorry for her. And yet Sarah found that she did. How typically thoughtless and male of Eddie to invite people over, tonight of all nights, without running it past his wife first. No wonder Annabel was irritated. Was he was trying to avoid being left alone with her? Delaying the inevitable? Or was he simply such an innately social animal, he couldn't help himself?

'Let's talk book,' said Charles, helping himself to a third glass of Eddie's excellent claret and attempting to lighten the mood. 'Do you know what you're going for in terms of tone?'

'What do you mean?'

'Well, you could pitch it various ways. You could go more Jeffrey Archer. Or more Jonathan Aitken. Or there's always the Alan Clark approach.'

'Not Clark,' Eddie said firmly. 'The man was a fraud and a bastard.'

'Damned funny, though. His diaries sold like hot cakes.'

'I know. But he claimed to love his wife and regret his affairs, then wrote a book boasting about them. That's not my style.'

Sarah French watched Annabel's face for any flicker of emotion, but found none.

'On the other hand I couldn't do an Aitken.'

'Too pious?'

'Exactly. All very well if one finds God in prison. But I'm afraid I didn't.'

'What did you find?'

Eddie thought about it for a moment. 'Compassion, I suppose. Camaraderie. And ambition. Renewed ambition. I enjoyed Jeffrey Archer's prison diaries, but I want this to be my own voice. I want it to be the book that gets me back in government. Or at least back in the party fold.'

'Blimey,' Charles French spluttered. 'That might be a tall order.'

'It might be,' Eddie agreed. 'I made a lot of enemies in Westminster.'

'And Fleet Street,' Charles reminded him.

'One enemy in particular, as we all know,' Eddie said darkly. 'But I'm also foolish enough to believe that I still have a number of friends, in both those worlds. Voters aren't looking for perfection. They're looking for someone who can learn from their mistakes. I've learned from mine.'

Have you? thought Charles French. But he kept it to himself.

'Besides, returning to politics is what I want,' said Eddie. 'And one should always go after what one wants in life.'

'What about you, Lady Wellesley?' Sarah turned to Annabel, infuriated by Eddie's self-centredness. 'Do *you* want to go back to Westminster life? After everything that's happened?'

To Annabel's own surprise, her answer was unequivocal. 'Yes. I do.'

Sarah was amazed.

'*Why?*' she couldn't help asking. 'After people were so poisonous to you.'

'I think it's because people *were* so poisonous,' Annabel

31

said truthfully. 'David Carlyle and his cronies destroyed our lives. Not just Eddie's life, but mine too. He robbed us of something that was ours. I want it back. We both do.'

Eddie saw the glint of fire in his wife's eyes and felt a powerful rush of desire. All of a sudden he wished his guests would bugger off and leave them alone.

'So why the move out here?' Sarah asked.

'We needed a change,' said Annabel, her earlier cool-ness back. 'If Eddie does go back into politics, we'll need somewhere private to retreat to. Somewhere that's just for us. Besides, I wouldn't want to live in London full time. And in any case, it may not happen. It's still early days.'

'There you are, you see,' Eddie smiled at Sarah French. 'You heard it from the horse's mouth. That little pleb Carlyle may have won the battle. But the war isn't over yet. Not by a long chalk.'

That night, in bed, Eddie pressed himself against his wife, slipping his hand up underneath her starched cotton night-dress.

'Can't you take this off?' he whispered in her ear.

Annabel didn't quite know why, but suddenly she felt like crying.

'No, Eddie. I can't.'

'Are you angry?'

'No,' she lied. 'I'm tired.'

'I'm sorry, Annabel.'

The words hung in the air above the bed like a cloud of ash, the last, lingering remnant of the catastrophe that had befallen their marriage. A volcano had erupted two years ago, wiping out Eddie's career and the life he and

Annabel had built together. The cloud was all that was left of that life.

We'll build a new life, thought Eddie. *We've done it before and we'll do it again.*

'I love you.' His hand caressed her breast through the fabric of her nightgown.

Annabel closed her eyes and bit down on her lower lip. Part of her wanted him, wanted to turn round and kiss him and make love and make everything all right. But that would require forgiveness and she hadn't got there yet. Not completely anyway. Annabel had married Eddie when she was very young, barely out of her teens. She'd built her entire life around him. But in one, disastrous year she'd seen that whole life wiped out. It was like planting a forest, watching it grow, and then waking up one morning to find that the chainsaws had been in and it was all gone. People accused her of being a snob, and perhaps she was. It didn't occur to anybody that she was defensive and standoffish for a reason. That she'd begun wearing armour because she needed it. Because Eddie had dragged her into a war zone and left her to fend for herself.

'Things have to change, Eddie,' she said, removing his hand from her breast and clasping it in hers.

'I know, and they will. You heard Charles tonight. It's going to be a slow road back to politics, whatever happens with this book. And in the meantime we can focus on our new life here. This house, the Swell Valley. It's a new chapter for all of us.'

I hope so, thought Annabel. *I really hope so*. But if this was day one of their new life: deranged neighbours wandering into the kitchen, Eddie inviting agents for supper, Milo getting rusticated again and reporters slavering outside the door like a pack of wolves, she had her doubts. They hadn't even bumped into David Carlyle yet, but that was bound to happen. On a clear day you could see Hinton golf course from Riverside Hall's attic windows.

'Goodnight, Eddie.' She let go of his hand and rolled over.

Eddie kissed the back of her head tenderly.

'Goodnight, my darling. It's good to be home.'

CHAPTER THREE

Laura Baxter watched the raindrops shudder their way down the grimy train window as the 5.02 p.m. from Victoria hurtled through the Sussex countryside. For once she didn't feel tired. Ever since she'd gone back to work, she'd been operating in a permanent fog of exhaustion, what with Luca still waking in the night and the long commute, not to mention the poisonous politics of the TV world. But today, none of that mattered.

She'd had an idea for a show. A bloody brilliant idea, if she did say so herself. She could hardly wait to talk to Gabe about it.

Ironically, it was the argument with Bill Clempson and his merry band of ramblers that had inspired her, although the idea itself had come to her in the midst of a disastrous meeting at Television Centre this morning. *Sisters*, a dark comedy drama that Laura had been working on with an old friend from the Beeb, and which looked certain to be green-lit a few weeks ago, had suddenly been binned by the powers-that-be at ITV drama.

'But you loved the pilot,' Laura protested. 'Jim Rose said it was the most original thing he'd seen since *Sherlock*.'

'It's a great show,' the commissioning editor agreed. 'It's just not quite the tone we're looking for at the moment. You mustn't take these things so personally.'

The problem was, Laura strongly suspected it *was* personal. John Bingham, Laura's long-term lover before she met and married Gabe, was out to get her. John had been head of Drama at the BBC when Laura first met him – charismatic, powerful, charming and married; unhappily so, according to him. Laura was young, impressionable and madly in love. It wasn't until she got pregnant and John callously cut her off, crawling back to his wife and torching Laura's career for good measure, that the scales had fallen from her eyes.

It all felt like a lifetime ago now. After she lost John's baby, Laura had moved back to Fittlescombe and met Gabe; the rest was history. She hadn't given John Bingham a moment's thought in years. Until family finances had forced her to go back to work and she'd discovered that, in the interim, Bingham had risen to become one of the most powerful men in the whole of British television. Now at ITV, where he'd sent the drama ratings through the roof and was considered little short of a god, John Bingham could make or break the careers of writers and producers with a nod or shake of his balding head.

He'd actually got in touch with Laura when she first went back to work, inviting her to a swanky, intimate lunch at the Oxo Tower 'for old times' sake'. Laura had been shocked by how old he looked – how old he *was*. The fit, rugged fifty-year-old she remembered was now over sixty, with a pronounced paunch and saggy, bulldog jowls that quivered when he laughed. *How was I ever attracted to him?* she thought, as he boasted about his success, bemoaned his marriage and assured her how bad he felt about 'that business with the baby' and how glad he was that it was all 'water under the bridge'.

'Do let me know if I can help in any way with your career,' he purred, placing a hand on Laura's knee and squeezing as he paid the bill. 'I've always thought you had tremendous talent.'

'Thanks,' Laura said frostily, removing his hand with a shudder and getting up to leave. 'And thank you for lunch, but I doubt our paths will cross, John.'

She was wrong. They had crossed. Not in person. But behind the scenes and in the most toxic way imaginable. One by one, every series that Laura became involved with was cut off at the knees. Television is a gossipy world and it wasn't long before the word was out – having Laura Baxter attached to your project, as a writer or a producer, was the kiss of death. John Bingham was out to finish her.

She wouldn't have cared so much if it weren't for the fact that she and Gabe relied on her income. Wraggsbottom, Gabe's beloved farm, was doing better than many others and keeping its head above water. Just. But if they wanted to take the boys on holiday, or buy a car, or decent Christmas presents, or even *think* about private education when the children were older, Laura needed to earn. And, thanks to John Bingham, she was running out of options.

That's when it came to her. The idea. A way to get round John, to do something new and commercial and exciting, to keep control of her own destiny. And, maybe, if she played her cards right, to make a lot of money.

She glanced at her watch. *6.15 p.m.* They'd be at Fittlescombe Station by half past and she'd be home before seven.

Please let Gabe like the idea. Please please please.

'No way. Out of the question. We can't possibly.'

Gabe sloshed a generous slug of Gordon's into a glass, topped it up with half-flat tonic from the bottle in the fridge and handed it to Laura. Then he made one for himself and sat down beside her on the sofa. They were in the kitchen at Wraggsbottom Farm, surrounded by a sea of Lego, Thomas trains, plastic dinosaurs and other small-boy paraphernalia. Lianne, the world's worst cleaner, had apparently been in today and 'done' the kitchen. Plucking a half-chewed apple out from between the cushions on the sofa and dropping it into the bin, Gabe wondered what *exactly* it was that Lianne had done.

'Why can't we?' Laura asked.

'Because. It's our home,' said Gabe. 'I just put my neck on the chopping block with our neighbours defending that very point, if you remember.'

'Of course I remember,' said Laura. 'That's what gave me the idea. Village drama! It's already like a soap opera, living here. So why not capture that?'

'I just told you why.'

Laura sighed, frustrated. 'But it would still be our home, Gabe.'

'Not if it were invaded by cameras it wouldn't be. I don't want some spotty little sound technician seeing you wandering around in the buff.' He ran a hand up his wife's thigh and looked at her hopefully.

Laura laughed. 'I wouldn't *be* wandering around in the buff.'

'Well that's even worse then. I'm sorry, Laur, but it's an awful idea.'

'No it's not,' said Laura. 'It's brilliant. I am a genius and you're not listening properly.'

Gabe grinned. He loved her confidence, and the way she didn't just back down. Gabe Baxter needed a strong woman. In Laura, he'd found one.

'It wouldn't be about our home life. It's about the village. But it's more than just a local drama. The centre of the show would be the farm. The valley around us, the changing seasons, the rhythm of life here. It's about selling the rural dream – like River Cottage, but bigger and more glamorous and aspirational.'

'I don't know, Laura.' Gabe took another big swig of gin and ran a hand through his hair. He couldn't even spell 'aspirational' and wasn't sure what it meant. It sounded like something you might need to help you breathe. He was dog-tired after a long day on the farm, and then getting the kids to bed. All he wanted was to have sex and go to sleep. 'I thought you hated reality TV.'

'I do. But that's because most of it is tacky and crap and derivative. This won't be. Plus, beggars can't be choosers. I'm finished in scripted television. John's seen to that.'

Gabe sat down beside her and slipped a hand under her shirt, expertly unhooking her bra from behind.

'Screw him. He's just jealous because he let you go. You're mine now and it bloody kills him.'

Laura closed her eyes as Gabe started caressing her breasts and kissing her on the neck and shoulders.

'I *am* yours,' she sighed, running her hands through his hair and feeling ridiculously happy. Was it normal, after ten years of marriage, to still fancy your husband this much? Reluctantly she wriggled out from under him.

'We have to talk about this, Gabe.'

Gabe groaned. 'Do we?'

'You know we do. We can barely make our mortgage payments.'

Gabe looked defensive. 'We're doing all right. The farm's surviving.'

Laura squeezed his hand. 'I know it is. And I know how hard you work and I think it's amazing. But we want to do better than all right, don't we? We want the boys to have a good life and a wonderful education. We want to go out to dinner sometimes. You want that Ducati, don't you?'

Gabe laughed loudly. 'Now you're just bribing me! You wouldn't let me get a motorbike if we had a billion pounds in the bank!'

'That's true,' Laura admitted. 'Because I love you and I don't want you to get squashed by a lorry. But the point is, we don't want to live from hand to mouth for ever, do we? Yes, the farm's surviving. But if it's going to be Hugh and Luca's future, we need it to thrive.'

Her enthusiasm was infectious.

'I still think it's ridiculous,' Gabe said. But he could hear himself wavering. 'We'd be Fittlescombe's answer to the Kardashians.'

'We would not!'

'Except you'd have a smaller arse.'

'Not if you keep making me drinks like this one I wouldn't,' said Laura. 'Anyway, my arse won't be in it. I'm strictly behind the camera. I'd produce it and you can present.'

'Me?' Gabe's eyes widened.

'Why not?' said Laura. 'You're gorgeous; you know all there is to know about the farm and the valley. And you'd work for free.'

'Oh, would I now?' said Gabe.

'Yes,' Laura giggled. 'You would. We're going to need a lot of cash to get it made, so we'll have to work on a tight budget.'

'I see,' said Gabe. 'And where would this cash be coming from? Not our savings account, I hope.'

Laura almost choked on her gin. 'What savings account? Luca's got more in his piggy bank than we have!'

'We'll raid his then,' said Gabe.

'We have two options,' Laura explained. 'Either we sell a big chunk of the show up front to an established reality player – Endemol or someone like that – or we raise the capital to do it ourselves. Now the Endemol option—'

'Let's raise the capital,' Gabe interrupted her.

Laura looked up at him hopefully. 'Really? You'll do it?'

Gabe kissed her. 'I know a lost battle when I see one. And if we are going to do it, it has to be our show. It has to be us in control.'

Laura gave a little squeal of excitement. 'It's going to be amazing, Gabe. I can see the trailers already.'

'So can I.' Gabe put on what he obviously thought of as a television announcer's voice. 'Coming soon: *Wraggsbottom Farm*, with Gabriel Baxter.'

Laura burst out laughing.

Gabe looked hurt. 'What?'

'Well, for one thing, we can*not* call it Wraggsbottom Farm.'

'Why not?'

'Why not? Because it's an awful, awful name.'

'It's the name this farm has lived by for well over a hundred years,' Gabe said pompously.

'I'm sorry darling,' said Laura. 'But no. And I won't let you present it either if you're going to do that dreadful American newsreader voice.'

Gabe pouted. 'That was my sexy voice.'

'No, it wasn't. Trust me.'

They sat in silence for a while, wrapped in each other's arms, thinking about what the future might hold. Laura didn't know whether to feel delighted that she'd talked Gabe round, or terrified because, if they really went ahead with this, it would all be on her shoulders. If the show was a disaster, or – heaven forbid – the farm itself suffered as a result, she would never forgive herself. It *was* a great idea. But it was also a big risk.

'Raising money won't be easy, you know,' she said, swirling the remnants of her drink contemplatively around her glass. 'If we can't find investors, we'd have to team up with a bigger production company or a network. There'd be no other way.'

Gabe stood up, stretched and opened the larder. Pulling out a family-sized bag of Doritos, he burst them open with a loud bang.

'Don't be such a pessimist,' he said cheerfully. 'Of course we'll find an investor. You said yourself it was a great idea.'

Laura wasn't sure what frightened her more. Having Gabe against the idea or having him for it. In five minutes flat he'd gone from 'it can't possibly work' to 'it can't possibly fail'. Sometimes his black-and-white nature terrified her.

'Anyway, I've already thought of an investor,' he announced blithely. 'He's local, he's rich and he's looking for a new business venture. I know that for a fact 'cause I heard it down the pub.'

Laura looked sceptical. 'Who?'

'Eddie Wellesley.'

Laura choked so hard that tonic bubbles flew out of her nose.

'Fast Eddie?'

'Uh-huh.'

'What does he know about television?'

Gabe shrugged. 'He's been on it a fair bit. Anyway, it doesn't matter. *You* know about television. Wellesley just needs to write a cheque.'

Laura Baxter watched her husband stuffing crisps into his mouth and felt overwhelmed with love. *I'm so happy with him*, she thought.

For a moment she felt a flicker of anxiety at the prospect of the two of them working together. In the unlikely event that this show actually took off, would they end up getting on each other's nerves? But she pushed the thought aside. *We're doing this for our future. For the boys.*

Besides, these would all be good problems to have. What Laura needed now was a hit show and a way out of the trap John Bingham had laid for her. And what Gabe needed was a new roof for the big barn. Short of planting some magic beans and kidnapping a golden goose, this was the only way.

'D'you really think Eddie Wellesley might be interested?' she asked Gabe.

He answered through a mouthful of Doritos.

'Only one way to find out.'

Eddie leaned back in his red brocade armchair, an amused look on his face.

'So you want me to back you?'

Laura blushed scarlet. How had she let Gabe talk her into this?

She was sitting in the library at Riverside Hall, a stunning, oak-panelled room lined with gold-leafed hardbacks and beautifully preserved first editions that Laura was quite certain were never read. Fast Eddie was more attractive in the flesh than she'd expected. Perhaps it was the half-suppressed smile, or the playful twinkle in his eye, but there was something innately flirtatious and fun about him that somehow made Laura feel even more embarrassed.

'I'm so sorry, Sir Edward, I shouldn't have come.' She stood up. 'I'm afraid I've wasted your time.'

'First of all, it's Eddie. And second of all, please sit down. You haven't wasted my time at all. It's not often I have beautiful young women come to me with business propositions.'

Laura sat.

'Tell me more about the show,' said Eddie. 'I think it has to be about more than just farming life.'

'Oh, it would be,' Laura assured him. 'The Swell Valley is unique. I imagine you know that already, as you moved here. People have always been fascinated by this area, by the combination of the rural idyll and the celebrity residents. The scandals.' She avoided meeting his eye. 'Tatiana Flint-Hamilton, Brett Cranley, Emma Harwich, Santiago de la Cruz. They're all synonymous with the valley. So yes, we're showing farming life, but we're also trying to package what it is that makes this place so special. It's a nostalgic snapshot of England, if you like: what England used to be, what we all still wish it were.'

'Like a Richard Curtis film, but in a reality format,' Eddie mused.

Laura looked delighted. 'Exactly! That's it exactly.'

'All right,' said Eddie. 'So how would it work, if I were to fund this? What would I get for my investment? Talk me through the nuts and bolts.'

He listened intently as Laura explained the process of producing a television series. *She's bright*, he thought, *and ambitious. And sexy.* He noticed the way her dark hair continually fell forward over her face and her breasts rose and fell quickly beneath her silk shirt when she became animated. She had very little make-up on and was simply dressed in a grey woollen skirt and a cream blouse. Eddie was a fan of the effortless look.

After ten minutes of straight talking, Laura finally drew breath. 'So. What do you think?'

'I think it's intriguing,' said Eddie. 'I'll give it some thought and come back to you.'

He stood up and offered Laura his hand.

'Oh. Right. OK,' she stammered. 'Thanks.'

She hadn't expected such an abrupt end to the meeting, and wasn't quite sure how to handle it. She was still standing there like a lemon, her hand clasped in Eddie's, when his wife walked in carrying a tray of tea.

Lady Wellesley took in the scene – a beautiful young woman, her husband in flirt-mode – and shot Laura a look that could have melted stone.

Christ, Laura thought. *Penny wasn't kidding. She really is intimidating.*

'Ah, darling.' Releasing Laura, Eddie wrapped an arm around his wife's stiff, distrustful shoulders. 'How sweet of you to bring us tea. But Mrs Baxter was just leaving.'

'What a shame,' said Annabel, in a tone that clearly translated as *good riddance.*

'I'll see myself out,' Laura mumbled awkwardly.

Had the meeting gone well or badly? She couldn't tell. Driving home, she wondered whether going into business with a politician might be more trouble than it was worth, especially if his wife disapproved. When it came to poker faces, Eddie Wellesley was a master.

Two days passed. Then three. Then four.

By Friday morning, Laura's 'work-from-home' day, she and Gabe had still heard nothing from Eddie.

'It's dead in the water,' said Laura.

'You don't know that,' said Gabe, although privately he agreed. If Wellesley wanted in, he'd have called by now.

'I do,' Laura said. 'The wife put the kibosh on it. I'm sure she thought I was flirting with her husband.'

'And were you?' said Gabe, giving Laura's bottom a playful squeeze as she leaned over to pick up yet more Lego from the floor. Hugh had tried to build a rocket before nursery this morning, with mixed results. 'You career women will stop at nothing to get what you want. How many times have I told you your place is in the kitchen?'

'Er, no times?' said Laura. 'The last time I cooked for you, you said the lasagne tasted like burned plastic.'

Gabe grimaced. 'Oo, God yes, that lasagne. That was rough. Not the kitchen then. The bedroom.' He circled his arms around her waist. 'I hate you getting on that train to London.'

'So do I,' said Laura, with feeling. 'But unfortunately, unless we can get this show off the ground, we need the money. Now sod off and spread some slurry, or whatever glamorous job it is you have on today.'

Gabe went out into the fields, leaving Laura to finish cleaning up while Luca had his morning nap. She really must sack Lianne. The house was a pigsty. Then again, thought Laura, catching sight of herself in the hall mirror, I fit right in. Still in her dirty Snoopy pyjamas and a dressing gown that was more hole than cloth (too lazy to get dressed, she'd pulled wellies and a coat on over the top to drive Hugh to nursery earlier), her overall look was definitely more Waynetta Slob than Grace Kelly.

A loud banging at the door made her jump. What had Gabe forgotten this time?

'Be quiet, you arse, you'll wake the ba . . . Oh!' She opened the door to find Eddie Wellesley smiling at her. That same half-smile that had made her feel such an idiot in his library. 'It's you.'

Immaculately dressed in corduroy trousers and a royal-blue cashmere sweater, and smelling faintly of toothpaste and expensive cologne, Eddie looked like a creature from another planet. A rich planet. A planet that owned an iron.

'May I come in?'

Laura glanced back at the sea of mess behind her. 'Er . . . the house is a bit, er . . .'

'I don't care about the house,' Eddie said briskly, easing past her into the hallway. 'I'm here to talk about selling the "glamour" of the Swell Valley.' The half-smile had become a full smile now and was openly teasing.

'You're in?' Laura hardly dared believe it.

'I'm in. So long as we can agree a few quid pro quos, naturally.'

Five minutes later, still in her pyjamas but having managed to brush her hair and wash her face, Laura brought two mugs of coffee into the relatively clutter-free dining room.

Eddie cut to the chase.

'I'll stump up a hundred grand to get things started. There'll be more to come as we need it.'

'We will need it,' Laura said honestly.

'I know. Money's not going to be a problem.'

What a great sentence, thought Laura. *I wonder if Gabe and I will ever be able to say it.*

'I want an exec producer credit, fifty per cent ownership and a say in all business-related decisions, including how we pitch this and to whom.'

'Did you have somebody in mind?' Laura asked.

'Not "somebody" as such,' said Eddie. 'But I have some ideas. You know the UK market, so I'll take your advice on how to sell this here. But I want us to pitch in America as well. The whole "packaging of a lost England" thing. I liked that a lot. And I think the Yanks will lap it up.'

'I see.' Laura sipped her coffee. 'The thing is, the US networks—'

'Will need a US name attached. I know,' Eddie interrupted her. 'Which is why I want to fly out to Los Angeles next week and interview some possible co-presenters.'

'Next *week?*' Laura almost choked on her Nescafé.

'No point faffing about.'

'Eddie, I appreciate your enthusiasm, I really do. And I couldn't be more delighted you want to be involved. But we really have nothing to show people yet.'

'On the contrary. We have you. We have this place,' Eddie waved an arm around Wraggsbottom's beamed dining room. 'We have a treatment, and funding, and we have your handsome and charming husband to bring it all to life.'

'You haven't even met my husband!' Laura reminded him.

'If you married him, I'm sure he's marvellous,' Eddie purred. 'And, as you say, he knows this valley inside out. The problem is he has no experience on camera. If we're going to sell this series globally, we'll need someone who does.'

'Right,' said Laura.

'Ideally a woman.'

Talking to Fast Eddie was like being run over by a very enthusiastic steamroller. A steamroller that was conveniently made out of money.

'Can I ask you something?' Laura said.

'Of course.'

'Why are you doing this? I mean, you don't need the money. Television's not your business. And you barely know us.'

Eddie laughed. 'All true, my dear. All true. But I'm a big believer in gut instinct. I like you. I like your idea and I think it has legs. Eventually I hope to go back into politics, but for the time being I need a new challenge.'

'Well, this will certainly be that,' said Laura.

'Have you thought about local opposition? How do you want to handle that?' Eddie asked. 'You realize that for every villager who's excited by the idea of television cameras in the village stores, there'll be five who feel violated and think you're defacing their community.'

Laura shrugged breezily. 'Gabe and I can take a bit of stick.'

'It might be worse than that,' Eddie said seriously. 'If we go forward with this, we all need to be prepared for a fight.'

They finished their coffees and Eddie got up to go.

'I'll get my lawyer to draw something up,' he told Laura. 'In the meantime, why don't you see if you can whip up any interest this side of the pond. And I'll book my flights to California.'

After he left, Laura sat frozen at the dining table for a full minute, feeling not unlike Dorothy after the twister deposited her in Oz.

49

Did that conversation really just happen?
Are we really going to do this?
She laughed out loud.
Screw you, John Bingham.
I'm about to produce the next big thing in British television.

CHAPTER FOUR

'Champagne, sir?'

Eddie Wellesley had barely stepped over the threshold of Michael Hart's Neo-Palladian mansion when he was accosted by a preposterously handsome young man bearing a silver tray.

'Thank you.' Eddie sipped at the dainty crystal flute as he walked down the white marble hallway, feeling like an extra in a Roger Moore movie from the seventies. The famous producer's house was the last world in vulgarity: ridiculously huge, opulent, gold-plated, and so eye-wateringly naff Eddie doubted whether it could ever have been built in England. At home, even pop stars and footballers and reality stars drew the line somewhere. But not in Los Angeles. Here, there were no lines. Eddie rather liked it.

Even better than the house itself, with its fish tanks and cream silk carpets and solid gold taps and hideous portraits of the lady of the house in various states of undress, were Eddie's fellow guests. Michael Hart clearly had a type when it came to the fairer sex. Lithe, obviously underage girls who

51

looked like models but were probably prostitutes, mingled with older women whose faces and bodies had all been surgically re-created, to greater or lesser degrees. With the exception of the waiters, who all looked like actors, and the sports stars (nine foot tall to a man and black as the ace of spades), the men were all short, ugly, old and fat. *And rich*, Eddie presumed, judging by the seven-figure cars pulling up to the valet station, and the improbably proportioned women on their stumpy little arms. The whole affair could be filed under 'Jeremy Clarkson's wet dream'.

Despite the hordes of people, Macy Johanssen was easy to find. Of course, Eddie already knew what she looked like. He'd spent hour upon hour in the last two weeks watching some truly ghastly American television in search of the right presenter for the Swell Valley series. Macy Johanssen had fairly leaped off the screen.

Macy's agent, Paul Meyer, had put it perfectly when he telephoned Eddie at his hotel this afternoon to suggest he 'swing by' the Hart party.

'If Macy shows up at all, she'll be there to talk business. Look for the only woman surrounded by at least four powerful men and with all her clothes on. And if that doesn't work, look down.'

And there she was, a tiny figure in a black Calvin Klein trouser suit with a fitted tuxedo jacket, holding court amongst a gaggle of enraptured executives from Sony. Her dark hair was cut in her signature sleek bob, her porcelain skin flawless and her crystal-blue eyes sharp and intelligent.

'Excuse me.' Eddie effortlessly parted the throng, his cut-glass English accent slicing through the air like a silver monogrammed knife through butter. 'Miss Johanssen? I'm Sir Edward Wellesley. I wonder, might I have a word?'

Macy turned and glared at him.

'We'll leave you to it,' the fattest, loudest Sony man said, smiling at Macy as he led his compatriots away. There was something about Eddie's voice and manner that commanded authority, even here.

'No, no, please. There's no need,' Macy called after them. 'Sir Edward and I have nothing to dis—'

She broke off when she realized she was talking to four retreating backs. Turning furiously to Eddie she said, 'Thanks for nothing!'

'Oh, come now, don't be angry,' Eddie said smoothly. 'I'm sure they'll be back. Whereas I may not be.'

Macy refused to be mollified. 'Paul sent you here, didn't he?'

Eddie smiled. 'I wouldn't say that, exactly.'

'Really, I could strangle the man.' Macy did nothing to hide her exasperation. 'He's supposed to my agent. He's supposed to represent *me*. I told him quite categorically that I have no interest in presenting your show. None whatsoever.'

'A message that he also passed on to me, in no uncertain terms,' said Eddie. 'Drink?'

'So why are you here?' said Macy.

'Because I'm tenacious. Like you. Because I flew several thousand miles to meet you, Miss Johanssen, and have no intention of going home without achieving that end. And because I happen to know you're making a mistake.'

'Really?' Macy raised an eyebrow. She liked a confident man and Sir Edward Wellesley was certainly that. Attractive, too, in an older, *Downton Abbey* kind of a way. 'And how do you know that?'

'Because this show is going to be huge. Not just in the UK, but here, too, eventually. If we get the format right, we could all make a small fortune.'

'Could, could, could,' Macy yawned. 'I think I might go home. I'm pooped.'

'Nonsense,' said Eddie. To Macy's amazement, he took her hand and started leading her towards the door. 'You're not tired, you're bored. Come and have a drink with me at my hotel. Give me one hour to pitch this show to you.'

'An hour?' Macy laughed. 'A good pitch should take thirty seconds.'

'If you're not interested after that,' Eddie ignored her, 'you have my word of honour I will leave you alone and never tear you away from another boring studio executive ever again.'

For a split second, Macy hesitated. Then she thought: *You know what, he's right. I am bored.*

Sir Edward Wellesley was certainly the least boring thing that had happened to her today. On that basis . . .

'OK. One hour.'

Eddie was staying at The Miramar, on the beach in Santa Monica. He and Macy found a quiet corner by a log fire in The Bungalow, the Miramar's hip Moroccan bar, and ordered martinis.

After some small talk and a *lot* of alcohol, Eddie handed Macy his iPad. 'So, this is the valley.'

Images of rolling green hills, burbling streams and sun-dappled woodland flashed across the screen.

'And the village. And the farm.'

'Wow.' Macy looked genuinely enraptured. She was drunk enough to be buzzed, but not so drunk that she couldn't appreciate what she was seeing. 'It's gorgeous. All those little stone cottages. It's like the village from *Beauty and the Beast*.'

'Like a fairy tale, you mean?' said Eddie. 'Exactly. And

when you see it for yourself you'll realize the pictures don't do it justice. The Swell Valley is everything that Americans love about England – it's quaint and idyllic and old-fashioned; but it also has glamour, the kind of glamour that simply doesn't exist here.'

'Who's that?' Macy interrupted him. An extremely attractive blond man had suddenly popped up in the slide show.

'That's Gabriel Baxter. Your co-presenter. He's lived in the valley all his life and owns Wraggsbottom Farm. His wife, Laura, is the writer/producer.'

'They called their house "Wraggsbottom?"' Macy asked incredulously.

'It's an old name. They inherited it.'

'Can't they change it?'

Now Eddie looked incredulous. 'Of course not. It's part of local history. That's what I'm trying to get at. "Celebrity" has become such a cheapened commodity, Miss Johanssen. But class, history, aristocracy . . . those things still have cachet. It's why you Yanks can't get enough of "Duchess Kate", as you so charmingly call her. Because you have no home-grown equivalent. *That's* why this show is going to sell. But we need you to sell it.'

His enthusiasm was infectious. Combined with the lethally strong martini and the intoxicating images she was looking at – not just Gabriel Baxter, although he certainly didn't hurt. But swans gliding beneath weeping willows, stone footbridges that looked like they must be a thousand years old, exquisite, beamed farmhouses, like something out of *Hansel and Gretel*. Macy sighed. It was all such a long way from her world.

'Why me?'

'Because you have class too,' said Eddie. 'Uniquely amongst attractive, female American television presenters, in my opinion.'

'Thank you.' Macy looked up from the iPad. Her eyes met Eddie's and she felt an instant, familiar jolt of desire. He definitely had something.

'I'm not complimenting you,' Eddie insisted. 'I'm being honest. You'll appeal to a British audience, and you'll bridge the cultural gap for an American one. Paul told me you're concerned about getting out of the US market and I understand that. But we will sell this show in the States, Miss Johanssen. We will.'

He reached across the table and grabbed her hand. Macy found her fingers entwining with his, returning the pressure.

'You have a room here, right?'

For an instant, Eddie thought about Annabel, asleep in bed at Riverside Hall. But only for an instant.

He signalled to the waitress for the bill.

Back in Eddie's bungalow, Eddie locked the door behind them.

'Would you like another drink?'

'No, thank you. I think we've both had enough.' Reaching up on tiptoes to put her arms around his neck, Macy kissed him on the mouth. It was so long since Eddie had had a woman – since he'd come home from prison Annabel had barely let him touch her – that his dick sprang up like a jack-in-the-box.

Macy grinned. 'Wow. That was quick.'

'I'll try to slow it down,' Eddie murmured, slipping a warm hand beneath the waistband of her trousers and caressing her perfect bottom.

'Not on my account,' said Macy, who'd already started to unbutton his shirt. 'It's nice to be appreciated.'

She wriggled out of her clothes in seconds. Eddie scooped her up into his arms in her underwear and laid her on the bed. She was so tiny, it was like lifting a doll.

'Christ, you're lovely.' He bent down to kiss the tops of her breasts, rising like two freshly baked rolls beneath the pale grey lace of her bra. Moving downwards, he kissed the smooth, flat plain of her belly, then down again. Macy could feel the roughness of his stubble against her inner thighs and his warm breath between her legs. She reached down to take off her underwear but Eddie stopped her hand with his. 'Not yet.'

The next few minutes felt like hours to Macy as he teased and caressed her till she wanted to scream with pleasure and frustration. At some point he must have taken his clothes off. Macy ran her hands over his back and shoulders and butt, pleasantly surprised by what great shape he was in for a man of his age. As for his dick, it was perfectly proportioned and solid as a rock, the kind of erection that would make a nineteen-year-old proud.

'Do you still know what to do with that thing?' Macy teased him. 'I'm guessing it's been a while.'

'Let's find out, shall we?' said Eddie, ripping off her knickers at long last and launching into her like an Exocet missile. Macy had to grab on to the headboard to prevent herself from flying head-first through the wall.

They made love for hours. It was a long time since Macy had had such good sex. Her last boyfriend, Chris, had been a thoughtful and imaginative lover. But Eddie fucked like a starving man who'd just sat down at a banquet. It was intoxicating and empowering, and she devoured him back, happy to have found a partner with a libido to rival her own.

When they finally released each other and collapsed, sweating and exhausted, onto the bed, Macy reached down for her purse and pulled out a long plastic cylinder. For a moment Eddie panicked it was a phial full of drugs. But then she put it in her mouth and inhaled.

'What on *earth* is that?' asked Eddie, as the end of the tube flashed with a neon blue light.

'It's an e-cigarette,' said Macy. 'All the nicotine but no tar. The only thing hitting your lungs is water vapour. We call it "vaping". Wanna try?'

'No!'

'It's good.'

'I'll take your word for it.'

'Listen,' Eddie began. 'Tonight was amazing. Truly.'

'Thanks.'

'You're a completely incredible woman. But I'm married. If we do end up working together . . .'

Macy held up a hand to stop him, simultaneously smiling and exhaling a cloud of steam, like an amused dragon.

'You have nothing to worry about. I had a great time, but I don't do commitment and I'm not interested in a rerun. We couldn't top that anyway.'

'No,' Eddie grinned. 'I don't suppose we could.'

'But discretion works both ways,' Macy said seriously. 'I don't tell, you don't tell, nobody gets hurt. That means no boasting in the locker room, no drunken confessions.'

'Of course not,' said Eddie.

'You don't want your wife to know. And I don't want people to think I slept my way into this job. That's not what this was about.'

58

'Not in the least,' Eddie assured her. 'So does that mean you'll come on board? You'll do the show?'

'That depends,' said Macy. 'I want equity. You'll have to negotiate the package with Paul. But if the price is right . . . yeah. I'll do it. I think the idea has promise. And, you know. I like you.'

'I like you too,' said Eddie truthfully.

Macy fell asleep almost instantly. *She's like a man in lots of ways*, Eddie thought, although thankfully not in all.

Eddie lay awake for a long time staring at the ceiling, his mind racing. He waited to be hit by an onslaught of guilt, but it never came. The truth was he'd enjoyed tonight. More than that, in some primal, deep-rooted way, he'd needed it.

He would not be unfaithful again. What happened with Macy had been a one-off. It had happened far away, in another world, and his wife would never know about it.

Eddie loved Annabel. As soon as she started sleeping with him again, he would become a one-man woman, the loyal, loving husband she deserved. Tomorrow was another day.

By the time he woke up the next morning, Macy Johanssen had gone.

Still in bed, Eddie picked up the telephone and left a message for Laura Baxter.

'I've found her,' he said triumphantly. 'I've found our girl.'

Slipping out of Eddie's bed at 5 a.m., Macy only took twenty minutes to get to her house off Laurel Canyon. In the dawn light, with no traffic on the roads, Los Angeles looked strangely peaceful, slumbering softly in the shadow of the San Gabriel Mountains, beneath the gently swaying palms. Closing the electric wooden gates behind her, Macy walked into her kitchen, kicked off her shoes and exhaled, still buzzing from her night with Eddie.

Macy's house was her sanctuary. Like her it was small but perfectly formed, a light-filled haven with white wooden walls, simple antique furniture and a crisp yet feminine feel. Mismatched jugs full of peonies and roses and sweet williams crowded every available surface, and vintage linens on the bed and table gave the place warmth. But the overwhelming impression was one of tidiness and calm. Everything in its place and a place for everything; Macy was a big believer in order and control, perhaps because her childhood had been complete chaos.

After her father walked out when Macy was three, her mother had turned to drink. Macy learned early on to fend for herself. Her formative years were spent shuttling between her mom's house, during Karin Johanssen's intermittent periods of sobriety, and a string of different foster homes across the LA area. For the most part Macy's foster parents had been decent people. It wasn't as if she'd been abused or anything. But there was no stability, no order. And so Macy had made her own, working like a demon at school, eventually getting a place at Yale and putting herself through college with a string of loans, grants and scholarships, all of which she'd researched and applied for herself.

The biggest blow of Macy's life had come at the end of her first year in college, when her mom died suddenly of a heart attack aged forty-seven. Only four people came to the funeral in LA. Two from her mom's AA group, one neighbour, and one from the funeral home in Encino where Karin Johanssen had been laid to rest.

After finishing her degree – if TV didn't work out, at least she would have a first-class education to fall back on – Macy moved back to Los Angeles and begun pounding on doors. With her beauty, wit, charisma and brains she was a natural as a presenter, and agents were soon lining up to sign her. Macy chose Paul Meyer to represent her, because he was honest and didn't pull his punches. She was still only twenty-three when Paul landed her a primetime, network gig, fronting the gameshow *Grapevine* for ABC. It was a huge break for a relative unknown. But as Paul had warned her at the time, one hit show did not necessarily guarantee a lasting career.

When *Grapevine* came off air, Macy suddenly found herself jobless. She waited confidently for more network offers to pour in. But as the months passed, her confidence began to wane. When Paul suggested she take a meeting with Eddie Wellesley, Macy had shut him down cold. She wanted another primetime show like *Grapevine*, not some two-bit gig in England with no names attached.

'But that's the whole point,' Paul had told her. 'You would *be* the name attached. You have nothing currently shooting here, Macy. That is the reality.'

Macy had frowned. 'Yes, but *Grapevine* . . .'

'. . . is over. Your last presenting gig finished almost six months ago. You need this.'

Macy had begged to differ. But clearly Paul and Eddie had conspired not to take no for an answer. After the incredible night she'd just spent with Eddie, Macy figured she should be glad about that at least.

Now, sitting down at her desk, with its glorious views over the canyon, she turned on her Mac and checked her emails.

Nothing work related. One from her trainer. Five from Chris, the lovely but far too demanding boyfriend Macy had been forced to get rid of last month. Chris had been an experiment, a toe in the water to test how it might be in a 'real' relationship. It wasn't a success. From now on she was back to her comfort zone of one-night stands. Life was enough of a struggle taking care of oneself. She didn't need dependants.

Finally one email that made her jaw tense and her stomach lurch.

Sender: ljjohanssen@me.com

Again. The bastard really didn't give up.

Furiously, Macy deleted the message, unread.

Her 'father' – he didn't deserve the name, but Macy didn't know what else to call him – had first attempted to get in contact last year. Per Johanssen, the man who had heartlessly deserted Macy's mother and destroyed her life, who had never sent so much as a Christmas card to Macy growing up, or lifted a finger to help when social services had taken her from her mom. *That* man now wanted to get to know his daughter. Now she had become famous and wealthy, Per had apparently rediscovered his paternal gene.

Macy tried hard not to hate men. She might keep them at a distance, emotionally, but she loved male company, the male sense of humour, and she very much appreciated the joys of having an accomplished lover in her bed, on as regular a basis as possible. But just thinking about her father filled her with an anger and loathing so wild, so intense, she scared herself.

How *dare* he email her?

How *dare* he inject his poison into her life, her inbox, her home? Who the hell did he think he was?

She switched off the computer feeling as if she'd just been molested.

Screw it, she thought. *I will go to bloody England.*

She trusted Paul Meyer and she liked Eddie Wellesley. That was as good a start as any. And she needed to get away, from Chris, from the misery of being out of work in Hollywood, and most of all from her so-called father.

What do I have to lose?

CHAPTER FIVE

The Reverend Bill Clempson, Fittlescombe's new vicar, looked out through the double-glazed windows of his ugly modern bungalow at the gardens of what used to be the vicarage. The stately Victorian red-brick house, covered in wisteria and surrounded by glorious formal grounds, was now owned by an investment banker named Chipchase. The Church had sold it years ago to raise some cash.

Fair enough, thought Bill. The Old Vicarage *was* enormous, big enough for two or three families. As a single man, Bill Clempson would have rattled around in it like a pebble in a shoe. Still, there had been no need for the bungalow replacing it to be quite so hideous and soulless; it was unquestionably the ugliest structure in the entire village. Not even the Reverend Clempson's beloved red Mini Cooper, gleaming proudly outside like a newly polished snooker ball, could lend his grotty little home much cheer.

The bungalow did, however, afford marvellous views, not only of the vicarage gardens but of St Hilda's Church and Fittlescombe village green beyond. It was mid-May now, and the entire Swell Valley was a riot of blossoming fruit trees. The pretty front gardens of the cottages along the High Street overflowed with colour and scent, the hollyhocks and rose bushes and foxgloves and jasmine all heralding the close of spring and the imminent approach of summer.

It's such a stunning place, thought Bill. *So unspoiled.* Then he thought about this evening's parish meeting and his resolved hardened. It was his job to ensure that Fittlescombe remained unspoiled, and preserved for everyone to enjoy. This awful reality television show that Gabe and Laura Baxter were proposing to start filming must not be allowed to get off the ground.

Of course, there were those in the parish who questioned his motives. The verger, Nigel Dacre, had as good as accused him of opposing the television show solely because Gabe was behind it. Everybody knew that Gabriel Baxter and the Reverend Clempson didn't exactly see eye to eye. 'Rambler-Gate' was generally considered to be fifteen-love to Gabe. This was Bill's chance to even the score.

'It's not about point-scoring, Nigel,' the vicar insisted. 'It's about what's best for our community.'

'But you don't know anything about it,' the verger protested. 'None of us does yet.'

'I know enough,' said Bill.

The show was to be called *Valley Farm*, and had been commissioned by Channel 5 (never a good omen). It centred around Wraggsbottom Farm, but would also take an interest in 'village life', whatever that meant. Intrusion, most likely. As far as the vicar was concerned, that was more than enough. It must be stopped, at all costs.

Bill's predecessor, the Reverend Slaughter, had studiously avoided village politics. Beyond Sunday services,

Fittlescombe's former vicar had limited his pastoral work to visiting the sick, giving the occasional speech at primary school assemblies, and judging the cake competition at the annual village fete.

Perhaps, Bill thought, it was part of the Lord's plan that he, Bill Clempson, should have taken over the reins at Fittlescombe just as the threat of this television show became real? Half the village – the same half that thought Gabe an ogre for refusing to let his neighbours walk on his land – were up in arms about the idea of having a television crew permanently based there, poking their cameras and micro-phones in where they weren't wanted and turning the village into a glorified theme park. Bill would be their voice, their leader. He would shepherd his flock through the danger posed by Gabe Baxter's rampant selfishness. A Channel 5 film crew in the village didn't quite constitute the valley of death, perhaps, but one fought one's battles where one found them.

Walking away from the window, Bill looked at his watch. Five o'clock. The meeting would start at seven, in the village hall. Although it had not exactly been kept secret, neither the Baxters nor Eddie Wellesley had been informed or invited. The village needed a battle plan, and you could hardly hope to formulate that with your enemy in the seat next to you, dunking Hobnobs into his tea.

The hall was already packed when Santiago de la Cruz walked in. Despite having lived in the valley for years, the Sussex cricketing hero still turned female heads. His arrival tonight was especially exciting as he'd brought an extremely attractive blond friend with him. In jeans and open-necked shirts, and smelling of cologne, the two of them looked more like rock stars than locals as they made their way towards the front of the room, where Santiago's wife, Penny, was saving them seats. Only when the blond removed his sunglasses did people realize that it was James Craven, England's most talented and charismatic all-rounder since Botham.

'You're late,' Penny whispered crossly as they sat down. 'It's about to start.'

'That's not late,' Santiago whispered back, kissing her on the cheek. 'That's on time. You remember James?'

'Of course.' Penny smiled. 'I can't believe Santiago dragged you to a village meeting.'

'Nor can I,' James groaned, rubbing his eyes. 'I'm so hungover, my breath must be fifty per cent proof. If anybody lights a match in here, the whole place will go up like Waco.'

'But it's seven o'clock at night,' said Penny. 'You've had the whole day to recover.'

'You wouldn't say that if you'd seen what I put away last night. That's what heartbreak can do to you.'

Santiago rolled his eyes. 'Oh, please. Heartbreak? You barely knew her.'

'Of course I knew her.' James looked hurt.

'Oh yeah? What was her middle name?'

'Esmerelda.' James grinned.

'Exactly. So stop moaning,' said Santiago. 'Besides, you're buying a cottage here. That makes you a resident.'

'I *looked* at a cottage,' protested James. 'Because you made me. I didn't buy it.'

'Whatever,' Santiago waved a hand dismissively. 'You will buy it. And someone needs to stand up to this lynch mob. Look at them all, just sitting there waiting to rip the Baxters to shreds.'

'I hardly think that's fair . . .' Penny protested. 'They're concerned for the village.'

'They're ignorant busybodies, bitter because Gabe turfed them out of his garden. And why bloody shouldn't he?' said Santiago robustly. 'I think a TV show will be great for the village. Why not? It could mean investment and jobs. Most of them are just envious they didn't have the idea first.'

'Good evening everyone. Thank you all for coming.'

Reverend Clempson banged a gavel self-importantly on the little wooden table at the front of the room. With his thinning hair, reedy voice and twitchy, nervous manner, he reminded Santiago of a meerkat. And not in a cute way.

'As you know, filming is due to start on the pilot episode of *Valley Farm* in a matter of weeks. Tonight's meeting is an open forum to discuss our response. Hopefully, as a community, we can come up with some practical and positive suggestions.'

'I have a suggestion.' Santiago raised his hand. His deep, booming Latin voice rang out in gloriously sexy contrast to the reverend's wheedling whine. 'Why don't we give this thing a chance, support our neighbours and stop acting like a bunch of playground bullies?'

The room erupted. Bill Clempson banged his gavel repeatedly to no effect as furious villagers tore into Santiago and into one another in a thoroughly unedifying shouting match. Who did Santiago think he was, sticking up for his rich mates and accusing ordinary villagers of bullying?

'Wraggsbottom Farm must be worth four million as it is,' Kevin Jenner, the butcher, pointed out furiously. The Jenners were a well-known Fittlescombe family. Kevin's cousin Danny was the landlord at The Fox. 'And we all know Sir Eddie's rolling in dirty money. Why should those fat cats be allowed to make even more money by exploiting the village and ruining it for the rest of us?'

'Oh, so it's about money, is it? I see,' said Santiago. 'And here's the reverend telling everybody it's about protecting the natural beauty of Fittlescombe! Last time I read the Bible, envy was a deadly sin.'

'So's greed!' someone yelled back.

Penny flushed scarlet with embarrassment, watching her husband take on all-comers. Why couldn't Santi let Gabe Baxter fight his own battles?

James Craven pulled a bottle of ibuprofen tablets out of his inside jacket pocket and swallowed two grimly. 'Do you think it's going to get physical?' he whispered to Penny. 'If it does, I warn you, I'm off. I'm a terrible coward. They don't call me Craven for nothing. I leave all that macho bollocks to your husband.'

In the end, as so often with village tensions, it was Max Bingley, the headmaster, who calmed things down.

'Look, this is ridiculous. Angela and I aren't happy about this programme being made here either. And our objections have nothing to do with wealth or how much people's homes are worth.'

'I bet they're not,' muttered Kevin Jenner.

Angela Cranley, Max's long-term partner, owned Furlings, the local manor, by far and away the most spectacular house in the valley, if not the entire county.

'For us, it's about privacy. However, I don't believe it's right or fair to hold meetings like this one without allowing the Baxters and Sir Edward to put their side of the case.'

The vicar opened his mouth to speak, but Max ignored him.

'It may be possible to reach some sort of compromise.

But only if we all behave in an open and reasonable way, and engage the other side in dialogue. The reality is, legally there's little or nothing we can do. The programme is being shot on Gabriel Baxter's land, and on public streets. Beyond keeping the cameras out of our own homes and property . . .'

'May I say something?'

A loud, authoritative voice rang out from the back of the hall. Everybody turned to see who had spoken.

David Carlyle, editor of the *Echo* and Fast Eddie Wellesley's most outspoken enemy, stood with his back against the door. In an expensive but naff grey suit that was cut too tightly, solid gold cufflinks and a garish red silk tie, Carlyle looked every inch the rich and powerful man that he was. When he smiled, as he did now, his teeth flashed brilliant white, giving him a look that was part toothpaste commercial, part wolf.

'With respect to the last speaker, there's a *lot* we can do. As a concerned local resident, I don't want this valley being defaced any more than you do.'

'Shame you built that godawful eyesore of a "McMansion", then,' James whispered to Penny under his breath. 'Architectural services care of Barbie and Ken.'

Penny giggled. 'Don't be mean. His wife's really lovely.'

Carlyle was still talking.

'With the help of my newspaper, and a carefully orchestrated campaign to raise awareness of what's really going on here, a scandalous abuse of wealth and privilege, I believe we can put an end to this, quickly and finally. Now, it will take money. But I'm happy to foot the bill for any action you can all agree on. And I'll make sure you get coverage, not just locally but nationally.'

For the second time that evening, order disintegrated. Reverend Clempson's attempts to assert any authority over proceedings evaporated utterly in the face of David Carlyle's confidence, charisma and cheque book, as villagers thronged eagerly around their new champion.

'What do you think of him?' Penny de la Cruz asked Angela Cranley as both women prepared to leave. Clearly nothing concrete was going to be decided at tonight's meeting.

'David Carlyle? I don't know him,' said Angela. 'But I think he means business. He reminds me a bit of Brett. I wouldn't want him for an enemy, that's for sure.'

'He hates Eddie Wellesley,' said Santiago. 'How can these people be so stupid?' He looked at his neighbours, thronging around Carlyle like devoted fans around a famous footballer. 'Can't they see he's using them to further a personal vendetta?'

'The whole thing is stupid,' Max Bingley muttered under his breath. 'And it's getting quite out of hand.'

David Carlyle was also trying to leave, shaking the vicar warmly by the hand and talking to him intently as he made his excuses to the assembled villagers.

'Look at bloody Clempson,' Max Bingley spluttered. 'He's blushing like a teenage girl who's just been asked on her first date. Whatever happened to impartial moral leadership?'

Angela Cranley rolled her eyes. She loved Max, but he could sound so terribly *headmasterly* at times.

Santiago was tapping away on his phone as they all filed out.

'What are you doing?' Penny asked him.

'Texting Gabe. Someone has to warn him.'

'Warn him of what?'

'The lynch mob.'

'That's a bit melodramatic,' said Penny. 'He already knows people are angry about the show, and the vicar's trying to curry favour with the congregation. He only has to walk into Preedys' or down the High Street to realize that.'

'Yes, but this is different,' said Santiago. 'This isn't just a few disgruntled neighbours and a desperate-to-please vicar with a Che Guevara complex. This is one of the most powerful editors in Fleet Street. David Carlyle's out to finish Eddie Wellesley. Gabe and Laura are going to get caught in the crossfire.'

David Carlyle leaned back in the taupe leather seat of his new Aston Martin Rapide and pushed his foot down harder on the accelerator. He felt good. Powerful. In control. Tonight's meeting had gone well. His new car roared impressively, surging forward at the tap of his foot like a tethered lion straining at the leash as he weaved his way through the Downs towards Hinton. He would go home, report his triumph to Louise, his loyal wife of over twenty years, pour himself a glass of Oban single malt, and set about the serious but enjoyable business of pissing on Eddie Wellesley's latest pet project.

The feud between David Carlyle and Eddie Wellesley had begun years earlier, back when David had worked as the senior spin doctor for Tristram Hambly, the prime minister. Eddie had been part of a group of senior Tories who'd pressured Hambly to get rid of David. The reason for their dislike was simple. They saw David Carlyle as a bully: unscrupulous, unethical, vile to his junior staff and all the interns and tea-makers at Number Ten. Yes, he was good at his job – brilliant, even. A political animal to his bones, David Carlyle understood the importance of controlling information: when to leak, when not to leak, who to stick close to and who to betray. His only political ideal was winning elections, and he would go to the ends of the earth to achieve this end, no matter who he worked for. But, as Eddie Wellesley put it to the PM, an old friend, 'Life's too short to be spent in the company of arseholes, Tristram.'

And so David Carlyle was 'reshuffled' and a marvellous woman from Saatchi's, Margot Greene, brought in to replace him.

Eddie Wellesley had won his little battle. But he had made himself a very dangerous enemy.

After David left Number Ten, his career had gone from strength to strength. He had landed the head of News job at the *Echo*, rising quickly to become editor when Graham Davies retired. Since taking over, David had tripled the paper's readership and made it a serious Fleet Street player once again. The success was sweet, but nothing could quite replace the thrill of politics, the Machiavellian *Sturm und Drang* of life at Number Ten, pulling the strings behind the scenes. Even so, David knew he would never go back. That time had passed, and new challenges awaited. But he never forgot or forgave the plot to oust him. David saw what had happened to him as a straightforward case of snobbery. 'Fast Eddie' Wellesley, Tristram Hambly and two-thirds of his enemies in Cabinet had all been at either Eton or Oxford together. David's father had been a printer and his mother worked in a butcher's shop. He'd heard the sniggers and snide remarks at Number Ten, about his grey shoes and his 'naff' ties and his use of taboo words like 'pardon' and 'toilet'. The bastards had been out to get him from the start.

'Don't let it bother you,' his wife Louise used to tell him.

'Who cares what they think?' Louise was from a similar background, the middle daughter of a carpet fitter from Dagenham. And the wonder of it was, she really *didn't* care. But David did. Desperately. He loathed the clubby-ness of the Tory party, and the myriad ways in which he was shut out of the PM's inner circle. But what infuriated him most of all was the way that ordinary, working-class voters – people like him – seemed to warm to Eddie Wellesley. They found Eddie witty and straightforward and charismatic, and forgave all his foibles as endearing eccentricities. Little did they know how much Eddie and his clique of posho-cronies despised them and all they stood for. It was up to David to set them straight.

He spent years, and hundreds of thousands of pounds of his paper's money, investigating Fast Eddie's tax affairs. When he finally nailed Eddie he did it in style, publishing a brutal exposé of his dodgy offshore schemes and bribing all his whores to testify against him. Eddie's resignation was a good day for David Carlyle, the day of his arrest an even better one. But the day that they carted the bastard off to jail? That had been the happiest day of David's life.

But now Eddie Wellesley was back, and trying to reinvent himself as a television producer. David felt his chest tighten. The barefaced gall of the man! He planned to do a reality show, no less: stooping to conquer, a real man of the people. David felt sick. Media was *his* world, *his* business. Just as politics had been his business, until Eddie came along and poisoned people against him with his lethal blend of snob-bery and charm. Eddie Wellesley was pure spite, wrapped up in a shining silver bow. And now, to top it all, the bastard had even followed David here, to the Swell Valley. Why couldn't Wellesley have bought a house in the fucking

Cotswolds like the rest of his posho Tory pals? No one wanted him in the Swell Valley with his TV cameras and his new posse of village cronies, lead by that popinjay Gabe Baxter.

David wondered exactly which Old Etonian strings Fast Eddie had pulled this time, to get *Valley Farm* off the ground. Apparently he'd already convinced some American bimbo to leave one of the big US networks and front the thing alongside Gabe, no doubt with an eye on the international market. Arrogant bastard.

The triumph and satisfaction David had felt, getting Eddie sent to prison, hadn't lasted long. Inexplicably, the great British public still adored him. If Eddie made a success of things in the TV world, no one would remember his fall from political grace. He'd be a survivor. Teflon Eddie, the comeback kid.

But he wouldn't make a success of it.

Not this time.

David Carlyle was going to see to that.

He wouldn't rest until that son of a bitch Wellesley was a broken man.

Pulling in through the electric gates of his Southern ranch-style home, David left his car in the driveway. He heard the satisfying '*beep beep*' of the Aston's automatic lock, followed by the gentle splashing of water from the dolphin fountain he'd had put in as a centrepiece in front of the house. Louise loved dolphins, and David loved Louise. She'd been with him since the beginning, since they were both kids, back when he had nothing. Louise had believed in him even then, when all he could offer her was a cramped room over a Falafel King in Tufnell Park. She'd sacrificed endlessly for his career, never complaining about his long hours, or the meagre pay in the early days, or the black moods that could grip him when work wasn't going well. Louise was the great miracle of David's life, always seeing the funny side, always in his corner. His success was her success, *their* success, and if Louise wanted a dolphin fountain then she would bloody well have one. David knew that the local upper-class mafia mocked his house, but he didn't give a rat's arse. If they preferred to live in draughty old piles full of damp and mould and mouse shit, that was up to them. They could keep their tatty Persian rugs and Jacobean furniture, and he would keep his state-of-the-art sound system, dolphin fountain and marble Jacuzzi whirlpool bath, complete with rainbow light feature panel, thank you very much.

Louise greeted him in the doorway, looking strained.

'You said you wanted tea at eight.'

In a pale pink dress and matching heels, and with her hair newly blow-dried, she'd clearly made an effort to look nice. Louise Carlyle was a big believer in working at one's marriage. 'Keeping the magic alive' wasn't easy, especially when you were married to an obsessive workaholic like David. But no one could say Louise didn't try.

'That's right.'

'It's nine thirty, David. The lasagne's ruined. What happened?'

'It was bloody brilliant.' David's eyes lit up. 'The whole village is up in arms about this TV show.'

'Are they?' Louise knew that there was some dissent. But she'd also heard plenty of people excited about *Valley Farm* and willing to give the idea a chance.

'Oh yeah,' said David. 'Eddie Wellesley's up to his neck in it this time.'

Louise sighed. *Eddie Wellesley. Again.*

'By the time I'm finished with him there won't be a voter

in England who can stand the fucking sight of him.' David grinned.

Louise Carlyle loved her husband and she was loyal to a fault. But David wasn't the one who had to live here, day in, day out. While her husband was up in London, churning out newspapers, Louise had worked hard to make friends in the valley, not just in Hinton, but in the livelier villages of Fittlescombe and Brockhurst too. It wasn't easy when one didn't have children. But Louise had joined the WI, and in recent weeks had started to become close to its chairwoman, Jenny Grey, and to the lovely Penny de la Cruz, who also helped with the church flowers. Louise knew that Penny's husband Santiago was friends with Gabriel Baxter, and that the Baxters were involved in this TV show of Eddie Wellesley's. If David started making waves again (forget 'if', he *had* started), the ripples were bound to affect Louise's own friendships. She wished, just once, that David would consider things like that. But she knew if she brought it up he'd feel unsupported and let down, and she couldn't have that. Sometimes it was exhausting, the degree to which David needed to be mothered.

He hugged her tightly. 'Lasagne, did you say?'

'Not any more. It's burned to a crisp. You said you wanted to have dinner, just the two of us.'

'Don't worry, love. Doesn't matter.' David was already moving past her, towards his study. 'I'll just have a Scotch and a packet of crisps. I need to get to work anyway. I want to do some research tonight on this Yank woman Eddie's bringing over. See what dirt my news desk can dig up.'

Louise Carlyle stood and watched as her husband walked into his study, closing the door behind him. He hadn't kissed her. Hadn't asked about her day. Hadn't apologized for being late or ruining the meal that she'd prepared for them.

He wasn't always like this, she reminded herself. *He's a good man, really.*

Louise had loved David for all her adult life, and a good few years before that, and she knew a side to him that few people got to see. *Her* David was romantic and passionate. He was funny and loyal and kind, forever doing little things for her, like leaving a sugar mouse on her pillow every time he went away on a trip, because Louise had mentioned on an early date how much she loved them as a child. Yes, he was ambitious and he worked hard. Louise suspected he was tough as a boss and she knew many of his staff disliked him. But it was only because his standards were high. David wanted a better life, for both of them. Becoming the prime minister's spin doctor had been a dream come true, but it wasn't some sort of gift. It was a dream he had worked for and felt he deserved. When Eddie Wellesley took that away from him, he took more than just a job. Other people saw David's anger. But Louise saw his pain. It was awful and it had changed him profoundly. After that there were no more sugar mice, no more thoughtful gestures. It was as if there was no room for anything but David's raging resentment, his need to exact vengeance. He'd made plenty of enemies in the course of his professional life, but with Eddie Wellesley it was different. Personal. Louise didn't hate Eddie Wellesley, but she did wish he would go away, far away, and never come back.

She gazed sadly at David's closed study door.

One day, when he finally got over this vendetta with Eddie Wellesley, things would go back to the way they used to be.

One day.

* * *

Laura stood outside the gates of St Hilda's Primary School, waiting for the bell to ring. Hugh had started nursery a few weeks earlier, and now toddled off to school three afternoons a week. The sight of him setting off from the farm with his pirate backpack, puffing his little chest out with pride, made Laura preposterously happy. What a magical place this was to grow up! Hugh and Luca had no idea how lucky they were, she thought, looking down at Luca asleep in his push-chair as a bee buzzed lazily past.

A group of mothers stood off to one side, chatting and occasionally shooting glances in Laura's direction. Hostile glances? Or was she imagining things? *I mustn't be paranoid.* Ever since Laura had sold *Valley Farm* to Channel 5, and word had got out in the village about the impending filming at Wraggsbottom, local feeling had been running high. It didn't help that the new vicar, desperate to curry favour with his parishioners, and still smarting from Gabe's rant about the Right-to-Roamers, had decided to stir up trouble, whipping up what would have been a few disgruntled murmurs into full-on war. Only yesterday, the notice that Laura had put up in the village stores, advertising for extras for the first day's filming, had been angrily torn down and replaced with a 'Save Our Village' poster. As if the village were under threat! Despite Call-me-Bill's efforts, however, Laura had faith it would all work out. No one loved the village and the valley more than she and Gabe. That was the truth, and one of the main reasons they'd wanted to make the show in the first place. With so many rich second homers, and farming in a terminal decline, Fittlescombe was in danger of becoming a ghost village, a theme park for wealthy Londoners that only came to life at weekends and holidays. Numbers at the village school were already dwindling.

Without new jobs, they would only fall further. *Valley Farm* could provide those jobs, both directly on set and indirectly through increased tourism and interest in the Swell Valley. Plus, once people saw how nice and respectful Laura's production team were, and how true the show was to the spirit of the valley and the people who lived and worked there, she was sure they would come round.

Besides, Eddie had promised to go door to door and turn on the legendary Wellesley charm once Macy Johanssen and the camera crew actually arrived in the village. If anybody could love-bomb Fittlescombe's naysayers into submission, it was Eddie. He and Laura had already become fast friends. Whenever she felt overwhelmed (producing a television show, taking care of two small boys and running the farm with Gabe all at the same time was no mean feat), Eddie somehow managed to calm her down. More than that, his belief in *Valley Farm* as a concept was so passionate and profound, so utterly unwavering, he boosted Laura's confidence simply by being in the same room. Thank God Gabe had had the balls to suggest approaching him.

One of the older children ran out into the playground, ringing the hand bell that signalled the end of the day. Moments later the children began to file out, youngest first. Laura waited to see Hugh's happy, excited little face running to greet her. But instead he emerged blotchy and red-faced. He'd clearly been crying.

'Darling!' Laura swept him up into her arms. 'What's the matter? What's happened?'

'Dickon said I can't go to his party any more.'

'Dickon Groves?'

Hugh nodded. 'Ev'un else can go. Only not me.' His lower lip wobbled pathetically. 'He's having a bouncy castle.'

'I'm sure that can't be right,' said Laura. 'Would you like me to go and talk to Dickon's mummy?'

Hugh looked doubtful. 'You stay here with Luca,' said Laura, setting him down on the grass. 'I'll be back in a moment.'

She walked over to where Sarah Groves was talking to some other mothers.

'Sorry to butt in,' she began with a smile, 'but I think Hugh's got the wrong end of the stick. He thinks Dickon doesn't want him to come to his birthday party any more.'

Sarah's face hardened. 'That's right.'

Laura felt a knot form in her stomach. Sarah Groves wasn't a friend, as such, but they'd always been on good terms. No more, evidently. The other mothers had lined up behind her, arms folded in a distinctly hostile manner. Laura felt as if *she* were at school, being cornered by the bullies.

'But . . . why? Has something happened?'

Sarah scoffed. 'Yes, something's happened. You and your husband have run roughshod over all of us. That's what's happened.'

'Now, hold on—' Laura began.

'No one wants this TV show, you know. No one. But you don't care, do you? As long as you're making a few quid.'

Laura was so shocked, for a moment she didn't know what to say. Then she looked across at her son standing by his brother's pushchair, his little shoulders slumped in disappointment and felt a surge of anger rush through her.

'My God. So you're taking out your petty grievances on an innocent four-year-old boy? How truly pathetic.'

Now it was Sarah's turn to look shocked. Her mouth dropped open with indignation. 'Petty grievances? How dare you! Who the hell do you think you are?'

But Laura had already walked away, scooping up Hugh

81

into her arms and marching furiously across the village green, Luca's pushchair lurching wildly at every bump in the grass.

She was still spitting tacks when she got back to the farm.

'What on earth's the matter?' Gabe was sitting with his legs up on the kitchen table, reading the racing results. So much for his 'ridiculously busy' day on the farm, the one that meant he couldn't go and pick up Hugh, or give Luca his lunch, meaning Laura had had to do it.

'That bloody cow,' Laura seethed.

'Buddy cow,' said Luca.

She filled him in while Hugh plonked himself down in front of *Scooby-Doo*.

'The witch,' said Gabe. 'I've got a good mind to go over there right now and tell her what I think of her. How *dare* she!'

'For God's sake don't,' said Laura.

Slumping down into the tatty armchair by the Aga, she suddenly felt exhausted. Santiago and Penny had come over last night, after the village meeting, and they'd all stayed up far too late drinking and taking the piss out of David Carlyle. Eddie kept telling her the furore over the show would die down, like the proverbial storm in a teacup. But Laura was worried. This particular storm seemed to have brewed pretty damn quickly. Fittlescombe was her and Gabe's home. It was the children's home.

'Are we making a terrible mistake?' she asked Gabe.

Gabe leaned down and kissed her.

'No. We're not. We're doing something exciting, and new, and different. People are afraid of change, especially round here. And when people are afraid, they lash out. Come on, Laur. We knew this was going to happen. Once the local economy starts improving and everyone's benefiting, they'll come around. It'll be all right.'

Will it? thought Laura.

She hoped so, and not just for Hugh's sake.

'Where are you going?' She noticed with alarm that Gabe had scooped up his car keys from the kitchen table. 'For God's sake don't go and cause a scene at the Groveses.'

'I wouldn't set foot in that house for all the tea in China,' said Gabe, his lip curling with disgust. 'I'm off to Toys R Us in Chichester. I'm going to buy Hugh the biggest fuck-off bouncy castle *on earth*. That little shit Dickon is gonna wish he'd never been born.'

Laura rolled her eyes.

Sometimes it was hard work, having three children.

CHAPTER SIX

Macy Johanssen pushed her dark hair out of her eyes and leaned back against the kitchen island with satisfaction. On the antique Welsh dresser opposite her, a pretty collection of mismatched china gleamed cheerfully, and a heavily scented jug of peonies made a perfect centrepiece for the table Macy had had shipped over from California.

After a week of solid unpacking, plumping up cushions, making beds and arranging treasures old and new, Cranbourne House was finally coming together. And what a house it was.

Eddie hadn't been exaggerating about the picture-postcard prettiness of the Swell Valley. If anything he'd played down the majesty of the ancient rolling chalk hills that locals called 'the Downs' – it seemed to Macy they went up as well as down, but who was quibbling? – and the quaint loveliness of the villages. Even the names sounded like something out of a storybook: Fittlescombe, Brockhurst, Hinton Down, Lower Cricksmere. As for Cranbourne House, the property Eddie and the network had rented for Macy on the edge of

84

Fittlescombe, it was really more of a large cottage – three cottages knocked together, in fact. It was all Macy could do not to cry when she saw the flint and tile-hung beauty, peeking out coyly from behind its veil of ivy and climbing roses. The garden was small but perfectly formed, and complete with both a pear and a walnut tree, as well as a buddleia smothered in butterflies. Whatever happened with the show, Macy was glad she'd taken a leap of faith and come to England. How could wonderful, happy things *not* happen to a girl in a place like this?

A loud knocking on the front door broke her reverie. Macy opened it to find Eddie standing on the doorstep with a very pretty woman. She was at least ten years older than Macy, yet there was something appealingly youthful about her. Possibly it was her wild mane of blue-black curls, or the lack of make-up on her pale skin, or the light smattering of freckles across the bridge of her nose. She wore jeans and a chocolate-brown sweater, and was clutching a laptop and phone in a rather businesslike manner.

'This is Laura Baxter, our producer, director, creator and all-round wonder-woman.' Eddie beamed.

'My boss, you mean?' Macy looked at Laura appraisingly. She'd never worked for a woman before and wondered whether she was going to like it.

'Exactly.' Laura smiled. Macy instantly liked her less. Laura might be the boss on paper, but Macy was the star of the show. She resented Laura's natural assertion of authority. And she wasn't keen on the doe-eyed way Eddie looked at her, either. Macy wasn't at all sure there was room for two beautiful women on the *Valley Farm* set.

'I thought it was time the two of you met,' said Eddie. 'As you know, we have our first official on-set meeting tomorrow morning at the farm. But we ought to put faces to names before then. May we come in?'

'Of course.'

Macy led them through to the drawing room, a small but pretty space overlooking the rear garden. It struck Laura how perfect the room looked already, all white linen sofas and artlessly arranged crystal. Clearly Macy had the same flair for decor as Lady Wellesley. *Is that what Eddie goes for, I wonder?* she thought idly. *The perfect homemaker, china-doll look? He wouldn't last long with me.*

'Tea?' Macy offered. 'Or fresh juice? I made some kale-ade this morning, it's delicious.'

'Sounds disgusting,' Eddie said cheerfully. 'I'm all right, thanks.'

'Me too,' said Laura. 'How are you finding England so far?'

'So far so good,' Macy said warily.

'Have you read over your script for the pilot?'

'Sure,' Macy lied. Evidently the small-talk part of the visit was already over. 'Eddie tells me you've never done scripted reality.'

'Funny,' Macy shot back. 'He said the same about you.'

Laura looked up sharply, as if seeing Macy for the first time.

'It's true, my background is in drama. To be honest, from a writing perspective, this is easier. But it presents other challenges. A lot rests on the interaction between you and Gabe, your chemistry on screen.'

'I don't usually have a problem with chemistry,' said Macy, catching Eddie's eye for the most fleeting of moments.

'Good,' said Laura.

She didn't warm to this girl. Eddie had described Macy

as 'very ambitious' – not a bad thing in itself, as long as she remembered who was boss. Laura had seen *Grapevine*. Macy was a talented presenter, no doubt about that. But Laura wondered how easy she was going to be to manage. She was clearly used to getting her own way. There would be no room for any diva antics on *Valley Farm*.

Laura stood up. 'Do you have any questions for me, before tomorrow?'

Macy stifled a yawn. 'No. I'm good.'

'In that case, I look forward to seeing you bright and early up at Wraggsbottom.'

Macy giggled. 'I still can't get over that name. It's like calling your house Ass-wipe. No offence.'

'None taken,' Laura said frostily. 'We'll see ourselves out.'

After they left, Eddie turned to Laura as they drove down the lane.

'You don't like her.'

Laura kept her eyes on the road. 'Why do you say that?'

'You weren't exactly friendly.'

'Nor was she. And I wasn't *un*friendly. Anyway, I'm not her friend. I'm her producer. This is my show, Eddie. I want to set the right tone, that's all.'

Eddie put a hand over Laura's and patted it reassuringly. 'I understand. But there's no need to hit back first. We're all on the same team here, Laura. We all need *Valley Farm* to succeed.'

No you don't, thought Laura. *You want it to succeed. That's a very different thing. Gabe and I need this money.*

The truth was, the set-to at the school gates had shaken Laura up more than she cared to admit. With each passing day she found her own confidence in the show's success waning, to the point where she was finding it really hard to sleep at night. While Gabe snored loudly beside her, Laura's mind was whirring. *My neighbours hate me, the bills keep rolling in, and I've staked my entire professional reputation on a reality show, a format about which I know precisely nothing.* Macy's quip just now about her lack of experience had hit home. Suddenly Laura felt desperately out of her depth. She knew she mustn't let Macy see that. Or Eddie, for that matter.

'OK,' she said aloud. 'I'll ease up. I just hope she cuts out the attitude with Gabe. He's not big on stroppy women.'

Eddie looked at her and grinned, but wisely said nothing.

'I can't believe this.' Laura ran an exasperated hand through her hair. 'I seriously can't believe it.'

It was the morning the film crew were supposed to come to see the farm for the first time, and a small but determined group of Fittlescombe villagers had gathered in the lane outside Wraggsbottom Farm to stage a protest. While Laura looked around a kitchen still littered with the detritus of yesterday's cake-baking efforts (stupidly, she'd thought a bit of home cooking might make a nice welcome for the crew, temporarily forgetting that her culinary prowess was very much on the King Alfred end of the scale), shouts of 'No TV in our Vall-ey!' drifted noxiously in through the open window.

'They're driving me mad.' She looked at Gabe despairingly. 'Should we call the police?'

Gabe poured himself another coffee, his third of the morning, and frowned. 'And say what? Unfortunately, it's a free country. People are allowed to protest about things.'

'Yes, but not at six in the morning, surely?' said Laura. 'That's when they started.'

'Don't remind me,' said Gabe.

Laura sighed heavily. 'Look at this sodding mess. Why didn't we clean it up last night?'

Gabe wrapped his arms around her. 'Because I was too busy disabling the smoke alarms.' Laura giggled. 'And you were hitting the gin.'

Through the kitchen window, they could see the tops of the protestors' placards, emblazoned with such cheery slogans as: 'GO HOME CHANNEL 5!' and 'SAVE OUR VILLAGE!'

'At least the kids aren't here,' said Laura.

'Exactly,' said Gabe. 'Look on the bright side.'

Greta, the Baxters' part-time nanny, had taken Hugh and Luca out to Drusillas Zoo earlier, with both the boys cheerfully chanting 'No TV!' as they got into the car.

It was now nine o'clock. The production team and Macy were due at the farm by ten, to do some walk-throughs of the property and set up for next week's pilot episode. Laura had a headache that could have felled an elephant, and Gabe's nerves, already frayed at the prospect of meeting his co-presenter and performing on camera for the first time, had not been helped by the relentless cacophony.

Opening the kitchen cupboards, he began pulling out a teapot, mugs, a packet of Jaffa Cakes and a tray.

'What are you doing?' asked Laura.

'Loving my neighbour. I'm going to disarm them with the power of McVitie's.'

Laura's eyes widened. 'Are you serious? You're taking them tea?'

'It's either that or spray them with slurry.'

Laura knew which option she preferred. But five minutes later, Gabe was outside the farm gates, tray in hand, smiling warmly at the sea of scowling faces.

'Tea, anyone? I'd offer you a home-made cake, but unfortunately my wife is a shit cook and they all turned out like charcoal.'

Reverend Clempson's eyes narrowed suspiciously. 'No, thank you.'

'Oh come on, Vicar. All that shouting must be thirsty work.' Gabe's eyes twinkled mischievously. 'Can't I tempt you with a Jaffa Cake?'

'He can tempt *me* with a Jaffa Cake,' one of the younger, female protestors whispered to her friend.

'Or without,' her friend sighed.

In faded jeans, wellington boots and a checked white and brown shirt rolled up to the elbows, Gabe looked fit and tanned and disgustingly rugged. One by one the female protestors put down their placards and accepted mugs of tea. By the time Macy Johanssen arrived at the farm, the scene outside looked more like a picnic than a picket line. Only the vicar and a few older men were still marching and chanting.

'Gabriel?' Macy offered her hand to the handsome, well-built blond man holding court among the women.

No wonder they picked him to present, she thought. *If all farmers looked like that, Dorothy would never have left Kansas.*

Gabe turned away from his admirers and fixed his eyes appreciatively on the petite, attractive girl in front of him. She had Laura's colouring, very pale skin with strikingly dark hair. But unlike Laura she was tiny and doll-like and immaculately well-groomed, all sleek hair and expensive clothes and perfectly manicured nails. You could tell in an instant that she didn't have children.

'You must be Macy,' he beamed. 'Lovely to finally meet you. Come on in.'

90

Macy followed him into the kitchen. In the ten minutes since Gabe had been outside, Laura had made valiant efforts to clean up. Gabe was relieved to see the kitchen looking almost habitable again and to hear the low hum of the dishwasher getting to work.

'Darling,' said Gabe. 'Macy's arrived.'

Laura, now sitting at the table engrossed by her laptop, didn't look up.

This woman's really beginning to annoy me, thought Macy, who'd been in a great mood up till then. She'd walked down the lane from Cranbourne House this morning. The sun was out, the meadows were full of wild flowers and the tall hedgerows teemed with butterflies and bees and twittering birds like something out of a Disney cartoon. But Laura Baxter was the ultimate buzz-kill.

'Sorry.' Gabe apologized for his wife's rudeness. 'We've had a bit of a crazy morning. Can I get you anything?'

'Tea would be lovely.'

Seconds later the first of the TV crew vans pulled into the farmyard and the chanting began again. Laura slammed shut her laptop with a clatter.

'No time for that, I'm afraid,' she said briskly. 'We have a ton to do today. Let's get to work.'

The rest of the morning passed in a whirl of activity, confusion and stress. While Laura and the film crew hotly debated set-ups and camera angles, Gabe and Macy were made to do take after take after take, some ad-libbed and some scripted. Macy was kicked in the shin by a lamb, urinated on by a piglet and yelled at countless times by Laura, who was distracted by the increasing din of the protestors. At some point a minivan had pulled up outside the gates, depositing at least twenty rent-a-mobbers, none of whom Laura or Gabe recognized. Soon afterwards, reporters from the *Echo* started taking pictures, climbing up onto walls and farm buildings and into trees like an unwelcome swarm of ants.

'Bloody David Carlyle,' Gabe seethed. 'He's orchestrating this whole thing, the little shit.'

'Who's David Carlyle?' asked Macy. Her eye make-up was starting to run and she was already regretting the black, long-sleeved dress with a low 'V' at the front that was far too hot and making her sweat unpleasantly under the arms and between her breasts.

'A shit-stirrer,' said Gabe. 'The Vladimir Putin of Swell Valley. I'll explain at lunch.'

Laura overheard them. 'We're not breaking for lunch, I'm afraid. We are way, *way* behind.'

'Bollocks to that,' said Gabe robustly. He understood Laura was stressed. A lot rested on all this. But people had to eat. 'Macy and I are starving. I'm taking her to The Fox for a bite.'

Macy waited for Laura to lose her temper, but instead she merely shrugged. 'All right. Work on your lines while you're there, then. And be back by two.'

Gabe kissed his wife lovingly on the cheek. 'Aye-aye, Cap'n. Come on,' he turned to Macy. 'Let's get out of here before the black hole sucks us back in.'

The Fox was unusually busy for a Monday lunchtime. People came to Fittlescombe's quaint, riverside pub as much for the gossip as the fare, and this week there were two exciting events to talk about: Gabe and Laura Baxter's new TV show, and next weekend's big wedding.

Logan Cranley, the stunning daughter of Brett and Angela

Cranley, was marrying her long-term boyfriend, Tom Hargreaves, this Saturday in St Hilda's Church. Logan's parents had divorced in a blaze of publicity three years ago. Her father, Brett, had moved to America with Tatiana Flint-Hamilton, the former wild-child heiress of Furlings turned international business phenomenon. Tatiana also happened to be Brett's daughter-in-law at the time, so it was something of a scandal all around. Supposedly, Cranley family relations were now cordial. But where Tatiana Flint-Hamilton was concerned, there was always the potential for drama. Logan's wedding would be the first time that all parties had been under the same roof since the divorce. The fact that this would happen in public and in the village was too thrilling for words.

Gabe led Macy to a quietish corner near the bar and they ordered from the blackboard. Fresh local crab salad and spring pea soup for Macy and an Angus beefburger and chips for Gabe.

'The food's average but the beer's great,' said Gabe.

'As long as you like it warm, right?' quipped Macy.

'Of course. This is England. We don't do ice.'

He's so easy-going, thought Macy. She wondered how on earth he'd wound up with a miserable nag like Laura.

As if reading her mind, Gabe said, 'You mustn't mind Laura. She's not normally like this, honestly. She's been so stressed about this show, poor darling, and the protests haven't helped.'

He told Macy about the other children picking on Hugh at school, and the malicious gossip Laura had endured around the village. 'It's water off a duck's back to me,' he said, in between large, satisfying bites of his juicy beefburger. 'But Laura hates conflict.'

Macy looked disbelieving.

'Normally,' Gabe chuckled. 'Plus, you know, she has a ridiculously romantic, idealized view of village life. She always has done, ever since she used to come here for summers as a kid and stay at her granny's place. She thinks Fittlescombe's perfect and everybody ought to love everybody else and spend their time skipping around maypoles.'

'And you don't?' asked Macy.

'Don't get me wrong. I love it here. But nowhere's perfect. This is a real community, not a theme park. I think being a farmer gives you a more realistic view of life generally, to be honest.'

'Is that why you wanted to do the show?' Macy asked earnestly. 'To educate people, from a farmer's perspective?'

Gabe looked confused. 'No. I'm doing the show to make money. Farming's bloody hard work for almost no money. This month alone I've got to tail and castrate all the lambs, get them ear-notched and tagged, spray the potatoes, do muck-spreading across the whole farm, repair three broken walls and clean out the livestock buildings. I'm knackered just thinking about it. By getting a camera crew to follow me around, I'm already doubling my earnings. And if the show does well and Fast Eddie sells the format overseas, who knows? We might make some real money for a change.'

'But you aren't worried about the protests?' Macy asked. 'Now that a national newspaper's involved, couldn't they shut us down before we begin?'

'Nah. If anything, it'll generate some free publicity, while it lasts. But things will calm down, trust me,' said Gabe. 'At least, they will if *he* winds his neck in.'

He turned to glare at Call-me-Bill Clempson, who'd just walked in with a couple of local farmers. Both had been friends of Gabe's before the furore about *Valley Farm* broke out.

'The vicar?'

Gabe nodded bitterly.

'But he looks so harmless. Like a little vole.'

'He's not harmless. He's a self-righteous dick,' said Gabe. 'Zipping around the village in his little red car like bloody Noddy, making me and Laura out to be some sort of landed gentry intent on keeping the peasants down.' He told Macy about the right-to-roam debacle. 'The truth is we haven't got a fucking bean of disposable income. I mean, the house is valuable, but our mortgage is massive and the upkeep costs a bomb. It's not as if we're running around buying diamonds and eating sodding caviar.'

Macy decided it was time to change the subject. 'You know, you're really good on camera.'

'D'you think so?' Gabe's anger dissipated as quickly as it had appeared. 'I was shitting bricks, to be honest with you. I've never done anything like this before. I couldn't bear it if I were a total failure and let Laura down.'

'No chance of that.' Macy patted his hand across the table. It was quite astonishing how often he mentioned his wife, and how obviously in love with her he was. 'You're a natural.'

Just at the moment their hands touched, the vicar appeared at their table, looking both smug and disapproving, as if he'd caught Gabe out at something illicit.

'Hello Gabriel. Miss Johanssen.'

'Bugger off, "Bill",' said Gabe. 'We're trying to have a quiet lunch.'

'I was only saying hello.' The vicar blushed. 'There's really no need for profanity.'

'That's debatable,' grumbled Gabe.

Macy gave an embarrassed smile. 'I hear you have a big wedding this weekend, Vicar?'

'Indeed I do.' Bill Clempson smiled back. Macy tried not to look shocked by how crooked his teeth were. Then again the British did seem to have a peculiar aversion to visiting the dentist's office.

'Shouldn't you be preparing for it then, instead of making a nuisance of yourself at my farm?' said Gabe. 'I'd stick to the day job if I were you, Bill.'

Bill Clempson bristled.

'Standing up for my parishioners *is* my day job.'

'Yeah, well. The Cranleys won't be best pleased if you fluff the "I do's".'

'I don't work for the Cranleys,' Call-me-Bill replied sanctimoniously. 'I work for God. Nor do I care in the least what wealthy and powerful people might think of me.'

'Unless their name happens to be David Carlyle,' Gabe shot back. 'I saw you blowing smoke up his arse earlier.'

'Gabe!' Macy looked horrified.

'Not very dignified for a man of the cloth,' said Gabe.

'Now look here—' the vicar began angrily.

'No, *you* look here!' Before Macy knew what was happening, Gabe was on his feet. Picking the vicar up by the lapels, like a ventriloquist manhandling his dummy, Gabe pinned him against the wall.

'You know nothing about this village, Clempson. Nothing! You're upsetting my wife and you're upsetting my children. So I suggest you crawl back under whatever rock you came out from, before I crush you like the pathetic little insect that you are.'

'If you care so much about your wife's feelings,' Bill Clempson stammered, 'perhaps you should reconsider how *you* choose to spend your lunch hours, Mr Baxter.' He looked meaningfully at Macy. 'Instead of lashing out at others.'

The insinuation was too much for Gabe. 'You little weasel! What are you implying?'

Bill Clempson let out a distinctly unmanly whimper as Gabe drew back his fist.

'Gabriel!' The landlord marched over.

'What?'

'Put him down.'

Gabe hesitated.

'Put the vicar down, Gabe, or you're barred. I mean it.'

Aware that all eyes were on him, Gabe released the reverend. Call-me-Bill slid to the floor like a sack of rubbish.

'We're leaving anyway.' Reaching into his wallet, Gabe dropped two twenty-pound notes on the table. Grabbing Macy's hand, he pulled her towards the door. As they stormed out of the pub, a camera clicked frenziedly.

A woman seated a few tables away watched them go, then turned to her husband.

'If *Valley Farm*'s half as dramatic as this, I'm definitely watching it.'

'Me too,' said her husband. 'That American bird's a knockout. Laura Baxter had better watch her back.'

Annabel Wellesley tried to relax. Driving her new Range Rover Sport through Brockhurst High Street towards Fittlescombe, she was aware of her rigid back and hunched shoulders, and the clenched set of her jaw that made her whole face ache.

It had been an immensely stressful few weeks. Ever since Eddie got back from his American trip, he'd been like a racehorse with the bit between its teeth about this damned television programme. A *reality show*! Could there be anything more common? More shaming?

Eddie had assured her that he wouldn't appear in front of the cameras. 'I'm just the money man, darling.' But Annabel understood that these sorts of programmes thrived on drama. It was only a matter of time before their private lives would be dragged into the maelstrom once again, a thought that brought Annabel out in a nervous rash.

And it wasn't just the invasion of privacy. Annabel resented Eddie's long absences from Riverside Hall, in particular the inordinate amount of time he seemed to spend in the company of the very pretty Mrs Baxter. They'd moved here for a fresh start, so that they could spend more time together as a couple, in private, and so that Eddie could focus on clawing back his political career. But instead, Eddie was never around, they were all over the newspapers again courtesy of the vile David Carlyle, and Eddie's 'return to Westminster' campaign had been put on a permanent back burner.

Things might have been easier for Annabel if life had been running smoothly at Riverside Hall. Unfortunately, it wasn't. Having hired and fired three utterly useless local cleaning women (the last one, Rita, had such terrible body odour that Annabel had been forced to follow her around each room with a bowl of potpourri and a can of Febreze, and the ones before that were so lazy and inbred they thought dusting was something one did to crops and polishing silver meant putting priceless bone-handled cutlery in the dishwasher), Annabel was once again run ragged doing everything herself.

And then there was Milo.

Since Harrow had booted him out, Milo had been enrolled on an A-level course at the local comprehensive school in Hinton. To his mother's certain knowledge, however, he'd attended this establishment a total of four times in the last three months, three of them to pick up a thoroughly unsuitable girl he'd started going out with, and once to cheer on the cricket team.

'They're so bad, Mum, honestly. They need all the support they can get.'

As admirable as her son's team spirit was, Annabel realized it was small consolation in the face of his wanton laziness, rampant entitlement and utter lack of ambition. Milo spent half of his days in bed, and the other half either down at The Fox or sprawled out in front of the television watching *Deal or No Deal* or box sets of American dramas. *Breaking Bad* was his latest obsession.

'It could be worse,' Milo told Annabel, seriously, when she berated him for the umpteenth time for wasting his life. 'At least I'm not a meth head.'

Annabel was at her wits' end. Eddie had promised to 'sort Milo out', but he'd been so distracted with this damn TV show he'd barely glimpsed the boy in weeks.

Last night Annabel had finally lost her temper and had a terrible row with Milo. Roxanne, the appalling girlfriend from Hinton Comp, had 'borrowed' Annabel's favourite string of pearls for a night out clubbing in London and failed to return them.

'She was mugged,' Milo told his mother solemnly.

'The only mug around here is you,' Annabel snapped. 'She clearly sold them herself. Probably for drugs.'

'Why would you say that?' Milo looked hurt. 'Roxie doesn't do drugs.'

'Of course she does drugs,' said Annabel contemptuously. 'All girls from her background do drugs. The only reason you don't know that is because you're from a different class. Not that anyone would ever know it these days.'

'I'm glad they wouldn't know it if it means being a crashing snob like you,' Milo shot back. 'You don't know anything about Roxanne.'

'I know she had no business wearing my jewellery. And I know she is never, *ever* setting foot in my house again. Do you understand?'

The ensuing row was truly awful. Eddie, as usual, had opted out, retreating to his study to 'work'. Well, no more. Annabel had had enough. The new maid, Magda, was arriving this afternoon, thank God. Eddie had promised to come home and take Milo out of the house for a good talking-to, while Annabel showed the girl around. She was Eastern European, which boded well for hard work, if not necessarily for honesty. Still, at this point, beggars couldn't be choosers.

Annabel exhaled deeply as the valley opened out below her and the red-tiled roof of Wraggsbottom Farm hove into view.

She'd decided to drive over to Fittlescombe herself to collect Eddie. Partly because, if he didn't talk to Milo today, she feared she might kill one or both of them. And partly because she wanted to see for herself what *Valley Farm* was all about. For a 'money man', Eddie was certainly spending a lot of time on set.

The worst part of finding out about Eddie's affairs was the humiliation of not knowing. All those girls. All those years. And Annabel had had no clue.

Well, it wasn't going to happen again. From now on, she intended to know *everything*.

'You idiot! You absolute, bloody idiot!'

Gabe couldn't remember the last time he'd seen Laura so angry. Macy, thankfully, had already gone home, so she wasn't there to see the meltdown. Most of the crew had gone too, but the lighting guys were still at the farm, setting up in the pig pens; as was Eddie Wellesley, who sat perched on a stool by the Aga, making calls and tapping figures into his iPad like an extremely well-heeled accountant.

'What if he calls the police?' asked Laura. 'He could have you charged with assault.'

'No one's going to charge anyone,' said Gabe. 'There wasn't a scratch on him.'

'We start filming in *a week*!' Laura screeched.

'I know!' Gabe shouted back. 'Do you think I don't know? You're not the only one working your arse off for this.'

Laura put her head in her hands. 'You are the face of this show, Gabe. People have to like you. You just beat up a clergyman in broad daylight because you didn't like the cut of his jib. How is that helpful?'

'He accused me of flirting with Macy. As good as accused me,' Gabe shot back.

'Well, I expect you were,' said Laura.

'I was *not*.'

'You'd flirt with your own shadow if you thought no one was watching,' Laura teased him. She knew she needed to lighten the mood. That her own stress was rubbing off on Gabe, and everyone, and making everything worse. But unfortunately Gabe took her comment the wrong way.

'Now you're being ridiculous,' he said crossly. Thrusting his hands deep in his pockets, he stomped off like a sulky schoolboy.

'He's only angry because he knows I'm right,' Laura said to Eddie, who'd sat and watched the entire contretemps in silence. Suddenly the stress of the day got too much for her. She pinched the bridge of her nose to try to stop the tears from coming, but it was too late.

'Oh God. Sorry,' she sniffed. 'I think I'm just exhausted.'

Eddie walked over and wrapped his arms around her. 'It's all right. Everyone's on edge. But Gabe's right, the vicar won't press charges. It'll blow over.'

'Will it?' sobbed Laura.

'Of course it will. But you must try to relax, you really must. You'll make yourself ill at this rate.'

'I know,' Laura nodded, burying her face in Eddie's shirt, which smelled incongruously of wood polish. He really was a lovely man.

'Edward!'

Releasing Laura as if he'd just discovered she was made of molten lava, Eddie turned round. Annabel stood in the kitchen doorway, a picture of rage. Gabe must have left the door to the yard open when he stormed out.

'Darling! What a nice surprise. I wasn't expecting you.'

'Obviously.'

That's all we need, thought Laura. *More misunderstandings.* She thought about saying something, trying to explain, but Annabel's expression made it clear she was in no mood to hear it.

'I need you to talk to Milo.' Annabel was talking to Eddie, but she couldn't bring herself to look at him. 'Right now.'

'Of course,' said Eddie, chastened. There was nothing going on between him and Laura. But after everything that had happened, he could hardly blame Annabel for thinking the worst.

Laura watched from the window as Eddie scurried across the farmyard after his rigid-shouldered wife. What a bloody awful day.

Valley Farm, 1. Marital Harmony, Nil.

* * *

Magda Bartosz clutched her small suitcase tightly in her left hand as she climbed out of her decrepit Ford Fiesta. It felt wrong, parking her rust-bucket of a car outside this spectacularly beautiful house. Like littering. But she was already late, thanks to an accident on the Lewes bypass, and there was nowhere else obvious to leave it. Smoothing down her skirt, Magda hurried up the steps to the front door, then hesitated.

Perhaps one doesn't knock at the front door of a grand house, when arriving for a trial as a live-in maid? Is there a back door? A servants' entrance? Or does that sort of thing only exist in Downton Abbey?, *she thought.*

Magda had been in England for a few years now, working as a companion-cum-housekeeper for an old woman who had since died. But English customs and traditions still baffled her, especially the ones that pertained to class. Magda herself had been born into an old and distinguished but impoverished family in Warsaw. Her proud, high cheekbones, smooth forehead and regal, aquiline nose bore testament to the better life once known by her ancestors. But everything that had once been refined and beautiful and pleasant about Magda's life had evaporated long ago. So long ago, and so totally, that she rarely even thought about it any more.

I'm here now, she thought.

I'm lucky to be here, in this heavenly place, with a roof over my head and food and wages.

I must make this job work.

I must make the family love me.

Crunching across the gravel, she followed the path around the side of the house, past the noisily rushing river. A heavy wooden door led directly into the kitchen. Magda knocked loudly, but there was no answer. Tentatively, she tried the handle. It opened with a creak.

'Hello?'

She stepped into the flagstoned room. It was spotlessly clean and smelled of fresh flowers and something baked and sweet and delicious. Something with cinnamon. For a moment she panicked that Lady Wellesley had already found a cleaner. But that couldn't be right. Magda had received an email only yesterday confirming today's arrangements.

'Helloo?' Setting down her suitcase, she ventured into the hall. The house appeared to be empty. A set of narrow, winding stairs led off to the right. Magda walked towards them. If there were a part of the house for servants, this was probably it. Suddenly she froze. A noise was coming from upstairs; a dreadful, primal moaning sound, as if someone had been injured.

Instinctively, Magda moved towards it. She heard it again, a woman's voice. Her heart was pounding nineteen to the dozen. What if an intruder had attacked Lady Wellesley? What if he was still in the house somewhere? But she couldn't run, nor could she call the police. At the top of the stairs now, her palms sweating, she burst into the room. 'Are you all r . . .?'

A naked blonde with a phenomenal figure was lying on the bed, her back arched and legs spread. She couldn't have been more than sixteen. On the floor at the foot of the bed knelt a boy, also naked, his head very firmly planted between the girl's thighs. The girl saw Magda first. Letting out an ear-piercing scream, she pulled the bed sheet around her like a shield. Startled, the boy turned round too.

'Hello.' He flashed Magda a sheepish smile. 'Who are you?'

'I'm so sorry,' Magda blurted, blushing to the roots of her hair. 'I didn't mean to . . . I thought someone had been hurt.'

Just then all three of them paused at the unmistakable sound of the front door opening and closing downstairs.

Seconds later a man's voice boomed through the house like a giant's. 'Milo!' Eddie roared. 'Where are you? I want a word. Now.'

The smile melted off the boy's face like butter on a hot stove. 'Fuck.' He turned back to the girl wrapped in the sheet behind him. 'Dad'll go ballistic if he finds you here. Hide!'

'Where the fuck am I supposed to hide?' demanded the girl. Not unreasonably, thought Magda, as – other than the bed – there wasn't a stick of furniture in the room. Clearly this was a largely unused part of the house. Magda also noticed that the girl's accent was distinctly *EastEnders*. Unlike the boy, who seemed to have a whole handful of plums in his mouth.

'Please. Help us.' He looked pleadingly at Magda. It didn't seem to bother him in the least that he was still stark naked.

'I . . . how?' Magda stammered. Sir Edward Wellesley's heavy footsteps could be heard thundering up the stairs.

'Stall him. Please. Just till I can get Roxanne out of here.'

Magda stepped out into the corridor, closing the door behind her.

Eddie was so engrossed in finding Milo – after a difficult journey home with Annabel he needed someone to take out his frustrations on – he didn't even notice the young woman standing in the hallway until he'd almost bumped into her and knocked her flying.

'Sorry! So sorry.' He threw his arms wide, like a footballer admitting a foul. 'I was looking for my son. Are you the new cleaner?'

Magda nodded meekly. 'I arrived a few minutes ago.'

'Marvellous. Lady Wellesley's going to be terribly pleased to see you. Did Milo let you in?'

'Er . . .' Magda hesitated.

'My son. Seventeen-year-old boy? Lazy, irritating, probably still in his pyjamas?'

'I haven't seen anyone.' Magda's heart thumped at the lie. 'I came in the kitchen door. It was open.'

Annabel appeared at the other end of the hallway.

'Ah darling,' said Eddie. 'This is the new cleaner. I'm sorry, I forgot to ask you your name.'

'Magdalena Bartosz. Pleased to meet you, Lady Wellesley.'

If this was Lady Wellesley looking 'delighted', Magda dreaded to think what she might look like annoyed. She was a beautiful woman, but her entire body seemed clenched, and her mouth was pursed in a tight 'o' of disapproval, like a cat's arse.

'What are you doing upstairs?' she demanded suspiciously.

'I . . . I thought I heard a . . . er . . . a cat,' Magda stammered.

'A *cat*?' Annabel frowned.

'Yes.'

'We don't own a cat.'

Magda blushed again. 'I must have been mistaken. I checked all the rooms in case it was shut in but they're all empty.'

'Hmm,' said Eddie. 'God knows where Milo's got to. Darling, why don't you show Magda to the cottage? I'm sure she must be tired after her journey. He turned to Magda. 'Do you have a case?'

'Yes, a small one. It's in the kitchen.'

'I'll carry it across for you.'

'Really, there's no need. I can manage.'

'I insist,' said Eddie.

Five minutes later, following her new employers across the lawn towards the gardener's cottage that she hoped might become her home, Magda looked over her shoulder. The girl, Roxanne, was clothed now and sprinting for her life away from the house towards the woods leading out to the lane.

Good, thought Magda. *She made it.*

It wasn't until that evening that she bumped into Milo again. After an exhaustive tour of the house and a veritable bible of instructions from Lady Wellesley about laundry, fireplace-sweeping and hand-washing crystal, Magda was washing up in the kitchen when Milo sauntered in. In jeans, bare feet and a dark green fisherman's sweater with holes in it, he looked lanky, like a young giraffe still not quite sure what to do with its legs.

'Thank you for before,' he said. 'I owe you one.'

'You're welcome.' Magda didn't meet his eye. He seemed nice enough, but she didn't want him to think she was some sort of co-conspirator. His mother had the power to hire or fire her. Magda could not afford to offend or upset Lady Wellesley, for anyone.

'My mother's not a fan of Roxie's,' Milo went on. 'She thinks she's beneath me.'

She was certainly beneath you this afternoon, thought Magda.

Sir Edward had described his son as lazy and disobedient. Magda could certainly imagine that to be the case, despite his charm.

'The thing is, we're in love,' Milo explained.

'It's really none of my business,' said Magda, drying her hands and reaching for the kitchen door. 'Goodnight.'

'I'll walk you to the cottage if you like,' said Milo. 'It's dark out there and it's the least I can do after you saved my bacon earlier.'

'No.' The word came out more sharply than Magda had intended. 'And please, don't mention this again. Goodnight.'

Milo watched, chastened, as she slipped into the darkness and out of sight.

CHAPTER SEVEN

Macy Johanssen adjusted the veil on her fascinator and surveyed the packed church surreptitiously from behind her order of service.

She'd been astonished to receive an invitation to Logan Cranley's wedding, having never met either the bride or groom. But Angela Cranley, the bride's mother, happened to pop into Wraggsbottom Farm during filming on Thursday and very sweetly asked Macy along.

'The whole village will be there, so it'll be a chance for you to meet everyone. And I know my ex-husband's curious to meet you.'

Not as curious as I am to meet him, thought Macy. Brett Cranley was one of the richest men in Australia, and a big investor in America too, not least in the media sector. For a consummate networker like Macy, Brett Cranley was exactly the sort of man she wanted to make a good impression on. She'd chosen her outfit carefully: a taupe silk dress that looked nothing on the hanger but that clung seductively to Macy's slender frame, making her look as though she'd been dipped in caramel; simple gold accessories; neutral Manolo pumps, and a wisp of netting from Philip Treacy over her dark bob that couldn't have cost more than five bucks to make but which was the most expensive item in Macy's entire outfit.

She'd been pleased with the result until she walked into St Hilda's Church and saw some of the most stunning, spectacularly dressed women she'd ever laid eyes on in her life. As for the hats, they made the Kentucky Derby look like a Puritan funeral.

A few faces were familiar. Sir Eddie and Lady Wellesley sat near the back with their son, Milo, a blond copy of his father with the same cheeky glint in his eye. It felt incredibly strange now to think that she had had a one-night stand with Eddie back in LA. Macy never thought of him in that way any more, and was as sure as she could be that the feeling was mutual. She liked Eddie, and was starting to consider him a real friend.

Apart from the Wellesleys, she recognized a number of the protestors who'd been hanging around the farm all week, as well as William Winter, her busybody next-door neighbour at Cranbourne House. But most of the congregation were strangers. Macy still felt like an interloper, playing catch-up on village gossip.

'Where's Tatiana Flint-Hamilton?' she whispered to Laura. 'I keep hearing people talking about her.'

'Not here yet,' Laura whispered back. 'I suspect she's planning to make an entrance and upstage the bride. That's her usual MO.'

Macy didn't know if Gabe or Eddie had said something, but in the last couple of days Laura had been a lot nicer to her. She'd been a lot nicer to everyone, in fact, and had that bleary-eyed, dishevelled glow that Macy suspected meant she and Gabe had been having a lot of make-up sex since the Vicar-Gate incident in The Fox. Macy couldn't help but feel a tiny bit jealous. Not only was Gabe incredibly nice and incredibly sexy, but it was a very long time since Macy had had sex, never mind the sort of sex that left you love-drunk and full of the joys of spring the next morning.

A Kate Upton lookalike in a show-stopping red dress distracted her from her self-pity. She was standing next to a balding, middle-aged man on the other side of the aisle. 'Who's that?' Macy asked Laura.

'Emma Harwich.'

'Not *the* Emma Harwich? The Gucci model?'

'And all-round slapper, yes,' said Laura. 'She's a local, unfortunately.'

'Is that her father she's with?' asked Macy.

Laura laughed, more loudly than she'd intended to. 'No,' she said, lowering her voice as people turned to look. 'That's Bertie Athol, aka the Duke of Moncreith.'

'He's a duke?' Macy sounded as impressed as only an American could. 'A real one?'

'Yup. More importantly, he's stinking rich and one of the biggest Tory Party donors,' said Laura. 'Oh, do look at poor Tom!' she said, turning to Gabe. 'I've never seen anyone so green. He looks like he's about to be shot.'

It was true, thought Macy. The groom did look an unfortunate shade of pureed pea, especially standing next to his tanned and handsome best man. Macy had expected English guys to be unattractive, a collection of hobbits with bad teeth and unfortunate facial hair, like Emma Harwich's duke. But she'd been pleasantly surprised since she moved to the

Swell Valley. More than half the men in the church today were good-looking, although none quite as good-looking as Gabe. Well, almost none. Macy found her gaze being inexorably drawn towards Santiago de la Cruz, smouldering in his morning suit on the other side of the aisle like a young Antonio Banderas.

James Craven, sitting in the row behind Santiago, leaned forward and whispered in his friend's ear, 'Someone likes you. Ten o'clock, dark bob, coffee-coloured dress.'

Santiago glanced at Macy, who immediately looked away.

'That's Macy Johanssen,' Santiago whispered back. 'She's the TV presenter for Gabe's show. Fast Eddie brought her over from America.'

'She's gorgeous.'

Santiago wrapped an arm around his wife's shoulders. 'If you say so.'

'Is she single?' asked James.

'I highly doubt it,' Santiago chuckled. 'Then again, neither are you, my friend. Remember?'

Santiago looked back and smiled at Luisa, the drop-dead gorgeous Argentine chick James had brought along as his date. Luisa smiled back briefly before returning to the pressing business of examining her cuticles and flicking her hair like an expensive but bored racehorse.

'She doesn't speak English, does she?' Santiago asked James, *sotto voce*.

'Not a word,' said James. 'Which has its pluses and minuses. D'you think you can get me Macy's number?'

At that moment Frank Bannister, the organist, struck up the opening chords of Handel's *La Réjouissance*. All chatter ceased as the entire church spun around in unison, craning their necks to get a first glimpse of the bride.

But instead of Logan Cranley, it was Tatiana Flint-Hamilton who came sailing down the aisle.

'Told you,' Laura whispered to Macy.

Making her way to her front-row seat next to the mother of the bride, Tati was escorted by none other than her ex-husband, Logan's brother Jason Cranley. The two of them were smiling and laughing like old friends.

'Christ,' said Gabe to Macy, under his breath. 'That's a turn-up for the books.'

'Why?'

'In a nutshell, *he's* gay, *she* married him for his money, then left him for his dad.'

Macy raised an eyebrow. 'Quite the modern family, these Cranleys.'

'You don't know the half of it,' said Gabe.

The entire congregation avidly scanned Tatiana's face for any sign of ageing. It was three years since she'd last been seen in Fittlescombe, at Max Bingley's short-lived wedding to Stella Goye. But her complexion and figure were both as flawless as ever.

'She's very beautiful,' said Macy.

'Yes,' said Gabe. 'She is.'

There was nothing else to say. In a simple buttermilk-yellow dress, with no jewellery and her hair loose, Tatiana outshone every other woman there, like the sun in a room full of candles.

As soon as she and Jason sat down, the organist switched to the 'Wedding March'. At last Logan walked in, beaming like a Cheshire cat on her father's arm. In floor-length, lace Alice Temperley, with a garland of daisies in her dark hair, Logan looked ravishing. She might not be as classically beautiful as her father's girlfriend, but no one could have looked happier or more deliriously in love.

Watching her catch her future husband's eye, Macy felt an unworthy stab of jealousy for the second time since she'd got to the church. It was hard not to wish you had someone on a day like today. She distracted herself by checking out Brett Cranley, who was far better-looking and more virile in the flesh than he was in pictures, and not nearly as old.

Life isn't all hearts and flowers, she reminded herself, firmly, thinking of the heartbreak that marriage had brought her own mother. *Logan Cranley'll find that out one day, even if she doesn't know it now.*

The service seemed to be over almost as soon as it had begun. There was one semi-hairy moment, when the vicar openly alluded to the *Valley Farm* controversy during the homily and Gabe looked as if he might be about to blow a gasket. Something about how wonderful it was to see all the village brought together in joy, at a time of such pain and discord. But other than that, Macy barely had time to drink in the beauty of the medieval church with its knights' tombs and stained-glass windows, or to enjoy the classic English hymns like 'Jerusalem', before the whole thing was over and Angela Cranley was walking back down the aisle behind her daughter, elegant and understated in a navy-blue shift dress and pillbox hat on Max Bingley's arm.

'What now?' Macy asked Gabe and Laura, following them out into the general crush.

'Now the fun part,' said Gabe, rubbing his hands together. 'Reception at Furlings.'

'We don't go home and change first?'

'No,' said Gabe. 'We leg it up the hill and hit the free bar before the good champagne runs out and Brett starts serving Cava.'

'I can hardly imagine Brett Cranley would stoop to Cava!' said Macy. 'He must be worth hundreds of millions.'

'He is,' said Gabe. 'But he likes to hold on to them. Brett's tighter than a gnat's chuff, believe me. And I say that as a friend.'

Outside the church it was a gloriously sunny late afternoon. The bride and groom were posing for pictures on the green, climbing up into a simple pony and trap, bedecked with flowing white ribbons. Apart from the ubiquitous cell phones, it was like a scene from a Jane Austen novel.

'I doubt Brett will be tight today,' said Laura. 'Not for his little girl's wedding, and at his ex-wife's house too. He'll be in full show-off mode. I reckon it's going to be quite a party.'

Seeing Macy about to be cornered by the vicar, Laura wisely dragged Gabe off in the opposite direction. Strolling along the lane up to Furlings, arm in arm with Gabe, Laura felt happier and more relaxed than she had in months. The pilot of *Valley Farm* would be shot on Monday, and miraculously all of the kinks surrounding filming seemed to have been worked out. Shooting indoors and outdoors, working with animals, which rarely did what they were supposed to when they were supposed to, capturing farm and village life without being intrusive, switching from scripted to unscripted action – all of these things were challenging. But the small Channel 5 production team had been a model of patience under trying circumstances. And Laura had finally come around to Eddie Wellesley's point of view about the local protests: that they made for good drama and should be included in the show, not edited out.

Gabe nuzzled into her neck as they walked up the hill among a growing crowd of wedding guests.

'You're gorgeous.'

Laura smiled. 'Thanks. But you're blind. I look awful.'

Laura had felt distinctly frumpy in the church, especially standing next to Macy. Her wine-red cocktail dress from Next, an old faithful that had done sterling service at countless weddings, christenings and work dinners, seemed tired and lacklustre compared to the beautifully cut, designer dresses of the other glamorous women. Teamed with slightly stained shoes and a ponytail, because she'd forgotten to wash her hair this morning and it was too dirty to let down, the overall look was definitely more farmer's wife than sex siren.

'You never look awful,' said Gabe. 'You were the most beautiful woman in that church, although I love that you don't realize it. If you knew how sexy you were, you'd be trading me in for a younger model in no time.'

Everybody moved to the side of the lane and cheered as the bride and groom clattered past in their horse-drawn carriage, ribbons streaming merrily behind them. Tom had lost his green pallor now and was gazing adoringly at Logan; they were lost in their own world. A few moments later they were followed by a gleaming dark blue Bentley.

'Isn't that Eddie?' Laura peered through the windows as the car passed. 'Why are they driving?'

'Lady Muck's too posh to walk with the hoi polloi, I expect,' said Gabe. 'That woman's so uptight she scares me. I can seriously picture her running amok with a machine gun one of these days.'

'Let's hope she's not armed today. David and Louise Carlyle have been invited to the reception.'

Gabe's eyes narrowed at the mention of David Carlyle's name.

'Gabriel,' Laura said sternly. 'The vicar's one thing. But

you may *not*, repeat *not*, assault the editor of a national newspaper.'

Gabe gave her a 'you're no fun' look.

'Don't tell me,' he said, running on ahead. 'Tell Eddie.'

CHAPTER EIGHT

Brett Cranley stood on the verandah of his former house surveying the wedding guests as they sipped his champagne. Angela, Brett's first wife of more than twenty years, appeared at his side. Together they watched their daughter Logan, hand in hand with her new husband, laughing as she crossed the lawn. 'She looks happy, doesn't she?' said Angela.

'She does,' Brett smiled. 'She and Tom are a good match. We've got a great girl there.'

'We have,' Angela agreed.

Their divorce had been painful, as all divorces were, but three years on, Brett and Angela Cranley were good friends.

'Jason's doing wonderfully too,' said Angela, pointing out their son, who was standing by the bar with his husband and Tatiana. 'He and George are so good for one another.'

'Hmmm,' said Brett.

He'd come to terms with the fact that his son was gay, but he would never be able to accept it with the same easy grace that Angela did. As ridiculous as he knew it was, he also felt jealous of the close bond that Jason still shared with

Tatiana. The sexual side of their marriage might have been a sham, but the affection between them was real. Watching the two of them talking intimately now, their arms wrapped around one another, Brett felt his chest tighten.

She's flirting deliberately, to bait me, he thought angrily. *She's still mad at me for letting Angela take Furlings in the divorce.*

Max Bingley, Angela's current other half, wandered over.

'Do you mind if I steal Angela for a moment? The photographer wants a picture of her and Logan together, just the two of them.'

'Of course,' said Brett. He watched Max and Angela walk away, hand in hand, and felt a twinge of sadness. It wasn't that he begrudged Angie her happiness. No one deserved it more. But he still felt guilty that he'd made her so *un*happy in the last years of their marriage, and perhaps just a little resentful that Max Bingley had succeeded where he had failed.

'Mr Cranley?' A very sexy dark-haired girl in a nude silk dress and gold necklace interrupted his musings. Brett instantly brightened. 'I'm Macy Johanssen. Sorry to ambush you, but I've heard so much about you I thought I'd take the chance to introduce myself. I'm co-presenting *Valley Farm* with Gabriel Baxter. I believe you two know each other?'

'Sure,' Brett purred. 'I know Gabe. You certainly seem to be ruffling some feathers around here with this new show.'

Macy rolled her eyes. 'The vicar's got the whole village whipped into a frenzy. With a little helping hand from David Carlyle.'

'Oh. I'm not sure you can blame the reverend – or David, for that matter,' said Brett. 'In my experience it doesn't take much for Fittlescombe folk to get their knickers in a twist.'

Macy laughed. Brett looked to see if Tatiana was watching

him being chatted up by this beautiful television presenter, but infuriatingly she was still glued to Jason.

'It's a stunning house,' Macy sipped her champagne. 'You must miss it.'

'Not really. I like America. It suits me. Besides, this house caused me a lot of grief one way and another.'

Macy nodded. She'd heard some of the saga.

'Tatiana still misses it desperately,' said Brett. 'She grew up here. Furlings is the love of her life. It means far more to her than I do,' he added – a touch sadly, Macy thought. 'Good luck with your show.' He kissed her on the cheek. 'I have to go and make a speech. Oh, and keep an eye on Gabriel Baxter. That man's the biggest rogue in Fittlescombe.'

I wish he were, thought Macy with a sigh. *Gabe seems about as likely to fool around as Pope Francis.*

Brett's speech was actually very touching. You could hear the warmth and tenderness in his voice as he spoke about his only daughter.

Laura was so engrossed, she didn't notice her handbag buzzing. Only after Penny de la Cruz tapped her on the shoulder and whispered *'Phone'* did she register the annoyed glances from the surrounding tables.

Grabbing her bag, Laura weaved her way through the tables in Furlings' Great Hall mouthing 'Sorry' until she reached the corridor.

'Greta? Is everything all right?'

'Erm . . . not really.' Laura could hardly make out the nanny's voice through the howling children in the background. 'Hugh had a bad dream and woke Luca up. I've been trying to settle them back off for the last hour but now Luca's thrown up and—'

'Don't worry,' said Laura. 'I'm on my way.'

'Can't she deal with it?' Gabe said crossly when Laura returned to the table. He'd been looking forward to dancing with his wife tonight. They almost never got to let their hair down any more, without the children. And Gabe missed Laura the wife, as opposed to Laura the boss. He'd been seeing too much of the latter recently and not enough of the former. 'Isn't that what we're paying her for?'

'It is,' Laura kissed him. She felt the same as he did, and was disappointed to have to leave early. 'But Luca's asking for me, and you know how much he hates being sick.'

'*I'm* asking for you,' Gabe said petulantly.

'I'll see you in bed later,' said Laura. 'I'll be the sleeping, naked woman smelling oh-so-slightly of vomit.'

Macy, sitting two tables away with the Wellesleys and a charming young couple named Will and Lisa Nutley, watched Laura leave. Taking her plate of wedding cake with her, she made a beeline for Gabe.

'What happened?' She took Laura's seat. 'Is everything all right?'

'Oh, yes, fine,' Gabe frowned, pouring himself another hefty glass of claret. 'Babysitter problems. How's your table?'

'OK,' said Macy. 'Not as fun as yours.'

'Drink?' He held out the bottle.

Macy laughed coquettishly. 'Why not?'

It was impossible not to flirt with Gabe. He looked incredible in his morning suit, so dashing and British and *big*. Something about the way the dark jacket hung off him emphasized his broad, farmer's shoulders and his masculine, stocky build. Macy was used to seeing him in work clothes – jeans and an old T-shirt and wellington boots. He looked

121

great in that too. But it was nice to see him 'off duty' for once, and incredibly rare to catch him alone, without Laura.

'Is it terribly rude to table-hop?' asked Macy.

'Probably. But you're not the only one,' said Gabe. 'Look over there. Poor old Bertie Athol's having a "Beam me up, Scotty" moment.'

Over on table nine, the Duke of Moncreith was giving Lady Wellesley what Eddie liked to call 'a damn good listening to'. The lovely Emma Harwich had evaporated into the throng, leaving her decrepit date to Annabel's unwanted attentions.

'We do miss Westminster,' Annabel told the duke wistfully. 'Do you still keep your beautiful flat in Albany?'

'Of course. You must come over for dinner when you're next in town,' said Bertie, dutifully.

'We'd adore that,' Annabel gushed. 'Tell me, have you been to Chequers recently?'

'Not recently, no.'

'I heard Martha Hambly's had some rather ghastly modern media room installed?'

'Hello Bertie.'

Seeing the Tory Party's single largest donor being cornered by his wife, Eddie raced over to the rescue. Annabel was usually a skilled political networker, but when it came to the aristocracy her snobbery sometimes got the better of her. She had an unfortunate tendency to use a sledgehammer to crack a nut.

'May I borrow my wife for a moment?'

The duke's eyes lit up. 'By all means.'

'What are you *doing*?' hissed Annabel, as Eddie dragged her away. 'We were getting along brilliantly.'

'I'm sure you were.'

'You do realize that Bertie Athol's a very important man? We need people like that in our camp if we're going to get you back into Cabinet, Edward. You must *try*.'

'I know,' Eddie kissed her on the cheek, 'and I will. I only came over because I can't find Milo. Have you seen him?'

'No,' said Annabel crossly. 'I haven't. But that's hardly a good reason to interrupt a very productive conversation. Now, if you'll excuse me, I must get back to the duke. Oh! He's gone.'

While Annabel went off in search of the hapless Bertie, Eddie wandered into the main house, looking for Milo.

Although Annabel might not believe it, Eddie was in fact very conscious of his image. He dreamed of a return to Cabinet, the way that a recovering alcoholic still dreams of a drink. The Duke of Moncreith wasn't the only person here tonight whose opinion mattered, and who might be helpful if Eddie played his cards right. The last thing he wanted was for his drunk son to end up making some kind of scene. Eddie had seen Milo hitting the bar hard earlier, before the speeches. Ten minutes ago, he realized with a sinking feeling that he hadn't seen him since.

'Milo!'

Eddie poked his head round the door of the kitchen, then the library. No sign. There was a queue for the gents, but Milo wasn't in it. Perhaps, if he *was* feeling the worse for wear, he'd gone upstairs in search of a loo.

A giggling couple passed Eddie on the stairs, coming down as he was going up. No prizes for guessing what they'd been up to.

Eddie walked along the upstairs corridor, opening doors, but all was quiet. The two family bathrooms were both empty, as were the rest of the bedrooms, thank God. Angela and Max's master suite was sensibly locked. Eddie was about to head back down the kitchen stairs at the other end of the hall, when a clattering noise stopped him in his tracks. It seemed to be coming from the laundry room. Pulling open the door, Eddie saw his son sprawled out on his back on top of a huge pile of dirty sheets. On top of him, still in the lace dress she'd worn at the church, Emma Harwich was frenziedly bucking and moaning, tossing her long blonde hair around like a rag doll in the wind.

'Jesus *Christ*!' said Eddie, closing the door with a slam.

A few moments later, Emma emerged, looking flushed but not particularly embarrassed.

'Lovely wedding,' she smiled at Eddie.

'He's seventeen,' Eddie said disapprovingly.

'I know,' Emma sighed contentedly. 'One forgets how much energy they have at that age. Don't be too hard on him. He's a sweet boy.'

And with that she glided down the stairs serenely, as if nothing had happened.

As soon as she'd gone, Eddie burst back into the laundry room. Milo was dressed, thank God, but the task of doing up the buttons on his shirt was proving too much for his drink- and sex-addled brain.

'Have you any idea what you've just done? *Any* idea?' Eddie fumed.

Milo looked perplexed. 'Is that a trick question?'

'She's Bertie Athol's sodding girlfriend!'

'Hmm.' Milo focused hard on his buttonhole. 'I might be wrong. But I don't think she's *that* into him.'

'I don't give a fuck who she's into,' Eddie exploded. 'If Bertie finds out my son's been bonking his girlfriend, I'm finished in the Tory Party.'

'I thought you were finished anyway? After prison,' Milo said guilelessly.

'You stupid, entitled . . .' Eddie muttered murderously.

'I don't know why you're so angry,' said Milo. 'Mum said you both wanted me to stop seeing Roxanne and find a nice, educated girl.'

'We did!'

'Emma's educated.'

'Well, she isn't nice,' said Eddie. 'Go home, now, before anybody sees you. We'll talk about this tomorrow.'

'But shouldn't I—'

'I said *go home*, Milo. It's not a bloody request!'

Downstairs, the party was in full swing. Brett and Tatiana were arguing loudly and drunkenly underneath the plum tree in the garden.

'If you loved me you'd buy it back!' Tati was yelling. 'You'd find a way.'

Her mascara was smudged and her hair windswept and messy. The cool, almost regal beauty she'd projected in the church was gone now. Tired of playing Grace Kelly, she'd reverted to type as a spoiled and demanding wildcat. But, if anything, the unhinged version was even sexier.

Brett grabbed her by both arms.

'It is *not* for *sale*, Tatiana! It's Angela's home. She's happy here, which – by the way – is something you never were. If only you'd wake up and take off those rose-tinted goggles for half a second . . .'

They battled on, with Brett only silencing her in the end by kissing her on the mouth so passionately and forcefully that Tati had no option but to give in.

Watching them, Penny de la Cruz said to her husband, 'I don't know how they do it. It looks exhausting.'

'What does?' said Santiago.

'The passion. The jealousy. The flaming rows. Brett must be well into his fifties!'

Reaching down, Santiago caressed his wife's bottom, delectably encased in midnight-blue crushed velvet.

'I don't know about the flaming rows. But we have passion. You're not exhausted, are you?'

'Of course not, darling,' said Penny, leaning into him. 'At least, if I am, it's not because of you,' she corrected herself, catching sight of her wayward daughter Emma sprawled out in the Duke of Moncreith's lap, very obviously drunk. 'Why can't she find somebody nice and normal? Preferably her own age? Like Logan Cranley did.'

'She can,' said Santiago. 'She just doesn't want to.'

Penny sighed. 'I suppose you're right. It's not always easy, this "finding true love" business.'

'No,' Santiago said distantly. 'It isn't.'

Penny followed his gaze to where Macy Johanssen was locked deep in conversation with Gabe Baxter. It was obvious from her body language and the adoring look in her eyes that she was smitten. Equally obvious was the fact that Gabe was now properly, profoundly drunk.

'Should we do something?' asked Penny.

Santiago considered. 'Yes. I think we probably should.'

Max Bingley was sitting on the verandah swing with Angela, sipping a cup of strong coffee. Although not officially the host of tonight's reception, Max did live at Furlings most of the time, and felt it was important for somebody to stay sober and on top of things. Tati had staggered off to the kitchen, where she was drunkenly reminiscing with the staff about her father and the old days. Brett was locked in an animated conversation with David Carlyle.

'Why d'you think Brett invited him?' Max asked Angela, marvelling again at the transcendent naffness of the editor's tight grey suit and clip-on bow tie. 'It's not as if they're friends. And he's such an oik.'

'Don't be snobby,' said Angela. 'It doesn't suit you. If you must know, I invited him.'

Max looked at her in astonishment. 'You? Why?'

'Why not?' said Angela. 'He's local . . . ish; he knows Brett socially and his wife, Louise, is a sweetheart.'

'Maybe, but he's baying for Eddie Wellesley's blood in a most unpleasant fashion. Did you know he's been offering money to people in the village to dig up dirt on the Wellesley marriage?'

'Are you sure?' Angela frowned. 'I can't imagine people here would go for that sort of thing.'

'So far they haven't. But *Valley Farm* is so unpopular, you never know what might happen eventually. It's not only this TV show that Carlyle wants to scupper. It's everything Wellesley touches.'

'Well, I think the whole thing's too childish and silly for words,' said Angela. 'They're both grown men. They should work it out. As for *Valley Farm*, I'm not thrilled about it either, but it's hardly a good enough reason to have the entire village set at one another's throats.'

Max kissed the top of her head. 'I agree, my darling.'

'If you really want to know why I asked so many people, that's why,' said Angela, her voice suddenly hoarse with emotion. 'I wanted today to be about coming together, and healing old wounds. Brett and Tatiana coming back here,

Jason and George, you and me, all happy for Logan and for each other. I thought, if we can do it, why can't the village? I'm so tired of everybody fighting and shouting all the time. Truly, if I hear one more person bitch about the bloody television cameras, I'm going to move back to Sydney and be done with it.'

'You don't mean that.' Max hugged her tightly.

'No,' said Angela. 'I don't. I just think life's too short for all this tension. Besides, I'm sure David Carlyle's got a nice side. He must do, to have such a sweet wife.'

Gabe made the mistake of standing up when Santiago and James Craven came over to his table. 'Mate!'

Stumbling forwards, he almost collapsed on top of Macy. Only James's quick reactions, inserting himself between the two of them, prevented her from being knocked to the ground. Instead Gabe slammed into James like a falling tree, before rocking back upright, where he was 'caught' by Santiago.

'I think maybe it's time to go home,' said Santiago, pulling Gabe's arm tightly around his shoulder and propping him upright, like a human splint. 'I'll drive you back to the farm.'

'Macy, y'know Santiago?' Gabe slurred. 'Santiago this-zzz Macy Yo hands . . . Yo handsome.'

'It's all right,' said Macy, getting up. 'I'm heading home too. I can get my cab to drop him off on the way.'

Santiago gave her a knowing look. 'I'll take him,' he said firmly. 'You two stay here and enjoy yourselves.'

James seized the moment, holding out his hand for Macy to shake.

'James Craven.'

'Macy Johanssen.'

'I think you'll find it's pronounced "Yo Handsome",' James quipped. 'Although Yo Drop-Dead Gorgeous might be more accurate. Today was the first time I've been to church since Christmas and, thanks to you, I was sinning through the whole service. If I end up burning in eternal hellfire, I'll know who to blame.'

Macy laughed. She was annoyed with Santiago for kidnapping Gabe, not to mention implying that she'd been planning to molest him during the cab-ride home. But it was hard to stay mad whilst being chatted up by an amusing and really quite sexy man.

'I saw you in church too,' she said. 'With your girlfriend.'

'Ah! Luisa,' said James. 'Not my girlfriend.'

Macy raised an eyebrow. 'No?'

'No. Easy mistake to make. She's my er . . . my . . .'

'Niece?'

'Goddaughter, actually,' James grinned. 'Terribly badly behaved. Her parents despair of her.'

'I'll bet they do.'

'They brought me in to provide some moral guidance.'

'Perhaps she needs it now,' said Macy. 'Isn't that her over there, eating the best man alive?'

She pointed to the dance floor, where James's neglected date was indeed comprehensively exploring the tonsils of Tom's best friend, Matthew Reed.

James shook his head. 'Tragic. A lost cause.'

'So, James, what do you do?' asked Macy.

'Me?' James was momentarily taken aback. As one of England's best-known cricketers, and with a slew of sponsorship deals under his belt, he hadn't been asked this question in quite a while. 'I do lots of things. I play a bit of cricket,' he said modestly.

'Really? I've always thought that looked like such a boring sport. Nothing happens! I'd rather have my teeth pulled.'

James laughed loudly. 'I think I might be a tiny bit in love with you. Can I get you a drink?'

As the evening wore on, most of the older guests drifted away, leaving only Tom and Logan's friends, family members and a few serious drinkers on the dance floor or propping up the bar. Just before 1 a.m., everyone spilled out into the driveway to wave off the bride and groom.

Eddie Wellesley swayed unsteadily as the young couple pulled away. He'd had too much to drink, and the sight of so much youth and happiness had made him feel uncharacteristically morose. He and Annabel had been like that once. Adoring. Contented. Complete. But he'd fucked it all up. Sometimes he felt that the only thing they still shared was their political ambitions. That and their love for Milo, although God knows that was being tested to the limit right now. They needed some time alone, really alone. A chance to get things back to the way they used to be. But right now there seemed to be precious little chance of that.

Annabel had been even angrier than Eddie when he told her about what had happened in Furlings' laundry room. But somehow her anger had veered off course and become directed at Eddie.

'What is he, some sort of sex addict?' she hissed. 'I suppose the apple never falls very far from the tree, does it?'

She'd driven home in a whirlwind of bitterness. The Duke of Moncreith had also made an early exit with Emma Harwich, probably wisely given her tendency to drop her knickers for any man who smiled in her general direction. After that, Eddie had talked briefly to Jason Cranley and his husband, a perfectly charming art dealer named George Wilkes, and then spent most of the night avoiding the vicar and his posse of angry locals, all of whom seemed intent on haranguing him about Monday's pilot of *Valley Farm*.

Now it really was time to go. Fumbling in his inside jacket pocket for his mobile phone, he ordered a cab back to Brockhurst. He was just considering popping back into the house for a last pee when he suddenly found himself face to face with David Carlyle.

'Hello, Eddie. Long time no see.'

Eddie had shown remarkable restraint so far, scrupulously avoiding bumping into David, or being drawn into any sort of drama. But now that Carlyle's smug, fake-tanned face was inches from his own, the urge to smash his fist into it was almost overwhelming.

He started to walk away. David called after him.

'How was prison?'

'It was all right,' said Eddie, his eyes narrowed. 'A better class of person than you meet at Westminster, most of the time.'

'Well, of course you'd know all about class,' said David, smiling nastily. 'You and your Old Etonian chums. It must have been quite a wake-up call, realizing that us plebs aren't the only ones who have to obey the laws of the land.'

'*We* plebs,' Eddie corrected him. 'Honestly, what *do* they teach one in comprehensive schools?'

The smile died on David's lips. He pushed Eddie hard, backing him up against the kitchen garden wall. Putting his face so close to Eddie's that Eddie could smell the onion on his breath, he whispered, 'I'll *finish* you, Wellesley. Do you hear me? First I'm going to sink your crappy reality show. And then I'm going to sink *you*.'

Eddie yawned. 'You know, David, you've become a ghastly

bore since Tristram fired you. I mean, you were always were a bully and an all-round toerag. That's why the PM got rid of you. But at least you used to be *interesting*. What happened, old boy?'

David drew back his fist to an audible gasp. A crowd of onlookers had gathered around to watch the showdown between Fast Eddie and his nemesis.

'Be my guest,' drawled Eddie. 'It's known as assault. I believe it's considered a crime, even when horrid, common little nobodies do it.'

David hesitated, then stepped back. Straightening his hair, he smiled again.

'You have no idea what I've got on you, Wellesley. *No idea*. That's the best part. Our campaign against your show is just a little teaser. But I'm going to make sure my readers and everyone in this country gets to know who you and your family *really* are. You take care now.'

Turning on his heel, he walked back into the house.

Macy came rushing over to Eddie with James Craven. 'Are you all right? Did he threaten you?'

'I'm fine,' said Eddie, dusting himself off. He noticed Macy and the England all-rounder were holding hands. 'How about you, my dear. Having fun?'

'Never mind me. I want to talk about you,' said Macy. 'What did Carlyle say?'

'Nothing important,' said Eddie. 'He's full of hot air, as usual. Ah, that's my cab. I must go.'

Taking his leave of Macy and James – another young couple with their whole futures ahead of them – Eddie looked back at Furlings as he drove away. Lit up like a magical palace in the darkness, it truly was the most stunning house, perfect in every way.

He wondered what David Carlyle had meant by his last threat. *To let people know who you and your family* really *are?* It was the 'family' part that worried him. Was it just hot air? Or was Carlyle alluding to something real, something tangible? All of Eddie's own skeletons were well and truly out of the closet. But the horrible thought struck him that Carlyle might have something on Milo. The boy had been running terribly wild lately, with tonight's debacle only the latest in a long line of potentially highly embarrassing antics. What if David knew something – something that Eddie didn't? Most people might consider a politician's child to be off limits, but not David Carlyle. There were no depths to which that man wouldn't sink, no fetid gutter in which he would not be quite happy to abase himself in pursuit of a story. Despite himself, Eddie felt a sharp pang of fear run through him.

Watching Eddie's car pull away, Macy leaned into James like a sapling propped against a giant oak. He smelled incredible – of cologne and desire – and his fingers were stroking the back of her neck. Macy closed her eyes. Something had been holding her back up till now, but she suddenly felt an overwhelming wave of arousal.

'Let's go to bed.'

James grinned, letting his hand slide down from her neck to her bottom.

'What a marvellous idea. My place or yours?'

'Mine,' said Macy firmly. James was cute, but not cute enough for her to do the walk of shame down Fittlescombe High Street tomorrow morning. 'We can christen my new bed.'

'A wedding and a christening in one day. We're quite the Christian soldiers, aren't we?'

'Mmmmm,' Macy kissed him. 'We should start a Sunday school.'

Gabe Baxter might be spoken for. But he wasn't the only fish in the sea. England, Macy decided, was turning out to be a lot more fun than she'd imagined.

Milo Wellesley had taken the long way home, via the Black Swan in Brockhurst, where the landlord took a relaxed view of both underage drinking and timekeeping, with last orders regularly called well after eleven.

As he staggered out onto the High Street at midnight, the cool night air and sudden total darkness both came as a shock. It was an effort to remember the direction of Mill Lane, and for a few moments Milo stood swaying uncertainly, coming to terms with how very, very drunk he was.

Eventually he pulled himself together sufficiently to find his way home, turning into the drive just in time to see his father speed past in a cab. Milo watched from the shadows as his mother opened the front door, stiff backed and brittle. He saw his father follow her inside, slowly, his shoulders slumped. They'd obviously had a row. Milo hoped it wasn't about him and Emma Harwich, but decided to loiter for a bit before going inside, just in case.

Noticing a light still on in Magda's cottage, he headed towards it, like a befuddled moth towards the moon. Unfortunately, a few yards from the front door, he tripped and hurtled headlong into a metal dustbin, sending it crashing noisily to the ground and spraining his ankle badly.

Seconds later the door flew open. Magda stood on the threshold in a dressing gown and wellington boots. Her pale skin looked almost translucent in the moonlight, like a beautiful ghost. 'Who's there?' she demanded, brandishing a frying pan menacingly in the darkness.

'It's only me. Milo.' He peered up at her. 'Sorry.'

'What are you doing here?' Magda lowered the pan.

'Hiding from Mum and Dad,' said Milo. His voice was still slurred with drink and his hair and clothes were all over the place.

'Do you know what time it is?'

'Er . . .'

'You'd better come in.'

Five minutes later, sitting in Magda's tiny kitchen with a packet of frozen peas on his ankle and a glass of Alka-Seltzer fizzing in his hand, Milo recounted what had happened earlier up at Furlings with Emma.

'Dad went ballistic.'

'I can imagine,' said Magda.

'I didn't know her boyfriend was some bigwig,' Milo protested.

'But you knew she had a boyfriend.'

'Hardly a boy. He's about a hundred and five,' Milo said bitterly.

'And what about Roxanne?' asked Magda archly. 'I thought you two were in love. Isn't that what you told me, when I covered for you the day I arrived?'

'We grew apart.' Milo smiled sheepishly from beneath a his floppy blond fringe.

Magda thought, *Gosh, he's good looking. No wonder Emma Harwich dumped her Tory grandee.*

Walking to the window, she saw the lights in Eddie and Annabel's bedroom go off.

'They're in bed,' she told Milo. 'You can sneak back in now.'

He looked at her plaintively. 'Can't I stay here tonight? I'm not sure I can walk on this ankle.'

'Absolutely not,' said Magda. 'I have work in the morning. Besides, if your father wakes up tomorrow and finds your bed hasn't been slept in, it'll only make things worse.'

Milo sighed. This was true. But something about being here with Magda made him feel stupidly happy. He didn't want to leave.

'You're very beautiful, you know,' he said, earnestly.

Magda's eyes widened, but she laughed it off. 'After what you've drunk tonight, all women are beautiful.'

'I mean it.'

'So do I. Now drink that Alka-Seltzer and get out of here, before you get into any more trouble. And try not to wake the whole village on your way across the lawn.'

Later, in bed, Magda found herself hoping that Sir Edward and Lady Wellesley went easy on their wayward son. Milo was like a puppy, infuriating and adorable in equal measure, with too much energy for his own good.

He has a lot of growing up to do, she thought. But his kindness touched her.

CHAPTER NINE

'So what exactly are we looking at here? Talk us through what's going on?'

Jennifer Lee, the trainee vet handpicked by Channel 5 to appear in *Valley Farm*'s pilot, because she was attractive in an ordinary, girl-next-door sort of way and inexperienced enough to make the sort of mistakes that viewers found endearing, answered Macy's question for the sixth time that morning.

'This is foot-bathing,' Jennifer explained, trying not to look directly at the cameras as she delivered her lines whilst simultaneously focusing on the struggling ewe's hindquarters as she splashed about in the highly toxic formalin solution. 'They don't much like it . . . as you can see.' Sweat poured down Jennifer's forehead and between her breasts. Her round, freckled cheeks were bright red, like twin apples, and her curly chestnut hair stuck to her face in great wet clumps. 'But it's very important to protect against bacteria and prevent scald, foot-rot—'

'Cut!' Laura yelled loudly.

'What? Again?' Exasperated, Jennifer let go of the ewe, which went careering off across the farmyard, almost knocking Macy flying before being intercepted by a skilful lunge from Gabe.

'I'm sorry,' said Laura. 'But there's still too much background noise. Perhaps we should move into one of the barns?'

Today was the first day of filming and the protestors were out in force. In a stroke of evil genius, Bill Clempson, the vicar, had provided drums, tambourines and some appalling form of screeching, penny-whistle-type instrument to his 'troops'. The noise was irritating to the human ear, but it clearly utterly terrified the poor animals. Jennifer was already covered in cuts and bruises beneath her protective coat and goggles, from where the panicked sheep had kicked her. So much for the glamour of television.

Dave, the sound engineer, put down his boom mic. 'I'll go and talk to them.'

'It won't do any good,' said Gabe.

'Probably not, but I'll give it a go.'

'One of you follow him,' Laura said to the two cameramen. 'At this point they're part of the show. Let's see if they give him anything interesting.' Turning to Macy, Gabe and the rest of the crew, she added imperiously: 'You lot can start moving everything into the barn.'

'I thought we were doing today outside?' Macy protested. 'You said you wanted the glorious weather and the exterior shots of the farm.'

'We'll use the footage but the dialogue has to be inside,' Laura said dismissively. 'It's just the way it is, I'm afraid. Let's not waste any more time. Now . . . where's Jennifer?'

The vet was gone.

'She's probably gone to the bathroom,' said Macy through gritted teeth. The 'easy-going' Laura from the weekend had clearly been kidnapped by aliens on Sunday night and replaced with the harpie of old. 'Or are we not allowed to pee now?'

'I don't want people wandering off willy-nilly,' Laura snapped. 'This is the sodding pilot episode. This is *it*! What we film today will decide the entire future of this show. Am I the only person here who understands that?'

Laura stomped off to the barn. Macy shot Gabe a murderous look.

'Think yourself lucky,' he said, returning Macy's scowl with a broad grin as he manhandled the ewe back into her pen. 'Some of us are married to her.'

How can you sound so pleased about it? thought Macy. *Talk about love being blind.*

On the grass verge outside the farm gates, the junior camera-man, Dean, filmed his colleague attempting to persuade the angry villagers to lay down their whistles and call it a day.

'It's a matter of principle,' the vicar intoned pompously, using his 'church voice' because he knew he was being filmed.

'Yes, but the animals are suffering,' explained the sound engineer. 'That's not fair, is it? None of this is their fault.'

'No indeed,' said the vicar, 'it's yours. You stop filming, we'll stop protesting.'

'But, Vicar, this is private property. The owners have every right to—'

'Gabriel Baxter should focus on his animals, not on the

pursuit of fame,' Reverend Clempson said primly. 'As Our Lord taught us, a good shepherd always puts his flock before himself.'

'Vicar! You must come!'

Hillary Wincup, an ample-bosomed stalwart of the Fittlescombe WI and staunch supporter of the new young vicar, came racing around from the lane. While she panted with exertion, her tweed-covered breasts bounced up and down like twin medicine balls, and were in danger of knocking her unconscious at any moment.

'Mrs Wincup. Don't upset yourself. Whatever's the matter?' The vicar arranged his features into a practised look of concern.

'It's . . . it's . . .' The exhausted woman fought for breath. 'Your car.'

Clempson's faux concern was replaced by the real thing.

'My car? What about my car?'

Poor Mrs Hillary Wincup looked close to tears. 'You'd better come and see.'

Jennifer the vet reappeared in the barn as the last sheep was ushered into the pen.

'Ah, there you are,' said Laura. 'Good. We're almost ready to go again. Could someone tell Dean and Dave they need to get back here?'

An ear-piercing scream made everybody look up. It came from the lane, and was followed by more deranged-sounding howls.

'What on earth?'

Laura raced outside, followed by the second cameraman, Gabe, Macy and Jennifer bringing up the rear. A tractor had been left parked to the side of the lane, its empty trailer still attached at the rear. The contents of that trailer – an enormous, steaming mound of silage – had been dumped unceremoniously on top of the vicar's beloved red Mini Cooper, which was now almost completely submerged.

'My car!' Bill Clempson wailed, wringing his hands like a mother over a lost child.

'Keep filming!' Laura told the crew, but they were already on a roll.

'It's destroyed!' sobbed the vicar. 'I can't . . . I'm speechless. Who would do such a dreadful thing?'

Standing directly behind Gabe and Macy, Jennifer muttered quietly, 'Maybe someone sick to death of being kicked in the shins by a flock of frightened sheep?'

Gabe looked at the young vet with renewed respect. 'You didn't!'

'Of course not,' Jennifer smiled sweetly. 'That sort of damage to property would be completely illegal.'

Macy burst out laughing. One of the photographers from the *Echo* snapped her mid-guffaw.

'It's not funny!' The vicar stamped his foot petulantly.

'It is a little funny,' said Macy.

'I demand to know who did this!'

'Now, now, Vicar,' grinned Gabe. 'Let he who is without sin cast the first stone and all that.'

Laura didn't know whether to laugh or cry. The pilot was supposed to focus on farm life, on the animals and the landscape and the simple rural rhythms of the valley. Instead it was turning into *The Benny Hill Show*.

What if the vicar pressed charges? This could come back to bite them in a big way.

On the other hand, the network *had* asked for drama.

Jennifer Lee smiled up at Gabe. 'Let's go back to the barn

and finish the foot-bathing. Before someone picks up another fucking tambourine.'

'Brilliant. That's bloody brilliant. We should have the man on the payroll.'

Eddie Wellesley hung up the phone looking excessively pleased with himself. He was in the kitchen at Riverside Hall, helping himself to a third slice of fruitcake – working on these damn memoirs was making him ravenous; he had rung Laura quickly to find out how the first day's filming was going.

'Well I think it's disgraceful,' said Annabel, after Eddie had told her the silage saga. She'd been in the pantry for the past forty minutes, hovering over Magda's shoulder while she folded the napkins and tablecloths, making sure everything was being done correctly. Annabel found she spent a lot of time following Magda, which she resented. Really, one ought to be able to trust one's staff. The more closely she watched, the more mistakes she found. The girl was a harder worker than her predecessors, but she could still be sloppy and looked permanently exhausted, which Annabel found irritating; although not as irritating as the sycophantic tone Eddie always used when talking to that bloody Baxter woman.

Eddie had promised only yesterday to spend less time on *Valley Farm* and to concentrate on his memoirs, devoting more energy and effort to the political comeback that both he and Annabel wanted. The role of a Westminster wife was not an easy one, as Annabel knew better than most. But it *was* a role, a purpose in life, and it came with a certain prestige that being the wife of a television producer could never hope to offer. After all the sacrifices Annabel had made, all the humiliation she'd suffered for Eddie's career, she wasn't prepared to walk away meekly, without a fight. The near-miss with Milo and the Duke of Moncreith's girlfriend over the weekend had focused both Eddie and Annabel's minds on just how important returning to politics was, for both of them. As had David Carlyle's mysterious threat to unleash some further, unnamed mayhem into their lives. Annabel had agreed to host a big political dinner as a sort of unofficial launch to Eddie's 'win back the Tory Party' campaign. But while Annabel slaved over a hot pile of napkins with the home help, Eddie was in his study, wasting time on the phone, gossiping about the stupid pilot. It made Annabel livid.

'Poor Reverend Clempson adores that car. It's a blatant act of hooliganism.'

'Oh, come on,' said Eddie. 'The man's a tit. Worse than that, he's completely in David Carlyle's pocket.'

'Who's in Carlyle's pocket?'

Milo walked in wearing a pair of odd socks and yesterday's dirty T-shirt, and sporting hair that looked like the business end of a lavatory brush. He'd been *persona non grata* with both his parents since his tryst with Emma Harwich at Logan Cranley's wedding, and had spent most of the two days since holed up in his bedroom playing 'World of Warcraft'.

'None of your business,' snapped Annabel. She did not want to discuss David Carlyle with Milo in front of the hired help. There was something about Magda that Annabel couldn't put her finger on, but that gave her the impression the girl didn't quite know her place. She was perfectly respectful, but there was a pride about her, an almost excessive dignity that put Annabel's back up. She seemed to have formed some sort of bond with Milo, too, which made Annabel uneasy to say the least. And then the other day she'd found her sitting quietly in the grounds, reading a book of poetry by John Donne. A maid! It made Annabel doubly anxious not to discuss sensitive family matters in Magda's hearing.

Eddie frowned at Milo. 'You look as if you've spent the night under Waterloo Bridge.'

'Do I? Well, I just woke up.' Milo poured himself a large bowl of Frosties and sat down blearily at the kitchen table.

'Just woke up? It's two o'clock in the afternoon!' said Eddie.

'I had a late night,' Milo shrugged. 'Hullo, Magda. You look nice.'

Magda looked up momentarily from her linens. Unlike his mother, who never missed an opportunity to criticize or make caustic comments, Milo always smiled when he saw her. After the incident with the bin, when he'd taken shelter at her cottage and confided in her about Emma Harwich, they'd grown closer. He was a sweet boy, albeit a lazy one.

'Leave Magda alone,' said Annabel crossly. 'She has work to do and so have you. You've got a busy day ahead of you.'

'No I haven't,' said Milo.

Eddie finished his cake and put his plate down on the table with a clatter. 'Yes, you have. As you've spectacularly failed to find anything meaningful to do with your life, having thrown your expensive education down the drain, you'll no doubt be delighted to hear that *I* have got you a job.'

'On *Valley Farm*?' Milo's eyes brightened. 'Brilliant. I've always fancied the idea of a career in TV. I take it I'll be working behind the camera? Although who knows, with my charm and good looks, maybe I'll be talent spotted.' He winked at Magda, who pretended not to notice.

'*Not* on *Valley Farm*,' Eddie said firmly. 'I wouldn't let you anywhere near that set if my life depended on it.'

Milo looked aggrieved. 'Why not?'

'Because you'd shag every female in sight, that's why not.' Magda blushed.

'That's rich, coming from you,' Milo shot back.

Annabel looked as if someone had squirted lemon juice in her eyes. How on earth was she supposed to teach Magda the proper respect with Eddie and Milo airing the family's dirty laundry right in front of her? 'Magda!' she barked urgently. 'Go upstairs and strip the guest beds.'

'Yes, Lady Wellesley.'

'And you can refill all the water jugs and empty the bins while you're up there.'

'Of course, Lady Wellesley.'

'I'd better come and check you're doing it properly,' Annabel snapped. 'Although, I dare say even you know how to empty a wastepaper bin.'

Milo watched morosely as his one potential ally left the room, followed by his stony-faced mother. Poor Magda. She must hate it here. He wished now that he'd asked her more about herself that night in her cottage, rather than wittering on about Emma Harwich and his parent problems. What kind of an arse must she think him? Then again, he'd been so drunk that night, he probably wouldn't have remembered anything she'd told him. Still, he pitied Magda. *He* wouldn't work for his mother for all the tea in china.

'You're going to be doing some hard work for once in

your life,' Eddie told him, once the women had gone. 'Real, physical work. And you're going to learn how unbelievably lucky you are.'

'What sort of hard work?' Milo asked suspiciously. He did not like the sound of any of this.

'Building schools.'

'Schools?'

Picking up his son's half-eaten bowl of cereal, Eddie tipped the remnants into the bin.

'Hey! I was still eating that!'

'In Africa,' said Eddie, ignoring him.

Milo's eyes widened. 'In Africa?' He laughed nervously. 'I'm not going to bloody Africa.'

'Oh yes you are,' said Eddie.

'I don't even speak African.'

Eddie put his head in his hands. Four years at Harrow and the boy was still as ignorant as a chimp.

'My friend Dominic Veesey runs a charity out in Sudan,' he told Milo. 'They need all the help they can get. He's expecting you next week.'

'Next *week*?' Panic began to set in. Milo tried to put on a mature, negotiating face. 'Dad, come on. I know you want to teach me a lesson and all that. And it's true I have been a bit laid-back about getting a job and school and stuff. But don't you think this is a bit drastic?'

'You'll be there for five months,' said Eddie. 'But if I hear from Dom that you've been slacking off, I'll extend it to six.'

'Dad!'

Milo felt sick. Eddie had been threatening something like this for months, but he never thought he'd really go through with it.

'I'm not going,' he said defiantly. Pleading was clearly having no effect. 'You can't force me onto that plane.'

'No, I can't,' admitted Eddie. 'But if you don't go, don't bother coming back here. And don't try to wheedle your way around your mother, either. We're agreed on this Milo. Either you go to Africa for five months and work your arse off, or you're on your own. Completely. No bed, no board, no allowance, no nothing.'

Eddie dropped a brown paper bag down on the table.

Milo stared at it, shell-shocked.

'A little going-away present,' Eddie explained. 'And now I must get back to my book before your mother garrottes me.'

Once his father had gone, Milo reached forward numbly and opened the bag.

Inside were six packets of condoms and a handwritten note.

Aids rates in Sudan no joke. If you can't be good, be careful. Dad x

He's serious, Milo thought bleakly. *He's really packing me off to the bloody Sudan!*

'I feel like I'm playing hookie,' said Macy, as James Craven ushered her into San Lorenzo's on Beauchamp Place. He'd shown up unannounced at the end of filming and whisked her off to London for a romantic dinner. 'Two hours ago I was elbow deep in sheep shit, and now here we are.'

'Here we are,' James smiled. 'One of the many lovely things about the valley is how easy it is to get up to town. God,' he blushed, 'I sound like an estate agent. This is the effect you have on me, you see. You make me nervous. I start talking absolute arse the moment I lay eyes on you.'

Macy watched the confident way James moved as the maître d' showed him to their table and decided there was nothing nervous about him. She liked his long legs and dry sense of humour and the way he instinctively took control of their relationship, if you could call it that; such as the way he'd simply assumed that Macy would be free tonight. Sex the other night had been great, if a little bit drunken. It had succeeded in distracting her at least partially from her growing crush on Gabe and her frustrations with Laura and with her so-called 'father', whose email harassment had not stopped with her move to England.

'You're a regular here?' she asked, sitting down while James immediately ordered wine and a bottle of sparkling water. 'People seem to know you.'

'Oh, everyone's a regular here,' James said breezily. 'This place is an institution. It costs a fortune and they only take cash, which is incredibly annoying. But it's the place to go if one wants to impress a girl.'

'Get a girl into bed, you mean?' Macy smiled coyly. 'You've already done that, remember?'

He reached across the table, grabbed her hand and said seriously, 'I'll never forget.'

Suddenly Macy wished they were back home at Cranbourne House and not sitting here in a posh London restaurant waiting to order appetizers.

'But the point is I'm afraid I rather jumped the gun and did everything backwards. I should have taken you out and wined and dined you first.'

'And then fucked me?'

James laughed. 'Must you be so crass? I'm trying to be a gentleman here.'

'And I'm not being a lady,' said Macy, with mock humility. 'I'm sorry. I'll try harder.'

A very attractive young woman in a black cocktail dress approached their table. 'I'm sorry to interrupt,' she said, looking nothing of the kind as she fluttered her eyelashes at James, 'but would you mind awfully giving me your autograph? I'm a huge fan.'

'Of course,' said James. 'What's your name?'

'Lavinia,' the girl purred. 'You can write in my book.'

Macy watched, astonished, as her date obliged, composing a note on the inside cover of the girl's novel. 'You're famous?' she asked, once Lavinia had skipped off to rejoin her friends. 'I thought you said you just played a bit of cricket.'

'I do,' James mumbled. 'For England.'

'Oh my *God*!' said Macy. 'Why didn't you say?'

'Because it's the most boring game on earth and you'd rather have your teeth pulled,' James quoted back at her.

Macy blushed. 'Oh, no, did I say that?'

'Don't be embarrassed,' laughed James. 'I love it that you don't care about cricket. It makes a change from the girls I usually date, believe me. Besides, I'm far more interested in your job. How did things go on set today? Do you think the pilot went well?'

'Well, it didn't go according to plan, that's for sure,' said Macy. 'Although that may not be a bad thing. I guess we'll know when we see the ratings.'

She told him about the silage incident with Reverend Clempson's car. 'You'd never think this girl, Jennifer, had it in her. She's this young vet, very green, very serious about animals . . . It was hilarious, though. Great television. The

149

vicar had a hissy fit. Gabe and I were hugging each other with laughter. Even Laura cracked a smile.'

James didn't like the idea of Macy and her handsome co-presenter hugging. It was quite apparent that she found Gabe Baxter attractive. Every time she mentioned his name her face lit up, and each mention of Gabe's wife, Laura, had the exact opposite effect.

I'll have to watch that, thought James.

Dinner was delicious. James made sure the Chianti kept flowing as Macy told him about her childhood and her life in Los Angeles. It was all so very far removed from James's world and experience: prep school, boarding school, university, cricket. That was it, his life in a nutshell. Macy's childhood sounded like some sort of wild melodrama by comparison. On the surface she seemed open, telling him about her mother, and how her mom's struggles and addictions had shaped her own life and fuelled her ambition. But James could tell she was holding things back. There was a control there, an inner editor carefully monitoring what was revealed and what remained hidden. She reminded him of a cat, outwardly affectionate but inwardly independent, even aloof.

I'll get through those barriers, he told himself. *I'll be the one she can trust, the one she opens up to.*

Leaving the restaurant hand in hand, they were snapped by photographers as soon as they stepped onto Beauchamp Place. Macy felt gratified, it was quite a while since paparazzi had bothered to take her picture, then realized to her annoyance that it was probably James they were interested in.

'Sorry about that,' he said, confirming her suspicions as he helped her into a black cab. 'They're not usually so full on.'

'Are you?' Macy asked archly. 'Usually so "full on"?'

'What do you mean?'

'Coming on to me at the wedding. Ditching your girlfriend. Showing up on set tonight. Dinner,' said Macy. 'It's all very romantic. But we only just met.'

James took her hand and pressed it to his lips.

'No,' he said seriously. 'I'm not usually this full on. But it's like you said, about living your dreams. If you want something badly enough, you *make* it happen.'

'I'm not sure I'm great girlfriend material,' Macy told him. 'Monogamy's never really been my thing.'

'Nor mine,' James said brightly. 'You see how much we have in common?'

Wilf, the Wellesleys' recalcitrant but charming border terrier, wagged his tail furiously with excitement as Magda bent down to put on his lead.

'I know,' Magda smiled, ruffling the dog's scruffy brown coat as she clipped the lead to his collar. Walking Wilf through the stunning Swell Valley countryside, through the winding paths of the ancient Brockhurst woods, was one of the few pleasures in her day. 'I'm ready to get out of here too, believe me.'

She was supposed to have taken the dog for a walk hours ago. Taking Wilf for his daily exercise was approximately item number seventeen on Lady Wellesley's impossibly enormous to-do list; after the laundry, ironing, silver polishing and countless other tasks, none of which was ever completed to Annabel's satisfaction. Inevitably Magda had fallen behind. It was physically impossible for a single human being to do as much work as Lady Wellesley expected in the allotted time, never mind do it to her exacting standards. Since she arrived for her trial week, Magda had finished every day trudging to her little cottage, behind, exhausted and demoralized. But she was determined to keep this job. Annabel might be a bitch, but Eddie seemed decent. And at the end of the day there was always Wilf, who seemed to annoy his mistress almost as much as Magda did.

The Wellesleys' border terrier reminded Magda of the fox terrier her family had owned when she was a very young child. *Ziga*. The sweet little bitch was a rare happy memory from Magda's childhood. From a time before her father started drinking, before everything unravelled like a casually dropped spool of wool.

Slipping on a pair of wellington boots and a thin cardigan against the slight evening chill, she opened the kitchen door. Wilf shot out across the lawn, pulling Magda after him like a puppet on a string.

Milo, also in boots and a wine-red sweater that Magda recognized as his father's brand-new one from Aquascutum, suddenly appeared at her side.

'Where's he taking you?'

'I'm taking him to the woods,' said Magda, yanking on Wilf's lead so hard he practically choked. 'Theoretically.'

'I'll walk with you,' said Milo. 'I'm meeting a friend at The Fox.'

Magda gave him a knowing, 'are you sure that's wise?' look, a clear reference to the last time he'd spent the evening in the pub and turned up on her doorstep too drunk to stand.

'Don't worry,' he grinned. 'I'll stick to half a shandy this time. Scout's honour.'

Magda began to feel uncomfortable. She was fond of Milo, but his mother had made it abundantly clear that she disapproved of any blurring of the lines between staff and family. Any sort of friendship between the two of them was obviously strictly off limits. Magda felt as if she'd unwittingly encouraged something that could threaten her position here, but she didn't know how to backtrack without hurting Milo's feelings.

'You know I'm leaving next week?' Milo said morosely.

'Yes. I heard. I wasn't eavesdropping,' Magda added hurriedly. 'Your parents were discussing it in the front hall while I was cleaning the floors.'

Milo thrust his hands angrily in his pockets. 'It's so bloody ridiculous. Africa! Dad didn't have to go *that* far. I could have volunteered for the Samaritans or something.'

They walked through the gates at the end of the drive and turned left along the lane. 'Well I think you're lucky,' said Magda.

'Lucky?' Milo looked at her wide-eyed.

'Yes, lucky. You get to travel, to meet new people, to do something really meaningful,' said Magda. 'There are people who pay a lot of money to go on these trips, you know.'

'More fool them,' grumbled Milo. 'I mean, no offence, but what the fuck do I know about building a school? Or building anything, for that matter? I've never been good with my hands.'

Magda wondered whether Roxanne or Emma Harwich would have agreed. Or any of the countless other girls that Milo's parents were convinced he'd been having his wicked way with.

He can be sweet, she thought, *but he's terribly spoiled. He's used to having life handed to him on a plate. A glimpse of the real world might bring the best out of him.* They walked on in silence until they reached the stile that marked the entrance to Brockhurst woods. Milo climbed over first then, reaching back, extended his hand to help Magda.

'You can let him off the lead here.' Milo nodded at Wilf, who had calmed down a little, but still looked as if he might take off after a rabbit at any moment.

'Lady Wellesley told me to keep him on it all the time,' Magda said anxiously.

'Mum would keep all of us on a lead all the time if she could,' Milo said with feeling. 'He's a dog. He needs to run. Go on, unclip him. I'll take the blame if he goes AWOL.'

Nervously, Magda let Wilf off the lead. After an initial, exuberant burst of speed he soon circled back and began trotting along obediently beside them.

'See?' Milo smiled. 'Good as gold. I'm sorry Mum's so vile to you.'

It was such a non sequitur, it took Magda a moment to realize what Milo had said.

'You must hate working here,' he added.

'Not at all,' said Magda quickly. 'I'm grateful for the job.'

'Grateful? Why? You're obviously far too educated to be a cleaner, never mind putting up with my parents' bullshit. You could do so much better.'

'It's not so easy for foreigners,' Magda said quietly. She knew Milo was trying to be nice, but he had no idea what he was talking about. 'And your parents are good people,' she added.

'Good people? Good people don't pack their only son off to Africa for five months for no good reason,' moaned Milo. 'They're selfish, that's what they are. All either of them has ever cared about is Dad's career.'

154

Suddenly Magda found herself becoming angry. She hadn't intended to have another personal conversation with Milo, but his entitlement was so infuriating and so insulting, it all came flooding out.

'Selfish? You want to know what selfish is? I'll tell you. Selfish is drinking away your family's savings so your children have nothing. Selfish is hitting your wife when she refuses to put up with it any more. Your parents aren't selfish, Milo. *You* are.'

'That's a bit harsh, isn't it?' Milo pouted. 'I thought you were on my side.'

'I am. And so are your mother and father. They've given you nothing but love and opportunities and you've wasted them all. Wilf! Come back here!'

Milo stood in stunned silence, watching a furious Magda run up the hill after the dog. By the time he pulled himself together and caught up with her, twilight had fallen. Below them, through the trees, the lights of Fittlescombe village could be seen twinkling cheerfully.

'Hey,' he grabbed her arm. 'Don't be cross with me. I'm sorry if I upset you.'

'You didn't upset me.' Magda looked away. Once again she seemed to have accidentally invited an intimacy between them that she didn't want.

'Was that your father you were talking about?'

'It doesn't matter.'

'It does,' Milo insisted. 'Of course it matters. I want to know about your life. Did your father drink?'

It sounded so benign when Milo said it. A simple, harmless question. 'Did your father drink?' And how should she answer it? 'Yes, my father drank.' It would be true. And yet those words would be so far from summing up the misery,

155

the utter anguish of Magda's childhood. The violence and abuse and hunger and insecurity that had prompted her to leave not just her family but her country, as soon as she'd been able. She couldn't bring herself to say it. Instead, a little less harshly than before, she said: 'You have no idea what this world is like, Milo. You think you do, but you don't. Africa will be good for you.'

They'd reached the bottom of the hill now. The woods had given way to meadows. A few yards ahead of them, a stone bridge crossed the River Swell at its narrowest point. Distant voices from The Fox Inn reached them through the still night air.

Milo slowed and turned to face Magda. There was a vulnerability in her face suddenly that he hadn't noticed before. In all their interactions so far, Magda had always been the strong one, the adult. But in that moment Milo felt an overpowering urge to protect her.

'Please don't mention this conversation to your parents,' she said nervously. 'I wouldn't want them to think . . .'

'Think what?'

'Nothing. I . . . just . . . my upbringing isn't relevant. I said more than I should.'

Milo didn't agree, but he sensed Magda didn't want to talk about it, so he said nothing. They walked on in silence into the village. It was further than Magda had intended on going. She must get back to Brockhurst soon or it would be fully dark.

'This is me,' Milo said, gesturing towards the pub. He was shocked by how much he didn't want to go inside. By how much he wanted to stay with Magda, just as he had done the night of the wedding. Except this time he wanted to listen to her, to show her that he wasn't the spoiled, feckless

teenager she thought he was, but a man, a man capable of
. . . of what?

'You'd better go in, then.' Magda was smiling at him
again now, but it was an indulgent smile, the kind a mother
might give when forgiving an errant son. Milo didn't like it
one bit.

'I don't like you walking back on your own,' he tried to
sound authoritative. 'It's dark.'

'Oh, I think I'll survive the mean footpaths of Fittlescombe,'
Magda joked. 'I have Wilf to protect me if anything gets
nasty.'

Reluctantly, Milo went into the pub. The door opened
just long enough for Magda to see him being greeted *very*
affectionately by a stunning blonde girl at the bar. It must
be Emma Harwich, the girl from the wedding who Milo had
sworn blind to Sir Eddie and Lady Wellesley that he'd never
see again.

No wonder they're sending him to Africa.

It *was* strange to think that next week Milo would be on
a plane to the other side of the world. Magda didn't like to
admit how much his presence at Riverside Hall had brightened her days. She didn't even see him that much, but
somehow his positive energy had been a counterbalance to
his mother's constant negativity, her fault-finding and
frequent flashes of irritation. Sir Edward was a positive
person too, but he was at home so little. Perhaps that was
why Lady Wellesley was so unhappy?

Clipping Wilf back onto the lead, Magda headed for home,
wondering what the next few months might bring.

Lying in bed at Cranbourne House, gazing up at the ceiling,
Macy couldn't sleep. Dinner had been lovely and sex even

lovelier. James had pulled out all the stops and put on a performance so athletic and ambitious that Macy had struggled to keep up. She'd lost count of how many times she'd come. But when it was finally over, she'd expected him to leave. Instead he'd kissed her, rolled over and fallen instantly asleep in her bed, as if it were the most natural thing in the world for him to be there, on a Monday night and with work the next day. Now he lay snoring quietly beside her, his broad chest rising and falling in a peaceful, sated rhythm.

Macy envied him. Not just his typically male ability to fall asleep at the turn of a dime. But the way he simply accepted things – like the two of them being together – without thought or question. She didn't think she had ever met a person quite so relaxed, quite so willing to take things day by day. The two of them had met less than a week ago, and yet already the handsome cricketer seemed to have slotted into Macy's life in an unnervingly permanent manner.

A phrase that her agent used to use drifted back to her: *There's such a thing as being too careful, Macy.* She could hear Paul Meyer's voice now, like something from a dream, or a past life. Paul had been talking about her professional life. But his words applied equally to Macy's chequered love life. She knew she was scared of commitment, and she knew why. But was she scared of happiness too? Would James Craven make her happy? She had to admit he was doing a pretty good job so far.

Her mind drifted back to the day's filming up at the farm. The furious little vicar hopping up and down beside his silage-filled car like a lizard on too-hot ground. Gabe laughing till the tears rolled down his cheeks. Gabe hugging her, smelling of wool and sheep dip and sweat and lemon verbena cologne. She smiled.

Not all men were like her father.

There's such a thing as being too careful, Macy.

At last she drifted into a fitful, dream-filled sleep.

CHAPTER TEN

Milo Wellesley's pre-Africa leaving party quickly morphed from being drinks with a few friends at The Fox to a full-scale shindig in Riverside Hall barn. Much against his father's wishes.

'For one thing, that building's an absolute deathtrap,' complained Eddie. 'One of Milo's idiot friends will get drunk and fall off a beam or something and we'll be sued for gazillions.'

'Of course we won't,' Annabel said brusquely. 'This isn't America. It's true the barn's a disaster, but that's exactly why we should have a party there. We're tearing it down in August. I'd rather the children wreak havoc in there than in the house. Wouldn't you?'

'They're not children,' Eddie said crossly. 'Milo's seventeen, for God's sake. And let's not forget why we're sending him to Africa in the first place. So he can bloody well grow up. I assume you haven't forgotten his behaviour at the Cranley girl's wedding?'

'Of course I haven't.'

'This trip is supposed to be a punishment. A consequence of his own immature, reckless, damn-fool behaviour. He doesn't *deserve* a bloody party.'

'Yes, well,' Annabel pouted. 'You didn't deserve a second chance at this marriage, but you got one, didn't you?'

Eddie bit his tongue. It irked him to have this thrown back in his face continually, but he was hardly in a position to protest.

'It's a few friends in the barn, Eddie, seeing Milo off,' Annabel said, a little more gently. 'Plenty of responsible adults will be milling around. Don't make a big deal out of it.'

Magda was also trying not to make a big deal out of it, although when the night of the party finally rolled round, she couldn't help but allow herself a small twinge of excitement.

Milo had invited her a few days ago, in a casual, throw-away way *en route* to play tennis.

'You must come. It'll be a good chance for you to meet some locals.'

Magda looked doubtful. 'I'm not sure.'

'Up to you. But you can't spend your entire life shut up in our gamekeeper's cottage like Rapunzel in the tower.'

This was true.

'Or down in the kitchen like Cinderella, dusting my mother's silver.'

She watched Milo sauntering off to his tennis match, in that easy, entitled way of his, seemingly without a care in the world. Even his annoyance about being banished to Africa had proved very short-lived, once it occurred to him that there was no studying involved and he'd be sure to come back with a killer tan.

161

But she mustn't be mean. *He's trying to be kind*, she thought, *inviting me. And he's right. I must get out more.* But the prospect still scared her. It would be the first time Magda had attended any sort of Swell Valley social event, and she would know nobody there except her bosses and Milo, who would have better things to do at his own leaving party than introduce her around.

Even so, she'd bitten the bullet and blown two weeks' wages on a clinging, chocolate-brown dress from Primark that made her feel like Sophia Loren. Her only pair of high heels were on their last legs, so scuffed that Magda had had to fill in the bare patches where the suede had rubbed off with black felt tip. But standing in front of the mirror now, with her dark hair swept back, a dash of lipstick and a simple pair of drop earrings sending the light dancing across her shoulders, she saw a confident, beautiful young woman staring back at her. That woman looked so different from Magda's usual, drudge-like self that she began to laugh.

'*And the Oscar goes to . . .*' she pouted into the mirror, striking a red-carpet pose, back half-turned as she looked over her shoulder.

Outside, the party had already started. Music thumped dully out across the lawn from the direction of the old barn, and numerous cars had already arrived, depositing gaudily dressed youngsters at the front of Riverside Hall while their parents drove down to the paddock to park. The girls were mostly very young, in tiny minidresses that showed off their long legs. Magda watched them from her window, as proud and dazzling as a flock of peacocks, and felt a moment's panic as they greeted each other with air kisses and giggles, flicking their long blonde manes from side to side.

162

What am I doing? I won't fit in! I'll have nothing to say to any of them.

But then she saw the vicar arriving, and Mr and Mrs Preedy from the village shop, and Penny de la Cruz, dressed as usual like a drunken scarecrow in a skirt she'd made herself, apparently from leftover curtain fabric, and smiling broadly at everybody. Clearly she and Annabel had made things up since their disastrous first meeting, on the surface at least. Magda remembered that not all of tonight's guests would be Milo's teenage groupies. Just about the whole valley was coming.

You look nice, she told herself. *You are nice. Now go and have fun.*

'I'm surprised to see you here, Vicar.' Jennifer Lee, the vet from *Valley Farm*, bumped into Bill Clempson on her way in. In a rather shapeless blue and white smock dress and Birkenstock shoes, Jenny wasn't looking her best tonight. But it still struck Bill how pretty her face was when she wasn't angry. 'Isn't this enemy territory?'

'Not at all,' Bill smiled warmly. 'Tonight isn't about our differences. It's about supporting young Milo. It's wonderful to see young people heading off to the developing world to do their bit. Don't you agree, Miss Lee?'

'Well, yes, I suppose so,' blustered Jenny, slightly wrong-footed. She wasn't used to seeing Bill Clempson smile. He actually wasn't nearly as ugly as she remembered him.

'Besides,' Bill went on, sensing he might be winning her round, 'my job is to represent Our Lord. And He didn't have enemies.'

'Didn't he?' Jenny frowned. 'What about the Pharisees?'

'Well, yes . . .' Bill stammered. 'I didn't mean—'

'And the Romans? And Judas?'

'Well, of course, if you're being literal . . .'

'And those old guys in the temple who gave him a hard time?'

'The High Priests.'

'If you say so,' Jenny shrugged. 'I'm a bit rusty on the old Bible stories, I'm afraid. But I'd say it's pretty difficult to get crucified if you don't have any enemies. Wouldn't you?'

'Well, I, er . . . I . . .' Bill Clempson blushed as the sentence trailed away.

Jenny instantly regretted going down this path. What did she care about Jesus and his enemies? She'd only said it for something to say, and now she'd shot the poor man down in flames, just as he was trying to rebuild bridges between them.

'I'd better go and mingle with my parishioners,' Bill said awkwardly. 'Enjoy the party, Miss Lee.'

'You too, Vicar,' Jenny called guiltily after him, helping herself to a flute of champagne from a passing waiter and downing it one.

Next time she saw Bill Clempson, she would be nice. Very nice.

He really wasn't such a bad fish after all.

At the far end of the barn, Milo was already tipsy, knocking back the gin and tonics with Will Cooper, an old school friend, when Roxanne, his most recent ex, sashayed in.

'Aye, aye,' Will nudged Milo hard in the ribs. 'Fireworks at two o'clock.'

With his freckled face, blue eyes, and long, floppy, reddish hair, Will Cooper had always looked ridiculously innocent and boyish. His nickname at Pinewood Prep had been 'Cherub'; at Harrow he was known as 'Bog' after his initials, W.C. But Will's butter-wouldn't-melt exterior concealed a mischievous, borderline filthy mind. Hence his lifelong bond with Milo.

'Shit,' muttered Milo.

Even he had to admit that Roxie looked fabulous in a gold lamé playsuit that might have been sprayed on to her slender body, sparkly seventies platform boots and a jauntily angled trilby hat. She'd quite rightly dumped him when she'd found out about his romp with Emma Harwich up at Furlings, and they'd barely spoken since. But the tiny gold shorts she was wearing tonight were already making Milo start thinking wistfully about a reconciliation. After all, she was here, wasn't she?

'Mum's going to go bananas,' he told Will. 'She'll think I invited her.'

'Didn't you?'

'Of course I bloody didn't. You should see her Facebook page. It's like a shrine to how much she hates me.'

'It's not her Facebook page I'm interested in seeing,' drooled Will, his eyes roaming lecherously over Roxie's endless legs, and hovering at the point where her upper thighs ended and the fabric of her playsuit began.

'I'm serious,' grumbled Milo. 'She started a chat called: "A hundred and one reasons to cut off Milo Wellesley's balls with a rusty penknife." It got, like, two hundred "likes" in twenty-four hours.'

'Ouch,' said Will. 'Well, it's obviously far too dangerous for you to approach her. I'll go over there and distract her. Take one for the team and all that.'

'All right, Milo.' Jamie King, one of Milo's more obnoxious Harrow acquaintances, swaggered over. 'Got any weed?'

'If I did I wouldn't share it with you, Kingo.'

Milo tolerated Jamie. He could be funny in certain, limited circumstances. But because his family lived close by and his dad was in the House of Lords, the two boys were forced to see a lot more of each other than either would have chosen.

Right now, Milo was a lot more interested in Will Cooper's intentions towards his only-just-ex than in Jamie King's weed-quest.

'You'd better not try to shag her, Bog,' he called after Will. 'Bog!'

But Will was already out of earshot, weaving his way through the guests, homing in on Roxanne like a testosterone-fuelled missile.

Things were not off to a good start. They were about to get worse.

'What is *that girl* doing here?' Annabel, overdressed for the occasion in a full, floor-length black skirt and matching embellished black sweater by Balenciaga, appeared at Milo's side. With her blonde hair scraped back into a severe bun and overly rouged cheeks, she looked like a particularly displeased ballet teacher. 'I told you explicitly not to ask her.'

'I didn't ask her,' Milo said meekly.

But his mother wasn't listening. She'd been horrified enough to find herself bumping into the fat little shopkeeper from Fittlescombe, Preedy, and his ghastly gossip of a wife. She assumed Eddie had invited them as some sort of childish, tit-for-tat gesture, to embarrass her, because she'd forced his hand on the party. Eddie was always upbraiding her for being a snob, and clearly got some kind of kick out of forcing poor Christopher Denton, the lord lieutenant, to make small talk with every local pleb he could lay his hands on. But she'd expected more from Milo.

'I stuck my neck out with your father to let you *have* this party,' she said furiously. 'And this is how you repay me? With bald-faced defiance?'

'Mum, I—'

'Get rid of her,' Annabel hissed.

Milo threw his arms wide. 'How can I do that? I can hardly turf her out.'

'Of course you can. Like you said, you didn't invite her.'

'I'll do it, if you like, Lady Wellesley,' Jamie King piped up, grinning obnoxiously. 'I'm an expert at grockle-disposal. Someone has to save Milo from himself, eh?'

Milo shot him a look that he hoped said: *You are a total penis.*

'Hello.' Just at that moment, Magda approached shyly, smoothing down a stray crease in her sexy chocolate dress. 'Are you having fun?' she asked Milo, not quite daring to make eye contact with Annabel.

'Not really,' mumbled Milo. He was too distracted to notice how stunning Magda looked. Unlike Jamie.

'Well hell-*o!*' His eyes fixed unashamedly on Magda's ample cleavage. 'And who might you be?'

'Magda, Jamie, Jamie, Magda,' said Milo without enthusiasm.

'Ah, Magda, good,' Annabel said brusquely, thrusting her empty champagne glass into Magda's hand. 'We need glasses cleared pretty much everywhere, and the canapé plates need replenishing. Karen, the catering manager, is in the kitchen. She'll tell you what to do.'

'Oh.' Magda blushed, turning to Milo, waiting for him to explain the mistake. That she was here as a guest. As his friend. But his eyes were still glued to Roxanne. Will was leading her onto the dance floor now, the little shit. *With friends like these, who needs enemies?*

Annabel stalked off, leaving Magda standing there, holding the empty champagne glass and wishing the ground would swallow her up.

Why didn't Milo explain? Why didn't he say something?

'She's your maid?' Jamie King turned to Milo. His expression had changed from admiration to disdain, and he sounded irritated, as if he'd been tricked.

'Hmmm?' said Milo, only half listening. 'Oh. Yes.'

Magda's stomach did a horrible flip.

That's how he sees me. That's how they all see me. I'm the maid.

'In that case, I could use a refill.' Downing his champagne in one with a small burp, Jamie handed Magda his glass too. 'Quick as you can, angel,' he added, rolling up his sleeves. 'I have some evicting to do.'

Her face burning, Magda turned and ran.

Milo turned on Jamie. 'You are *such* a cock. Do you know that? You say one word to Roxanne and I swear to God I will fucking flatten you.'

He didn't even notice Magda had gone.

Magda dropped the empty champagne glasses on the table nearest the entrance and ran out of the barn, her heart pounding. Humiliation burned like acid in her chest and pricked her skin like a nettle rash.

How could Milo do that to her? How could he put her in that situation?

She crossed the lawn and bolted back into her cottage, slamming the front door behind her and leaning against it as if she were trying to keep out a tidal wave. A tidal wave of shame. Pulling off her stupid shoes, she flung them down on the ground, tears of frustration pouring down her cheeks.

It's not really Milo I'm angry with, she thought bitterly. *It's myself.*

Milo was just a kid. Kids were supposed to be foolish and insensitive. Magda might not be that much older than him in years, but in life experiences they were worlds apart. She, unfortunately, was an adult. And adults had to face reality. What had possessed her to think that she'd be accepted as an equal by these people? These closed, upper-class, rich English people like the Wellesleys, with their clipped manners and their rigid rules and their cruel, thoughtless etiquette? That she could become 'one of them' if only for a night?

Who did she think she was? Cinderella?

This cottage, this valley, might *look* like something out of a fairy tale. But it wasn't. Any more than Milo Wellesley was a handsome prince.

'No one's going to rescue you,' Magda told herself scathingly, speaking the words aloud as she pulled savagely at her dress, ripping it off her body. 'Grow up.'

Scrunching the dress into a tight ball, she lit the kindling in the wood-burning stove and shoved it inside. For a few moments she watched as the cheap fabric burst into flames. Then she closed the heavy, cast-iron doors and went to bed.

CHAPTER ELEVEN

It was a blazingly hot summer, the warmest anyone could remember in the Swell Valley for a generation. For the local children, home from school, this meant unending fun. Hosepipes in the garden, swimming in the river, delicious, melting Mr Whippy ice creams from the van on Fittlescombe village green. Local pubs also did a roaring trade, with The Fox's beer garden heaving day after day. Tesco in Chichester had a run on Pimm's that made the local papers, and the valley fire brigade were called to a slew of barbecue-related incidents, one of which almost resulted in the oldest medieval tithe barn in Sussex being reduced to a heap of ashes.

For local farmers, the soaring temperatures were less welcome. Harvesting and baling of straw was dusty work in the ninety-degree heat, and the livestock suffered as much as the labourers. Lambs could get dehydrated very quickly and, even with regular irrigation, the potato crops suffered. As for the usual August ploughing, the earth was so dry and hard it was like trying to churn one's way through concrete.

With the first episode of *Valley Farm* due to air at the end of August, the cameras had rolled all summer, capturing the tough conditions at Wraggsbottom and elsewhere. The heat wave was a key part of the show, but so were the ongoing tensions in the village. High temperatures led to frayed tempers on all sides, with Laura's patient camera crew twice almost coming to blows with the vicar's increasingly strident posse of objectors. One episode focused on Macy Johanssen's kitchen windows being pelted with eggs. Gabe thought the whole thing was hilarious, and the ensuing village whodunnit too Nancy Drew for words. 'As you can see from these egg boxes, they were purchased locally,' he joked to camera in a conspiratorial whisper. 'It's not so much Professor Plum in the library with a candlestick, as Mr Preedy in the front garden with half a dozen Speckled Sussexes.'

There were times when Laura was convinced they were making great television. Gabe and Macy had terrific on-screen chemistry, the sort of larky, teasing relationship that producers kill for. As for the show itself, it had lashings of local drama, enough rural charm to open a chocolate-box factory, and real, educational, factual content. All the fun and lightness of reality television, but with a crucial ingredient that made *Valley Farm* different from all the others: intelligence.

But at other times she was sure they'd blown it. What if viewers ended up siding with the protestors? Had Jennifer's stunt with the vicar's car taken things too far? Did it make Gabe and Laura look spiteful, or snobby, or elitist, or greedy; all the things that David Carlyle's journalists were accusing them of on a daily basis in the *Echo*?

It was the pre-season publicity that worried Laura most. Eddie and Gabe both seemed to view it as a gift. 'Who cares what people are saying about the show?' Gabe would tell Laura night after night, in an effort to reassure her. He loved his wife intensely, and it pained him to see her so stressed all the time.

'*I* care. It's bad enough having half the village hate us. Do we really need half the country?'

'The point is, people have a view. They know about us already, and they're curious. You can't buy that sort of PR. Once we air, they'll get to see for themselves what a storm in a teacup this whole thing has been. It'll be Carlyle and Call-me-Bill who come off with egg on their faces, not us.'

'You don't know that,' said Laura. 'What if it *is* us?'

'Then we'll just have to drown our sorrows in money,' said Gabe, kissing her. 'Because we're going to be making a lot of it, either way.'

This was another thing that worried Laura. Money. Gabe was touchingly convinced that the show would make their fortunes. But Laura knew just how risky and fickle the television business could be. Meanwhile revenues from the farm, their day job, were dropping like a stone. And while the property itself had gone up in value, Laura and Gabe were mortgaged up to the eyeballs. Making the repayments had been a strain even when Laura had a steady job at ITV. Since starting *Valley Farm*, her weekly salary had dropped to precisely zero. Eddie Wellesley and Channel 5 were bankrolling production, but Laura and Gabe's remuneration was all profit-share.

What if there were no profits to share?

What if it was all a big, huge disaster of Laura's own making? She'd have alienated all her neighbours and friends, and for nothing; poor Hugh and Luca would never go to

THE SHOW

another birthday party again, and she and Gabe would end
up broke and at each other's throats.

The week after filming ended, Laura was at home on Mummy
duty with the boys when Hugh's reedy little voice drifted
in from the playroom.

'Look, Mummy! Maisie's on the television.'

'She can't be, darling. Our programme won't be on telly
until next week, remember?'

Laura was in the kitchen, mindlessly peeling potatoes to
make a shepherd's pie for supper. It was too hot for shepherd's pie really, but she couldn't look another salad in the
face and needed something to do that didn't involve die-cast
trains or worrying herself sick about *Valley Farm* finally airing.

'She is!' Hugh insisted. 'Come and look.'

Laura wandered back into the playroom. Luca was
gnawing a stickle brick to death in the corner. Hugh had
been engrossed in CBeebies, but had accidentally switched
to SkySports on the remote and now seemed to be watching
a one-day match live from The Oval.

'Look! It's Maisie. Right there.'

Hugh pointed to the screen. There indeed was Macy – for
some reason Hugh had never been able to pronounce her
name – jumping up and down with delight in the stands.
Australia had been all out for a meagre 230 after England
had put on an impressive 352 in their 50 overs, and James
Craven had been named man of the match.

Laura watched Macy skip onto the pitch and fling her
arms around James's neck. She looked ravishing in a floaty
blue and white sundress, her usually porcelain skin tanned
a light, golden brown from all the long hours of outdoor
filming.

Looking down at her own meat-stained apron and unshaven legs beneath a shapeless old denim mini, Laura suppressed an unworthy stab of envy. She knew that Macy and James's high-profile relationship meant more publicity for the show. It was a good thing that Macy was constantly photographed looking gorgeous at glamorous events, and even better that she did it on the arm of a bona fide British sporting hero. And it wasn't as if she, Laura, wanted to spend her life whizzing up to London parties, drinking champagne and getting her picture in the papers. But still, it rankled slightly that Macy and Gabe got to have all the fun, while she sweated bullets behind the scenes, or ran around after the children.

Gabe was also up in London today, at some swanky Channel 5 drinks do in the Chelsea Physic Garden. He claimed not to want to go – 'It's a pain in the arse, if you must know; there's so much to do at the farm' – but Laura couldn't help but think he had had the better end of the deal, versus her own day of playing *Thomas the Tank Engine* for four hours straight with two fractious little boys, in heat that would have made Gandhi lose his temper.

'I love Maisie,' Hugh sighed.

'Do you?'

'I do. She's like a beautiful queen. And she's always laughing.'

'Is she?' Laura frowned.

'Uh-huh,' Hugh nodded. 'Just like Daddy.'

'Well, what about me?' Laura was ashamed to hear herself asking. 'Don't I laugh?'

Hugh looked confused by the question. 'Not really. I mean, not all the time, like Maisie. You're a bit more seriouser.'

'Oh.'

174

'You laugh if someone tickles you,' Hugh added kindly. 'Do you want me to tickle you now? I will if you like.'

'Not right now, sweetheart.' Laura kissed him. She felt stupidly emotional and annoyed. Where the hell was Gabe? He should have been home hours ago to help with the kids. No doubt he was laughing away somewhere, three sheets to the wind on Pimm's and champagne, clowning around with the Channel 5 execs. *They're probably in a strip club by now*, she thought irrationally. *Spearmint bloody Rhino.*

The phone rang. Laura jumped on it.

'Where the bloody hell are you?' she snapped.

'Er, at home, in my library. Should I not be?'

Eddie's voice was deep and smooth and instantly calming, like an Irish coffee. He sounded amused but not mocking. Laura exhaled and let her shoulders relax. She hadn't heard from him in weeks. He'd been busy finishing his prison memoirs, locked away in his study at Riverside Hall or up in London with his literary agents. Laura had missed him dropping round to the set, sprinkling his charm and easy confidence over everybody like fairy dust. It was good to hear his voice.

'Oh, it's you! Sorry.'

'Who were you expecting?' asked Eddie.

'Only Gabe,' Laura sighed. 'He's late, as usual. Anyway, how are you? How's the book?'

Eddie made a groaning sound.

'It can't be *that* bad,' said Laura.

'It's not bad, exactly,' said Eddie. 'I'm just not sure it's good enough. If it's going to be my ticket back into politics, it needs to say exactly the right things to exactly the right people. But at the same time, I do feel it has to be truthful. I met a lot of good people in prison. It's . . . difficult.'

'My my,' Laura teased him. 'I believe I just heard the fabled sound of the political conscience! I thought you people had your scruples removed at birth? Or at least on entering the Commons. Like wisdom teeth.'

'Or foreskins,' said Eddie.

'Ouch.'

'Exactly. Happily, I remain intact in that department. Which I dare say is more than you needed to know!' He laughed loudly.

I really must try and laugh more, thought Laura. *Out of the mouths of babes, and all that.*

'Anyway, I was ringing to see how you and Gabriel were and to see if you wanted to come up here next Sunday and watch the first episode with us?'

'That's terribly kind of you,' Laura began.

'Annabel's not exactly cock-a-hoop about it, as you know,' said Eddie. 'But she's agreed to host a small drinks do.'

Laura felt suitably astonished, although it was true that Eddie's wife had notably softened towards the show recently. Ever since Milo Wellesley had been packed off to Africa, in fact, Annabel seemed to have cheered up immeasurably. Perhaps having the house to themselves had been all that the Wellesleys needed to revivify their marriage. Laura indulged in a momentary fantasy of how easy and relaxed her life with Gabe would be if the children disappeared for a few weeks. Although she knew if it really happened she'd spend the whole time pining for the boys. Gabe would be even worse.

'You've probably already made plans to watch it up in London with the Channel 5 lot . . .' Eddie said.

'Actually,' said Laura, 'between you and me, the only plan I've made is with my sofa and a sick bag. I'm terrified, Eddie.'

'But why? It will be a triumph, my dear, you'll see.'

'I'm not even sure if I can sit through it myself, never mind watch it in public,' said Laura. 'I've been biting poor Gabriel's head off for weeks. I'm a wreck! As for the reviews the next day, I've already told Gabe to go into the village early and set fire to every newspaper he can find.'

'That's it then,' said Eddie. 'It's settled. You must watch it with us.'

'No, really. I—'

'We will raise a great number of glasses of excellent champagne, to the show and to you and to all your hard work. We will celebrate, and reviewers be damned. All that matters is the ratings, anyway.'

'Spoken like a true television producer,' said Laura.

'I'll expect you on Sunday then. Six o'clock at Riverside Hall; dress for success, sick bag optional.'

'Eddie really, I . . .'

The line had already gone dead.

'I can't face it, Gabe. I actually can't. Let's just go home.'

Laura and Gabe were standing outside the front door of Riverside Hall. Gabe had reached forwards to ring the bell when Laura grabbed his arm, her face white with panic.

Pulling her into a hug, Gabe stroked her hair soothingly. 'We can't go home. Lady Wellesley's expecting us. You know as well as I do one does *not* disappoint Lady Wellesley.'

'Oh God, I'd forgotten about her,' Laura wailed. 'That makes it even worse. She always looks at me like I'm Pol Pot. I can't watch the show with Cruella de Vil breathing down my neck!'

'The only person breathing down your neck is going to

be me,' said Gabe, 'in a good way. The show will be great, Laura. Tonight will be great. Trust me.'

He rang the bell. The door was answered almost immediately by a pretty but fragile-looking young woman in a full maid's outfit.

'Please come in. May I take your coats?' she asked nervously, like a call-centre worker reciting a script.

'We don't have coats,' said Gabe. 'It's ninety degrees out here. I could murder a cold drink, though, if there's one going.'

'Of course, sir.' The girl blushed. 'Follow me.'

She led them into a comfy sitting room. A large TV was mounted on the wall above the fireplace, already tuned to Channel 5. Laura switched her attention to the soft linen sofas and armchairs strewn with brightly coloured scatter cushions that were dotted invitingly around the room. On a coffee table in the centre, a vast Wedgwood jug overflowed with wild flowers, and scented Diptyque candles flickered on the windowsills. Along the garden side of the room, floor-to-ceiling French doors had been flung open, allowing the scents of jasmine and honeysuckle and newly mown grass to drift inside on the warm evening breeze.

Macy and James were already here, sipping cocktails and chatting to Santiago and Penny de la Cruz in one corner. Eddie had his arm around his wife, who was smiling broadly.

'I don't think I've ever seen her crack a smile before,' Gabe whispered in Laura's ear. 'Have you?'

'Never,' Laura whispered back. 'Perhaps she's got wind.'

Gabe laughed loudly, making Eddie look up.

'Ah, there you are! At last. Kick-off's in five minutes. What can I get you both to drink?'

'Gin and tonic for me, please,' said Gabe. 'Well, if it isn't the man of the hour!' He wandered over to congratulate James Craven on his recent performance, leaving Laura alone with Eddie and Annabel.

'What can I get you?' Eddie asked her.

'Nothing. Just water.' Laura's nerves were back with a vengeance.

'Nonsense. We're celebrating. You must have something. A glass of champagne, at least?'

'Mrs Baxter just said she didn't want a drink, Eddie,' Annabel said curtly. Her earlier smile was gone now, replaced with a familiar expression of withering disdain. 'Magda! Don't just stand there gaping! Fetch some iced water, please. Quickly!'

Laura watched awkwardly as the maid scuttled away. Lady Wellesley spoke to her as if she were a dog. So much for the happier, more relaxed Annabel. Clearly Milo's absence had only defrosted the ice queen so much . . .

'It'll be fine, don't worry,' said Eddie, ignoring his wife's wrath and wrapping a paternal arm around Laura's shoulders. 'Today's quite the day for good news.'

'It is?' Laura looked puzzled.

'Yup. I've sent my agents the first two-thirds of the book and they love it,' Eddie beamed. 'This time next year I could be back in politics full time.'

'That's brilliant.' Laura smiled back. 'You must be thrilled,' she added to Annabel.

'I'll be thrilled when the book's finished and published and we have our old life back,' said Annabel waspishly. 'And when all this television nonsense is behind us. I don't mean to be rude, but your ghastly programme's been a terrible distraction for Eddie.'

She had never liked Laura, and she knew for a fact that

the feeling was mutual, so she resented Laura's attempts at 'chumminess' now. If Westminster life had taught Annabel anything, it was that an enemy was infinitely preferable to a false friend.

Laura was just wondering what Annabel might say when she *was* trying to be rude when Eddie jumped in.

'Yes, well,' he said smoothly, kissing his wife's cheek. 'With any luck it will prove to have been a lucrative distraction. That's not the only good news either. We had a letter from Milo today, finally. Apparently he's loving Africa. We could hardly believe it, could we, darling? He sounds like a different boy.'

Magda, who'd just returned with the water jug, froze at the mention of Milo's name. After the awful humiliation of his leaving party, she'd been too angry and upset to say a proper goodbye to him. Of course, more than two months had passed since then. She no longer felt the same burning mortification that she had at the time, when that dreadful boy Jamie had looked through her as if she were nothing, as if she were dirt. But the memory still stung. She wondered what it would be like when Milo came back. Whether he really *had* changed. Thinking about his return from Africa bothered her more than it should have.

'Magda! Don't stand there like a lemon.' Annabel's irritated voice brought her back to the present. 'Pour Mrs Baxter her water. She's been waiting long enough.'

'Really, I'm fine.' Laura gave an embarrassed laugh. Why was Eddie's wife so poisonous to the maid? Did she just dislike all women? *It must take a huge amount of energy*, Laura thought, *to live one's life at such a pitch of distrust*. Then again, perhaps being married to a serial philanderer like Eddie had taken its toll? Laura tried not to judge Annabel too harshly.

After all, she herself had been pretty vile to Gabe recently behind closed doors, and with much less reason. You never really knew what went on in other people's marriages, no matter how hard you tried to peek behind the curtains.

The familiar theme tune signalled that the news had ended. Everyone turned towards the TV.

'That's it. We're next!' said Eddie, rubbing his hands and sinking down into one of the sofas, a stiff Annabel beside him. 'Magda, make sure everybody has a full glass. Come on, you lot. Find a seat.'

James, who was sprawled across Annabel's perfectly pristine Chesterfield as though he spent every day reading his newspaper there, squeezed Macy's hand. 'Are you nervous?'

She looked at him as if he were mad. 'Not at all. It's not the first time I've been on TV, you know, honey.'

'Of course not. But it's still a big deal. This time tomorrow you could be a household name.'

'I wouldn't hold your breath,' said Macy.

The truth was, she was nervous. She could tell that Gabe was too. He played it cool in front of Laura. But he needed this show to be a hit. In their different ways, and for their different reasons, they all did. For Gabe and Laura it meant paying off the mortgage. For Macy it could be the gateway to an international career. For Eddie it was a stepping stone back into politics. Even Annabel wanted the show to do well, if only to have an answer to all its many detractors.

'I wonder if we'll be in it?' Penny whispered to Santiago. 'They did film me once or twice in the village, out and about with Emma.'

'They won't show you,' Santiago whispered back, stroking

Penny's rosy cheek. 'They want viewers to look at Macy. One look at you and no one would give her a second glance.'

Penny laughed so hard she almost choked on her vodka and tonic.

'I do love you.' She dabbed the tears from her eyes.

'I'm serious,' said Santiago.

'I know you are,' said Penny, squeezing his hand as the opening credits of *Valley Farm* finally began to roll.

'You're hurting me.'

'Hmm?' David Carlyle didn't take his eyes off the screen.

'David! Let go! You're crushing my fingers.'

'Hmm? Oh. Sorry.'

Belatedly, the formidable editor of the *Echo* released his wife's hand. Poor, loyal Louise Carlyle had put up with her husband's foul temper for days now, as the date for *Valley Farm*'s first episode drew nearer. Now that they were actually sitting here, in their own front room, watching Gabriel Baxter and Macy Johanssen stride through the familiar fields of the Swell Valley, it was as if David had entered some sort of trance.

Throughout the summer, you would never have guessed that the Tory government was on the brink of collapse. Or that war might be about to start again in the Middle East. Or that the little boy abducted from his bedroom on Teeside two weeks ago would miraculously be found alive and unharmed. As far as David was concerned, the *only* news that mattered was the launch of his hated rival's TV show. the *Echo* covered other stories, of course. But not since CNN's obsession with the missing Malaysian aircraft had a major news outlet focused so intensely and so consistently on one single issue. David had worked tirelessly to portray Eddie

Wellesley as the greedy, elitist, self-serving pig that he was. He'd done all he could to smear the reputations of Gabriel Baxter and his wife by association, and to stir up anti-American sentiment towards Macy Johanssen for worming her way into the affections of England's favourite cricketer since Santiago de la Cruz.

He'd succeeded in turning *Valley Farm* into a story, and the exploitation of the Swell Valley and its residents into an issue. But the true measure of the *Echo*'s campaign would be the public reaction to the show itself. David sat still as a statue, glued to the screen like a wide-eyed child watching the moon landings.

'Oh, look!' said Louise as Furlings appeared in shot, looking impossibly romantic swathed in early morning mist. 'Doesn't it look pretty! And there's Angela Cranley. I didn't know she was going to be in it.'

'Nor did I,' David seethed. Angela was rich as Croesus, but with her soft, Aussie accent and gentle manner, chattering away about sustainable gardening and the camaraderie of village life, she came across as a likable everywoman. By the time they showed her and Max Bingley pleading for calm and tolerance at the village protest meeting in the next scene, viewers were already firmly on Angela's side. Bloody Laura Baxter was a better producer than David had given her credit for.

'It's outrageous,' he muttered. 'Look at that! They're making Bill Clempson out to be a total fool. He sounds pompous and ridiculous.'

'I thought you said he *was* pompous?' Louise observed innocently.

'That's not the point.'

Laura had saved the scene where the vicar discovered his

car submerged in silage until right before the commercial break. Louise Carlyle gasped, whispered, 'No!', clapped a hand over her eyes . . . and then burst out laughing.

'You think that's funny?' David asked accusingly.

'I . . . well, no. I mean, a bit,' Louise blushed. Living with David recently had felt like trying to keep a wild bear as a pet. Everything seemed to make him angry.

The next shot was of Gabe Baxter and Macy Johanssen catching one another's eye and dissolving into uncontrollable giggles. It took a superhuman effort for Louise not to join them.

'Would you like a cup of tea?' she asked, unsure what else to do.

David looked up as if seeing her for the first time. 'Yes. Thanks, love.' Reaching out, he squeezed her hand. It was so unexpected, Louise thought she might cry.

'I'm sorry if I'm on edge,' said David. ' It's just . . . I have a lot riding on this not working. I don't mean to take it out on you.'

'I know,' Louise squeezed back. 'I understand.'

Once she'd retreated to the kitchen, David sat alone on the couch, digging his fingernails into his palms until they bled.

Fuck. Fuck, fuck, fuck.

He picked up the phone and called his secretary.

'I need you to set me up a lunch.'

'Of course, Mr Carlyle. With whom?'

'John Bingham at ITV.'

'Very good. And when would you like—'

'As soon as possible. Book somewhere swanky. Let me know when it's done.'

He hung up.

* * *

At Reverend Clempson's bungalow, a few of the more hard-core protestors had gathered to watch the show together and enjoy Bill's home-made organic hummus and aubergine dip.

'Our cottage looks nice,' Rita Bramerton cooed to her husband, Reg, as Macy Johanssen was shown walking down Fittlescombe High Street, admiring the beautifully planted front gardens. 'Look at your hollyhocks! Don't they look grand?'

'They do,' Reg agreed.

'For heaven's sake. It's not about how pretty the flowers look!' Bill Clempson said, more sharply than he'd meant to. 'Can't you see you're being manipulated?'

'Sorry, Vicar,' Reg Bramerton said meekly.

A retired bus driver and keen amateur gardener, Reg now mowed the village green and tended to the churchyard flowers as a volunteer. David Carlyle had run an entire feature on the Bramertons in the *Echo* last week, as the ordinary, elderly working-class face of the Swell Valley, and the kind of people that *Valley Farm*'s producers were cruelly exploiting. They'd certainly worked tirelessly to support the local protest campaign, mainly at the urging of the vicar. Rita had baked cakes and handed out flyers, and Reg had hammered together 'Save Our Valley!' placards. But now that they were actually here, watching the programme they'd devoted so much time and effort to stopping, the Bramertons were a little baffled as to what, exactly, they'd been saving the valley *from*.

They weren't the only ones.

'It could be worse, Vicar,' John Preedy from the village stores observed – although he wasn't sure the same could be said for the vicar's tasteless dip. You'd get more flavour from a can of Polyfilla. 'At least the farming segments are informative. They let Gabriel talk about what he knows, don't they? It's not all just pretty Americans and fluff.'

'It could *not* be worse,' Bill Clempson said petulantly. Watching himself hop up and down beside his car like a demented jack-in-the-box, his cheeks red and his voice high and squeaky like a puppet's, had been a deeply shaming experience. If these people couldn't see what the producers were doing – the protestors, the very locals he'd been trying to protect from exploitation – then what hope was there that ordinary viewers would see the harm in *Valley Farm*?

'It's not only me they're mocking.' He turned to address the little group squeezed into his tiny sitting room at the bungalow. 'Look at the way the cameras are zooming in on Hillary there?'

They looked. Hillary Wincup could be seen flapping her arms hilariously as she ran across the farmyard, her enormous bosoms flying, like a distressed hen escaping a burning coop. 'They're laughing at you, Mrs Wincup. That's what reality television *does*.'

At last a few frowns and mutterings of 'shame' began to replace the initial thrill of seeing themselves and their neighbours on screen.

'You must understand,' Bill Clempson went on earnestly. 'If this programme becomes successful, it won't stop here. Do you really want these cameras to become a permanent part of your lives? This village will be turned into a theme park. And you'll be like monkeys in a zoo. These people are laughing *at* us, not with us. And they're raking in fat profits at *your* expense, for themselves and the Baxters.'

'That's a bit strong, ain't it, Vicar?' Reg Bramerton piped up again.

'I don't believe it is, Reg,' said Bill. 'You mustn't let Gabe Baxter's easy manner fool you. A man may smile and smile and be a villain, you know.'

Six simple faces looked at him blankly.

'Shakespeare?' Bill Clempson sighed deeply. 'Never mind.'

The celebrations at Riverside Hall went on well into the night. They wouldn't know final ratings, or read any reviews, until the morning. But Channel 5 had already been on the phone, clearly ecstatic about the early numbers, and the reaction on social media was crazy. Even though Gabe didn't know his trending from his elbow, #ValleyFarm was going stratospheric. And everyone felt they'd made a show that was not only worth watching, but had done what it set out to do – show the real Swell Valley, its people, landscape and rhythms in all its unique, magical glory.

James had a match the next day so left early and alone. Gabe and Laura offered Macy a lift home to Cranbourne House but she decided she'd rather walk. It was still partially light, and the summer heat lingered into the night, rising up from the baked earth like steam from newly baked bread.

She ought to feel happy, and was irritated at herself for the niggling sense of depression and self-doubt that hung over her like an unwanted cloud as she strolled along the lane towards Fittlescombe.

The show was great. Everyone loved it, she told herself. *Your career's back on track, you have a great boyfriend, a gorgeous house, a wonderful new set of friends. What the hell is wrong with you?*

Her mind wandered to Los Angeles and her agent – she must call Paul tomorrow, and start to think about strategies for marketing *Valley Farm* in the US – and it occurred to her suddenly that she might be homesick. She loved England and the valley far more than she'd ever thought she would. Since dating James, she'd even caught herself using words like 'lovely' and 'loo'. She'd better watch that, actually. She didn't want to morph into Madonna from the Guy Ritchie years and start wearing a flat cap and rattling off cockney rhyming slang like Dick Van Dyke. But there were things about America that she did miss and thought about increasingly. Stupid things like Kashi breakfast cereal, and Greens 3 from Pressed Juicery, and yoga and *Sixty Minutes* and Steve Inskeep on NPR news. Perhaps a trip home was all she needed? Time away from work, and England and James. *And Gabe*, her subconscious added for her helpfully. Gabe, with his blissful marriage and his cute kids; Gabe with his perfect face and dirty jokes and utter, utter, total unavailability.

Macy sighed. *I'd better book my flight.*

CHAPTER TWELVE

David Carlyle watched contentedly as the waitress poured the wine. He liked The Wolseley. It was old school and posh, with properly trained staff, not Eastern European models with short skirts and stuck-on tits, like the girls they had serving at Box 50, the hot new members' club for 'London's media elite', which his publicity officer had pushed him to join. David was firmly of the belief that a hooker's place was in the bedroom, not at the helm of a decanter.

'Domaine Armand Rousseau.' John Bingham raised a bushy eyebrow admiringly. 'I'm impressed.'

'Get used to it,' said David Carlyle, raising his own glass. 'Once you're director-general, it'll be top-class burgundy all the way.'

John Bingham laughed. 'I seriously doubt that.'

'Why?' said David. 'The Beeb might be strapped for cash, but they can still put on a good show at the top. Attracts foreign investment.' He winked.

God, thought John Bingham. *He really is such a common little man.*

'It's not the wine budget that I doubt. It's me being approached as DG. I just can't see it happening.'

'I can,' said David, ordering oysters on the half shell followed by beef Wellington. He'd have preferred to skip the carbs – the *Echo*'s editor prided himself on his physique. Not many men in his line of work could boast washboard abs at nearly fifty, but he wanted ITVs legendary head of Drama to see him as a man's man. Infuriatingly, Bingham ordered steamed sea bass and spinach. 'I have it on very good authority they're going to approach you. That's why I'm here.'

John Bingham gave him a knowing look. 'Why is it I get the feeling that this is going to end up having something to do with Fast Eddie?'

David's upper lip curled. He loathed Wellesley's soubriquet almost as much as he loathed the man. 'Probably because Eddie Wellesley's the other big name in the ring.'

John almost choked on his wine. 'You can't be serious! I know *Valley Farm*'s the new "hot show" right now. But that's down to Laura, not Eddie Wellesley. The man has no television experience whatsoever.'

It pained David to hear *Valley Farm* described as the new 'hot show', but unfortunately this was a matter of simple fact. Not since *Downton Abbey* had a programme become such must-see viewing so quickly. 'Ground-breaking' was how Caitlin Moran had described it in *The Times*. 'Reality, documentary, comedy, drama . . . you don't know what it is, you only know you love it.' 'Baxter and Johanssen are television gold,' cooed the *Guardian*. 'The best presenting team since *Top Gear*,' according to the *Radio Times*. The *Echo* still covered local impact stories, but it had reached a point where articles overtly hostile to the show were becoming counterproductive. The British public had taken the Swell Valley and its cast of characters to their hearts, and Eddie Wellesley was basking smugly in its reflected glow.

It was mid-October now. Seven episodes had been broadcast, with a further five to go before the series finale. Each week ratings had jumped exponentially. That meant that the Gabriel Baxter/Macy Johanssen dream team would remain on air until almost Christmas, even though actual filming had finished in the valley this week. If David wanted to derail Eddie Wellesley's career, he needed a change of tactics. He also needed an ally – one with as much motive to destroy Eddie as he had.

'I quite agree,' he told John Bingham smoothly. 'He knows nothing about television. The man's a politician. But then again, the director-generalship's very much a political appointment, as you know.'

'Hmmm.' Bingham frowned. This was true.

John Bingham was also irritated about the furore over his former lover's new show. John Bingham had always seen himself as the star in their relationship. *He* was the industry powerhouse. Laura had been his protégée. Professionally speaking, he viewed her as an insignificant pilot fish swimming in his wake. It was irritating enough that she'd returned to TV at all after their affair ended – an unnecessary embarrassment. But that she should then both reject his advances *and* become supremely successful in her own right stuck in John Bingham's craw. 'Well, I don't see that there's very much I can do about it. If Wellesley's cronies all want him at the Beeb, then that's what'll happen.'

'Not necessarily,' said David.

His oysters arrived. Picking one up from its bed of shaved ice, he slurped it noisily out of the shell. 'Eddie's goal is to get back into government. The BBC job would be a stepping stone for him, nothing more. Something to re-establish his respectability and credibility. It would put him back at the heart of the establishment.'

'I still don't see—'

'It's politics, John,' David said impatiently. 'If you want the top job, then you need to play Wellesley at his own game. You have contacts in the Tory Party – good ones. Use them.'

John prodded his fish thoughtfully. It was true. William Berkeley, the party chairman, was an old friend from Cambridge. And Leonard Thring, the chief whip, still owed him money on a private equity deal.

'You must do everything you can to discredit Eddie Wellesley.' David spelled it out for him. 'I'm working on something, a book, that should make your job a lot easier when it comes out. But you need to lay the groundwork in the meantime.'

'What sort of book?' John Bingham's ears pricked up.

David tapped the side of his nose smugly. 'All in good time.'

'Eddie's got his own book, you know,' said John Bingham, biting back his irritation. He found David Carlyle insufferable. It was incredible how a man could be so superior and yet at the same time so pathetically chippy. 'His prison memoirs. If his publishers have any sense, they'll tie in the PR with *Valley Farm*. If even half of those viewers buy his book, it'll top the bestseller lists for sure.'

'Which is why timing's so important,' said David. 'The DG appointment will be announced in November. My guess is Eddie's book will be out right before Christmas. That's peak book-buying season, and right after *Valley Farm* comes off the air, so fans will be wanting their fix. You and I need to act now. If we sit on our hands, the bastard'll be a runaway train by Christmas.'

They talked strategy for the rest of the lunch. When the bill arrived, David paid and they stepped out onto Piccadilly and into separate cabs. It had started to rain.

John Bingham watched the rain trickle down the taxi window, deep in thought.

Was he really being considered for the BBC's top job? It was the first he'd heard of it. But David Carlyle seemed very certain. The odious little man certainly had influence, and a finger in all sorts of pies.

John Bingham had spent his entire life in television. If this was his chance, his shot at the gold medal, he was not about to sit by and see it snatched away by some insignificant ex-girlfriend and her political crony.

His mind raced as the cab rolled on.

'It *is* you! Oh my God. I can't believe it. Will you do a photo with me and my friend?'

'Of course.' Gabe smiled at the two girls. He knew it was childish, but he still enjoyed being recognized, even if it was by a pair of giggling schoolgirls. He was on the train from Victoria back to Fittlescombe for tonight's wrap party after a day at the rugby. Being on a hit TV show had a number of perks, Gabe was learning, including being offered swish corporate boxes at Twickenham from 'sponsors' he barely knew.

'I'm Tania and this is Rochelle,' said the first girl, draping herself over Gabe's lap as she handed her friend her phone. 'We love *Valley Farm*. You should have seen how much Rochelle cried when them lambs died! She was well upset.'

As 'Rochelle' snapped away, it occurred to Gabe that perhaps being photographed wrapped in a fifteen-year-old girl in school uniform might not be the *best* image for Laura to see on line or in the newspapers. Or the network, for that matter.

Laura was always going on at him about his 'media profile' and being more 'conscious'. Gabe hated it when she spoke in that way. It made him feel like a naughty schoolboy, having the ways of the world explained to him by an exasperated schoolteacher. *Valley Farm* was already a tremendous success – far more popular than any of them had dared hope. But Laura was being so damn serious about it. She had an unfortunate knack of sucking all the fun out, and making Gabe feel guilty for enjoying his moment in the sun.

'You wanted me to present it,' he'd reminded her last night, after they'd rowed yet again, this time about something Gabe had said to a journalist in a newspaper interview. 'But now that I'm good at it and people like me, it pisses you off.'

'For God's sake,' sighed Laura. 'It does not piss me off that you're good at it. Or that people like you.'

'Could've fooled me,' grumbled Gabe.

'It pisses me off that you let some pretty hack from the *Mail* get you drunk and then you made comments about Macy's figure. Specifically, her breasts! That is not cool, Gabriel.'

'I didn't make a comment. The journalist made a comment. She said she thought Macy had great tits. I just agreed with her.'

Laura rolled her eyes.

'What's wrong with that?' asked Gabe.

'What's wrong with that is the headline, you dickhead,'

said Laura. '"I love Macy's boobs, says Baxter". How would you like to read something in the paper where I talked about some guy's dick?'

'Now you're just being silly.'

'I am *not*. And this isn't just about us either – it's about the show. *Valley Farm* is wholesome, family television. That's what we're trying to see here. It's about gambolling lambs and maypoles and village traditions. It is not about Macy Johanssen's bloody tits!'

'Why don't we stand up?' Gabe said hurriedly, removing the girl from his lap as Laura's words came ominously back to haunt him. 'Then I can get both of you in the shot. May I?' He took the phone from her friend, quietly deleting the pictures before handing it to a fellow passenger, who quickly snapped three new images. Lots of smiling, zero touching.

Very family friendly, thought Gabe.

The wrap party was being held at Wraggsbottom and he was really looking forward to it. The last thing he wanted was to get dragged into another row with Laura. Everything was going brilliantly, but it had been hard work and an immense amount of stress. Tonight was all about sitting back and relaxing, enjoying the fruits of their labours. Gabe realized how much he'd been missing the old Laura recently – his fun, irreverent, sexy, relaxed wife of pre-*Valley Farm* days. Tonight he was hoping to catch a glimpse of her again. They both needed it.

'Right.' Laura put her hands on her hips and surveyed the scene with satisfaction. 'Gin and tonic time, I think.'

Tonight's wrap party was a low-key affair. Channel 5 were throwing a much grander end-of-season bash at The Dorchester next week. But tonight was for any local cast, crew and their immediate families who felt like turning up and celebrating the end of filming in the time-honoured British manner of getting completely plastered at someone else's expense, dancing to preposterously cheesy eighties music and passing out on the floor in the middle of an ill-advised midnight game of Twister.

Despite the informal nature of proceedings, and the fact that no press whatsoever would be allowed inside the farm gates, Laura had made an effort. For once she'd decided to splash out and bring in outside help: a local firm of cleaners to get the farm looking its best and a caterer to sort canapés and drinks. Earlier this afternoon Laura had found herself running her fingers in wonder along polished wood surfaces that she hadn't seen in years, so long had they been buried under piles of unopened gas bills and dog-eared copies of *Thomas the Tank Engine* magazine. And the mini Gruyère soufflés she'd sampled in the kitchen earlier were so good they'd brought tears to her eyes.

With the children packed off to Laura's mother for the night (not an ideal solution, but the nanny was on holiday again and it wouldn't kill the boys to OD on sugar mice and unsuitable television for twenty-four hours), she'd even had time to try to look nice for once. Yesterday she'd driven guiltily into Lewes and spent far too much money on a dark green jersey dress that clung to her body perfectly and made her feel sexy and mysterious. Then, this morning, while Gabe had been at Twickenham, she'd had her hair cut and highlighted and raced home to shave her legs, which were in an awful state. *I look like a Shetland pony*, she thought, horrified, clipping a third Gillette Mach 3 head onto her razor. *I don't need a Ladyshave, I need a bloody Flymo.* No wonder Gabe had started noticing other women's boobs. Here he was, a newly minted sex symbol, married to a yak.

Well, not tonight, thought Laura, dousing herself in YSL Rive Gauche, Gabe's favourite scent, and dusting talcum powder over her newly trimmed bush. On the plus side, all the stress and exhaustion and excitement of producing *Valley Farm* while raising two small boys had left her slimmer than she'd been since before she had babies. She could afford to indulge in a cheese soufflé or two.

The sweet girl from the catering company disappeared into the kitchen and returned with a large gin and tonic, ice cubes clinking merrily against the cut-crystal glass. Laura had just sat down and taken a first, delicious sip, when the door opened and Gabe burst in.

'Sorry I'm late, some problem at East Croydon station. I swear to God, Southern are the . . . bloody hell! What happened to you?'

'What do you mean? Nothing.'

'You look amazing.'

'I thought I always looked amazing,' Laura said coyly, standing up and giving him a little twirl.

'You do. But this is . . . better. That dress is pure porn.'

'It is not!' Laura giggled. 'It's elegant.'

'Like hell it is. It's sexy. Take it off.'

He grabbed her, running a hand up beneath her skirt while the other snaked around the back of her neck and he pulled her in for a kiss.

'Don't be silly.' Laura pushed him away half-heartedly. It was ridiculous how happy she felt. 'People'll start arriving in a minute.'

'I'll lock the doors.' Gabe grinned.

'No you *won't*,' laughed Laura. 'Go upstairs and get changed.'

'Only if you promise to get completely filthy with me later.'

'I promise,' said Laura. 'Go.'

'I mean it, you know.' Gabe gave her a knowing look as he went upstairs.

So do I, thought Laura. Suddenly she couldn't wait for tonight's party to be over.

By eight o'clock the party was in full swing. Santiago and Penny showed up early and brought Penny's twenty-five-year-old son, Seb, who proceeded to knock back the home-made sangria at a terrifying rate.

'It's a legacy from his university days,' Penny explained sheepishly to Laura. 'Anyone would think he'd read Binge Drinking at Newcastle.'

'Gosh, I don't mind,' said Laura. 'He's young.'

'Not that young,' Penny sighed. 'He's supposed to be an investment banker. I mean who'd invest money with *that*?'

She glanced over at Seb, who was singing along loudly and drunkenly to '*Red, Red Wine.*'

Laura laughed. 'Well, Gabe still drinks like a fish and he never even went to uni. Come to think of it, I'm pretty sure he failed his A levels.'

'Done all right, though, hasn't he?'

Gabe was talking to Macy Johanssen and James Craven. In dark blue jeans and a crisp Turnbull & Asser shirt teamed with a burgundy cashmere jumper, he looked movie-star handsome this evening, tossing back his blond hair and laughing loudly at some blue joke of James's. 'Is he enjoying presenting?'

Laura rolled her eyes indulgently. 'He's like a pig in shit. He loves it. All the attention, especially from girls.'

'You trust him, though?' Penny's eyes narrowed.

'Oh, God yes,' said Laura. 'I mean, he's an awful flirt. Really dreadful. It's like an illness. But I think that's part of what makes him so good on screen. It is odd, though,' she added thoughtfully, 'having the whole country fall in love not just with one's house and village and lifestyle, but with one's husband too.'

'I'm sure,' said Penny.

'I supposed you must be used to it with Santiago. Girls flinging themselves at him, I mean.'

'Actually, I don't think one can ever really get used to it,' Penny said seriously. 'It's always in the back of one's mind. The idea that something *could* happen. You try not to let it get to you, to take it as a compliment and all that. But it's hard.'

Laura hadn't expected such honesty, especially not from Penny, whose marriage to Santiago had always seemed so perfect. It was disconcerting. All of a sudden she felt depressed, as if someone had let all the air out of her happiness balloon.

'Hello, ladies!' A beaming Eddie Wellesley walked up behind them, wrapping one arm around Laura's shoulders and the other around Penny's. If anyone could refill one's balloon, it was Eddie. 'Red Red Wine' was booming out over the sound system, and Eddie was swaying slightly to the beat, clearly a little the worse for wear himself. 'I trust you're both enjoying yourselves?'

'How much have you had?' Laura teased him. 'And where's Lady Wellesley? Not in the mood for a party?'

Eddie gave her a reproachful look. 'Annabel's under the weather.'

Angela Cranley, who'd drifted over to join them, caught this last remark. 'Really? She seemed fine when I saw her at the Conservative Ladies Luncheon earlier. I hope it wasn't something she ate. I told Max the coronation chicken tasted a bit dodgy.'

'I think it's a touch of flu,' said Eddie.

'Oh, please,' Laura rolled her eyes. 'She didn't want to come because she loathes the show. If you can't lie convincingly, Eddie, don't lie at all. I thought that was the first rule of politics?'

Eddie laughed. 'So cynical for one so young, Mrs Baxter. Well, you're right, Annabel doesn't have flu. She just finds these sorts of thing difficult.'

What sorts of thing? thought Laura. *Parties? Or anything involving me?*

It was obvious that Annabel didn't like her. That she resented Laura's friendship with Eddie, almost as much as she resented his involvement in the show in the first place.

Oh, well. Too bad, thought Laura. *You can't please everyone.*

It was a warm autumn evening and Santiago had slipped out into the garden for a crafty cigarette under the apple tree. When Penny found him he was peering back in through the drawing-room window, half hidden behind a rhododendron bush.

'What on earth are you doing?' she asked. 'You look as if you're casing the joint.'

'I'm watching. Look at that.'

Penny looked. Gabe and Macy were locked in conversation. Gabe's head was bent low to hear what Macy was saying. He had one hand resting lightly on the small of her back and from time to time he was nodding intently in reply.

'I don't like the look of that,' said Santiago.

'They're only talking,' said Penny. Although she had to admit there *was* an intimacy to the body language. Her earlier conversation with Laura came flooding back to her.

Santiago stubbed out his cigarette. 'I'm going in there.'

Penny looked at him aghast. 'To say what? For heaven's sake, darling, there's no law against talking. They're colleagues. Don't stir up trouble. It's none of our business.'

But Santiago was already striding back in through the French doors.

'I think Laura wants you,' he said to Gabe, physically inserting himself between Gabe and Macy. 'Something about running low on tonic water.'

'Really? We had plenty this morning. Where is she?'

'Out in the garden last time I saw her,' said Santiago.

Gabe scurried off. Looking irritated, Macy was about to follow suit when Santiago grabbed her by the arm.

'James's a good man, you know.'

Macy's frown intensified. 'I know. That's why I'm with him.'

'Yes, but *are* you with him? Really?'

'What are you talking about?' Macy snapped, trying to extricate herself from Santiago's grip. 'I don't have time for riddles.'

'I'll spell it out then,' Santiago whispered in her ear. 'I think you're in love with Gabriel Baxter.'

Macy laughed derisively.

'It won't come to anything, you know. Gabe might flirt, but he loves his wife.'

'This is ridiculous,' said Macy. 'You don't know what you're talking about. Let go of me.'

Santiago released her arm. 'Fine. But what you're doing is unfair to James. Not to mention poor Laura.'

201

'I'm not *doing* anything,' Macy said indignantly. 'For your information, James and I are very happy together. *Very*. And as for "poor Laura", I'd save your sympathy if I were you. Believe me, that woman can stick up for herself. If anyone's suffering in that marriage, it's Gabe, not her.'

'You don't know what you're talking about,' snapped Santiago.

'Is everything all right?' James came over, wrapping both arms around Macy's waist. 'You two aren't arguing, are you? Santi can be a pig when he's been drinking.' He smiled.

'We're not arguing.' Macy shot Santiago a frosty look. 'Everything's fine.' Turning round she stood up on tiptoes, coiling herself about James's neck and kissing him passionately on the mouth. 'Let's go home,' she said huskily.

James lit up like a light bulb. 'I'd love to. But are you sure? This is your wrap party, after all.'

'Positive,' purred Macy. 'I'm tired of all these people. I just want you.' She turned to Santiago. 'If you'll excuse us.'

James grinned over his shoulder at his friend as Macy pulled him away, like a cavewoman dragging home her kill.

'There you go,' said Penny, reappearing at Santiago's side. 'I saw that kiss. You have nothing to worry about.'

Santiago thought: *I'm not so sure.*

Macy and James went back to James's place, a rented gamekeeper's cottage overlooking the river at Brockhurst. From the bedroom window you could see the gabled roof of Riverside Hall. The lights were still on upstairs.

'Cruella's still up,' said Macy. Stripped down to her Elle Macpherson underwear she was kneeling on the window seat, gazing out across the valley. 'Probably devising some elaborate torture for poor Eddie when he gets home.'

'Annabel is a witch, isn't she?' agreed James. Walking up behind Macy he leaned down and nuzzled her neck. He could feel his dick start to harden instantly. How had he ever managed to land himself such a stunning, incredible girl? She looked insanely sexy in her white lace bra and knickers.

'Why do you think he married her?' asked Macy, sighing contentedly as James unhooked her bra and cupped both her breasts with his warm, rough hands.

'She probably cast a spell on him,' murmured James, who was rapidly losing interest in the Wellesley marriage. 'Something involving frogs and eyes of newt.'

Macy giggled.

'Or maybe it's all an act and she's red-hot in bed,' James whispered, moving his hands down and slipping beneath the flimsy lace fabric of her underwear, expertly caressing her clitoris. 'Maybe they're fucking like stoats up there every night. Although at his age I doubt it.'

'He's not that old,' said Macy defensively, as an unwanted memory of Eddie making love to her in Los Angeles flashed into her brain. She'd enjoyed it at the time, but now the thought of having ever been with Eddie felt obscene.

'He's not that young,' James said reasonably.

Turning round, Macy wriggled out of her underwear completely and slid naked into his arms, wrapping her legs around his waist like a rainforest native about to shimmy up a palm tree. 'I'm kinda done talking.'

Grinning, James staggered backwards onto the bed with Macy still on top of him. His hard-on was so big now it was tricky to get his jeans off, like taking down a tent with the poles still up. But finally he too was naked. Gasping with pleasure he slid inside her, watching while she arched and

203

bucked and moaned on top of him like the world's hottest rodeo rider.

Macy closed her eyes and immediately saw Gabe Baxter's face. She opened them again, panicked.

'You OK, babe?' asked James.

'Mmm-hmmm,' Macy nodded, forcing herself to focus on the present and the incredible sensations flooding through her body.

Bloody Santiago de la Cruz! Why did he have to put dumb ideas into her head? She was not in love with Gabe. Attracted, maybe, in an idle, offhand way. But everyone had people they were attracted to, besides their partner, didn't they?

Scared he was going to come too soon, James suddenly pulled out of her and flipped her over onto her stomach. Relieved he could no longer see her face, Macy buried her head in the pillow. Propping himself up on his elbows so that only part of his weight was on her, James nudged her legs wider before pushing inside her once again, forcing himself to slow his thrusts into a calmer, more controlled rhythm. It was torturous and wonderful. Macy groaned. Waves of pleasure lapped all around her, never quite breaking on the shore.

'I love you,' James murmured in her ear.

'I love you too.' The words were out before she knew she'd said them. Macy felt her hips move faster and faster with a mind of their own, willing her body towards orgasm and release. But if her body was in heaven, her mind was in hell. Images of Eddie Wellesley and Gabe Baxter continued to jump out of her like ghouls on a ghost-train ride, tormenting her, making her doubt everything. And Santiago's voice: *'I think you're in love with Gabriel Baxter'* playing like a stuck record, over and over, until she wanted to scream. Then suddenly, too quickly, James exploded inside her, clinging onto the headboard for support as his whole body shot forwards like a torpedo. Macy's own climax came then, too, wave after wave, each one bigger and harder than the last. The faces and voices were finally gone.

'Jesus.' James collapsed on the bed beside her, gasping for breath. He was drenched in sweat, as if he'd just been swimming.

'Yeah.' Macy lay beside him, her own heart pounding. 'Jesus.'

'I meant it, you know,' said James, once he'd finally got his breath back. 'I do love you.'

Macy stared at the ceiling, trying not to cry. She didn't know if she felt wildly happy or desperately sad. Only that the maelstrom of emotion inside her was too much to bear. And that she didn't want to be alone in this world any more.

'James?' Her voice rang out in the still night air. 'Will you marry me?'

CHAPTER THIRTEEN

Eddie Wellesley lay in bed feeling profoundly happy. It was November, not yet a whole year since he'd walked out of Farndale, but it felt like a lifetime ago. So much had happened in that time – moving to the Swell Valley, meeting the Baxters and Macy, becoming a television producer, and now, launching his memoirs. Outside, a chill wind rattled against the windowpane. But the dreary weather could do nothing to dampen Eddie's spirits this morning.

Annabel lay in his arms, warm and naked and *happy*, something Eddie had feared she might never be again. Last night, after Eddie's appearance on a new Channel 4 chat show to promote his memoirs, he and Annabel had driven back to Riverside Hall and had had the best, most passionate sex they'd had in years. Decades, probably. Eddie hadn't realized quite how much he'd missed it – missed her – till now. Nothing meant anything compared to this. To the two of them being together and happy and a team.

'I adore you,' he whispered in her ear.

Turning round, Annabel kissed him softly on the lips. 'Good.'

Annabel was happy too. Despite what people thought, she'd always loved Eddie. His affairs had hurt her, but she'd stayed because, in the end, she'd never stopped loving him or feeling loved by him. And because he said he was sorry, and she believed him. She knew she could come across as cold and unfeeling. It was one of the reasons why so many strangers blamed *her* for Eddie's infidelity. *She's so cold, she's such a snob, she drove him to it.*

But Eddie had always seen past that. He'd seen the warmth in Annabel where no one else had – perhaps he'd even created it? – and that private understanding had made him feel special. In Eddie's eyes, Annabel was something rare and wonderful, a secret treasure chest to which only he had the key. She loved him for that more than anything.

Even so, it had been a long road back to their old intimacy. When Eddie had got involved in *Valley Farm*, and started hanging out with all those television people, especially Laura Baxter, Annabel had been terrified of losing him all over again. In television, Annabel felt excluded. But politics? That was a world where they both belonged, for better or worse. A world where Annabel had an important role to play, as wife, hostess, team mate. With the memoirs finally finished and publication scheduled for next week, last night's television appearance had been the first concrete step in Eddie's political comeback. That alone had been a huge boost to Annabel's spirits. The fact that it had been such a triumph made her positively giddy with hope, and renewed love for her husband.

'What's your greatest regret?' the chat-show host had asked Eddie.

'I don't believe in regrets,' Eddie said briskly. 'I broke the law and I paid the price. But I'm not complaining. I learned a lot in prison, and I made some great friends.'

'Still, if you could turn back the clock, surely there are things you would have done differently? That you wish you hadn't done?'

Eddie had thought about it for a long time. Then, with disarming sincerity, he'd said: 'I wish I hadn't hurt my wife.' Zooming in, the camera caught the tears in his eyes. 'But that's a private matter between the two of us.'

Watching in the green room, Annabel had fought back tears of her own. Eddie had said sorry countless times. But last night, for the first time, she had known he really meant it.

She met him in the corridor as soon as he walked off stage.

'Did I do all right?' he asked nervously.

'You were wonderful.'

He pulled her to him, pushing her hair back tenderly behind one ear and locking his eyes onto hers. *'You're* wonderful. It's all going to be different this time round, you'll see. I love you and I'm going to protect you. From everything.'

This transformative moment in Eddie and Annabel's relationship had turned out to be transformative for Eddie's career too. According to this morning's viewing figures and reviews, the public had been deeply moved by his marital remorse. Eddie's political agent, Kevin Unger, had called at crack of dawn, waking them both up.

'You went down a storm,' Kevin gushed. 'Huge ratings for last night's show. Over eighty per cent of viewers found you "sincere and credible". Ninety per cent liked you! That's unheard of for a politician.'

'Especially a bent one,' quipped Eddie.

Kevin laughed. 'No one cares any more.'

'Except David Carlyle.'

'David who?' the agent scoffed. 'Get Annabel to serve the party chairman a few bottles of really good burgundy at tonight's book launch and, I'm telling you, you're home and dry. They'll be throwing safe seats at you like girls chucking their knickers at a One Direction concert.'

Now, lying in bed next to Annabel, Eddie ran a hand lovingly down her bare back. 'Can I do anything for you?' he asked.

'Such as what?' she asked archly.

'Anything you like,' Eddie grinned. 'We don't have much to do today before the party, do we?'

'Not much to do?' Annabel rolled her eyes. 'Honestly, Eddie, these things don't magically happen by themselves, you know. It's not just a book launch; it's the rebirth of your political career. The Home Secretary's coming, and the party chairman. This is a crucial evening for us. Crucial.'

'I know that,' Eddie said gently.

'Then there's the spin doctor, speech writer, or whatever he is. The bald chap with the permanent sneer and the American wife.'

'You mean Phil Blaize?'

'Yes. Him. The wife's bound to have "allergies".'

'Why is she bound to have allergies?' Eddie laughed.

'Because they always do. American women are so tiresome about their eating habits.' Annabel sighed heavily. 'Really, Eddie, I've been run off my feet for months preparing for this damn party and I'm still nowhere near ready.'

'I thought Magda was supposed to be doing most of the legwork?'

TILLY BAGSHAWE

'Magda?' Annabel rolled her eyes extravagantly. 'Don't get me started. Honestly, if I had a pound for every time I've had to correct that girl, or go back and do a job myself because she simply cannot follow simple instructions . . .'

Eddie stopped her with a kiss. He knew the postcoital glow wouldn't last for ever, but he wanted a few more hours of it at least.

'I'll make breakfast,' he said brightly. 'How about pancakes? Thinking of American eating habits.'

Annabel burst out laughing. 'Edward! You have no idea how to make a pancake.'

'Yes I have.' Eddie pulled on a dressing gown. 'You use eggs and . . . things.'

'What things?'

Eddie looked vague. 'Milk? Look, I can make a fucking pancake, all right. I'm not an imbecile. You just relax and leave it to me.'

Milo Wellesley hopped down from the passenger seat of the cab and waved cheerily to the lorry driver as he drove away.

He'd been lucky to get a lift almost all the way from Heathrow to Brockhurst. Gary, the jovial, enormously fat driver, was taking a load of Topps Tiles to a warehouse in Chichester and was happy to have the tanned, skinny blond boy along for the ride. Having been dropped at the top of the hill, by the side of the A27, Milo had less than two miles to walk down into the valley till he reached Riverside Hall.

Before Africa, he would never have hitchhiked. But a lot of things had changed for Milo in the last few months. He'd returned to England happier, healthier and immeasurably

more resourceful. He was determined to prove to his parents
– and certain other people – that he was no longer the
needy, entitled public schoolboy of old. He was a man of
the world now. A man with opinions and ambitions and
plans for the future – a future that lay spread out before
him, just like the glorious patchwork of fields, woods and
streams he stood gazing at now.

Hoisting his backpack onto his skinny shoulders, he started
down the hill at a jog. It was still only nine in the morning
and the air was cold enough for him to see his breath. After
the dryness of Sudan, the sense of damp in the air felt
wonderful. Milo drank in the mist and the breeze and the
promise of rain or even snow like a bumblebee gorging itself
on nectar after a long spell in the wilderness. But it wasn't
only England he was pleased to see, or his home, or his
family. It was Magda.

He'd gone to look for her the morning after his leaving
party, to say goodbye, but she'd taken Wilf out for an early
walk and he'd missed her. At the time he'd been so caught
up with the Roxanne drama – Roxie had hooked up with
his friend Will Cooper that night deliberately to bait him –
and he hadn't thought much about missing his parents'
home help. But being away had changed all that.

Out in Africa, as the days and weeks rolled past, Roxanne
had faded from his memory and Milo's thoughts had turned
more and more to Magda. He pictured her giving him a
stern talking-to on their walk to The Fox a few days before
the party, the night he'd met Emma Harwich for a drink. It
wasn't just that Magda was beautiful, although she was
certainly that. It was her combination of strength and vulnerability, her quiet dignity that had begun to give her an almost
mystical aura in Milo's memory. He'd been too blind to see

it back in England. Too caught up in his own shit, chasing girls like Emma and Roxanne for no better reason than that they were sexy. But after long, gruelling days lugging bricks in the African sun, the long nights had given him plenty of time for reflection.

He'd been blind. Blind and stupid. Roxanne was a nice enough girl, but she had never inspired him to become a better person the way that Magda did. Nor, despite her antics with Will, had she ever presented much of a challenge. Magda, on the other hand, was nothing but challenge. She was a grown woman, an intelligent woman, a woman to be conquered. A woman *worth* conquering.

Not that he was obsessed or anything.

Milo was going to show Magda that he was a changed man. It made him cringe to think about that night outside The Fox now, when he'd still been mooning over Emma Harwich. Emma Harwich! How pointless and vacuous his fling with Emma seemed now. Although, in a roundabout way, it had turned out to be a good thing, as he'd never have been sent to Africa if it weren't for Emma.

Bizarrely, Emma's face had been one of the first things Milo had seen when he'd landed this morning. She and her ancient boyfriend, the Tory donor, were on the front page of the *Daily Mail*, shaking hands with some movie star or other. Milo had found himself staring at Emma's image like a man who has just realized his old master painting is actually nothing but a cheap fake. She was pretty enough, of course, in a regular-featured, generic, model-y sort of way. But, next to Magda, her beauty was as lifeless and blank as the painted face of a doll.

The closer he came to Riverside Hall, the more excited Milo felt. As the lane twisted and turned, and the ground seemed to fall away beneath his feet, familiar smells joined forces with the sights and sounds of the valley. Wet grass and mulch and wood smoke and horse manure, all mingled together into an intoxicating soup of home and countryside and belonging. Suddenly Milo realized he was starving. A mental picture of a warm bacon sandwich shimmered before his eyes like a mirage in the Sahara. He broke into a jog, then a run.

Both his parents' cars were parked in the drive at Riverside Hall, although he couldn't see Magda's rickety old Ford Fiesta. An awful thought struck him. What if Magda had left while he'd been gone? What if his mother had fired her? Or she'd grown tired of Annabel's ceaseless, unreasonable demands and taken off, leaving no contact number or forwarding address?

If only he'd told her how he felt about her before he left! But the truth was, he hadn't known then. Not really. He'd been so immature back then, bemoaning his trivial life problems like some sort of navel-gazing moron, after Magda had shared something so personal and profound with him.

I was an arsehole. A complete fool.

But that was the old Milo.

The front door was unlocked. Dropping his backpack on the floor with a clatter, Milo woke Wilf, who'd been sleeping quietly in his basket under the coat rack. Opening one eye and turning his head to the side in the very faintest possible display of curiosity, the border terrier farted loudly and went back to sleep.

'Well, that's charming,' Milo grinned. 'That's all I get after five months in the bloody back of beyond? So much for man's best friend.'

Hearing laughter from the dining room, he opened the door and stood frozen. *Was this a dream?* There was his dad, perched on the edge of the dining table, detritus from breakfast strewn all around him. And *there*, on his father's *lap*, was Milo's mother, wearing a short silk dressing gown that could only be described as skimpy, with her hair down and unbrushed, giggling – actually laughing, out loud – at something his dad was whispering in her ear. Clearly Milo wasn't the only one who'd changed since the summer. His parents seemed to have morphed into two teenagers. Or at least into people who liked each other and laughed at each other's jokes.

'Mum?'

Annabel and Eddie spun round in unison. 'Milo!'

'What on earth are you doing home?' asked Eddie. 'We thought your flight was next weekend?'

'It was. I changed it. Thought I'd surprise you,' said Milo. 'Evidently I succeeded.' He raised an eyebrow laconically.

'You're so thin!' Annabel exclaimed, leaping off Eddie's lap and belting her robe more tightly around her. If Milo wasn't hallucinating, which was quite possible at this point, he could have sworn he saw his mother blush. 'Didn't they feed you over there? And you're so brown! Look at you.'

'It's Africa, Mum. It was hot.'

'Yes, but don't they have sun cream? I hardly recognize you. Oh, good grief, your fingernails!' Annabel picked up Milo's hand in disgust. He almost felt relieved. Here was the mother he remembered. 'You look like you've been ploughing a field with your bare hands. And your hair's far too long. Go up and have a shower right away and I'll book you in at the barber's in an hour to have it off.'

'I don't want to "have it off",' said Milo. *Other than with Magda.* 'Where's Magda?'

'Magda? In the kitchen, cooking for tonight,' said Annabel. 'Why?'

Milo felt the relief wash over him like a cool wave. She hadn't left, then.

'What's tonight?'

'Your father's book launch. Except it isn't really a book launch; it's more a vitally important political dinner.'

'Oh.'

'So you aren't to pester Magda. She's far too busy to waste time yabbering away to you.'

'Am I invited? To this vitally important dinner?'

Eddie and Annabel exchanged glances.

'Do you want to be?'

'Of course.'

Eddie looked astonished. The old Milo would rather have eaten his own hand than sit around with a bunch of boring politicians.

'All right,' he said. 'You can come. But only if you behave yourself impeccably.'

'And cut your hair,' added Annabel.

Milo kissed his mother on the cheek. 'I'm not cutting my hair. But I will be on my best behaviour. Now, you'll both have to excuse me. I'm afraid I have an urgent appointment to keep.'

Eddie grinned. He was delighted to see Milo back home, but he clearly found this new, mature version of his son highly amusing.

'An urgent appointment, eh? May one ask with whom?'

Milo grinned back. 'With a bacon sandwich.'

Well. It was half true.

* * *

Magda was sitting at the kitchen table, almost invisible behind an enormous mound of peeled prawns.

'Hello, stranger,' said Milo, trying to project a confidence he didn't feel.

She looked up and gave him the briefest, most perfunctory nod of greeting before returning immediately to her work.

Milo's heart plummeted. 'Are you angry with me?'

'No.' Magda continued peeling.

'Well, you're acting like it. I've been gone for months! Don't I get a hug at least?'

Magda's eyes blazed into his. 'A hug? Oh, I see. A hug's all right down here in the kitchen, where nobody can see, is that it?'

Milo frowned. 'What are you talking about?'

'What do you think I'm talking about?' Exasperated, Magda pushed aside her bowl of shells. 'Your party. Your "friend" Jamie and your mother treating me like the hired help.'

'Aren't you the hired help?' Milo asked tactlessly.

Magda was furious. 'I wasn't that night. I was your *guest*. You invited me! I even brought a new dress.' To her own surprise, there were tears in her eyes. She hadn't thought she still cared so much about this. But seeing Milo again brought it all flooding back. 'Can you imagine what an idiot I felt? How embarrassed I was? You stood there and disowned me.'

Milo looked at her helplessly. He didn't remember any of this! He had a vague mental picture of Jamie King being a dick, but that was about Roxanne, not Magda.

'I'm sorry,' he said eventually. 'I didn't *mean* to disown you! I didn't realize. I guess I didn't think.'

'No.' Magda returned to her prawns. 'You never do.'

Now it was Milo's turn to get impassioned.

'That's not true,' he said, snatching the bowl away from her to force her to listen. 'I mean, maybe it was true back then. But it's not true now. I do think. I've thought about you. A lot.'

Magda blushed scarlet. This was not the response she'd expected at *all*. Why on earth had she started this stupid conversation in the first place?

'OK, well. I can't talk now,' she mumbled. 'I am *so* behind with this soup and then there's the pastry cases to make for the beef Wellington and all the prep work for the trifle and that's before I even start the cleaning.' She knew she was rambling but she couldn't seem to stop. 'You should see the list your mother's given me. You wouldn't be—'

Milo cut her off. Marching round the table he pulled her to her feet and in to his chest before she had a chance to protest.

Despite herself, Magda could feel her heart beating nineteen to the dozen as he hugged her. Milo looked different. He very thin, and tanned, but it was more than that. He seemed older somehow, despite the silly student beads and the straggly, gap-year hair. He smelled of sweat and toothpaste and something with patchouli in it, and she was finding it harder and harder to stay angry with him.

'Do you forgive me?' he spoke into her hair.

'I suppose so,' Magda mumbled, disengaging herself as soon as she politely could and sitting back down.

'So,' she asked, a little too brightly, returning to her work. 'How was your trip?'

His face lit up. 'Amazing. Life changing, actually. You

haven't lived till you've seen Africa,' he added, more than a touch pompously.

Magda suppressed a smile. 'Is that so?'

Now it was Milo's turn to blush. He wasn't sure how he'd pictured their reunion exactly. But not like this. He wanted to show Magda that he'd changed. That he wasn't the spoiled, entitled boy who had left five months ago. The boy who was so blind, he'd deeply humiliated her at his own leaving party without even realizing it. He wanted her to see that he was a man now, an adult with opinions and real-life experiences who should be taken seriously. But standing in front of her now, Milo felt younger and more foolish than ever. It was all going wrong!

He cast around desperately for something to say.

'Mum seems on very good form. She and Dad looked very loved-up just now.'

'She does seem a lot happier lately,' Magda replied cautiously. It wasn't her place to gossip about Lady Wellesley – with Milo, or anyone else for that matter.

'I'm going tonight. To the dinner,' blurted out Milo. He wished Magda would look at him.

'That's nice.' Magda continued peeling.

'I'm trying to take more of an interest in politics.' He could hear how stilted the words sounded. He felt like a little boy, dressing up in his father's clothes, desperately trying to play the part of the grown-up. But he ploughed on anyway. 'I need to understand Dad's world better. So I can make a difference. When I was in Africa—'

'Milo.' Magda cut him off mid-sentence. 'I'm glad you're back. And I'm glad it was a good trip. Really. But I simply don't have time to talk at the moment. Help yourself if you want something to eat, but then, please, let me finish this.'

'Of course.' Milo forced a smile. 'We'll catch up later.'

Winded with disappointment, he left the room. He didn't want the bacon sandwich any more. All of a sudden he'd lost his appetite.

Magda waited for the door to close before wiping her hands on her apron, leaning back in her chair and closing her eyes.

What's wrong with me? she thought bitterly.

A few minutes in Milo's company and her emotions were churning like washing in a machine. She felt angry and happy and nervous, all at the same time. Worse than that, she had no idea how to react around him, what to say, how to *be*. Either she was *too* close to him, *too* intimate – that hug had been painful – or she came off as cold and aloof and ended up hurting his feelings, as she had just now.

He was the one who had treated *her* badly. And yet here she was feeling like a Class-A bitch.

Guiltily she returned to her mountain of prawns.

William Berkeley, the Tory Party chairman, sank back contentedly in Eddie Wellesley's battered leather chesterfield armchair, puffing on a Padrón 1964 Anniversary cigar. They really ought to have waited till after dinner. But the chance to slip away to Fast Eddie's study and enjoy a decent smoke beforehand had been too good to pass up. Truth be told, William Berkeley wasn't much for literary parties. Too much noise and clatter, and too many stupid women banging on about Orange prizes and God knows what.

'House looks lovely,' William observed, through a thick cloud of cigar smoke. 'Annabel's excelled herself as usual.'

'Thanks. But we're not here to talk about the house,' said Eddie.

'And the book's clearly going to be a triumph.'

'Or the book. Or the TV show,' Eddie added.

'Thank God for that,' muttered the chairman, only half under his breath. He really had less than nothing to say about a reality television programme that was apparently hosted by a young lady who'd been named after a department store. Or perhaps a parade.

'I want to know where I stand with the party, William.' Eddie lit his own cigar and took a long, satisfying puff. 'Am I forgiven?'

William Berkeley made a purring sound, like a cat being presented with a saucer of cream. It was pleasant to have men like Wellesley paying one court.

'Well now, Eddie, you have many friends and supporters in the party, as you know. You've already had your membership restored.'

Eddie gave William a knowing look. 'That's not quite the same thing as being forgiven.'

'Perhaps not. But Garforth's here tonight, isn't he?' said William. 'That should tell you something.'

James Garforth, the new Home Secretary, was the highest-profile political guest to have graced Riverside Hall to date.

'Hambly isn't, though,' said Eddie.

'One step at a time, old boy,' William Berkeley patted his paunch reassuringly. 'Tristram's always been a supporter of yours, you know that. But he *is* the PM. And you *did* go to prison.'

Eddie scowled. Patience had never been his strong suit.

'I think the book will help,' said William. 'It strikes the right tone. Sorry, but not grovelling.'

'Will it get me a safe seat?'

'I'm really not at liberty to say,' Berkeley began, before

breaking off in the face of a withering look from Eddie. 'Oh, look, all right, yes. Barring disaster, you're being talked about for Chichester and Swell Valley at the next election. No one likes Piers Renton-Chambers. He's been a terrible damp squib.'

'Really?' Eddie's face lit up like a small child's on Christmas Eve. 'That's wonderful news!'

'Yes, and very much off the record,' William reminded him sternly. 'You'll have a lot of sucking up to do to the local parliamentary party, aka the swivel eyes.'

'Of course, of course,' said Eddie.

'And there can't be a whiff – not a single, solitary fart's worth – of scandal.'

'Of course not. What do you take me for?' Eddie had the cheek to look affronted.

Both men smoked on in silence for a few moments. The noise of the drinks party drifted in from the drawing room, a blur of voices and laughter, growing louder as the alcohol flowed. The majority of the guests were due to leave by eight, leaving only a hardcore of VIPs for the sit-down dinner at nine.

After a while, William asked idly, 'By the way, have you heard anything about David Carlyle's book?'

'No,' said Eddie. 'I'm surprised he can read, never mind write. What is it?'

'That's the thing. No one knows. It's shrouded in mystery.' William waved a fat hand around dramatically. 'Apparently it's with Doubleday, but they're denying all knowledge.'

'They've probably all died from shame,' said Eddie. 'It's probably some torrid potboiler for plebs: *Fifty Shades of Grey Shoes*.'

'Now, now,' William chuckled.

'Maybe he used a pseudonym. Chip. O. N. Shoulder.'

'Ha!' The chuckle became a full-on laugh. 'That's very good. But seriously. He doesn't have anything on you, does he? Anything that didn't come out at the trial?'

'No,' Eddie said sourly. 'If you remember, I was thoroughly disembowelled at the trial, thanks to that bastard. There's nothing.'

'Good.' William Berkeley clapped his hands, smiling broadly. 'Then we've nothing to worry about. Is it almost suppertime, do you think? I could eat a horse.'

'Well! Isn't this nice? All the heaving throngs have gone, and we can finally relax.'

Annabel smiled stiffly down the table at her illustrious guests, looking anything but relaxed. The book launch drinks had gone off without a hitch, but the really important part of the evening was just beginning.

The chairman, William Berkeley, sat on Annabel's left. She'd intended to launch a full-on charm offensive at him during the bouillabaisse. But then William and Eddie had drifted in to dinner thick as thieves, so she'd refocused her attention on the Home Secretary, James Garforth, on her right. Whatever it was that had propelled young Garforth to the top of the political tree, Annabel decided, one could rule out charisma. Whether it was the lingering Birmingham accent or the glazed look of naked ambition in the eyes, Garforth was as drearily humourless as a feminist book group discussing the latest Tony Parsons. Worse, he used embarrassing business clichés, talking about 'going forward', and 'thinking outside the box' on immigration. 'That's exactly the sort of issue where we Conservatives need to blue-sky it,' he concluded triumphantly. 'Don't you agree?'

Further down the table, Eddie's political agent, Kevin Unger, was making small talk with Rita Blaize, wife of the Number Ten spin doctor and all-round electoral guru, Philip. Phil Blaize scared Annabel. She couldn't read him at all, yet she had a sneaking suspicion that he might well be the most important man in the room. Which made it all the more distressing to have to watch him being bored to death by a distinctly tipsy Camilla Berkeley, the chairman's wife, who only ever wanted to talk about hunting.

'Of course, it was different when I was a gel,' Camilla boomed. 'I gort my first hunter at nine. Happiest day of my life! The whole county used to see off the hunt in those days. It wasn't just the landowners. All these animal rights Johnnies who bang on about class, they couldn't be more wrong. Hunting's not elitist! Never has been. It's urban bloody ignorance, that's wort it is. Now if you have the PM's ear, you really *must* get him to look into it.'

Meanwhile, at the far end of the table, Milo appeared to have the Home Secretary's wife in stitches, which pleased and panicked Annabel in equal measure. And Eddie was devoting far too much time and attention to Lisa Unger, the agent's wife, one of the few people present with literally nothing to offer him politically, instead of rescuing the spin doctor from Camilla Berkeley's tweed-clad advances.

When at last Magda staggered in carrying a vast silver soup dish, Annabel could have wept with relief.

'Ah! The bouillabaisse. Marvellous. You may start serving, Magdalena.'

Milo took one look at Magda, then directed a furious glare at his mother. Not only had she made the poor girl get dolled up in full black and white maid service, which looked patently ridiculous at such a small, informal dinner, she'd clearly also driven Magda to the brink of exhaustion. Her eyes looked small and red, wisps of hair clung to the sweat on her forehead like seaweed on a wet rock and her hands were trembling, whether from nerves or physical strain it was hard to tell.

'Let me help you.' He stood up, earning himself an irritated look from his mother and a panicked one from Magda.

'I'm fine, thank you.' The soup tureen clearly weighed a ton. Staggering towards the table, Magda tried to remember what Lady Wellesley had instructed her this morning about serving. *Start at the head of the table and move left. Or was it right? No, definitely left.*

'Come on,' Milo insisted. 'That's far too heavy.'

'For heaven's sake sit down, Milo. Magdalena can manage,' snapped Annabel. She didn't know why, but something about Magda always seemed to bring out the worst in her.

'No she *can't*,' Milo snapped back. 'Open your eyes!'

The guests were all staring at her now. Magda could feel their eyes on her; her heart was hammering against her ribs like a jumping bean in a cage. Why did Milo have to make a scene? Lady Wellesley hated scenes. In a rush, she reached forwards to set the dish on the table, but lost her footing. After that everything seemed to happen in slow motion. There was a collective gasp from around the table as the silver lid clattered to the ground and the tureen tumbled forwards, depositing a cascade of scalding bouillabaisse directly into William Berkeley's lap.

'*FUUUUCK!*' The chairman of the Conservative Party let out a roar of pain, leaping to his feet and scrambling to undo his trousers. Seconds later they were around his ankles, along with his underpants, as he hopped from foot to foot, naked and howling. While most of the guests stared transfixed at this unexpected display of burned wedding tackle, Lisa Unger, thinking quickly, whipped the champagne bottle out of a nearby ice bucket, ran around the table and emptied the icy water directly onto the chairman's crotch.

'I think he might need to go to hospital,' said Philip Blaize, the first words he'd spoken since he sat down.

'Somebody call an ambulance!' boomed Camilla.

Annabel turned on Magda, tight-lipped and furious. 'Clean it up,' she hissed.

'I'm sorry. I don't know how it happened. I—'

'Now!'

With a sob, Magda ran from the room.

As the ambulance carted away poor William, it was hard to tell what distressed him more: the blistering pain in his balls or the prospect of being ushered into a confined space with his drunken bore of a wife. In any event, with the Berkeleys gone, dinner continued, with conversation considerably more lively following the unexpected drama.

'That's a nice way to launch a comeback,' Philip Blaize teased Eddie. 'Maiming the party chairman!'

'I expect it's the most action William's had in the trouser department in many a long year,' Eddie cracked back.

Annabel laughed along – Eddie had always been better at handling these things than she was, and would no doubt pluck victory from the jaws of disaster. But she remained livid with Magda for her clumsiness, and with Milo for setting the whole thing off, trying to play Prince Charming to the maid's Cinderella.

Magda went through the motions, serving the beef and the pudding and coffee, moving silently around the room like a wraith. Eddie tried to smile at her reassuringly, but she didn't dare to meet his eye, or anyone's.

Later, when the guests had retired to the drawing room for cognac, Milo found her in the kitchen. Sitting at the table, staring dumbly into space, she still looked shell shocked.

'Are you OK?' he asked, pulling up a chair beside her.

'She'll fire me. I know it. I'm going to lose my place.'

'She won't fire you,' said Milo. 'I know my mother. She might rant and rave a bit, but she won't want to start again with someone new. Anyway,' he looked at Magda questioningly, 'would it be the end of the world if she *did* fire you? You can't like working for her. You're much too good for this job.'

Magda shook her head. 'Life isn't about what you "like". It's about what you need.'

'OK. But why do you need this job so badly?'

Magda opened her mouth to speak, then closed it again. It was a good question, a fair question. But she couldn't answer it. Not without lying, and she wasn't prepared to do that, not to Milo.

'You don't understand.'

It came out like an accusation. Milo looked hurt. 'Explain to me, then.'

I want to, thought Magda. *I really do.* But if she told Milo the truth, there was a chance that he'd let something slip, that eventually his parents would find out. And she couldn't risk that. For their sake as much as her own.

'Forget it. Forget I said anything.'

Reaching out, Milo took her hand. Not questioningly or tentatively, but firmly, with a confidence Magda hadn't seen in him before. 'I'm not a kid, Magda. I'm not the boy I was before I left. I want to help you.'

For the briefest of moments their eyes met. He was so

226

earnest, so endearing. For the first time in a long time, Magda realized, she had made a true friend.

'I'm happy you're home, Milo,' she said truthfully. 'I just pray to God you're right about your mother.'

It was nearly two in the morning by the time the last guests left. To Eddie's amazement, it was the Home Secretary, James Garforth, and his wife, who were the last to stagger to their car.

'Terrific evening.' James patted Eddie warmly on the back. 'Shame about poor old Berkeley,' he added, in a tone that clearly implied it wasn't a shame at all. 'Your boy, Milo's, very impressive, by the way. Wonderful to meet a young person who cares about today's big issues.'

'Milo?' Eddie failed to keep the astonishment out of his voice.

'Yes. You can tell him I'll look into that internship. We need to expand our bandwidth over at the Home Office; get some young blood flowing, new ideas.'

Eddie looked at him blankly. *Bandwidth?* He couldn't imagine what had possessed Tristram Hambly to promote a man who spewed out such a ceaseless flow of twaddle.

'Jolly good,' he said blithely, helping Garforth into his car. 'Thanks again for coming. Drive safely.'

Back inside, he cornered Milo on the stairs on his way up to bed.

'Did you ask the Home Secretary about an internship?'

'Yeah,' said Milo. 'I thought, you know, one might as well ask. There's so much reform needed in immigration,' he added seriously. 'They could probably use an extra pair of hands.'

Eddie rubbed his eyes in disbelief. '*You*'re interested in immigration?'

'Well. A bit. And, you know, it's all good for the CV,' he added sheepishly. 'Night, Dad.'

Eddie gazed after him in wonder as he went to his room. Whatever Dominic Veesey had been putting in Milo's water out in Africa, he and Annabel had better order a job lot.

Upstairs in bed, Milo lay awake, his mind racing. The truth was he couldn't care less about immigration, or his CV. But he needed a job, a real job, something important and meaningful that would impress Magda.

Before tonight, he'd imagined that he loved her.

Now, he knew.

It was time for the rest of his life to begin.

CHAPTER FOURTEEN

Macy Johanssen pulled her cashmere scarf more tightly around as she strolled along Walton Street. It was December, and with Christmas just round the corner, London had been transformed into a fairy-tale city, a gloriously kitsch and glowing version of its usual self. Tiny stores – to Macy's American eyes they literally looked like dolls' houses – had stuffed their window displays with every kind of festive delight: trays of sweet frosted marzipan fruits, bright baubles in every shape and colour, clockwork toys, pretty knitted children's dresses and coats and brightly wrapped boxes garnished with holly and ruby-red berries. After a morning spent trying on wedding dresses in Notting Hill, Macy had decided to walk to her lunch date at Scalini through Kensington Gardens, transformed into a wonderland over-night by the sort of heavy frost that left everything white and sparkling beneath a dazzling blue winter sky.

It was impossible not to feel happy on a day like today. Hope hung in the air like the sweet cinnamon spice wafting out of Patisserie Valerie's. Not that Macy had any reasons to feel *un*happy. Being engaged to James was more enjoyable than she'd thought it would be. Random strangers would rush up to Macy on the street and congratulate her, which was disconcerting at first, but in the end she'd come to quite enjoy. Then there were the wedding magazines to pore over. Nothing fed Macy's perfectionist, homemaker obsession quite like the prospect of organizing a wedding. For months now she'd gone to bed dreaming of hand-tied posies and The Wedding Company table arrangements and Alice Temperley dresses with just the perfect amount of lace detailing. James, needless to say, was unmoved by all of the above and happy to leave it all to Macy. He was also away a lot with his cricket, most recently on a tour of Sri Lanka, in which England were leading a triumphant 3–1 in the five-match Test series. While his long absences were regrettable, they did at least mean that Macy could get on with things unhindered by tiresome male meddling. Of course, there were still some things they needed to talk about – not least their future living arrangements. James's cricket effectively tied him to England while Macy still had her long-term sights set on a US TV comeback – but Macy was enjoying this period of calm before the storm, and in no rush to emerge from her fantasy-wedding stupor.

At Scalini, she peeled off her coat and scarf and let the maître d' lead her to her table. Eddie Wellesley was already seated and armed with what looked like a large G&T.

'My dear,' he beamed. 'You look as lovely as ever.'

'Thanks. You look like you just bought a dollar for ninety cents.'

'Excuse me?'

'You look pleased with yourself!' Macy explained.

'Oh, I see. A bit like "you lost a shilling and found sixpence", but the other way round.'

'If you say so. So what happened? D'you sell another million copies of your book?'

Eddie's prison diaries-cum-autobiography had been this Christmas's surprise smash hit, an instant runaway bestseller. Suddenly his face was everywhere, on buses and billboards, or laughing jovially from the couches of countless chat shows. Everybody, it seemed, had missed Fast Eddie Wellesley.

'Not yet. But I'm working on it,' he grinned. 'Of course if the bloody publishers had let me call it *Fast & Furious* like I wanted, we'd have sold loads more.'

'Of course you would,' Macy laughed. 'Cowards!'

They ordered pasta and lots of delicious-looking things involving cheese and truffles. Eddie insisted on wine, but Macy only sipped at hers. They were here to talk business. She wasn't about to let Eddie charm her into something she might regret, or get her too pissed to ask him the tough questions she needed to.

'How's the *Christmas Special* coming along?' Eddie kicked things off innocuously enough. 'Is it all peace and goodwill down at Valley Farm?'

Macy raised a sceptical eyebrow. 'Hardly. When is it ever? There are fewer protestors now. The poor old vicar shows up from time to time with a couple of old biddies from the WI, but that's about it. But the dragon's still as demanding as ever.'

'By the "dragon" we mean the lovely Laura?'

Macy rolled her eyes. 'Lovely to you, maybe. She's a harridan to everyone else. I suggested to Gabe that we get the kids involved in the Christmas show somehow. They're great boys and I think it'd be cute to see them spraying glitter trees on their bedroom windows or making holly wreaths with the farm hands. Plus it's a half-hour longer than usual, so we have airtime to fill.'

'Sounds good to me,' said Eddie. 'Did Laura say no?'

'No one's asked her yet. Everyone's afraid of her, Eddie, even her own husband. Gabe promised me he'd broach the idea with her but, so far, nothing. We film tomorrow.'

'You can hardly blame Laura for not agreeing to something she hasn't even been asked about,' Eddie pointed out reasonably.

'Sure I can. She's so busy yelling at poor Gabe, I suspect he hasn't been able to get a word in edgeways.'

Eddie looked at Macy thoughtfully. England had changed her, he decided, and for the better. She was softer now than when he'd first met her in LA, less brittle and highly strung. She'd gained a little weight too. Not much, just enough to give her a more contented, womanly glow. It suited her. He hoped that part of her happiness was due to her engagement to James Craven. But he couldn't help but notice that, since they'd sat down, she'd mentioned Gabe's name scores of times and her fiancé's not at all. He decided to cast a fly over the water.

'I'm surprised to hear that,' he said. 'The Baxters seem to have a very happy marriage to me.'

Macy took the bait instantly.

'That's because you barely know them,' she said sourly. 'I see them every day.'

'And it still hurts, does it?' Eddie probed gently.

Macy blushed. 'I don't know what you mean.'

'I think you do.'

Stretching out her left arm, Macy flashed her engagement ring pointedly in Eddie's direction.

'In case you haven't noticed, I'm off the market. I've already found my handsome prince.'

'Is that so?'

'Yes,' she said defensively. 'For your information, it is. Speaking of happy endings, how's *your* marriage going? You've been keeping your extra-curricular activities very quiet lately.'

'I haven't had any,' said Eddie.

'Is that so?' Macy mimicked him snidely.

'It is,' said Eddie. 'Not since you.'

There was an awkward moment when neither of them quite knew what to say. It was an unspoken rule between them that their one-night stand was never brought up, and it irritated Macy that Eddie had broken it now. Then again, she had pushed him. But she didn't appreciate Eddie grilling her about Gabe, or doubting her relationship with James. Hearing your own, hidden thoughts exposed is never pleasant. Eddie Wellesley had always had an uncanny and disconcerting habit of seeing right through her.

'Anyway. Enough chit-chat,' she said brusquely. 'You promised me if the first season went well we would take the show to the States and try to raise some interest back home.'

'I did,' Eddie conceded.

'Well, the first season went well. Better than well.'

'It did,' he agreed again.

'So . . .?'

'So, I'm happy to do another trip to your illustrious home-land.'

Macy looked surprised. 'You still want to sell the format? I figured, with your book and getting back into politics and all, you'd kinda lost interest.'

'Not at all,' said Eddie. 'Although, once you're Mrs Craven, won't you be rather tied to living here? You are marrying an English sporting hero, you know.'

'Yes. And he's marrying an American TV presenter with a career and a life of her own.' Macy smiled, but there was a

233

defiant gleam in her eye that did not bode well for marital harmony, in Eddie's view.

'You've discussed it then?' he asked. 'Because you know you already have a profit share if we sell the format. Your Rottweiler of an agent did a good job for you there. You don't have to present if you don't want to. You could continue presenting here.'

'And here was I thinking you wanted me to stay away from Gabriel Baxter?' Macy said archly.

Eddie topped up her glass and raised his own. 'To America. And the future.'

Macy tapped her glass against his. 'To America.'

'You *are* kidding?' Laura Baxter put her head in her hands, leaving a sticky residue of marzipan frosting all over her hair. 'I actually need to know that this is a joke.'

It had been a long and stressful day. With filming due to start on the *Valley Farm Christmas Special* tomorrow, Laura had a mountain of work to do, but had done none of it, thanks to having rashly agreed to produce thirty miniature Christmas puddings for the St Hilda's Primary School Festive Fayre. Gabe's suggestion this morning, that she simply buy them from M&S in Chichester, had put Laura in a foul mood. Partly because she wished she'd thought of it herself (ideally before she'd spent a small fortune on ingredients and waxed thirty miniature pudding bowls). And partly because it strongly implied that Gabe thought her culinary skills weren't up to it (true but annoying.) And partly because her PMT had now reached levels that were the hormonal equivalent of weapons-grade plutonium. They'd had a horrible row and then Gabe had sodded off to London and some swanky Christmas party at the Chiltern Firehouse, which had been in the diary for ever but which Laura had completely forgotten about and which meant she was also left juggling the boys solo for an entire day.

Now Gabe had returned, made an ill-advised joke about King Alfred after taking one look at Laura's disastrously charred efforts, and then casually dropped the bombshell about Hugh and Luca being filmed tomorrow.

'Why should it be a joke?' he asked, standing back slightly so Laura wouldn't smell the booze on his breath. 'I think it's a great idea and so did Mike Briarson.'

'Mike? You discussed this with Channel 5 already?'

'Not formally,' Gabe backtracked. 'Mike happened to be at the Firehouse party and I . . . mentioned it.'

'You didn't agree we'd do it, though?' Laura pressed him.

'Erm . . .'

'Gabe! We agreed, right at the beginning, no filming the children.'

'I know, but—'

'You were even more insistent about it than I was, if I remember. You said you didn't want them turning into the Osbournes. No filming, No exceptions.'

'Yes, but that was before.'

'Before what?'

'Before everything! Before the show started, before we knew anybody. The production crew are like family now.'

'I can't believe I'm hearing this.' Laura closed her eyes and wiped a sticky hand across her brow.

'I'm sorry, but I don't see what's so terrible about Dave and Dean doing a few takes of Hugh making a Frostie the Snowman card, or taking feed out to the sheep pens.'

'Then you're a bloody idiot,' Laura snapped. 'And you're not sorry.'

'It's a one-off, for fuck's sake,' Gabe snapped back.

'It's the thin end of the wedge.'

'Why do you have to be so bloody negative about everything?'

Behind them, Luca – sitting on the kitchen floor with his face covered in icing sugar – started to cry. 'Don't shouting!'

'You see?' said Gabe, scooping his son up into his arms and placating him with a Thomas train and a handful of Smarties from the bowl on the table. 'You're upsetting the kids.'

'*Me?*' Laura looked at him, incredulous. It took every ounce of her willpower to take Luca and Hugh calmly into the other room and settle them both down in front of a DVD before returning to the kitchen and exploding at their father.

'Firstly, no one is filming the boys. I won't allow it, end of story.'

'It's not "end of story",' Gabe said furiously. 'I promised Mike Briarson.'

'Then *un*-promise.'

'Why should I? I think it would be good for the kids to be involved.'

'Well, I don't and I'm their mother.'

'So? I'm their father.'

'Well, *I'm* the fucking series producer, which means *I* have the final say. And I say: Over my dead body will the boys be filmed.'

'Macy said you'd be like this,' Gabe muttered, only half under his breath.

'I'm sorry, what was that?' said Laura. '*Macy* said? So this was Macy's idea? She put you up to it?'

'No one "put me up to" anything,' said Gabe. 'You should hear yourself, Laura. You talk to me like a fucking schoolboy sometimes.'

Laura bit her lip. She knew this was true. But then Gabe could be so utterly exasperating. And he always seemed to pick the very worst moments to spring these things on her. Too angry and het up to apologize, she opted to go back on the attack.

'Macy fancies you,' she blurted out. 'She does these things to cause trouble between us.'

'Well, if she does, it's a damn good strategy,' Gabe said nastily.

'At least you finally admit it,' said Laura. Suddenly she felt close to tears. She couldn't understand how the conversation had spiralled downwards so quickly.

'Admit what?'

'That she fancies you. That you fancy each other.'

'Don't be absurd,' said Gabe. 'The girl's about to get married. She's been swept off her feet by cricket's answer to George Clooney, remember?'

'Cricket doesn't have an answer to George Clooney,' said Laura. 'And if it did it wouldn't be James Craven. Besides, they barely see each other.'

'He's on tour!' Gabe felt as though he was talking to a madwoman. 'What has any of this got to do with the boys making a cameo appearance tomorrow?'

'It has everything to do with it. You're just too blind to see it. I swear to God, Gabriel, ever since you got a taste of fame you've become insufferable.'

'*I've* become insufferable? Do you know what you're like to work with?'

'For,' snapped Laura. 'Work for.'

'I rest my case!' said Gabe.

But Laura hadn't finished. 'I mean it. Before any of this started, the children, *me* and the children, we always came first. But now all you seem to care about is the stupid show and how you look. To the network, to Macy, to all your sodding *fans.*' It would not have been humanly possible to inject more disdain into the word. 'You go to a celebrity party, you tell a big shot at Channel 5 what you think he wants to hear. Then you go back to Macy for a pat on the back and to get eyelashes fluttered at you and your ego massaged. To hell with the promises you made to *me*. To hell with what's best for our sons. Just as long as the Gabe Baxter show keeps rolling along, and you're still the great big star!'

Gabe looked at her for a long time. Then he said, quietly but with complete conviction, 'You are *such* a bitch.'

Laura felt as if she'd been kicked in the stomach. Her eyes welled up but she was determined not to give him the satisfaction of tears.

'Fine,' she said. 'Film the boys. Go ahead. I'm sure you'll make Macy very proud.'

She walked past him towards the study. It was time to put the boys in bed anyway but, even if it hadn't been, she needed to hold them. To smell their sweet, soft skin pressed against her cheek. To feel their little hands clasped in love – unchanging love – around her neck.

'Laura, come on,' Gabe called after her, suddenly contrite. 'Let's talk about this.'

She'd made him feel so angry before. But now, in some way he didn't fully understand, the tables had been turned. Now he felt like the bad guy. The bully. The vain, self-centred wanker she'd just accused him of being.

'You know I love you,' he told her.

But the door had already closed.

* * *

Filming day for the *Valley Farm Christmas Special* dawned clear and very cold. Dave and Dean, the sound engineer and cameraman, swathed in thick layers and wearing fingerless gloves, blew on their hands as they gingerly moved their equipment across the farmyard at Wraggsbottom.

'Gorgeous day!' Jennifer Lee, the series vet, beamed as she climbed out of her filthy Land Rover. Wearing a bright yellow scarf and matching woolly hat, teamed with a red ski jacket and wellington boots with snowflakes on them, she looked like a cross between a children's television presenter and a lunatic. The bouncy smile didn't help.

'What are you looking so chipper about?' asked Dean. 'It's fucking arctic and we've got ten straight hours of filming ahead of us.'

'Well, Mr Grinch. It just so happens I love Christmas,' Jennifer trilled, skipping over to the pigsties, where Gabe and William, one of the hands, were already busy feeding the sows. 'Don't you, Gabe?'

'Hmm?' Gabe looked up absently from the troughs.

'Love Christmas,' clarified Jennifer, de-scarfing as she knelt down to examine one of the animal's hooves. 'The valley looked so pretty this morning, all frosted and bright, I could have cried.'

'Soppy cow,' said Dean good-naturedly, handing her a mug of tea from the flasks Laura had left out earlier. 'Can't you feed them a bit later?' he added to Gabe. 'We should get it on film. God knows we have enough hours to fill. Nothing happens on a farm in December.'

'Plenty happens!' said Gabe. 'There's fence-mending.'

'Not exactly gripping television, is it mate?' Dave, the sound engineer piped up.

'We need to harvest the brassicas.'

'Again . . . unless you can get Macy to do it in her underwear. Or Jen, here. You could dress up as a sexy Christmas elf.' He nudged the vet playfully in the ribs.

'Kiss my arse, Dave.'

'Oh, go on!' said Dean. 'You'd be great. Santa's dirty little helper!'

Gabe guffawed with laughter.

'What's so funny?'

Laura walked over to the pigpens. In baggy jeans and an oversized man's sweater, clutching a clipboard in one hand and a phone in the other, she looked tired and stressed. The moment she arrived, the mood changed.

'Nothing,' muttered Gabe. 'We were just taking the piss out of Jen.'

'Oh. OK. Well, Macy just arrived. So if you're ready, let's get a few scenes in here, with Macy and Gabe doing the feeds together. And then we can move inside mid-morning.'

'Inside?' The crew's faces lit up.

'We're doing some sequences with Hugh and Luca. Decorating our tree, that sort of thing. Mike at Channel 5 wanted a bit more human interest.'

'Brilliant.' Everyone nodded enthusiastically. Gabe met Laura's eye for the briefest of moments, then they both looked away. They'd had a horrid night, both too hurt and proud to reach out and make things up with the other.

'And then you can shoot in the village after dark,' Laura continued briskly. 'Get the Christmas lights and the carol singing. Macy's doing most of that scripted. We can run through it later.'

* * *

By the time Eddie dropped in at half past eleven, they'd already been filming for three hours. Gabe and Macy were taking a break together in the kitchen, running through the afternoon's scenes while Gabe stuffed his face with Mr Kipling's mince pies and Macy nibbled restrainedly on a single ginger biscuit.

'Aren't you hungry?' Gabe asked her, through a mouthful of sweet pastry crumbs.

'Of course I'm hungry,' said Macy. 'I'm a girl. I'm always hungry.'

'Then eat!'

'That crap? No thanks. Besides, James gets home tomorrow. I need to look my best.'

'You look great,' Gabe said truthfully. 'You always look great. Too good for James bloody Craven, if you ask me,' he added, jokingly.

Macy flushed with pleasure and took another minuscule bite of her biscuit.

'So you talked Laura into it?' She looked over to the play-room table, where the boys were engrossed in making glittery paper chains under the watchful eye of Dean's Camera 2.

'We discussed it,' Gabe said tactfully. 'She was cool with it in the end.'

Macy raised a knowing eyebrow but said nothing. Eddie came over.

'Is Laura about?' he asked. 'I wanted a quick word.'

'In the study,' said Gabe. 'Someone from the parish council's kicked up a fuss about filming on the green this evening. She's on the phone trying to smooth things over.'

Laura hung up just as Eddie walked in.

'Silly old bat,' she seethed at the phone.

Eddie could see at once how tired she looked. 'Everything all right?'

'Oh, yes, fine,' said Laura unconvincingly. 'Just another outbreak of festive Nimbyism in good old Fittlescombe, the south of England's friendliest village.'

'I came to see if I could change your mind about letting your boys appear on the programme, but I see you decided to go ahead. I must say I'm pleased. Christmas without children's like having Christmas pud without the brandy butter. Sort of . . . flat. They look awfully sweet in there, beavering away.' He smiled broadly.

Laura didn't.

'Oh, so you knew about this too, did you?' she said crossly. 'Who told you?'

'Well, er . . . Macy might have mentioned something,' said Eddie, wrong-footed.

'Macy!' Laura fumed. 'First she gets Gabe on her side, then Mike Briarson, then you. By the time old muggins here gets to hear about it, it's a done bloody deal!'

Eddie tactfully closed the study door. 'Keep your voice down,' he said. 'They're still rolling next door.'

'Never mind that I'm the boys' mother,' Laura ranted on, ignoring him. 'Not to mention the creator of this sodding show, and Miss No-Pants-On's so-called boss! I mean, what a joke, right?'

'Johanssen – No-Pants-On,' Eddie chuckled. 'That's quite good.'

But, to his horror, Laura burst violently into tears.

'It's not fucking funny!' she berated him. 'I'm fed up, Eddie. Fed up of it being three against one. Fed up of being cast as the bad cop, the horrible nag, while Gabe gets to swan around having all the fun and making everybody laugh. Especially *Macy*.'

242

Eddie frowned. So he wasn't the only one who'd noticed Miss Johanssen's continued attraction for her handsome co-presenter.

'It's *me* who does all the work,' said Laura. '*Me* who picks up the pieces, whether it's the show or the children. I'm not bloody superwoman. I have feelings!'

'Of course you do.' Eddie hugged her. Not entirely sure what else to do, he started stroking her hair. 'Of course you have feelings. No one's saying you don't. And no one's trying to gang up on you.'

'Yes they are,' Laura sniffed defiantly into his cashmere sweater. 'That scheming little cow . . .'

'All right, well *I'm* not,' said Eddie, cutting her off. 'And at the risk of getting my head bitten off, is it possible you're overtired?'

'You make me sound like a toddler,' Laura said sheepishly. 'But I suppose so. I didn't sleep much last night.'

She wrapped her arms tighter around Eddie and closed her eyes. It felt so good to let go for once, and to be comforted and understood. If only Gabe weren't so damn stubborn! Why couldn't he be like this? Kind and soothing and—

'Oh my God! Sorry!' The door to the study opened suddenly. Jennifer Lee, the vet, stood on the threshold, a look of horror and embarrassment plastered across her kind, open face. 'I didn't mean . . . shit.'

The door slammed closed again.

Laura looked at Eddie. 'You don't think she thought . . .?'

'I'm pretty certain that's exactly what she thought,' said Eddie, grimly. 'Should I go after her?'

'No.' Laura pulled herself together, disengaging reluctantly

243

from the safety of Eddie's embrace. 'No point making a mountain out of a molehill. I'll explain to her later. We're filming all afternoon, worse luck.'

In fact, it wasn't until the very end of the day, when Jen was getting back into her car to set off home, that Laura had a chance to speak to her.

The filming in the village had been disrupted – or enlivened, depending on how one chose to look at it – by a set-to between Laura and some disgruntled members of the Parish Council, after one of Gabe's sows had made a break for freedom and run across the village green, trampling a good third of the Christmas model village display. After much farcical dashing about with nets and blankets, Jen had finally apprehended the Wraggsbottom One, but not before the Reverend Clempson had come marching out of St Hilda's Church like a self-appointed avenging angel, and attempted to read the riot act, not only to Laura and Gabriel but to the entire *Valley Farm* crew. Some wag had suggested that the assembled village choir start up a chorus of 'Silent Night' in the midst of the ensuing shouting match. All in all it had been an eventful night, and the cameras had kept rolling till well past nine. Then there were the usual long, drawn-out goodbyes that marked the end of the series, as well as the end of the year. It would be almost two months until the *Valley Farm* crew got together again.

'Jen!' Laura called across the deserted farmyard. It was pitch-black outside now, and the lights from the house cast only a dim glow over the treacherously icy ground. 'Could I have a quick word?'

'Er . . .' Jen stiffened. 'I'm a bit late actually.' She'd stayed later than everyone else, to make a last check on the poor, traumatized sow that had caused all the trouble, and was longing to go home. It had been a very long day, and the thought of having to talk about what she'd seen in the study earlier was mortifying.

'It'll only take a moment.'

Laura was at the car now, with her hand on the door. She cut to the chase.

'I wouldn't want you to misinterpret what you saw before. In the study. Eddie and I . . .'

'Please.' The darkness hid her blushes, but Jen was sure Laura could feel her embarrassment. 'It's none of my business.'

'But that's just it,' said Laura. 'There is no "it". I was upset and Eddie was being his usual, kind self. There is absolutely nothing romantic or . . . anything . . . going on between us.'

'Right.'

Laura hesitated. Was that 'right' as in 'I believe you?', she wondered. Or 'right' as in, 'I agree to lie for you?' Or maybe it was just 'right' as in, 'I want to go home.'

'I do, sort of, have to go now,' Jen said awkwardly.

'Of course. Sorry.' Laura stepped back from the car. Jen hopped in, closed the driver's door and sped away, with what Laura couldn't help feeling seemed like undue haste. But perhaps she was imagining things? The same way Gabe said she was imagining things between him and Macy? 'Merry Christmas!' she called after the vet as an afterthought. She doubted Jen could hear her over the noise of the engine.

Once the car had gone, Laura stood there for a moment, the first still moment she had had all day. There was no moon, but the stars dazzled in the sky, bright and mesmerizing above the rolling pastures of the valley. Laura thought about the shepherds in the Bible story, in another peaceful valley far away and long ago, looking up at the night sky on that first Christmas morning. She wasn't really religious, but for a brief, lovely moment, she felt a kinship with those simple men. As if some magical line connected them through the ages. It wasn't only a human connection either. It was about the animals too, and the land, and the peace of this beautiful place. Gabe would have understood, although he probably couldn't have put it into words any more than she could.

As she turned towards the house, it started to snow. Thick, wet, heavy flakes began drifting lazily to the ground, like feathers from a pillow. Snow usually made Laura happy. But tonight, for some reason, the joy wouldn't quite come. Instead she felt an unpleasant sense of foreboding. As if a change were coming, and it wasn't good.

Eddie's right, she told herself. *I'm overtired.*

Wrapping her jacket more tightly around her, she hurried inside.

CHAPTER FIFTEEN

'Merry Christmas.'

Gabe kissed Laura on the cheek as they walked through the lichened gate into St Hilda's churchyard. A light snow still clung to the ground and covered the tops of the grave-stones like piped icing, but Ambrose Bray, the church gardener, had thoughtfully cleared and salted the path that led from the gate to the church door. The Christmas morning service didn't start till ten, but the tiny village church was already packed to the rafters. If they didn't get a move on, there'd be no chance of squeezing into a pew together.

'Merry Christmas, darling.'

Laura kissed him back and they hugged tightly as the boys skipped ahead of them. They'd made up after the *Christmas Special* debacle, to Laura's immense relief. The show had aired last night to fabulous ratings. Thanks to all the drama with the runaway pig, the scenes with Luca and Hugh in them had been cut to a few snatched seconds anyway, so the whole ridiculous argument had been for nothing.

How silly I was to get so upset and let my imagination run away with me, Laura thought now. *There's nothing wrong.* She made an early New Year's resolution to count her blessings more and to trust in the good things in her life, especially Gabriel. Yes, he drove her mad sometimes. But she also loved him madly, and she knew he felt the same. This morning he'd brought her a cup of tea in bed on a tray – with flowers, no less – and told her she looked sexy which (at that hour) was a flat-out lie. *You don't have to say sorry to be sorry*, Laura realized. Gabe was trying. Everything was going to be fine.

'Oh my goodness!' she gasped, as they stepped through the heavy wooden doors into the church itself, squeezing into a back pew next to one of Hugh's school friends and his family. 'Doesn't it look gorgeous?'

Even Gabe had to admit that their arch-enemies, the WI protestors, had done a spectacular job with the festive decorations. Heavy garlands of greenery – ivy and dark holly and incredibly scented fir – hung beneath each of the ancient stained-glass windows. Bright sprigs of berries clashed gloriously with the wreaths of white roses pinned to the crumbling stone walls, and simple stacks of beeswax candles burned cheerfully on each of the deep window ledges and along the nave. On the altar, four taller Advent candles in deep red flickered over a beautifully carved Nativity scene. Both Gabe and Laura remembered the same wooden figures of Mary and Joseph and the three kings from their own childhood Christmases. This year, the local children had made Victorian decorations of cinnamon sticks and oranges tied with gold ribbon and studded with cloves. Hung from the altar and the ends of the pews, and mingling with the scent from the pine garlands, they made the church smell wonderful, like sitting inside a freshly baked Christmas pudding.

On the other side of the church, the smell was making Santiago de la Cruz feel sick.

'I may have to go home,' he whispered to Penny, as the organist struck up the opening bars of 'Hark! the herald-angels sing'. 'I seriously think I might throw up.'

'You can't,' she whispered back. 'Louise Carlyle's solo's up next, "I Saw Three Ships". The poor thing's terrified. We must stay and support her.'

'Can't you support her?'

Penny frowned. 'It's not just Louise. You promised to drive old Mrs Cole back to her cottage after church, remember? It's your good deed for the day.'

Santiago groaned.

'It's your own fault for drinking so much last night. Honestly, drinking crème de menthe at your age . . .'

Seb, Santiago's stepson, had proposed an ill-advised Christmas Eve game of 'Spin the Bottle', in which forfeits were to be alternate shots of crème de menthe and Baileys. Unfortunately for Santiago, at twenty-five Seb Harwich had the constitution of an ox and, like a lot of young investment bankers, the alcohol tolerance of a Russian sailor. After a couple of Alka-Seltzers and a bacon sandwich, the boy looked as fit as a fiddle this morning, and was singing lustily on the other side of his mother.

The service cracked on, with Louise Carlyle's solo performance widely considered a great success. Her husband might be a polarizing figure in the valley, but people had come to love Louise. She was so kind to everyone, and so modest, and she tried so hard to fit in, it was impossible not to root for her. The Reverend Clempson was also at a good pace for once, keeping his sermon short but sweet. Bill wasn't so old that he'd forgotten what it was like to be a child himself, itching to get home to unwrap his presents. He hadn't the heart to torture people with a long sermon on Christmas Day. On a rather more selfish note, he'd been invited up to Furlings for lunch by Max Bingley and Angela Cranley, and was looking forward to sinking into their grand Knole sofa with a glass of vintage champagne and the *Times* Christmas jumbo crossword in front of a roaring log fire.

The Baxter children were out of their seats and running for the door before the last strains of 'Deck the Halls' had finished playing. In the front pew, Angela and Max chatted and exchanged Christmas greetings with the Wellesleys and their son, Milo, who seemed to have turned into a grown man overnight. Angela was in particularly good spirits, as both Logan and Jason had come home for Christmas with their respective husbands, as well as Max's daughters, Rosie and May, and their husbands and children, transforming Furlings back into a family home, if only for a few glorious days.

'I hadn't realized how maternal you are,' said Max, kissing her with evident pride. Everyone knew that Max Bingley and Angela Cranley were the happiest unmarried couple in the entire Swell Valley.

'Grand-maternal at this point,' joked Angela. 'I wish Logie would hurry up and get pregnant.'

'Give her a chance,' laughed Max, taking her hand and leading her down the aisle. 'They've only been married five minutes.'

Penny de la Cruz rushed past, a blur of flowing orange sweater and rather odd dark green knitted skirt. 'Sorry,' she mouthed to Angela. 'Rushing. I've got Macy Johanssen coming for lunch and I forgot to defrost the pecan pie!'

Outside in the snow, Bill Clempson was smiling and shaking hands with everyone, even Gabe Baxter. Christmas was a time for reconciliation, after all, and it was a joy to see the whole village coming together. He was particularly touched when Jennifer Lee, the young vet who'd argued with him so bitterly during filming, thrust a gaudily wrapped bottle of sloe gin into his hands.

'It's home-made,' she blurted, clearly rather embarrassed at her own boldness. 'It's sort of an apology present.'

'An apology?' Bill looked puzzled. 'I'm not sure that's necessary, Miss Lee. We haven't seen eye to eye about *Valley Farm*, it's true. But there's no crime in having different opinions.'

'Yes, but I was mean to you. At Milo Wellesley's leaving party. You were trying to be nice and I was . . . annoying.'

'I don't remember that,' Bill muttered awkwardly. He'd always been a rotten liar.

'I'm afraid there's more.' Jen blushed scarlet. 'The silage. On your car.'

Bill's eyes widened.

'That was me.'

'You?'

Jen nodded, biting her lower lip. 'I was so cross with you at the time. For scaring the animals. But it was awfully childish and, well . . . I'm sorry.'

'Oh. Well.' Now it was Bill's turn to blush. 'Apology accepted.'

The car incident had been mortifying at the time, but it was a long time ago now. He'd always assumed that Gabe was behind it and was astonished to learn that it had in fact been this really rather pretty young woman, who had such a passionate love for animals. Watching Jen hopping from foot to foot in the snow, her marvellously ample bosom heaving beneath a plum-coloured cashmere sweater that clashed with her flushed cheeks, he wondered why he'd never before noticed how attractive she was.

'Perhaps, in the New Year, you'll come and have a glass with me?' he heard himself saying. 'We can bury the hatchet properly.'

'I'd like that,' Jen smiled. 'Merry Christmas, Vicar.'

'Please. Call me Bill.'

'All right, Bill. And I'm Jen.'

'Merry Christmas, Jen.'

Watching her scurry off to her car, Bill Clempson decided this was turning out to be quite the merriest Christmas he could remember.

Magda closed her eyes and let the enchanting sounds of the King's College Choir wash over her. The tiny CD player in her cottage sitting room was not exactly the height of acoustic sophistication. But Sir Edward had kindly lent her a *Carols from King's* collection, assuring her that it was *the* sound of a traditional English Christmas. With its simple, unaccompanied boys' voices, 'Jesus Christ the Apple Tree' didn't require Bose speakers or surround-sound. Its purity rang out as crisply and clearly as a church bell on the still morning air.

Magda cherished her moment of peace, knowing it would probably be the last of the day. She was officially 'off' for Christmas, but with nowhere to go and no one to see, she had agreed to cook for the family. Incredibly, it would just be Sir Edward, Lady Wellesley and Milo at Riverside Hall this Christmas. Since Eddie's book had been published, and his political comeback launched, he and Annabel had dived headlong into a positive orgy of entertaining. Occasionally, for the bigger weekend parties, they brought in extra help. But it was always Magda who bore the brunt of the work, with one long weekend blurring into the next in a constant round of laundry, cooking, bed-making, fireplace-sweeping and general exhaustion. Desperate to be forgiven after the soup incident – apparently the poor party chairman had suffered second-degree burns to his scrotum and had needed a partial skin graft – and still insecure about her position, Magda had worked without complaint. But she'd been delighted and astonished in equal measure to hear that Christmas week was going to be 'family only', with Milo coming back from his London internship but no other guests expected.

The carol ended. With a sigh Magda got up and turned off the CD player. It was past eleven, time for her to return to the kitchen and put the potatoes she'd basted with goose fat earlier into the oven. Grabbing her apron from the hook by the door, she was surprised to hear a knock. Lady Wellesley usually marched right in, and Sir Edward never came to the cottage.

'Merry Christmas!' Milo, just returned from church, stood on the doorstep. He was holding a parcel, beautifully wrapped in striped green and gold paper and with a big red bow on the top. Dressed formally in a dark suit and tie, and with his hair cut shorter (much to his mother's delight, presumably), it struck Magda how much older he looked than the last time he was home. In a good way.

'For you.' He held out the present eagerly. 'I do hope you like it.'

'I didn't get you anything,' Magda said awkwardly. 'I wasn't expecting . . .'

'I don't want anything,' said Milo. 'Except for you to take this before my arm drops off.'

Belatedly, Magda took the gift, setting it down on the hall table. He followed her inside.

'Aren't you going to open it?'

'Not now,' said Magda. 'Later. I have to put the roast potatoes on and start trimming the Brussels sprouts. I was just on my way back to the house.'

Milo looked crestfallen, but he didn't press her. Since landing the internship at the Home Office he'd been staying with his godfather Charles Murray-Gordon in a flat on Cadogan Square. Charles M-G was an ex-Flemings banker and terrible old roué, who'd taken it upon himself to provide his godson with a wealth of unsolicited advice on how to charm the opposite sex. As this was a field in which his godfather had a proven track record of success (three wives to date and a string of decades-younger girlfriends accompanying him to Annabel's every night), Milo had decided to heed his words of wisdom, among which were: 'Never chase a girl when she says "no". Doesn't matter if it's sex or a cheese sandwich. Don't chase.'

Milo offered Magda his arm. 'I'll walk you over.'

She smiled playfully. 'I think I can find my way across the lawn.'

'Are you always so independent?' said Milo.

'Always.'

'Well, it's Christmas, and you selfishly failed to get me a present, so you can jolly well humour me,' said Milo, taking her hand and forcibly linking her arm with his. 'That was a joke by the way. About the present.'

'Yes,' she laughed. 'I got it.'

It was nice to be flirted with, even if it was by a boy

barely out of school and someone who, she knew for a fact, had flirted with every female, young or old, within a twenty-mile radius.

But still. It was nice.

Back at the house, Eddie helped Annabel out of her coat, a sumptuous vintage fox fur that had once been his grandmother's, and tuned the Sonos system to the Sinatra station.

'Oh, Gawd. Must we have Frank and Bing *again*?' Annabel rolled her eyes. 'How about some lovely carols?'

'We just had carols at church,' said Eddie. 'I want something I can dance to.'

Grabbing her hand and slipping one arm around her waist, he twirled Annabel around the hall, gliding across the parquet flooring like a very British Fred Astaire. Annabel tutted and mumbled 'don't be so ridiculous' a few times, but deep down she felt profoundly happy. The fact that Eddie had kept Christmas sacrosanct and just for them this year felt hugely symbolic. Since Milo's return from Africa, a little of the old strain had crept back into their relationship. And even though Eddie's political comeback meant an enormous amount to both of them, Annabel felt relieved and grateful that, for the first time, he seemed to be putting their marriage first. Putting *her* first. It was the best Christmas present she could have wished for.

The phone rang. Reluctantly, Eddie released her. 'If it's my mother, you'll have to talk to her,' he told Annabel. 'I have an urgent appointment in the log shed.'

'Why should *I* have to talk to her?' Annabel began. But Eddie had already answered. It wasn't his mother. It was Kevin Unger, his political agent. Even in the 24/7 world of politics, a call on Christmas morning was rare.

'I see.' Eddie nodded stiffly, hunched over the phone. 'Hmmm. Hmmm. I see.'

Annabel watched and listened, so still she was barely breathing. After what seemed like an eternity, he hung up.

'What's happened?' Her throat was dry with nerves.

Eddie turned and looked at her solemnly. 'Well . . .' He took a deep breath. 'I'm back in.' His face erupted into a smile so broad it looked painful. 'They won't announce anything officially before the New Year. But Piers Renton-Chambers is standing down. I've got unanimous support to replace him amongst the local constituency party. You're looking at the new Tory candidate for Chichester and Swell Valley.'

'Oh, Eddie!' Annabel flung her arms around his neck.

'What are we celebrating?' Milo emerged from the kitchen, chased out by a distracted Magda.

'Your father's been selected as an MP,' his mother gushed.

'Almost,' said Eddie.

'We're officially back in politics! Or we will be in January.'

'Congratulations, Dad.' He shook Eddie's hand. It seemed like the manly thing to do. 'That's brilliant news.'

'Isn't it?' Annabel said delightedly.

Milo was on the straight and narrow. Eddie was heading back to politics. The ghastly world of television could be left behind them, as could the scandal that had nearly destroyed them all. At last, at long last, everything was coming right.

What a difference a year could make!

Unlike the Wellesleys, David Carlyle had had a *very* social Christmas. Following the *Echo*'s official, star-studded bash at the Savoy on the 20th, David and his wife, Louise, had hosted Christmas drinks for three hundred at Millstones, their grotesquely huge McMansion on the edge of Hinton golf course. Fully staffed with a fleet of caterers, waiters, butlers and valet parking, and complete with a twenty-foot artificial tree, tastefully decorated in blue and silver and surrounded by mechanical elves, the event had – in David's eyes at least – been a triumph. Lou looked gorgeous in her lilac gown with all the Swarovski crystals. And not one person had mentioned the name Eddie Wellesley to David throughout the entire evening.

Now, on Christmas Day itself, they'd just finished a sumptuous six-course lunch, attended by twenty of the most influential people in British media, including Laura Baxter's ex and ITV's head of Drama, John Bingham, with his wife, Abigail, and Murray Wylie, CEO and owner of Wylie Pike, the most successful literary agency in London. If Louise was tired she didn't show it, graciously smiling at all her guests' jokes, flattering the men and complimenting the women on their clothes, or their various children's achievements. Not for the first time, David felt immensely proud of her, and pleased with himself for marrying her. Sitting down alone at the kitchen island once all the guests had gone, treating himself to a small bowl of leftover Christmas pudding, David Carlyle thought in contrast about Eddie Wellesley's wife – the snobby, poisonous Annabel. She was almost as bad as her husband. Those two deserved each other.

Louise, changed into her favourite velour tracksuit and Ugg boots, wandered in and smiled at him. 'You must be shattered, darling,' she said. 'I know I am.'

'Actually I feel great,' said David, stifling a satisfied burp. 'Lunch went brilliantly. You were amazing. We should celebrate.'

Getting up, he mooched over to the drinks cabinet and pulled out a bottle of Courvoisier.

'Brandy? It's four o'clock,' protested Louise.

'It's Christmas,' said David.

'Exactly. Time for a cup of tea, a mince pie and *Only Fools and Horses*.'

'I'm serious,' said David. 'I want to celebrate.'

A shadow of apprehension passed across Louise Carlyle's face. 'Why? What is it? Why are you grinning like that? Has something happened?'

'Not yet.'

David filled two cut-crystal tumblers with the smooth, amber liquid. Handing one to his wife, he raised the other in a toast.

'To the New Year! And everything it might bring.'

Louise's frown deepened. She didn't like it when David got all cryptic. *Please God let this not be about Eddie Wellesley again.* Louise, too, had enjoyed hosting a party where, for once, that name hadn't been mentioned. She'd dared to hope that, at last, that particular ghost was buried. But David's tone worried her. David sat back down and pulled her onto his lap. 'Just drink with me, will you? Be happy.'

David himself was deeply happy. That smug bastard Wellesley thought everything was coming up roses. Whereas, in fact, he was standing on the train tracks about to get hit – and neither he, nor anyone else, had the slightest inkling. There were few things in life more satisfying than successfully keeping a secret. But David Carlyle had done it. All he had to do now was sit back and watch the fireworks, with his lovely Louise by his side.

'I am happy,' said Louise cautiously 'I just want to stay that way. It's been a lovely Christmas, David. Let's not ruin it, eh? Let's not stir things up again.'

'I don't know what you mean.'

'Hmmm,' said Louise. All of a sudden she decided she needed that brandy after all.

Macy pushed open the gate wearily and walked up the path to Cranbourne House. *Thank God I ignored the neighbours and put those uplighters in*, she thought, as the warm glow from the garden lights led her safely to the door, in what otherwise would have been pitch-darkness. The lamps were beautiful as well as practical, turning the higgledy-piggledy tile-hung building into something out of Grimms' *Fairy Tales*, warm and welcoming and inviting amid the bare trees and snow. Macy felt like Snow White, coming home to the dwarfs after a long day wandering in the woods.

Not that there were any dwarf. Or that Christmas Day at the De la Cruz's had been like being lost, or anything other than lovely. Penny, as always, had made a huge effort and been as kind and generous and thoughtful a hostess as it was humanly possible to be. She'd even gone to the trouble of getting in a pecan pie for pudding, 'so that Macy can have her traditions, too.' Macy was really touched, and grateful to have been invited, especially as she only really knew Penny and Santiago through James, who'd had to go abroad again for yet another charity cricket thing in Dubai and couldn't make it.

Ever since she got engaged to James, in fact, all his friends had been lovely to her. Santiago was sweet and funny as always, making terrible jokes about the presents and doing impressions of the Reverend Clempson that reduced Macy to tears of mirth. Penny's son, Seb, was also great fun, outrageous and stupendously politically incorrect. Even Emma Harwich's pouting during the Queen's Speech had failed to dampen the festive family atmosphere. (Emma's elderly, aristo lover, Bertie Athol, had stupidly managed to lose most of his money in a hedge-fund disaster in November, leaving Emma no choice but to dump him. Finding herself dateless for the Christmas party season, she'd returned home to the bosom of her family, a decision that had evidently filled her stepfather with about as much joy as his impending trip to the orthodontist for root-canal work.)

Perhaps it was *because* of all the kindness, and the loving family atmosphere, that Macy felt so deflated now? Either that or the effort of keeping one's game-face on all day, being polite and smiling and making conversation, when secretly all you really wanted was to crawl under the duvet with a box of Maltesers and wait for it all to be over. Alone.

You're being pathetic, she told herself sternly, unzipping her Charles Jourdan boots and lighting the logs in the wood-burning stove before flopping down on her overstuffed sofa from Shabby Chic, the most comfortable object on earth. *This house is gorgeous; this village is gorgeous. You have great friends here, a handsome fiancé and a job most people would kill for.* But today of all days, her homesickness refused to be talked into submission.

Macy's thoughts kept drifting back to childhood Christmases with her mother. The early ones, before her dad left, were a blur of colours and sounds and smells: red and gold tree baubles, Nat King Cole on the car radio, pumpkin pie and cinnamon and her mother's favourite lilac perfume. Her mom's laughter. In later years there was less laughter, and eventually none at all. Although, God knew, Karin Johanssen had tried to hold things together for Macy's sake, especially at Christmas, in the end the booze had destroyed everything. The four Christmases Macy spent with foster families had been OK. There were presents, and a big dinner, and everybody was kind and inclusive. But there was an emptiness inside, a deep longing for the family she'd lost that gave a bitter aftertaste to every sweet thing.

Maybe *that* was what had depressed her about today? The kindness, the politeness, the whole let's-invite-poor-Macy-cause-she's-on-her-own-ness of Penny and Santiago's gesture had reminded her of a period of her life she would rather forget.

Her ghosts of Christmas past might not bring back wholly happy memories. But they were still her ghosts, her past. Macy missed the States. She missed the tacky lights that everyone put up, complete with reindeer statues, in the front yard. She missed the cheesy piped music everywhere, and *It's a Wonderful Life* on the TV, and *A Charlie Brown Christmas*, and the Salvation Army ringing their bells outside. This year she didn't think she'd heard Vince Guaraldi on the radio even one time. How could anyone celebrate Christmas without Charlie Brown music, for God's sake?

She missed her little house in Laurel Canyon. That house had been her sanctuary, her fortress, her respite. Now it was five thousand miles away, but it felt even further, almost as if it were in a different dimension, part of a life she'd dreamed once and woken up from. Or was this the dream? England, James, *Valley Farm*.

Gabriel Baxter.

Going upstairs, Macy switched on the computer in her bedroom and then started running a bath. The Organic Pharmacy made an amazing lavender essential oil that made the whole house smell like an Aman hotel and never failed to relax her. Starting to unwind at last, she undressed and pulled a cashmere robe and slippers on while she checked her emails. She would Skype James later. It was nearly six o'clock now, nine o'clock in Dubai. He had a big team dinner tonight and wouldn't be back at his hotel till eleven at the earliest.

Checking her inbox she saw two messages from her father's lawyer. *Austin Jamet.* It was a name Macy had come to hate. Per had finally stopped contacting her directly, but he hadn't given up. Against her better judgement, she opened the latest message.

'*Miss Johanssen. I have an important communication for you from your father that is to your advantage. I urge you to contact this office urgently. Regards, Austin Jamet, Partner.*' There was a phone number for her to call at the bottom of the message.

Macy deleted it angrily.

'*Important communication', indeed. Important to whom? Not to me.*

Pushing her father out of her mind, she walked back into the bathroom and stepped gingerly into the steaming, lavender-scented water. It felt incredible. Naked except for her engagement ring, she twisted it around and around on her finger, admiring the emerald-cut diamond from every angle. By next Christmas she would be Mrs James Craven. She tried to picture herself married, but the image wouldn't come. Would they be back in LA by then? Would Eddie have sold the *Valley Farm* format? Perhaps Macy would be presenting a similar show from somewhere in Northern California. Big Sur, maybe, or Napa? That part of the fantasy she could do. But when she tried to slot James into the picture, oh-so-British James, with his cricket and his club and his beloved nights at the pub, everything fell apart.

Stop over-thinking things, Macy told herself, closing her eyes and sinking deeper into the water. *It will all work out. You just need to go with the flow.*

Outside her window, the bells of St Hilda's Church struck six.

Macy wondered what Gabe was doing right now. Probably bathing the boys with Laura. Laura irritated the shit out of Macy, but she was a good mom, and she made childhood magical for those two kids. Macy imagined her and Gabe kissing and laughing, playing snow bubbles with Hugh and Luca and telling them stories about Santa and the North Pole. She felt a stab of envy for their perfect family life, so sharp it made her wince.

Christmas. Who needed it? It was just another stupid day.

Magda had turned out the lights and was about to go upstairs and crawl gratefully into her bed when she saw Milo's present by the door. Slipping it under her arm, she took it with her. She would open it in her room. End the long, tiring day on a happy note.

Carefully untying the ribbon, she peeled off the pretty striped paper and gasped.

Inside was a beautiful book of John Donne poems. Leather bound, with gilt-tipped pages and a fleur-de-lys design etched into the cover, it was clearly very, very old. Reverently, Magda opened the cover and ran her fingers over the time-stained opening pages, looking for a printing date.

There it was: 1635! John Marriot was named as the printer. It was a second edition. It must be worth five thousand pounds at least.

Inside, Milo had slipped a postcard. On it he had written simply 'Because I know you will cherish it. Happy Christmas. M.'

There was nothing romantic about the note. But it didn't escape Magda's notice that he'd slipped it into the page with

'The Good Morrow' on it, one of Donne's most famous love poems. *'If ever any beauty I did see, Which I desir'd, and got, 'twas but a dream of thee.'*

From the darkened window of his bedroom, Milo watched Magda. He saw her open the book, registered the delight and astonishment on her face as she turned its fragile pages. He held his breath as she read his note. Had she seen where he placed it? Was she reading the poem? Before he could work it out, she stood up abruptly and turned out the light.

Ironically it was his mother who'd tipped him off to the fact that Magda liked poetry and particularly Donne. 'Pretentious madam! I suspect she feels it makes her seem more interesting and sophisticated. But I mean, really. Who's watching?'

I am, thought Milo.

His godfather, very generously, had lent him the money to buy the book from Peter Harrington on Fulham Road, Chelsea. At his current rate of earnings, Milo would be paying it off until he was about a hundred and four, but he didn't care. It had been worth it, just to see the joy on Magda's face tonight. Good old Charles had also advised him on the wording of his note and the most romantic poem in which to place it. Milo had skimmed through the book himself beforehand and failed to understand a bloody word of it.

'What does "troth" mean?'

'Are you sure you and this girl are a good match?' his godfather asked cautiously. 'Might she be a bit too intellectual for you?'

'She's perfect,' Milo explained.

Of course, Charles hadn't known *whom* the book was for.

No doubt he'd have disapproved as much as Milo's mother, what with the age gap and the difference in their circumstances and all the rest of it. But if he met her – when he met her – he would understand. Milo was sure of it. They would all come around, in the end.

'You're perfect,' he whispered now to the shadowy space where Magda's light had just gone out. 'You're perfect and I'm going to save you and rescue you and make you love me.'

Closing his eyes, he sank back into his own bed and a deep, blissful sleep.

PART TWO

CHAPTER SIXTEEN

'This is the last call for flight VS4 to Los Angeles. Would all remaining passengers for Los Angeles please proceed to Gate 27 immediately.'

Macy frowned. There was still no sign of Eddie. They'd agreed to meet for breakfast in the Business Class lounge at eight – their flight, the first of the day, left at nine thirty – but he hadn't shown up, or called to say he'd be late.

It was the third week in January, and Macy and Eddie were on their way to LA to pitch the *Valley Farm* format to US networks. Macy was excited to be going home, even if it was a short trip, jam-packed with work.

'Just don't go native on me,' James had joked when he'd dropped her off at Terminal Three. 'Make sure you come back.'

'Don't worry.' Macy kissed him, more tenderly than usual. 'I'll come back.'

Since he got back from Dubai ten days ago, she and James had spent a lot of intense time together, most of it in bed. Sex was still the one area where everything was always great between them: easy, passionate and fun. But sometimes Macy feared that they used it as a bit of a prop. Time spent making love was time *not* spent talking about their future, or trying to find things to do as a couple that they both enjoyed. Absence had made the heart grow fonder, but it had done little to bridge the gap between Macy's world and James's, or to help them understand each other better.

James had been really hurt a few days ago when Macy had bitten his head off after he'd suggested they might invite her father to the wedding.

'He's your dad,' James said simply. 'You have to forgive him some time.'

'No I don't,' Macy said furiously, tapping away on her laptop like a woman demented. 'And he is not my "dad". He's a sperm donor. He never raised me. He never gave a shit about me.'

'Well, he obviously gives a shit now,' James pointed out, reasonably. 'Getting his lawyers to keep sending you emails. He's not giving up, is he? It wouldn't kill you to hear whatever it is he has to say.'

'Yes, it would.'

James sighed. 'He's not going to live for ever, you know.'

'Well, he can't die soon enough for me,' Macy said waspishly.

'You don't mean that.'

'Don't tell me what I mean! If you loved me at all – if you *knew* me at all – you wouldn't even suggest this.'

That was the stinger. She regretted the words as soon as she'd said them. But she had said them. James's wounded feelings were written all over his face. He'd done what he always did when they had an argument – gone off for a walk by himself for a few hours and returned calm and happy and as if nothing had happened. And Macy had been as sweet as she could to him since, prompting her tender goodbye to him at the airport this morning. But this particular fight had affected both of them.

Macy was glad of the chance to throw herself back into work; this trip with Eddie was supposed to provide it. They had an insane schedule lined up, including back-to-back meetings with everyone from NBC and ABC to Showtime, HBO and Fox, as well as trips to CAA and all the big agencies and publicists. It was exciting and nerve-racking and all-consuming, and they couldn't afford to waste a single hour, never mind a day. But now bloody Eddie was about to miss the damn plane.

Where the hell is he?

All Macy's texts and emails of the last hour had gone unanswered, which was unlike Eddie. Like most politicians, he pretty much slept with his phone glued to his ear. Belatedly, the thought crossed Macy's mind that something awful might have happened to him. What if he'd had a heart attack and been rushed to hospital? Or what if his car had crashed *en route* to Heathrow? She hadn't considered that. Perhaps she should call someone . . .

'May I ask you to board now, madam?'

A very camp air steward shimmied over. Looking up, Macy noticed that the gate was almost deserted.

'Of course. Sorry. I was hoping . . . never mind.'

Flustered, her eye was caught by a copy of the *Echo*, left open on the seat next to her. It was the picture, in particular, that made her stop. Picking it up, she began to read as the steward led her towards the gangway.

'Is everything all right, madam?' he asked, when Macy failed to produce her boarding card.

'Oh shit,' Macy murmured, her eyes glued to the paper. 'Shit, shit, shit.'

Eddie Wellesley looked at the red lights flashing in front of his eyes and wondered where he was. He was so hung over after last night's big bash at Brooks's, it took him a moment to realize that he was in bed in his London flat, that the red lights were the numbers on his digital alarm clock, and that he was late for his flight.

Very late.

'*Fuuuuck!*' He sat up suddenly and then immediately lay back down again as a wave of nausea washed over him. Why hadn't the fucking alarm gone off? He was sure he'd set it. Then again, he was also sure he'd removed his suit trousers last night *before* putting on his pyjamas, but looking down now he could see that this was not, in fact, the case. The entire room was spinning. Scratch hung over. He was clearly still drunk.

Last night had been Rupert Galston-Smith's sixtieth, and the 2010 Gevrey-Chambertin Fonteny Premier Cru had flowed unstintingly, followed by enough Château d'Yquem to fill a small swimming pool. What had Eddie been thinking, letting Macy talk him into such an early bloody flight to America?

Moving more slowly, but with a pained sense of urgency, he managed to brush his teeth, splash cold water on his face, and keep down a glass of Alka-Seltzer. After that he dressed quickly (a shower and shave would have to wait till he got to LA), grabbed the suitcase that Annabel had carefully packed for him days before and walked out onto Sloane Street.

Thank God for Annabel, he thought, hailing a black cab

and climbing gingerly inside. It felt wonderful to have her behind him again, to have her on his side. So much had changed between them in the past few months, starting with Milo going to Africa, and then with all the good news on the political front. Little by little, cocooned together up at Riverside Hall over Christmas, Eddie and Annabel had become a team again. She still had her moments, of course. Mention of Laura Baxter's name could occasionally make her fly off the handle, and poor Magda always seemed to put her back up. But generally the change had been little short of miraculous – and not a moment too soon. Eddie didn't just love his wife. He needed her.

'Heathrow, please. As fast as humanly possible. I'm very late.'

His stomach was still doing back-flips but, with the windows open, he felt fairly confident he would make it to Terminal Three without being sick. He'd better call ahead to Virgin, let them know he was on his way. Switching on his phone, he saw he had a long string of texts from Macy and a veritable barrage of missed calls. Before he had time to read even one of the messages, his handset started to ring.

'Wellesley.' Eddie barked the word out, as if worried that even one more syllable might prompt him to empty the contents of his stomach.

'Eddie, it's Kevin Unger. I've been trying to reach you all morning.'

This not being a question, Eddie didn't answer. His political agent sounded stressed. Then again, Kevin always sounded stressed.

'Have you seen this morning's *Echo*?'

'No.'

Yes/no responses were about all Eddie could handle. He hoped Kevin continued in this vein.

'Are you sitting down?'

'Yes.'

He smiled. He was hitting his stride now. But as the agent kept talking, the smile quickly died. Two minutes later, Eddie was as sober as he'd ever been in his life.

'That piece of shit Carlyle's gone too far this time,' he seethed.

'Is it libellous? Think carefully, Eddie.'

'Of course it's bloody libellous! Every poisonous, mean-spirited word.'

'Then we're going to need to issue a statement. Right away.'

'OK. I'll call you back.'

Eddie hung up. He needed to talk to Annabel. He needed to talk to a million people, but Annabel first.

'Change of plans,' he told the cabbie. 'We need to go back to town.'

Grimly, he dialled the Riverside Hall number.

'You'll be wanting this.' Mrs Preedy handed Laura a slightly torn copy of the *Echo*. 'It's my last copy. We're sold out.'

Laura asked innocently, 'Why? Is there something special in it?'

Unloading her basket of groceries at the counter, she was distracted by Hugh's constant refrain of 'Match Attax!' as he hopped up and down, pointing a sticky finger at the coveted football cards.

'You haven't heard, then?'

'Heard what?'

'Pages two to six. That'll be eight pounds sixty, please. Are you wanting the Match Attax cards?'

But Laura wasn't listening. Mindlessly leaving a ten-pound note on the counter, and handing the cards to Hugh to shut him up, she walked home to tell Gabe, still holding the paper open with one hand and reading as she went.

'I'm just reading the *Echo*,' she told him. 'They're serializing David Carlyle's new book. It's an exposé.'

'I know. Of Annabel Wellesley's misspent youth. Eddie just called me,' said Gabe.

'Have you *seen* what Carlyle's written?'

'Not verbatim.'

Laura started reading under the lurid headline, 'LADY WELL-SLEAZY!': *Lady Wellesley, known for her cold and haughty demeanour during her husband's court case, when Fast Eddie's secrets were being laid bare, has skeletons of her own. As a working-class teenager, Anna Green ('Annabel' was a later affectation) actually SLEPT her way into high society, taking elocution lessons and 'reinventing' herself as 'posh', before seducing TWO married aristocrats, destroying their families in the process.* Lady Liar *reveals the secrets that Lady Wellesley and her tax-dodging husband hoped to hide from voters. Her obsession with money and class. Her desperation to hid her own, humble background, including disowning her own PARENTS. This is the Wellesley Family History they never wanted you to see.'*

Laura's eyes were drawn to a picture of a young Annabel, in hotpants and a clinging T-shirt, her arms wrapped tightly around an unknown man. With her waist-length blond hair blowing everywhere and her carefree, mischievous smile, she looked utterly unrecognizable as the tightly wound harridan of a wife that the Swell Valley, and the country, had come to know. She looked *happy*. She looked *fun*. Was *this* the woman Eddie had fallen for, Laura wondered. And if so, what had happened to her?

'Fucking hell,' said Gabe. 'Poor Eddie.'

'Poor Eddie! Poor both of them,' said Laura. 'I must say I'm astonished. I can't imagine Annabel seducing anybody, can you? She was bloody sexy, though, back in the day.'

She showed Gabe the picture.

'Eddie says it's all nonsense,' said Gabe. 'Completely made up.'

'It can't be,' said Laura. 'Carlyle's not that stupid. He wouldn't dare publish if he weren't sure of his facts. The publisher would have checked them too.'

'That's what I thought,' Gabe admitted. 'But Eddie was adamant. Says he's suing for libel.'

As he spoke, two television vans pulled up on the High Street. Within minutes they were followed by more. A reporter for the *Daily Mail* came over and asked Laura for directions to Riverside Hall. Laura smiled and sent them the wrong way.

'Has anyone told Macy?' she asked Gabe once they'd gone.

'Shit,' said Gabe. 'I didn't think about that. I wonder if her plane's already left?'

Macy sat in her business-class seat, glued to her tablet. David Carlyle was being interviewed on the BBC. In a pale blue suit and silk tie he looked tanned, confident and relaxed, leaning back on the studio sofa and smiling at James Neil.

'Clearly these allegations, the things you've written about Lady Wellesley in your book *Lady Liar*, some of them are fairly serious,' James Neil was saying. 'You call her a home-wrecker. At one point you imply that she blackmailed a former lover; that he gave her money to keep quiet about the affair.'

'That's right. I was as shocked as you are, James, and as I know our viewers will be. To put it bluntly, these aren't the kinds of people we want running the country.'

'Are you concerned about legal action?'

'Not at all.' David Carlyle spread his arms wide in a gesture of innocence. 'There's no law against writing the truth. Or, in this case, exposing the lies behind a carefully constructed public image. I'm a hundred per cent sure of my sources, as are my publishers. There's nothing in my book that wouldn't stand up in court, and the Wellesleys know it.'

'Even if that's the case, some people would argue that it's unethical to go after the wives and families of politicians. Lady Wellesley isn't a public figure. She's never stood for office. Isn't this "truth" just the latest chapter in a personal vendetta being waged between you and Sir Edward?'

'Not at all. I'm a newspaper editor. It's my job to bring people the truth.'

'But isn't this ancient history, David? About somebody's private life?'

'No,' David responded, a slight edge creeping into his voice. 'It's a story about two people pretending to be something they aren't, for personal gain. The problem with people like the Wellesleys, James, is that they don't believe the usual rules apply to them. We saw that with Sir Edward, over his tax affairs. Now we're seeing it from his wife. Breaking up marriages. Ditching her own parents in her desperation to rebrand herself as upper class. It's scandalous. Voters need to understand. These people are not who they say they are.'

Unable to stand David Carlyle's sanctimonious smirk a moment longer, Macy switched to ITV and was amazed to see an ashen-looking Eddie being interviewed. A reporter had cornered him in the street as he was getting into his car.

'I've already made a statement.' Eddie sounded tired. 'There is no truth to these revolting allegations. None whatsoever. My wife and I will be taking legal action. Beyond that, I have nothing to say.'

'So you don't know about these married lovers?'

'There were no married lovers!' Eddie snapped.

'David Carlyle says he stands by his sources,' the reporter shouted after Eddie as he climbed into his Bentley.

'Then I suggest his "sources" buy a clothes peg,' Eddie shot back, giving a flash of his old, mischievous self. 'Anyone standing next to that oik should beware of the smell.'

Macy laughed, but it wasn't funny. She felt terrible for Eddie, but also nervous about what it might mean for the show. Here she was, flying to LA alone to pitch *Valley Farm* to US networks, with a potentially damaging scandal playing out back in Britain. In Macy's experience, American TV execs were deeply wary of bad publicity. What, exactly, was she supposed to say to them about Sir Eddie Wellesley's absence?

It would help if she could reach Eddie in person. Or Gabe, or Laura, or anyone. But it seemed as if every phone in England was switched to voicemail this morning. Not even James was picking up.

Switching off her iPad as the plane's engines roared into life and they juddered along the runway for take-off, Macy wondered whether what the *Echo* had published was true. On the one hand she couldn't *imagine* the brittle and superior

Annabel Wellesley as plain old Anna Green, a mechanic's daughter from Barnsley on the make. And Eddie was too experienced and savvy a politician to deny a story he knew to be true.

On the other hand, David Carlyle was hardly likely to risk his editorship and a major lawsuit by printing something overtly libellous. Especially something as salacious and incendiary as this extract from *Lady Liar*. And, according to the publisher, there was more to come. The teasers suggested that Annabel might even have been involved in some sort of 'escort' business. Not prostitution, but making herself available to wealthy, upper-class men as arm candy. It implied that she'd married Eddie not out of love, but as part of some sort of social climbing master plan.

Macy hoped that wasn't true. Eddie certainly wasn't a blameless husband. But he loved his wife, of that Macy had no doubt.

She closed her eyes as the plane swept up into the clouds, uncomfortably conscious of the empty seat next to her.

Eddie was driving far too fast on the A3 when the car phone rang.

'Annabel?'

Milo could hear the near panic in his dad's voice when he answered, 'No, Dad, it's me. Are you OK?'

'I've had better mornings. I take it you saw the news?'

'Yeah.' There was a momentary pause. Then Milo said: 'Is it true?'

Eddie couldn't have been more shocked if someone had thrown a glass of iced water in his face. 'Is it *true*? Of course it's not bloody true! How can you even ask that? This is your mother we're talking about.'

'I didn't say I thought it *was* true,' Milo defended himself.

'But you wondered?' Eddie shot back.

The truth was, he *had* wondered. Milo had never really understood his mother. He'd always had the sense that there was a huge part of her that was a closed book to him and to everyone. And, in some ways, Carlyle's version of events made sense. If she'd spent her whole life playing a role, and worrying about being found out, no wonder she was always so highly strung and irritable.

'Is Mum OK?' Milo asked nervously.

'I don't know.' Eddie's anger was gone now, replaced once again with worry. 'I can't bloody reach her. There's no answer at the house, and you know she never has her mobile switched on.'

'She's probably out for a walk or something,' said Milo.

'That's what I'm afraid of,' said Eddie. 'She obviously doesn't know yet, or she'd have called me. Which means she could get ambushed by the press at any minute, completely unprepared, completely unprotected. I'm on my way home now.'

'Do you want me to come down?'

'No,' said Eddie. 'Stay where you are. Lie low and don't so much as blink at the press.'

'Of course I won't.'

'And if your mother calls, ring me immediately.'

'It'll be OK, Dad,' Milo heard himself saying. Hanging up, he wondered whether it would.

The moment Milo rang off, Eddie heard the sirens.

This can't be happening. But a glance in his rear-view mirror confirmed it. Two squad cars, lights flashing, were pulling him over. Eddie groaned. For one, mad moment he considered hitting the accelerator and trying to outrun them, but he quickly came to his senses. Pulling over, he wound his window down.

'Morning, sir. Did you realize you were doing over . . . oh! Sir Edward.' The policeman did a double take.

'I'm sorry, officer,' said Eddie, running a hand through his hair. 'I know I was speeding, I accept the points, but I'm desperately worried about my wife and I'm trying to get home. I don't know if you've read this morning's *Echo* . . .'

'Yes, sir.'

The policeman liked Eddie Wellesley. Everybody liked Eddie Wellesley. His wife was another matter, but the poor bloke was obviously beside himself with worry.

'If you like, sir, my colleague and I can escort you home. We'll make better time that way.'

Eddie was touched. 'That's incredibly kind. Thank you.'

Following the police through dreary suburbs and then open countryside, Eddie cast his mind back to the early days with Annabel. Who had she been going out with when they met? It was all so long ago, but Eddie was sure he'd have remembered if it were anyone aristocratic, or married. Not that it would have put him off. He'd fancied Annabel so madly, he'd have wooed her no matter who she'd been bonking. But no. If there'd been married men, or high-profile affairs, he'd have known. Of course he would.

There were faint shadows of truth in elements of Carlyle's hateful story. It was true, for example, that Annabel was estranged from her parents. They hadn't come to the wedding, and Eddie had never met them – although he knew they lived in a small estate in Scotland and that the father had been in the Scots Guards. *Perhaps*, he thought

281

now, *I should have been more curious? Asked more questions.* But then again, why should he? How was he to know that some deranged little pleb with a chip on his shoulder the size of Cornwall was going to crawl out of the slime thirty years later and publish a load of garbage about Annabel having working-class roots, and changing her name, and *blackmail*, for heaven's sake! The *Echo* piece made her sound like Mandy bloody Rice-Davies. The whole thing was absurd.

Grimly, Eddie drove on, his anger burning more fiercely with each passing mile.

The first thing Eddie saw when he pulled up at Riverside Hall was the predictable fleet of reporters and cameramen huddled outside the gates. The second thing was Wilf, racing across the lawn to greet him, wagging his tail as if all were right with the world; the third was a panicked-looking Magda.

'Where's Lady Wellesley?' Eddie asked her.

'I don't know. I . . . I don't think she's home.'

Magda explained that she'd left early this morning for a long walk over the Downs with Wilf. When she'd returned twenty minutes ago, she'd found the house surrounded by press. Darting inside, she'd looked for Annabel but found no sign. She'd managed to keep the gates closed and the press pack at bay, but they kept yelling their questions over the walls. It was like being under siege.

Leaving the police to deal with the media, Eddie ran into the house.

'Annabel!'

No answer.

Her car was in the drive and she never went for a walk without Wilf. She must be here somewhere. He did a quick scout around the ground floor then bounded up the stairs, two at a time.

'Annabel! Darling? Are you here?'

Nothing.

Perhaps she *had* gone out? But where would she go, on foot and without the dog? The only possibility was into the village, but if that were the case then the TV crews would have pounced on her instantly.

Eddie walked into their bedroom. The bed had been slept in, the covers pulled loosely together afterwards. Everything looked as it always did. There was nothing on the nightstand or Annabel's dressing table to suggest where she might have gone, no sign of a struggle or anything untoward. Her mobile phone was there, plugged into its charger, but that wasn't unusual. She never took it anywhere. After the court case the poor thing had developed an allergy to telephones. Somehow they never seemed to bring good news.

Then suddenly Eddie saw it, taped to the door of the master bathroom: an envelope. *For Eddie and Milo.*

Ripping it off, he tore it open frantically. Inside, on a neatly folded, single page of writing paper, Annabel had written only six words.

'I love you both. I'm sorry.'

Eddie felt his knees buckle beneath him and the bile rise up in his throat. He tried the bathroom door. It was locked.

'Annabel!' It was more of a scream than a word.

Outside, the two policemen looked at each other. Without a word they started to run towards the house.

Eddie ran at the door, throwing his whole weight against it. It took three attempts before it finally gave way. By the time he found her, limp and lifeless on the floor, the pill bottle still in her hand, the police were right behind him.

'Call an ambulance!' Eddie yelled at them, desperately starting mouth-to-mouth.

But deep down he knew it was too late.

CHAPTER SEVENTEEN

David Carlyle could hear the *tap, tap* of his handmade leather shoes on the polished marble as he crossed the lobby of the *Echo*'s London office. Everyone from the reception staff to the security guards to the groups of employees waiting for the lifts watched him pass in stunned silence.

'Cheer up!' David grinned, addressing himself to all of them and apparently revelling in their discomfort. 'Nobody died.'

Miraculously, this was true. Annabel Wellesley had defied the odds by surviving her huge overdose. Overnight her condition had gone from 'critical but stable' to 'comfortable', which was doctor-speak for out of the woods. But the backlash against the *Echo* for running the story in the first place was growing by the hour. No one cared any more who Lady Wellesley had or hadn't slept with when she was eighteen, or what her father did for a living. There was a new villain of the piece, and his name was David Carlyle.

David didn't give a rat's arse. Eddie Wellesley was suffering and Eddie Wellesley deserved to suffer. If the British public didn't think so, it was because they didn't know him like

David did. The paper's circulation was up by well over a hundred per cent, and David's book, *Lady Liar*, was flying off the shelves all over the country. If there was one thing British readers really excelled at, it was rank hypocrisy.

'You've all got work to do.' He clapped his hands together loudly, like a cotton grower summoning his slaves. 'So stop gawping and get back to your desks.'

At his own desk five minutes later, David began taking the first of what would be a long morning of calls. The first was from his publisher, Damian Blythe.

'Sir Edward Wellesley's dropped the lawsuit.'

The relief in Blythe's voice was palpable.

David laughed. 'What did I tell you? It's only libel if it's not true, Damian. By the way, did I mention I'm thinking of counter-suing for defamation?'

The publisher's relief evaporated. 'You can't do that.'

'Why not? Eddie's been all over the TV, calling me a liar and a scumbag and God knows what. I want an apology.'

'His wife almost died,' Damian Blythe pointed out. 'In case you hadn't noticed, David, people don't like you very much at the moment.'

'So?' Carlyle scoffed. 'I'm not running for office. What do I care? As long as they're buying my book and my paper, I'm laughing. So should you be.'

However, to his immense irritation, David's lawyer gave him the same advice as his publisher.

'A defamation suit would be a disaster.'

'You mean I'd lose?'

'You might win the battle. But you'd lose the war. Wasn't your entire aim in this to derail Eddie Wellesley politically?'

'My aim was to tell the truth,' David said archly. 'I'm a journalist. That's what I do.'

'*Touché*,' said his lawyer. 'Very good. But be aware that if you take Wellesley to court over this, you run the risk of cementing his popularity with voters. Public sympathy right now is overwhelmingly on Eddie's side, David. Overwhelmingly.'

David clenched his fists. He knew that this was true. His desk was littered with polls confirming it. But he still found it hard to credit.

'His wife's a whore and he tried to cover up for her,' he snarled. 'How stupid can people be?'

'Come on,' said his lawyer. 'Wellesley didn't know. It all happened years before he met her.'

'You can't seriously believe that?' said David.

The lawyer paused. 'It doesn't matter what I believe,' he said carefully. 'People believe it. Don't go to court, David. It's not in your interests.'

David Carlyle hung up.

Fuck it. The wilfully blind voting public could think what they liked. The fact was that they all bought his book, and his newspaper, because deep down they were desperate to know the Wellesleys' dirty little secrets. Eddie was in hell this morning, while he, David, was getting richer and richer.

I'm the winner here, he told himself.

There was something wonderfully old-fashioned about Worthing Hospital. Eddie wasn't sure whether it was the neatly ironed uniforms of the nurses with their pocket watches and hats, or the fifties feel of the architecture, or the cups of tea provided from a pot on a trolley rather than the ubiquitous dispensing machines. But he felt safe here, protected from the press as far as possible, and amongst friends.

Annabel's private room was small and sparsely furnished,

287

but like the rest of the place it was cheerful and clean. A simple vase of peonies, Annabel's favourite flower, basked in the winter sunshine beneath the window, from Penny de la Cruz of all people. Annabel felt dreadful when she remembered how vile she'd been to Penny the day they first met, right after they'd moved in to Riverside Hall. It all felt so very long ago now. Cards from other friends and family littered every available surface. To Eddie, the room smelled of hope and kindness. A new day. He was incredibly grateful for the miracle that had been performed here. Worthing's doctors had brought Annabel back from the dead.

Nothing mattered apart from that. Nothing at all.

'We should talk, Eddie.'

Annabel's voice was as weak as she was. Propped up on oversized pillows, her skin still waxen-white, she looked as tiny and fragile as a child's doll.

Eddie shook his head. 'There's nothing to say. Just rest.'

'There's everything to say.' The pain in her eyes was beyond tears. Eddie couldn't bear to look. 'It's true, Eddie, it's all true. Well, apart from the stuff about my parents. They were the ones who abandoned me, not the other way round. Although the Scottish estate and all of that was a lie . . .'

'Please, darling. Rest. It doesn't matter. None of it matters.'

'It does to me. I lied to you. About who I was, about where I came from. But not because I didn't love you, like they said in the paper. Because I *did* love you. I thought . . . I was afraid you'd reject me if you knew.' Her bottom lip trembled. She looked about twelve.

'I fell in love with *you*.' Eddie took her hand, close to tears now himself. 'Your name, your background . . . I couldn't care less about those things.'

'But the affairs. I *did* take money from those men, Eddie. I did. I was young and poor and desperate to change my life. But it's no excuse. Can you forgive me?'

'There's nothing to forgive,' Eddie said fervently. 'It was before we met, Annabel. We all do stupid things when we're kids. If anyone should be asking forgiveness, it's me.'

'How do you work that out?' Annabel smiled weakly.

'I should never have tried to go back into politics, back into public life. I knew Carlyle would stop at nothing. Stupidly, I thought it might be Milo he'd go after. I never dreamed it would be you. But I put you at risk, put all of us at risk.'

'That's ridiculous.' She closed her eyes. The effort of conversation was exhausting. 'Politics is your life. Our life. It was what we both wanted.'

'Yes, well, not any more,' said Eddie. '*You're* my life. I love you so much, Annabel. Please, don't leave me.'

They sat in silence for a while. Then a mask of anguish descended again over Annabel's features as a new thought occurred to her. 'Milo! Oh God. What must he think of me? Have you seen him?'

'Milo's fine,' said Eddie. 'He's coming in this afternoon to see you.'

'Oh, no. No, no. I can't face him, Eddie. Not yet.'

'Yes, you can,' Eddie said gently. 'You can face anything after this, my darling. We all can. Do you know, I'm actually starting to think that David Carlyle's done this family a favour?'

Annabel's eyes widened.

'I mean it. No more secrets. No more lies. No more politics.'

No more politics . . .

289

Collapsing back onto the pillows, Annabel wondered what a life without politics might be like. Was it good news, or bad? Did Eddie even mean it? Was he capable of it? Was she? The picture was too vague and unformed to hold on to, like trying to imagine the afterlife.

It was still slipping through her fingers as she drifted back into a deep, dreamless sleep.

Laura sat in the front row at the school play feeling her irritation build.

'Is this seat taken?'

Rachel Cantor, another St Hilda's mum who'd been one of the leading voices in the early anti-*Valley Farm* campaign and had never approved of Laura, pointed at the empty seat beside her.

'Actually, yes, sorry,' said Laura. 'I'm saving it for my husband.'

'Yes, but he isn't here, is he?' Rachel said crossly. 'It's not really fair to save seats for parents who can't be bothered to show up, when so many of us who *are* here are having to stand.'

Laura smiled thinly. 'The seat's taken.'

Rachel huffed off to rejoin her gaggle of gossips at the back of the hall, muttering furiously about 'entitlement' and the 'bloody Baxters'. Earlier Laura had heard the women bad-mouthing Annabel Wellesley, and had only just restrained herself from giving them a piece of her mind. One of Laura's New Year's resolutions was to try to relax more and to pick her battles.

Tonight's battle was going to be with Gabe.

They'd had a lovely Christmas and New Year. Gabe was clearly making an effort to be more thoughtful and less selfish, and Laura was snapping less. The break in filming meant more sleep and less stress, which had worked wonders for their relationship. But in the last few days, things had started to slide. With Eddie stuck in England, closeted away at his wife's bedside, Macy had flown to LA alone. But, without a producer, the meetings would be a disaster. She'd called Laura for help.

'Please come. I wouldn't ask if I didn't need you.'

This, Laura knew, was true. Macy no doubt relished a week in Laura's company about as much as Laura looked forward to spending that time with Macy. The fact that it was LA, a city Laura loathed with a passion, and that it meant a whole week away from the kids, only made things worse. But there was nothing for it. With enormous reluctance, Laura had agreed to go in Eddie's stead. But if she was looking for support from Gabe, she didn't get it.

'I can't believe you're moaning. I'd love to have a week in the California sunshine, hanging out with Macy,' he said, tactlessly.

'We won't be "hanging out",' Laura said crossly. 'And we won't be sunning ourselves either. It's work.'

The LA trip meant that Laura suddenly had a hundred and one things to do, not least pack. But as usual when she needed Gabe to take over with the boys, he'd done one of his disappearing acts, swanning up to town for more mysterious 'meetings'. He'd promised her faithfully he'd be home in plenty of time for tonight's performance of *Tom Thumb* – Hugh, bless him, was in the title role. But, yet again, he'd broken his word.

'Excushe me. Shorry. Coming through.'

Right on cue, Gabe arrived at the village hall, making the sort of entrance that only he could. Handsome, dishevelled, grinning and quite obviously the worse for drink, he clattered his way through the rows of metal chairs like the proverbial bull in a china shop.

'Made it!' he said proudly, sitting down next to Laura and adding, too loudly, 'You look sexy,' as he ran a hand unashamedly up her thigh.

'Stop it,' Laura whispered, blushing scarlet. Despite her annoyance, his hand felt wonderful against her skin, warm and rough and just the right amount of possessive. Even drunk and late, he still had the ability to turn her on like a flipped switch. 'And keep your voice down.'

'I love you,' Gabe slurred, only slightly quieter.

'You're drunk,' said Laura. Although it was hard to keep her anger going as he planted kisses on her neck.

The lights went down. A few minutes later Hugh toddled onstage dressed like an acorn with a brown papier-mâché cone on his head and two large green felt leaves sewn onto the back of his T-shirt. Gazing at the audience without a hint of stage fright, he started to sing, his reedy little voice floating through the air like the most fragile of butterflies unfurling its wings.

Gabe welled up. Clasping Laura's hand he said, 'I can't believe how big he is.'

'Neither can I.'

'I wish you weren't going to America.'

'That makes two of us.'

Laura returned the pressure of his fingers as she stared up lovingly at their son. Marriage to Gabe was like a roller-coaster, even after all these years. Ten minutes ago she'd been furious with him, with every reason. But now she felt nothing but love. Sometimes she resented the way he could flip her emotions like a pancake. She knew that, far too often, it meant he got away with murder. But at the same time it was part of what held them together as a couple, part of their romantic glue. And she didn't want to go away for a whole week on the back of a row.

Gabe hoped she couldn't hear his heart pounding. He knew he'd cut it too fine tonight. Laura wouldn't have forgiven him if she'd missed Hugh's play, and he wouldn't have forgiven himself either. But these industry parties were an important part of making the show a success. Laura didn't want to admit it, but it was true. As *Valley Farm*'s presenter, schmoozing with the network was part of Gabe's job. Of course, he'd probably have a better chance of convincing Laura of that if he weren't three sheets to the wind every time he got home . . .

New Year's resolution number 104: Drink less.

Leaning into him, Laura hoped Gabe hadn't done anything stupid up in London while he was drunk. The Wellesleys' scandals were more than enough for the show to have to deal with right now. In the past, unexpected displays of affection from Gabriel had a nasty tendency to spring from a sense of guilt.

Think positive. That was one of Laura's New Year's resolutions.

Closing her eyes, she allowed the sweet sounds of Hugh's song to carry her away.

CHAPTER EIGHTEEN

Paul Meyer dripped with sweat beneath the punishing midday sun as he jogged behind his client through Nichols Canyon. It was January, supposedly the depths of winter, but as usual nobody had sent Los Angeles the memo. Today's temperatures were set to top ninety degrees.

How do people do this for fun? the legendary agent thought, watching another group of tanned, smiling, lithe-limbed young people bound past him like a flock of Disney-happy gazelles, while his own lungs screamed with pain with every breath. Seriously. He felt like he was inhaling razor blades. And meanwhile Macy Johanssen just kept getting faster.

It must be a Gentile thing, Paul decided. A scorching canyon in the Hollywood hills was no place for a Jewish man pushing sixty. It was a testament to his affection for Macy, whom he hadn't seen in a year, that he had let her talk him into it.

'Stop!' he called after her, leaning over with his hands on his knees and wheezing like a concertina. 'I need a break.'

Macy jogged back down the hill. 'C'mon, Paul. We just

started!' she teased, skipping from foot to foot like an Energizer Bunny on pause.

'Uh-uh.' He shook his head. 'We just finished. I want to talk.'

'So talk.'

'To your face, not your ass. Lovely as your ass is,' he added, still panting.

Once Paul got his breath back, they continued along the path at a leisurely walk. It was a glorious day, hot and clear, with blue-sky views all the way from the mountains to the ocean. Just being back in Nichols Canyon on a day like today made Macy's heart open and her spirits soar. She knew she'd missed LA, but she hadn't realized quite how much until this moment. She felt like a mole, emerging into sunlight for the first time, blinking joyously at the warmth and the light and the clear, dry, flower-scented air.

'So,' said Paul, 'you've got your first big meeting on Tuesday. NBC. You prepared?'

'You know me. I'm always prepared,' Macy beamed. 'I would have preferred to have Eddie with me. He's great at this stuff. But, you know, under the circumstances . . .'

'How is he?' Paul Meyer knew all about the scandal involving Sir Eddie Wellesley's wife. It hadn't made the news stateside, but anything that affected Meyer's clients affected him. 'I always liked that guy.'

'Me too,' said Macy. 'I haven't spoken to him, but I hear he's OK. Staying with Annabel.'

Meyer raised an eyebrow. In Hollywood people got divorced because their wife put the wrong number of shots in their latte.

'True love, huh?'

'I guess,' said Macy. 'Laura Baxter's flying out to take the meetings with me.'

The look on her face told Paul Meyer all he needed to know about Macy's feelings towards *Valley Farm*'s creator. He quickly changed the subject.

'So, can I see the rock?'

Macy stopped and held out her left hand. The diamond was suitably impressive, but Paul couldn't help but notice that she seemed less than enthusiastic about showing it off, or discussing her engagement.

'Gorgeous,' he observed. 'He's a cricket player, right?'

Macy nodded. 'He's a big deal in England. The David Beckham of the cricket world.'

'Nice. You happy?'

'Of course,' she said, an edge of irritation creeping into her voice.

'When's the wedding?'

She shrugged. 'This year some time. Probably summer, but it depends what happens this week. Work commitments come first.'

'Does Becks know that?' Paul joked.

'His name's James. And yes, he does. He's marrying a career woman.'

'Yeah, but—'

'No buts,' said Macy. 'He'll have to take me as he finds me.'

Another group of runners cruised past them, the third in as many minutes. Not one of them gave Macy a second glance. She pouted at her agent.

'I'm invisible here now, aren't I? Everyone's forgotten me.'

Paul Meyer gave her an indulgent look. All his clients were insecure, but Macy Johanssen was one of the few whose vulnerability he found endearing.

'It's been a while. But that will all change once we get you a US deal for *Valley Farm*.'

'*If* we get a deal,' Macy said gloomily.

'Excuse me? That's not the Macy Johanssen I know. Of course you'll get a deal! Two beautiful chicks like you and Laura Baxter? You'll have those network suits eating out of your hands like bunnies at a petting zoo.'

'Hmmm.' Macy sounded unconvinced.

'Besides which, it's a great format, it really is,' said Paul. 'A California version of *Valley Farm* would go down a storm here. It's totally fresh. You'll have a bidding war on your hands in no time, believe me.'

Macy smiled. She loved Paul Meyer. Out of all her Hollywood and TV friends, she was the only one who actually trusted her agent. Paul had the same ability to lift her up and make her feel good about herself that Eddie had. It was why she'd wanted so badly for Eddie to be here for these pitch meetings. Not because she needed her hand held. But because Eddie's presence always made her a better version of herself.

'Come on.' She clapped Paul on the back with exaggerated heartiness. 'One last sprint to the top of the ridge and I'll buy you lunch.'

In the event, they passed on lunch. Paul had an urgent appointment with a shower, followed by another with a movie actress who would not tolerate being kept waiting.

Macy swung by Lemonade on Beverly for her favourite poached salmon and kale salad, before driving back up Doheny to Sunset and then on to Laurel Canyon. By a rare stroke of luck, her little house in the hills was between tenants, which meant she could stay at home rather than a hotel.

It was lovely to be back, amid her familiar pictures and furniture and books. But it was also weird. Jarring. As if something were not quite right, not quite as it should be. It had taken her a full day to realize that the thing that was different was her. When she'd left this house only a year ago, England had been a strange and unknown country and Macy had been a single woman with no more thought of settling down than a seed blowing carelessly on the wind. Now England was almost as much her home as Los Angeles, and she was preparing to marry one of its most famous native sons.

She told herself that these were all good things. Wonderful things. That soon she would re-establish her career in the States, too, and that somehow she and James would make their transatlantic careers work, and it would all be perfect and she would live happily ever after. But there was a part of her, deep inside, that hadn't got the script. For some reason she couldn't quite grasp, being in this house seemed to feed that part.

Settling down at her dining table, a rustic beauty from Restoration Hardware, she pushed her doubts aside as she wolfed down her Lemonade lunch. All the exercise and fresh air had left her famished, and food like this simply didn't exist in England, for all Jamie Oliver's efforts. Opening the screen doors to her rear deck, she allowed the scents of jasmine and honeysuckle and newly mown grass to waft into the room. The combined pleasure-bomb of the delicious food and warm breeze quickly banished any lingering negativity. Once she'd finished her meal and cleared her plate away, sated and happy, it occurred to her she probably ought to shower. Peeling off her Lululemon jogging pants, she padded upstairs in her underwear.

Bathrooms. That was something else the Brits hadn't got quite right. In England, the expression 'power shower' meant anything that turned on and produced water, and you were lucky if you got even that. Most homes in the Swell Valley, including Cranbourne House, still had iron baths with separate taps that either scalded or froze you to death, depending on which you turned on first. Standing now on her gleaming, porcelain-tiled floor, while hundreds of hot jets of water pounded down mercilessly onto her aching muscles, Macy closed her eyes in pure delight. The sensation was so wonderful, it took her a full fifteen minutes to drag herself out and get dry. If she didn't have so much work still to do to prepare for the NBC meeting, not to mention a string of emails from Laura that demanded replies, she could happily have stood in that shower all day.

As it was she dried off, slathered herself in Ole Henriksen grapefruit body lotion and slipped on a purple silk robe that barely covered her groin and hung open loosely across her breasts. There was no one here to see it, but the touch of the soft silk against her bare skin always made her feel sexy. Maybe she'd keep it on for her Skype call with James later? Or take it off. It was odd how the times she most wanted sex with him were the times he was thousands of miles away.

Skipping back down to the living room, she reached the bottom of the stairs and froze.

There was someone in the house. A man.

At first she thought she'd imagined the tall, dark figure moving past the deck. But then she saw him clearly, stepping through the open glass doors, looking around him stealthily, no doubt for something to steal. He wore jeans and a hooded top, but Macy could see from his hands that he was black.

How could she have been so stupid, leaving the doors open? This was Hollywood, not Fittlescombe. He hadn't seen her yet. Crouching back into the shadows, Macy grabbed a heavy glass ashtray from the side table in the hall. He was facing away from her now, bending down over her desk. With a strength and speed born of pure terror, Macy launched herself at him with a wild, war-like shriek, her raised arm brandishing the glass ashtray like a hand grenade.

The man spun around, a look of panic on his face.

'Stop! Please!' He just had time to cover his head with his arms before the glass came crashing down, missing his skull but painfully slamming into his wrists.

'Get OUT!' Macy roared, lifting the ashtray for a second strike as the man yelped in pain. 'Get out of my house, you asshole!'

This time he reacted more quickly. Lunging to one side, he reached out and grabbed Macy's arm forcefully, easily knocking the ashtray out of her hand. The next thing he knew he had his hands full of wriggling silk as she lashed out wildly, kicking, biting and scratching like a deranged cat. A manicured fingernail clawed at his cheek, drawing blood.

'Please! I'm not here to hurt you. The door was open!'

Macy continued lashing out blindly.

'I'm a lawyer. I represent your father. Per Johanssen.'

Macy stopped hitting him. Nervously, the man let go of her. She stepped back, pulling her robe more tightly around her and looked at him, her eyes narrowed with suspicion.

'You don't look like a lawyer.'

'What do lawyers look like?' he asked.

'They wear suits.'

'Not on the weekend.' He risked a smile and extended his hand. 'Austin Jamet.'

Macy shook his hand but did not return the smile. On closer inspection he did not look much like a housebreaker. His skin was smooth and coffee coloured, and freshly shaven that morning. He had a full mouth and playful dark brown eyes and his hands were manicured to perfection. The hoodie, she noticed now, was made from very fine-weave summer cashmere.

'I have a doorbell, Mr Jamet.'

'Austin.' He was still smiling, rather unnervingly. 'I know you do. I rang it, repeatedly. There was no answer.'

'I was in the shower.'

'So I see.'

Macy ran a hand angrily through her wet hair.

'I'm sorry I scared you,' he went on. 'But when I saw the rear doors were open, I figured—'

'You'd barge in uninvited?'

'I have something important to deliver to you, Miss Johanssen. I realized this might be my only chance.'

'If it's from my father, it's not important to me,' said Macy. 'You shouldn't have come here.'

The familiar Skype ringtone prevented the lawyer from answering. Macy disappeared into the kitchen. Austin Jamet could hear she was talking to a boyfriend. There were lots of 'babys' and 'sweethearts' being thrown around. Almost too many.

'I'm sorry, baby,' he heard Macy cooing. 'I miss you too, soooo much. But I have a situation here . . . I'll call you right back. Uh-huh. Of course I do.'

301

She hung up.

Returning to the living room, she looked in an even worse mood than before.

'You're aware I have a restraining order against my father?'

'I am.'

'Forbidding him to contact me?'

'Yes.'

'Then what are you doing here?'

'I'm not your father, Miss Johanssen. I'm his attorney. The order doesn't extend to legal representatives.'

Macy sighed. 'Look, Mr Jamet . . .'

'Austin.'

'Mr Jamet. There is nothing that Per Johanssen has to say to me that I want to hear.'

'I understand that. But there are things you don't know. Things that, if you *did* know them, might make you think differently.'

'Think differently about what?' asked Macy.

'A lot of things.'

Pulling out a business card, the lawyer scribbled something down on the back of it and handed it to her.

Macy's eyes widened. She started to laugh. 'Mr Jamet, I am not having dinner with you.'

He smiled back at her. 'Table's at eight. My name. I can see myself out.'

Nobu Malibu had to have one of the most stunning locations of any restaurant in the world.

Perched just feet above the Pacific Ocean, surrounded by swaying palms and white sand, diners on the sleek outdoor deck could watch passing pods of dolphins leap and play for their amusement as they sipped at their cocktails, while a bruised purple sun bled into the horizon. Flames from the fire pits danced in the darkness, while inside the finest Japanese food was being lovingly prepared by the best sushi chefs outside of Tokyo.

Macy had arrived early, thanks to an Uber driver who was clearly a frustrated Formula 1 wannabe and had torn down Pacific Coast Highway like a bullet. Now, sitting alone at a table overlooking the ocean, staring at the single white orchid and tea-light candle in front of her and sipping on sake, she began to wonder what on earth had possessed her to show up tonight.

It was true she'd always been a sucker for the confident approach. Austin Jamet's assurance that she would meet him for dinner was almost a dare. A thrown-down gauntlet that Macy simply had to pick up. But it wasn't as if this were a date. She was with James now, well and truly spoken for. And Jamet was her father's attorney, which made him something close to an enemy, at least on paper.

Macy didn't like the idea that perhaps it was this that had prompted her to slip on a simple, grey Calvin Klein cocktail dress and Jonathan Kelsey heels and impulsively tap the Uber X app on her phone. That there might be a part of her that was curious about this message, whatever it was, that Per Johanssen was so desperate to give her. Something so important that an attorney would show up at her home, uninvited, on a Saturday, to try to deliver.

She was curious about Austin Jamet, too. What sort of a lawyer gave up his weekends to do his client's bidding, and break every known professional boundary in the process? Didn't Austin have a wife? A family? What would he have been doing tonight if he weren't having dinner with her?

The questions were still rolling through Macy's brain like

tumbleweed when she saw him, weaving through the tables towards her with the same smile he'd had at her house this afternoon. He was even better-looking this evening in a pale blue linen shirt and khakis, like a preppy Jamie Foxx. Macy noticed that quite a few women stopped or acknowledged him as he passed. All the young, beautiful ones, basically. The ones with tiny shorts and sheets of waist-length blonde hair and long tanned legs like perfect sticks of caramel.

Not married, thought Macy, *but he definitely has a life of his own.*

'You came!'

He seemed genuinely delighted to see her.

'I have no idea why,' said Macy.

'Doesn't matter why,' said Austin. 'You're here. Let's order. We have a lot to talk about.'

Macy felt a twinge of disappointment at his business-like tone, followed by annoyance at herself for feeling it. This wasn't a date, for heaven's sake.

Macy ordered the black cod and seaweed salad, and Austin got them a huge plate of assorted sushi that looked incredible, like a platter of glistening jewels. The food arrived quickly but Macy found she was too nervous to eat. Austin got straight to business.

'Your father is dying.'

Macy shrugged. To her, Per Johanssen had died a long time ago.

'He has terminal lung cancer and is now in the very final stages,' Austin went on. 'He wants to see you.'

'Wants to see my money, more like,' Macy scoffed. 'What's he after? Better medical care? Round-the-clock nursing? Some expensive new drug?'

Austin frowned, apparently taken aback by her callousness.
'There arc no drugs,' he said quietly. 'And Per doesn't
need money.'

'What then?' Macy heard herself getting angrier.
'Absolution? I'm sorry, but he can't have that either. Was
that the important message? That he's dying?'

'No.' The lawyer speared a California roll with a chopstick
and demolished it in a single bite.

'What then?'

Austin wished he could tell her. He liked Macy enormously. Had liked her from the second he saw her, and not
just because she was ridiculously sexy. She reminded him
of her father, a man whom Austin Jamet admired greatly
and had come almost to love. It was true that Per Johanssen
was a client, but he was also more than that – and *so* much
more than his daughter gave him credit for.

Like most children of divorce, Macy had been raised
exclusively on one side of the story. Her mother's. But
heartbreak, alcoholism and depression could all play havoc
with the truth. There was another side to Macy's family
history, and it was Per's place to tell it to her. If she gave
him the chance, before their time ran out.

'He'll tell you himself, when you see him. This is his
address.'

He pushed a piece of paper across the table. Macy unfolded
it. *St John's Hospice, Santa Monica*. Macy passed it back to
Austin.

'Tell him no.' The anger had dissipated. Macy sounded
sad and a little weary. 'I'm sorry. I know you're trying to
do your best for him. But it's too late for that.'

Sensing correctly that it would be counterproductive to
push her further tonight, Austin ordered more sake and

changed the subject. He wanted to do the best he could for Per. That was why he was here, after all. But he was also very attracted to Macy, and more than a little intrigued. At first they made small talk about LA, and their different perspectives on the city.

'I went to the East Coast for law school,' he told Macy. 'Froze my ass off. When I graduated I moved back here first plane I could catch. You can't beat LA for the weather. Or the women.'

Macy raised a sceptical eyebrow 'I don't believe for a moment that you're that shallow, Mr Jamet.'

'You don't?' Austin grinned.

'There must be more to LA than that. More that pulled you back here.'

Austin looked suddenly serious. 'Not really. I'm not that close to my family. We grew up in Venice, but it was totally different back then. No million-dollar beach shacks or artists' studios or Abbot Kinney restaurants charging eighty bucks for a steak.'

'What was it like, then?' Macy sipped her wine.

'Tenth grade. Two kids in my algebra class got an F on a test. Went home, got beaten up by their dads. Real bad.'

Macy shrugged. 'That happens.'

'Uh-huh. Next morning they walked into class and blew the math teacher's head off.'

Macy gasped.

Austin speared another roll and flashed her a naughty smile. 'We all got As in algebra after that.'

After forty minutes, Macy felt as if she'd asked him a thousand questions and he'd answered all of them. And yet by the end she still knew almost nothing really important about him.

'Your turn.'

Austin pushed the molten chocolate cake towards her, but Macy declined.

'Tell me about Macy Johanssen.'

'You look like a man who does your research,' Macy teased. 'Didn't you read my file?'

'Oh, I know your résumé,' said Austin, proceeding to rattle off Macy's date of birth, education and career highlights. It was more than a little unnerving. 'But I don't know *you*.'

'I'm an open book,' Macy lied. 'Ask away.'

'OK. Why'd you move to England? Were you running away from something here in LA?'

'Not at all,' Macy stiffened. 'I thought *Valley Farm* would be a good career move. And it was.'

'A good personal move too, by all accounts,' said Austin. 'I understand you're getting married?'

'That's right.' Macy reached her arm across the table, showing him the ring. Austin took her hand, resting her slender fingers on his flat, warm palm, like a delicate flower resting on a lily pad.

'That's quite a rock.'

Macy smiled.

'He's English?'

'Very.'

'And you like living over there?'

'I love it,' said Macy. 'The Swell Valley, where we shoot *Valley Farm*, is like something out of a fairy tale. Seriously, I don't think Hans Christian Andersen could have dreamed this place up.'

'But?'

Macy frowned at him. 'What do you mean "but"? There are no buts.'

Austin frowned back at her. 'Come, come now. If we're going to be friends, you're going to need to be straight with me. You're in town to sell the show in the US, correct?'

Macy nodded.

'So you want to move back here?'

'For a while maybe,' Macy said defensively. 'I want to spend time in both places.'

'With your very English husband-to-be?'

'That's right. What's wrong with that?' Macy bristled a little. More fool her for getting into a Q&A with a lawyer. Austin was making her feel as if she were on trial.

'Nothing,' he said breezily. 'I heard you Skyping back at the house. He sounded like a nice guy.'

'You were eavesdropping?'

'Actually, you were projecting,' Austin said gently. 'It was almost like you wanted me to hear how affectionate you guys were. How happy.'

Macy blushed. Gosh, he was observant. 'Don't be silly.'

An awkward silence fell. Austin pulled a smokeless cigarette out of a box in his pocket and offered one to Macy.

'Do you vape?'

She shook her head and laughed. 'I used to. I gave up when I moved to England. My God, I haven't seen one of those in a while.'

She remembered how horrified Eddie Wellesley had been the night she first met him, when she'd offered him a smokeless cigarette after they slept together. *Jesus, did I really sleep with Eddie?* What a long time ago that seemed now.

Austin inhaled deeply, a cloud of steam snaking softly from between his lips.

'You're not sure about him, are you?'

THE SHOW

It took Macy a moment to realise he was talking about James.

'What? Of course I'm sure,' she said. Her stomach gave an unpleasant lurch, as if someone had opened a trap door beneath her feet and she'd just plunged through it.

'Is there someone else?'

'No!'

'Someone at work?'

Macy pushed her plate away and folded her arms. This game had stopped being fun. Who was this man, to ask her such personal questions, and make such wild assumptions about her life?

Realizing he'd gone too far, Austin apologized. 'Sorry. I didn't mean to offend you. I guess it's force of habit, the probing questions. Kind of an occupational hazard.'

They managed to finish the evening without incident, but the earlier ease between them had gone. Macy felt upset, as if she'd been tricked into revealing more of herself than she meant to. At the same time, it bothered her that this man, this complete stranger, should make the same observation that Eddie Wellesley and Santiago and others had made to her. Austin's words hung in her head now like an accusation:

'You're not sure, are you? . . . Is there somebody else? . . . Somebody at work?'

She was pleased when the bill came and it was time to leave. Even more pleased when her phone informed her that her Uber driver was only one minute away. Outside, the cool night air blowing off the Pacific ruffled Macy's hair and soothed her spirits. Really, what did it matter what Per Johanssen's handsome lawyer thought about her?

'This is me,' said Austin, as the valet brought round a

gleaming, midnight-blue Aston Martin. 'May I offer you some advice, Macy? In case I don't see you again?'

'It's a free country,' said Macy.

'Go and see your father, before it's too late.' He slipped into his car, stretching out his long legs in front of him with the same, easy grace with which he seemed to do everything. 'And don't get married unless you're absolutely sure.'

Macy opened her mouth to say, 'I am sure.' But while the words were still forming, Austin drove away.

All the way back to Laurel Canyon, Macy felt her mood worsen and the tension in her body increase. What a horrible evening! What a mistake to have gone, when she could have been at home doing something useful, like preparing for her pitch meetings. On top of it all, Laura was arriving tomorrow. This would be the first time the two women had been alone together without Eddie or Gabe there as a buffer. Just the thought of Laura's hostile, critical presence at these important meetings was enough to drain what was left of Macy's confidence like a lanced boil.

In a few short hours, all the joy she'd felt at being back in her home city had gone, to be replaced by something very close to dread.

Thanks for nothing, Austin Jamet.

CHAPTER NINETEEN

Amazingly, Macy slept well. Waking at six, she went for a run through the canyon, had another incredible shower and a light breakfast and by eight o'clock was at her desk, working on the pitch. For once, the words and ideas seemed to flow out of her. This was easy! She knew what she loved about *Valley Farm*. And she knew what viewers loved about it. All she had to do was stand up in front of the network execs and tell them exactly that. How hard could it be?

By the time she stopped typing at two o'clock, she was so awash with confidence and a sense of achievement that she decided to take the bull by the horns and go and meet Laura's flight herself. That way she would look eager and co-operative and she could head off any negativity from the start. It would also give her a chance to brief Laura on the way to Shutters on the Beach, the fancy hotel in Santa Monica that Eddie had booked her into, and generally love-bomb her producer to such a degree she'd have no chance to find fault with anything.

We're going to sell this show, Macy told herself, over and over, listening to Kiss FM as she tore down the 405 towards LAX. *We're going to sell this show and make a fortune, and I'm going to be famous again. This time next year, everyone in America's going to recognize my face, just like they do in England.*

It was only as she was pulling into the parking structure at Tom Bradley International Terminal that she realized she'd forgotten the Skype call with James that they'd scheduled for this afternoon. Oh, well. He would understand. She'd call him later, once Laura was settled at her hotel, and explain.

When she got into the arrivals hall, the screens told her that the Heathrow flight had already landed. The first-class passengers were already beginning to drift through the double doors. *Perfect timing.* Nipping into the Ladies room, Macy went to the bathroom and tidied her hair with her fingers. She hadn't had time to put on any make-up, rushing on an impulse from her desk to her car, and was still in the casual striped maxidress and flip-flops that she'd pulled on after her shower. Not that Laura would care.

She contemplated buying a bunch of flowers, then decided that was overkill. Grabbing a bottle of water from the kiosk instead, she found a spot right in front of the barriers and waited. Seconds later, the double doors swung open. For the second time in twenty-four hours, Macy felt the invisible trap door give way beneath her. For there, sauntering into the arrivals hall with a small suitcase, looking tired but as gorgeous as ever in an old pair of jeans and a white linen shirt, was Gabe.

The moment he saw Macy's face, he burst into a grin.

'What are you doing here?'

'I could ask you the same thing,' said Macy. Suddenly horribly conscious of her make-up-free appearance and shapeless dress, she didn't return his smile. 'Where's Laura?'

Gabe's face darkened. 'She couldn't make it. We had a row, actually. A big one. She refused to fly out so I decided to come instead.'

'Oh!' Macy was ashamed at how cheered she was by this news.

The truth was she really needed *Valley Farm*'s creator at these network pitches, or at least one of the show's producers. Besides being another warm body in the room, Gabe didn't add much value to the meetings, especially as he would not be a part of any US-based presenting team. Macy ought to feel furious with Laura for bailing without even letting her know. But anger was the one emotion she could not seem to find, looking at Gabe's kind, funny, familiar face.

'Are you taking me to my hotel then?' he asked Macy.

'That was the plan,' she said, looking down so he wouldn't see the shadows under her eyes.

'Great,' said Gabe. 'You can fill me in on who we're meeting on the way. And I'll fill you in on Laura.'

By the time they pulled up outside Shutters' famous coral tree, Macy's buoyant mood of this morning had completely deserted her. First, her agent, Paul Meyer, had called just as they were pulling out of the airport to tell her that not only had NBC cancelled their Tuesday meeting but that ABC had pulled out of the running again.

'Someone in their commissioning department belatedly read a British newspaper,' Paul told Macy ruefully. 'I'm sorry, Macy, but you know the score. These guys are so risk averse, they're all looking for a reason to say no. Lady Wellesley just handed them a whole bunch.'

'But that's ridiculous! She has nothing to do with the show! Even Eddie's only an EP, for Christ's sake.'

TILLY BAGSHAWE

'You're preaching to the converted,' Paul told her. 'Don't panic. Showtime and HBO and Netflix are all still in the mix. And Fox. You and Laura just need to charm the pants off them.'

'Yeah,' said Macy. 'About Laura. Slight change of plan.'

Paul had been upbeat, but Macy knew he was worried and that most of his confidence was due to the fact that he knew he was on speakerphone with Gabe. Once he'd rung off and Gabe told her what had actually happened with Laura, Macy found herself in the rare position of being on his wife's side. Apparently, after the play at the village hall, Gabe had been in the bathroom downing Alka-Seltzer when his phone had buzzed downstairs. Laura had picked it up and found herself looking at a picture of a very young girl in her underwear, signed off with xs and os.

'She didn't even give me a chance to explain!' Gabe protested.

'Explain what?' said Macy. 'You're sexting with another woman. Case closed.'

'First of all "sexting" is not a word.'

'Of course it's a *word*,' laughed Macy.

'Not a real one. And, anyway, I wasn't doing anything with other women. This stupid trollop sent a picture to *me*.'

'How did she have your number?' Macy asked the obvious question.

'Well, I . . . I don't know.'

'You don't know?'

'I don't remember exactly. I was quite drunk. I mean, I meet girls all the time. You know what it's like when you're on TV. But I've never done anything and I never would.'

'Hmmm.' Macy sounded about as convinced as Laura had. 'It's still disrespectful, though, isn't it?'

'Not you too . . .' muttered Gabe.

It emerged that in the tempestuous aftermath of this discovery, Laura had thrown the remainder of her toys completely out of the pram, accused Gabe of allowing fame to go to his head – and his dick – and of *Valley Farm* being 'toxic' to their marriage, and announced she was pulling the plug on the whole thing. Not only would she not consent to sell the show abroad, but she was having serious second thoughts about a second UK series. And Gabe could consider himself fired as a presenter.

Macy went white. 'Can she do that?'

'No,' Gabe said robustly. 'I have a share in the show. So does Eddie, and Channel 5, and you.'

'I have, like, half a per cent,' Macy reminded him.

'The point is, Laura has no right to pull the rug out from under all of us, just because she's irrationally jealous and insecure in our marriage,' Gabe fumed. 'I told her that if she wouldn't take these meetings with you then I would. So here I am.'

Macy was too stunned to say anything. This was a disaster. With Eddie halfway out of the door and Laura determined to punish her errant husband, pitching *Valley Farm* would be like trying to run a marathon with both legs tied together. At this point it was far from clear whether Macy and Gabe actually had anything left to sell.

Gabe, however, seemed determined to throw a positive light on everything.

'Thanks so much for the lift,' he said, kissing Macy on the cheek. 'It'll all be all right, you'll see. Why don't I get a few hours' kip and then we can meet for supper, make a plan of attack. Eight o'clock all right?'

For the second time in two days, Macy found herself

accepting a dinner date from a handsome man other than her fiancé, much against her better judgement.

They went to the Blue Plate Oysterette on Ocean Avenue. Feeling more confident in subtle but flawless make-up, Hudson jeans that hugged her figure in all the right places and a red silk shirt (sexy but not trying too hard), Macy was determined to keep things businesslike. She was not about to make the same mistake she had with Austin Jamet last night and let her guard down.

Her resolve wavered for a moment when Gabe walked in looking rested and impossibly handsome in a Thomas Pink shirt and dark jeans, his hair still wet from the shower. But she quickly regained her composure, and even managed to stick to sparkling water while she talked Gabe through her plan for tomorrow's meeting with Fox.

Gabe ordered a light beer with his clam steamers and listened attentively. It was vital for these meetings to go well, so he could justify his impulsive decision to jump on a plane. For all his outward bluster, he knew he'd fucked up by flying out here after the row with Laura. The boring, eleven-hour flight had given him plenty of time for reflection. Deep down he knew perfectly well that giving out his number to young women was not cool. That the only appropriate reaction after Laura saw that picture should have been a grovelling and abject apology. But some stupid male impulse had taken over – part pride, and part fear; some idea that if he admitted he was wrong Laura would leave him – and had made him lash out. And then, when Laura had threatened to pull the plug on *Valley Farm*, he'd panicked. Little by little, without him even really noticing it, Gabe had allowed his self-worth to get caught up with the show.

Farming had always been his life, his identity. But that had changed. The truth was, Laura was right and he resented her for that. Now that he'd had a taste of fame, albeit a modest one, he didn't want to let it go. He enjoyed the attention, and he was tired of feeling guilty about it.

After the meal, Macy walked him back to his hotel. It was only a few blocks and it was a beautiful evening, warm, with a soft breeze ruffling the tops of the palm trees like an affectionate mother patting her child's head.

'Do you think Eddie will stay with the show?' Macy asked him. Proud of herself for sticking to business thus far, she wasn't about to blow the evening at the last minute. She loved James, and anybody who thought differently was just plain wrong.

'I don't know,' said Gabe. 'I hope he will. At the moment he says nothing's changed, but this stuff with David Carlyle's book must be hell for him. You'd think after Annabel's overdose Carlyle would have the decency to stop the serialization in the *Echo* at the very least. But he's still printing new stories every week. Trying to poison them to death, drip by drip.'

'But if Laura pulls out . . .?'

'She won't,' said Gabe. '*Valley Farm* is her baby. She loves it more than any of us, and she wants it to succeed.'

'She didn't come out here,' said Macy. 'That's a pretty strong statement.'

'She was angry,' said Gabe. 'Which was my fault.' He ran a hand through his hair in frustration. 'God, I can be such a dick sometimes. I don't know why I do it. The fact is, Laura's right. I *do* like being recognized. I *do* like the attention I get from being on the show. And I'm proud of it, you know? I suppose you could say I'm ambitious.'

They had reached Shutters now, and came to a stop

beneath the white wooden sign at the front of the hotel, where the road met the sand.

'There's nothing wrong with ambition, you know,' Macy told him. Even in heels, she only came up to Gabe's chest, so she had to tilt her neck back to look at him. Standing just inches apart, staring up into his beautiful, sad eyes, it was a physical effort not reach out and touch his face. 'You shouldn't be so hard on yourself.'

'Thanks,' said Gabe. Without thinking, he pushed aside a stray lock of dark hair blowing across Macy's face. It was a momentary gesture, but Macy's entire body tensed. There could be no mistaking the violent sexual energy between them in that instant, like a lightning storm.

'Sorry,' Gabe mumbled, stepping back.

'No,' Macy said awkwardly, her voice hoarse. 'It's fine.'

'I'll see you tomorrow, then,' said Gabe, turning away from her and walking towards the hotel so fast he almost broke into a jog. 'Get some sleep,' he called over his shoulder with forced cheeriness.

'You too!' said Macy.

Ten minutes later, in the safety of his suite, Gabe sank down on the foot of his bed and put his head in his hands.

What's wrong with me? he thought miserably. *What the fuck is wrong with me?*

He longed to call Laura. Just to hear her voice and to tell her he was sorry. He *was* sorry, for more things than he could even put into words. But it was quarter to five in the morning in England right now. Under the circumstances, he probably wouldn't get a very warm reception if he woke her and the kids up before sunrise. *I'll call in the morning, as soon as I wake up.*

* * *

Lying in her bed in Laurel Canyon, Macy stared at her bedroom ceiling and waited for the pain to go away.

It didn't.

Eventually she fell asleep anyway.

Fox Studios sits on a fifty-acre lot off West Pico Boulevard. Like the other big studio lots, it is a world unto itself, complete with sound stages, corporate offices, hospitality buildings, production suites and stores selling every conceivable item of 20th Century Fox-branded merchandise. Gabe's eyes were on stalks from the moment Macy parked the car. You needed a map to get from the parking structure to the executive offices, and the route was both long and distracting. Gabe followed Macy past a teen band making a music video, involving what looked like a pack of wolves running down a hill, being chased by three kids whose body weight must have been at least fifty per cent hair gel.

'Do you get tame wolves?' Gabe asked Macy, a faint edge of nerves to his voice as they walked past.

'This is Hollywood,' said Macy. 'You get anything you want if the studio's paying.'

Gabe was soon distracted by a half-built house in which a bunch of actors he recognized were shooting an episode of a famous soap opera. After that it was the backstage doors for *American Idol*, where the next crop of hopefuls were lining up for the first round of televised auditions.

'Is that Ryan Seacrest?' Gabe whispered to Macy, as a slim, tanned man in a sports jacket slipped into the building, glued to his cell phone.

'Don't know, don't care,' said Macy, not looking up. 'Focus, OK? We're here.'

Tim O'Donnell, the head of Scripted Reality for the Fox

Television network, occupied a suite of palatial offices on the sixth floor of the tallest building on the lot. The *Valley Farm* format would be a stretch for Fox. Their bread and butter were competitive, Simon Cowell-style shows. Macy and Paul Meyer had both been frankly astonished that Fox had agreed to a meeting at all, let alone that they'd wheeled in a big gun like O'Donnell.

After signing in downstairs, in a glass-walled lobby so awash with sunlight it was impossible to walk through it and not feel uplifted, Macy and Gabe took their ugly, laminated name tags and stepped into a clear glass elevator that whisked them to the sixth-floor reception.

Upstairs everything was darker and more businesslike. A stunning Asian girl with dead eyes and a curtain of dark hair like a silk veil emerged from behind her poky desk to offer them 'coffee, water or green tea', with a smile so false it made Gabe's eyes water.

'She's a bit scary,' he whispered to Macy. 'Talk about shock and awe. Her teeth are so white they must glow in the dark.'

'Ask O'Donnell,' Macy whispered back. 'I'm sure he knows what they look like in the dark.'

Gabe laughed loudly, earning himself a withering look from the Asian girl and a panicked one from Macy.

'Keep your voice down,' she hissed.

'Sorry,' Gabe hissed back.

It was weird to think that until relatively recently he'd been an unknown farmer in Sussex, and now here he was, taking Hollywood meetings with network executives as if it were the most natural thing in the world. His life had changed so much. And yet fundamentally, inside, Gabe felt the same.

320

Laura doesn't think so, he reflected sadly. *She thinks I've changed, big time.*

He must try not to think about his problems with Laura. Not here. One thing at a time.

The Asian girl was still giving him evils.

'She looks like she wants to put bamboo shoots under my fingernails,' Gabe whispered, trying to make Macy laugh, or at least crack a smile. Aware that some invisible line had been crossed last night, he was trying to make things normal between them again by reverting to their usual banter. Gabe badly needed things to be back to normal with someone. He'd called Laura four times this morning and left messages, but she was obviously still too angry to take his calls.

'I'll put bamboo shoots under your fingernails if you don't zip it,' Macy whispered back, only half joking. 'This meeting is crucial for us. Please, focus.'

'I *am* focused,' protested Gabe. 'I haven't even checked the cricket score and England are—'

Behind the reception desk, a door opened and a small, bald, unprepossessing-looking man in a terrible suit stepped forward.

'*Valley Farm*, right? From England?' he gestured vaguely towards Macy. 'Tim O'Donnell. C'mon in.'

The meeting was short.

Macy gave her prepared spiel and Gabe gave his. They were both charming, informed and poised in their delivery. Gabe, in particular, radiated pride in the show and did a good job of glossing over Eddie and Laura's absence. *He's a natural salesman*, thought Macy, as her nerves fell away.

Tim O'Donnell listened, nodded and smiled. At the end

321

he asked a couple of questions and gave the show some glowing compliments.

'And your agent is . . .?'

Macy reminded him. O'Donnell dutifully wrote Paul Meyer's name down.

'Great. Well, thank you both so much. We'll be in touch.'

Gabe smiled broadly at White Teeth as they got into the elevator. Hitting the star button for the lobby, he turned to Macy, glowing with pride, like a delighted puppy presenting his mistress with a swiftly retrieved ball.

'That was amazing! He loved us,' he said brightly. 'When do you think we'll hear back?'

'Never,' Macy said bluntly. 'He's not interested.'

'But . . . all those things he said about how original the concept was, and how TV here needs more of this kind of show?'

'They always say that shit,' said Macy. 'If a show's going to sell, it sells in the room.'

Gabe looked so crestfallen that Macy almost forgot her own disappointment. 'Hey, we tried. We still have HBO and Showtime and Shine America. Think of it as practice.'

Think of it as practice.

Back at home that afternoon after dropping Gabe at his hotel, Macy tried to take her own advice.

It was one meeting. Their first meeting. She couldn't expect to hit a home run the first time she stepped up to the plate. She might hope to, maybe, but not expect.

She Skyped James, hoping that talking with him might cheer her up or at least put things into perspective. But his team had just been badly beaten, and Macy spent most of the call trying to lift *his* spirits, with mixed success.

'I'm so tired of travelling,' he told her, miserably. 'I know it's an awful thing to say when I'm doing my dream job. But all I want is to go home and stay there. I miss everything. Marmite, *News at Ten*, rain, the gossip in the Preedys' shop.'

'And me, I hope,' said Macy.

'Of course you. I'm so horny I could sleep with the chambermaid.'

'Please don't!' said Macy.

'I'll do my best, but no promises,' James teased. 'I love you.'

'I love you too.'

Macy closed her laptop, feeling no better. She ought to go over her pitch for tomorrow's meetings, tweaking the little things where she felt she'd lost O'Donnell's attention at Fox today, or failed to impress as much as she might have. But she didn't have the energy. Still, she had to do something or she'd go mad. Wandering into the kitchen, she began pulling glasses out of the cupboard and checking them for smears, cleaning and polishing any less-than-perfect specimens until they shone like diamonds.

She was so engrossed in the task that at first she didn't notice the phone ringing. When she finally heard it, she walked into the hall and picked up with a heavy sigh. Whoever it was, she didn't want to talk to them. Not today.

'Macy, it's me.'

Paul Meyer's voice positively vibrated with excitement.

'I just got a call from Tim O'Donnell.'

'You did *not*.'

'He loved it. Loved *you* in particular. They're gonna make an offer.'

Macy let out a little squeal of delight. She didn't think

she'd been more surprised since the day she heard that George Clooney had decided to get married.

'Did he talk terms at all?'

Paul made a noncommittal, agent-y sort of noise. 'Kind of. There are a few kinks to work out, like there always are.'

'Kinks?'

'He wants Gabe Baxter as part of the US presenting team.'

Macy exhaled heavily. She knew that would never happen. Ambitious or not, trying to take Gabe out of Wraggsbottom Farm would be like trying to uproot an oak tree. Impossible. Even if, by some miracle, you succeeded, the tree would never survive.

'Don't sweat it,' Paul Meyer said smoothly. 'These are all details. We'll get around it. The point is, Fox want the format. You landed the big fish, baby.'

The moment Macy put the phone down, there was a hammering on her front door.

Still in a daze, she opened it to find a triumphant Gabe hopping up and down with excitement. One look told her he'd already heard the news.

'How did you know?' she asked him.

'White Teeth rang my hotel,' he beamed. 'I think she likes me!'

'I'm still in shock,' said Macy. 'This never happens. Like, never.'

'Let's celebrate!' said Gabe. Macy walked towards her drinks cabinet, but Gabe put a hand on her arm. 'Uh-uh. I mean, really celebrate. Let's go out. Where can I get the best margarita in LA and see shit-loads of celebrities?'

Macy grinned. 'That would be the Chateau.'

* * *

To her surprise, Laura had had a good day today.

The first twenty-four hours after she found that terrible picture on Gabe's phone had been horrific. The pain she felt, looking at that vile girl, was so visceral, so intense, it had frightened her. Was it normal that Gabe still had the power to shred her heart into a million pieces, and shatter her happiness like a carelessly dropped Christmas-tree ornament? In her late thirties, with a glittering career and two children, wasn't she supposed to be more mature than that, more emotionally independent, more protected?

Apparently not. When Gabe had reacted not with remorse but with petulance, and had even had the nerve to get on a plane to Los Angeles and try to pitch *Valley Farm* – *her show* – without her, Laura had wrapped her anger around her like a shield and held on to it for dear life.

That was it. That was *it*. No more. She would wind up the show, cut Gabe off from the celebrity he'd started to crave like some pathetic, attention-hungry junkie, and reclaim her life. Their lives. Eddie Wellesley was retreating into his family cocoon after a crisis. Why shouldn't she?

I started this train and I can stop it, Laura told herself, with more than a trace of desperation. *I have control here.*

In those first awful days she'd wanted to punish Gabe, to hurt him, just like he'd hurt her. She refused to answer his calls from LA. But as the week rolled on, in the silence and emptiness of their bedroom, she began to mellow. Gabe's voicemails were becoming more and more contrite. And the distance from him was doing her good. Gabe had been an idiot, but she didn't believe he'd actually cheated on her. If, by some miracle, he and Macy did get a bite in LA from one of the networks, she would probably consider it. But only on *her* terms. She began to feel more cheerful. She was still furious with Gabe. But she also knew how much she loved him and how much, despite everything, he loved her. Perhaps, in the end, their relationship would come through this stronger?

Sprawled out on the sofa in the living room, a gin and tonic in one hand and a large bar of Cadbury's Fruit & Nut in the other, Laura weighed up her options. Go to bed – it was already nearly midnight and Luca and Hugh were bound to be awake at the crack of dawn tomorrow – or watch another episode of *Borgen*.

Borgen won easily. There weren't many situations in life, in Laura's opinion, that couldn't be improved with a combination of gin, chocolate, and Kasper Juul pouting sexily from the screen. Katrine was handling him all wrong. Laura would have done a much better job at keeping him in check.

When her phone rang, and Gabe's US number popped up on the screen, she decided the time had come to answer it. He wasn't forgiven, but some small sign of a thaw in relations was probably called for.

'Hello?'

'Laura?'

Gabe's voice sounded distant and almost drowned out by a cacophony of background noise: laughter, music, shouting. A party? But surely it was only tea-time in LA?

'Laura? Are you there?'

'Yes, I'm here.' She kept her tone neutral. 'Where are you? I can hardly hear you.'

'I'm at the Chateau Marmont. We're shelebrating!' Gabe slurred.

'Who's we?'

'Me and Macy and . . . some people.' In the background,

Laura could clearly hear female laughter, followed by what sounded like a splash.

She stiffened. 'Are you drunk?'

Gabe either ignored the question or couldn't hear it through the din. 'Fox want the show,' he told her excitedly. 'We've sold it! At least, I think we have. Isn't that great?'

Before Laura could answer, Macy grabbed the phone. She was clearly also drunk. This was quite some party Laura was missing.

'Hi, boss! Did he tell you? Tim O'Donnell at Fox *loved* us.'

Laura felt her anger start to return. So much for Gabe's remorse. He was obviously having the time of his life out there.

'I was totally stressing it before we went in, but O'Donnell didn't ask one question about Eddie or the scandal or why you weren't there. Thank God Gabe came out, he was *amazing*,' Macy gushed. 'You'd have been so proud of him.'

Would I, indeed? Laura thought furiously.

Gabe came back on the line. 'I mish you.'

'Really?' Laura said archly. 'Well, I suggest you go home and sober up then. And you can tell Macy and the rest of your cheerleading squad that *Valley Farm* isn't sold until I say it is. Now, if you'll excuse me, it's late. I'm going to bed.'

She hung up.

Tears of anger and frustration welled in her eyes.

How dare he call her, drunk and triumphant and surrounded by women, after what he'd just done? What a fool she'd been, forgiving him so easily, convincing herself that things might actually be better. She should never have taken his call.

Turning off Kasper Juul, she downed the last of her drink and went miserably to bed.

*   *   *

Gabe stood by the pool, phone in hand, looking shell shocked.

'What happened?' asked Macy, oblivious. 'D'you get cut off?'

'I don't know,' said Gabe. 'Maybe.'

But he knew that wasn't what had happened. Laura had hung up on him. She wasn't pleased that he and Macy had done so well today. She didn't forgive him. She was still angry. She would always be angry.

He headed back up to the bar and began to drink in earnest.

At some point in the evening, the party moved to Shutters. Some of the starlets who Macy and Gabe were hanging out with learned that Gabe had a suite there, and the rumour went around that a Fox expense account was paying for everything.

Gabe had no idea how he got back to Santa Monica. He thought he remembered Macy opening a car door for him. There were lights, and a warm seat and he slept for a while. He might have eaten a hot dog. In any event, at some point he found himself sitting at a bar on the sand, being told by the bartender that it was time to close up. Looking up, he was surprised to see stars and a bright half-moon in the sky. It was late, and cold. The hangers-on from the Chateau had all gone. Macy was still there, passed out on a sun lounger, an untouched cocktail on the table beside her.

'Your check, sir.'

Gabe unfolded the white slip of paper. His eyes were swimming, but he was pretty sure he saw a four-figure number in the 'total' column. He was also pretty sure the number started with a seven.

'Fuuuuck.' He groaned out loud.

'What?' Macy woke up suddenly.

'We just drank seven thousand dollars worth.' Gabe closed his eyes. 'I feel sick.'

Getting unsteadily to her feet, Macy came over and put an arm around his shoulders.

'Who cares? You sold the show, remember? You're rich.'

'I'm not rich,' said Gabe.

'Well. You will be.' Macy smiled. She had a very pretty smile, Gabe thought.

'Laura's going to go spare.' He looked at Macy forlornly. 'We didn't get cut off before. She hung up on me. She's so fucking angry.'

'She's always angry,' said Macy. Her hand had moved from Gabe's shoulder to his neck. He closed his eyes as her cool, slender fingers stroked his bare skin. It felt wonderful. 'You deserve so much more, you know.'

Gabe turned to face her. Both Macy's arms were around his neck now. Instinctively, he slipped his own arms around her waist. Staring down at her face, still smiling that lovely smile, he felt poleaxed with desire. It wasn't just that she was very beautiful, or that he was very drunk, although both of those things were true. It was the look in her eyes: adoring, desirous, her pupils dilating wildly in the darkness like something out of a Japanese Manga cartoon. It was the way her back arched slightly when he held her. The way her breath quickened. *She wants me.* Reflected in Macy's eyes, Gabe was everything he wanted to be.

He bent down to kiss her and she exploded into his arms like a lit firework.

'Take me to bed,' she whispered in his ear. Her hands

were inside his shirt now, clawing at his back, pulling at him with wild desperation. 'Please.'

Gabe nodded, so turned on he could barely breathe.

It was already done.

CHAPTER TWENTY

Macy opened her eyes dreamily. A sense of deep peace and wellbeing flowed through her. For a moment she wasn't sure where she was. But then she saw Gabe lying next to her, sprawled out on the pillow, and the sunlight chinking through the white wooden shutters of the hotel bedroom, and it all came back to her in a rush.

Last night had been incredible. Not just sexually, although that was pretty spectacular. But the way Gabe had looked at her, the tenderness between them . . . it was more than she'd dared to hope for, even in her wildest fantasies.

He loves me, she told herself, savouring this new reality like honey on her tongue as she gently traced a finger down his back. Deep down she'd always known that she loved him. But last night was the first time he'd shown her that the feeling was mutual. As Gabe started to stir, she allowed her mind to wander, picturing a future for the two of them. It would be in England, of course. Even in fantasy, Macy couldn't paint Gabe into an LA life. But that was OK. With James she'd hankered after home and her own career because, lovely as he was, James wasn't 'the one'. But, with the right man – with Gabe – Macy realized she could live anywhere. Just imagining herself in the kitchen at Wraggsbottom Farm, married to Gabe, making breakfast for the two of them, flooded her with a contentment she didn't think she'd ever felt before. Somewhere in the background of the fantasy, Laura and the children and James swirled uncomfortably, but a wave of happiness swept them aside like scraps of driftwood on a dazzling blue sea.

Gabe groaned. Still half asleep, he reached out and idly stroked Macy's belly. Then suddenly he sat up, as if an alarm clock only he could hear had just gone off in his head.

'Shit!' Running his hands through his hair he looked around him wildly.

Macy touched his shoulder gently, her face alight with love. 'It's OK,' she smiled. 'Paul Meyer cancelled the other meetings, remember? You can go back to sleep.'

Gabe turned and looked at her, and in an instant all Macy's fantasies shattered, the shards piercing her heart like a million tiny daggers of glass.

'Oh God.' He wasn't crying, but his whole face was twisted into a mask of utter, unmistakable anguish. 'Shit. Shit, shit, *shit*.' Jumping out of the bed as if it were on fire, he began frantically pulling on his clothes like a man deranged.

'It's OK,' Macy said again, automatically.

Gabe stared at her bleakly. 'It's not OK. We should never . . . I should never . . . FUCK!' He shouted the word so loudly, the walls shook. Macy burst into tears.

'Oh God, I'm sorry.' Dressed now, he sat down on her side of the bed. 'It's not you,' he said contritely. 'You're lovely. This is my fault. There's something wrong with me.'

'No there isn't,' said Macy.

Gabe shook his head bitterly. 'There is. FUCK! I am such a fucking dickhead.'

'Why? For wanting some support? Some affection? Some love?' Macy could hear the desperation in her own voice but she couldn't stop the words from coming out. 'Laura takes you for granted! She doesn't love you. Not the way I do.'

'Don't say that,' Gabe pleaded.

'It's the truth. I love you so much, Gabe.'

Gabe stood up again and started pacing like a trapped animal. The guilt was unbearable. Combined with his hangover he felt like he'd just swallowed a pint of battery acid.

'I'm sorry, Macy. I am. I think you're incredible. But I love Laura.'

Macy looked down at her hands, suddenly fascinated by the web of lines on her palms. How was it possible to go from being so perfectly happy to so utterly crushed in just moments, she wondered, as if all this were happening to someone else, a character in a play. She knew she ought to get up and get dressed, to get out of Gabe's hotel room, to end this awful, gut-wrenching scene, to exit stage left. But she couldn't seem to move.

'Laura can never know about this,' said Gabe, an audible tremor of fear in his voice.

Macy nodded.

'Never.'

'I understand.'

Turning away from her, Gabe picked up the phone by the bed. 'Yes, I need Virgin Airlines, please. Ticketing. I have to fly back to London tonight.'

* * *

Five hours later, Gabe stared out of the plane window as they climbed through the clouds. Beneath him, Los Angeles disappeared like a bad dream.

Guilt still squatted in his chest like a malignant tumour. Guilt towards Laura, to Hugh and Luca, to Macy, and to James Craven, whom he didn't know well but who had always struck him as a really decent guy. None of them deserved this. But his panic of this morning had subsided.

Nobody knew what had happened besides him and Macy, and Macy wasn't going to say anything. She wasn't the vengeful type.

With any luck this offer from Fox would firm up. Then Macy could front the US version of *Valley Farm*, marry James, and their lives would naturally drift apart. Laura and Eddie would hire a new co-presenter to work with Gabe on the original UK show, and everything would be fine. Jennifer Lee, the vet, might even want to step up and do it. Ever since the showdown with the vicar she'd been a big hit with viewers. Right now, all Gabe had to do was go home, keep his mouth shut, smooth things over with Laura, and spend the rest of his life being the model husband she deserved.

If Fast Eddie Wellesley could do it, so could he.

Gabe closed his eyes and drifted into a fitful sleep.

By the time Gabe emerged into the arrivals hall at Heathrow, he felt almost human again. Just seeing the grey, rainy weather when they touched down had been reassuring, a return to reality after the madness of the last forty-eight hours. A kind stewardess had brought him two bacon sandwiches and a large mug of strong black coffee before landing, further strengthening his resolve.

You fucked up, he told himself, swinging his bag off the carousel, *but you can fix it.*

Then the electric doors to arrivals swung open like the gates of hell.

Hundreds of flashbulbs exploded in Gabe's face, blinding him.

'Gabe! Do you have any comment about the *Sun*'s pictures?'

'Where's Macy? Can you confirm you're having an affair?'

'Do you love her, Gabe?'

'Have you spoken to your wife?'

The questions shot through the air like bullets. There were cameras and microphones and a human wave of people, pressing around him from all sides, like vultures trying to pull him to pieces. Putting his head down like a bull, Gabe charged through them.

'Will you get a divorce, Gabe?'

Gabe spun round towards the voice so fast he could have got whiplash.

'Absolutely not.'

Another battery of flashbulbs. Through the maelstrom, Gabe suddenly caught sight of a familiar face. Before he knew what was happening, Santiago de la Cruz was at his side, taking his bag and wrapping a protective arm around his shoulder as he steered him towards the lift leading to the parking bays. Gabe didn't think he'd ever been so pleased to see a person in his life.

'Santiago!' The vultures temporarily switched targets.

'Have you spoken to James Craven?'

'Is the engagement off?'

'Fuck off, all of you,' Santiago snarled.

'Gabe! Gabe!'

Santiago bundled Gabe into the lift, blocking the reporters' path with his body until the doors closed behind them.

The sudden silence was deafening. Gabe looked at his friend, still in shock.

'Thanks for picking me up.'

'I came as soon as I saw the paper,' said Santiago. Grimly, he pulled a copy of this morning's *Sun* out from his inside jacket pocket. 'You'd better take a look.'

Gabe shook his head. 'Not now. In the car.'

He knew that, once he opened that newspaper, the next chapter of his life would begin. It was a chapter he desperately, desperately didn't want to read.

The car journey back to Fittlescombe was one of the longest in Santiago's life. Watching Gabe was torturous. As he sat slumped over in the passenger seat, staring at the photographs of himself and Macy kissing passionately at Shutters' beach bar, as if by looking hard enough he could somehow will them away, his remorse hung in the air of the little Volkswagen like a living thing.

And then there were the questions! God, they were awful. *How had Laura taken it? Had he or Penny seen her?*

Santiago told him the truth. But he knew that with each answer he was twisting the knife into a dying man.

Laura had taken it badly.

Yes, Penny had seen her this morning. She'd collapsed in Penny's arms.

'Is she going to leave me?'

The misery in Gabe's voice was just horrendous.

'I don't know, mate,' said Santiago. 'She might.'

There was a long silence. Eventually, Santiago filled it, probing Gabe as tactfully as he could about what had happened.

'So, you and Macy. Has it been, you know . . . going on for a while?'

'No!' Gabe looked appalled. 'Christ, no!'

'Because the papers are suggesting—'

Gabe cut him off. 'There is no "me and Macy".'

Santiago raised an eyebrow.

'It was nothing,' Gabe insisted. 'Just a stupid, stupid mistake. I was very drunk. We both were. Laura and I had been fighting. Macy was just . . . there. I mean, she's a nice girl. I like her, I do. And, you know. She's beautiful. But I love my wife.'

His voice was starting to break. Santiago put a hand on his leg.

'I know you do. It'll be OK.'

Gabe's mind snapped back to Macy, saying the same thing to him less than twenty-four hours ago, lying naked in his bed.

It'll be OK.

But it wouldn't. Nothing would ever be OK again.

A cluster of press had gathered in front of Wraggsbottom Farm's closed gates, huddled together against the bitterly cold February wind. Against Santiago's advice, Gabe got out of the car and spoke to them briefly.

He was not having an affair with Macy Johanssen.

He deeply regretted what had happened in Los Angeles.

He couldn't make any further comment till he'd spoken to his family.

'I really need you guys to leave now,' he said, agreeing to pictures. Once they had their shots, the reporters all wished him luck and respectfully dispersed.

'That was incredible,' said Santiago. 'They'd never do that for me!'

'That's because you keep telling them to fuck off.' Gabe smiled sheepishly for a moment, before the gloom descended again. 'They're only doing their job.'

'Do you want me to come in with you?' asked Santiago. 'Or I could wait out here? Just in case . . .' He left the thought hanging.

'Thanks,' said Gabe. 'But you've done enough. I'll take it from here.'

He waited in the farmyard as Santiago drove away and the gates swung closed behind him. Then he walked slowly up the path to the front door, past Luca's discarded tricycle and the egg-carton wind-chimes that Hugh had made on his first day at primary school, re-taped for the umpteenth time to the beam over the front porch.

All he wanted in that moment was to see his sons. To hear their sweet little voices and press their soft faces to his own and hug them like he would never, ever let them go.

His hand shook as he slipped his key in the door and let himself into the hallway.

'Laura? Boys?'

Inside, the familiar chaos of family life was everywhere. Toys, wellington boots and odd socks littered the floor. This morning's breakfast dishes were still on the kitchen table, and Laura's papers sat piled up messily on her desk, next to the picture of the two of them on their wedding day. But without the usual soundtrack, of shouts and squeals and TV in the background, everything looked wrong.

Gabe ran upstairs, but he already knew no one was home. This wasn't a momentary silence, but a heavy, total absence of sound. It was the silence of abandonment. The silence of loss. Of death.

Get a grip, Gabe told himself. *She's probably out at a friend's house, avoiding the press.* But then he walked into the bedroom and saw the mess of clothes strewn across the bed and floor. In the boys' room, the chest of drawers had been completely emptied, the drawers jutting out at Gabe like shocked, gaping mouths, appalled at what he'd done.

Gabe gripped the wall, nauseous.

They're gone.

Carefully, trying not to run, he went back downstairs to the kitchen, picked up the phone and started calling.

He would find her. He would talk to her. He would make this right.

He had to.

Laura's parents lived in a rather horrible, modern house on the Kent border. It was beyond Laura why anyone would choose such a soulless home, especially in a part of the country so chock-full of charm. Even the name was awful: Holmlea. It sounded like cheese. But Laura's mother liked it because it was 'low maintenance', whatever that meant, and because she and Laura's father could walk to the railway station that took them straight back to London, the city they had just escaped from in order to enjoy a country retirement, in under an hour.

Hugh and Luca weren't keen on their grandparents' place either, although Grandpa's cuckoo clock and the two tortoises in the garden, Gin and Tonic, took the edge off their boredom for the first few hours at least. Even so, when they saw their father's car pull up outside, both boys hopped up and down with delight at the prospect of being taken back to Wraggsbottom.

'Daddy! Daddy's here!'

Hugh ran to the door, oblivious to the strained looks between his mother and grandparents.

'Are we going home now?'

'No,' Laura said brightly. 'We're staying the night at Granny's, remember? I told you.'

Hugh's face fell, then brightened. 'Can Dad sleep in my room?'

Before she had time to answer, Gabe was out of the car. Running outside, Hugh launched himself into his father's arms, swiftly followed by a toddling Luca.

Gabe stood and hugged them for a long time, burying his face in their hair, smelling and kissing them with an intensity that brought tears to Laura's eyes. Finally, after what felt like an age, he set them down on the tarmacked drive. He and Laura looked at each other. Neither of them spoke.

'Come and see the tortoises!' Hugh tugged at Gabe's hand. 'They're having a strawberry-eating race. Tonic's winning.'

'Let Mummy and Daddy talk first.' Laura's father scooped Hugh up and dangled him upside down over his shoulder, producing gales of giggles. 'We can have some of Granny's chocolate cake while we're waiting.'

Easily trumped by the prospect of a slice of cake, Gabe watched his boys disappear inside the house and the door close behind them. He felt a terrible sense of dread.

It got worse when Laura started speaking.

'What do you want, Gabe?'

She sounded tired. Resigned. Eerily without emotion.

'I want you to come home. I want to talk to you. I'm sorry, Laura. I love you.'

She held up a hand for him to stop. 'Please. Don't.'

'Don't what? Don't say I love you? But I do, desperately.'

She gave him a small, sad smile. 'Not desperately enough, it seems.'

He took a step towards her but she immediately moved back. 'It was a mistake. It meant nothing. Look, I'm not minimizing it, but I was drunk out of my mind. So was Macy. I was upset after our conversation . . . Please, Laura. Look at me.'

She did, and Gabe instantly wished he hadn't asked her to. Her gaze was so clear, so *blank*. There was no anger there, no fight. For Laura, it was already over.

'We'll come home in a few days,' she said. For an instant Gabe's hopes soared. 'Once you've gone,' Laura clarified, sending them crashing down again.

Gabe opened his mouth to speak but she shut him down.

'I know you're sorry,' she said. 'And I know you love me. I love you too. But I can't do it, Gabe. I wasted my entire twenties on a man who lied to me. Who wasn't what he seemed to be. The pain was so bad I thought I would die, but I didn't. I survived. And I promised myself, never again.'

'Oh, come on!' Gabe raised his voice. His fear was making him angry. 'You can't seriously be comparing me to John Bingham? The man was a total arsehole. And he was married.'

'So are you,' Laura said quietly.

'Yes, and I've been faithful,' said Gabe. 'For ten years! And then, yes, I made a mistake. One mistake. One night. And I know I was wrong and I'm sorry, but come *on*, Laura. Surely you aren't going to throw away our life, our family over that?'

For the first time, a flash of real anger crossed Laura's face. 'I'm not throwing away anything, Gabe. *You* did that! This is all *you*. So if you're looking for someone to blame, I suggest you start with the mirror.'

Gabe looked away. There wasn't much he could say to that.

'Wraggsbottom's your home,' Laura went on, once she'd calmed down. 'I understand that. Once everything's sorted out, I'll find somewhere else for me and the children. I want us to try and be civilized about this, for their sakes.'

'Civilized about what?' demanded Gabe.

She didn't answer.

'Laura, this is crazy. We have to talk.'

'Go home, Gabe.' She gave him a pitying look and started walking back to the house.

'No!' he shouted after her. 'I won't go! Not without the boys. I'll sleep out here if I have to.'

When she turned back to look at him the pity was gone. It had been replaced by something close to disgust.

'I'd like to believe that not even you would be that selfish,' she said. 'You've caused enough pain for one day, Gabriel. Go. Home.'

Back at Wraggsbottom two hours later, Gabe sat down at the kitchen table. The children's cereal bowls were still there, the day-old Frosties glued to the sides like barnacles on an abandoned ship.

That's what this house is now, thought Gabe. *An abandoned ship.*

And I'm the captain, left to sink here alone.

His phone buzzed in his pocket, the one-millionth urgent message of the day from someone. Macy, Eddie, Santiago, Channel 5. Everyone had called. Everyone but Laura. Standing up, Gabe walked outside to the pond, drew back his arm and threw the phone as far as he could. It made a satisfying *plop* as it hit the water.

He waited until the ripples had all gone and the pond was still again, like glass. Looking down, he saw his reflection. Laura's voice rang in his ears.

If you're looking for someone to blame, I suggest you try the mirror.

For the first time, Gabe started to cry.

CHAPTER TWENTY-ONE

James pulled up outside Cranbourne House in a silver Jaguar XJ and turned off the engine. Rain poured down in a solid grey sheet, sluicing the windscreen and pooling on the road in deep, lake-like puddles. The weather suited James's mood. He sat for a moment, gathering his thoughts, letting the rhythmic pounding of the raindrops soothe him.

God, he was tired. Exhausted. It was a full week since the news had broken about Macy's night with Gabe Baxter, but tour commitments had meant that James hadn't been able to fly home until last night. Of course he and Macy had spoken. There had been tears and apologies and dreadful, pain-filled silences. But it was James who'd cut their conversations short. This was not something that could be worked out on a computer screen or over a long-distance telephone line. He needed to see her.

A few reporters had shown up at the airport when he'd landed and asked their inane questions. But the upside to being stuck in Dubai for a week was that by the time James got home the story was lukewarm, if not quite cold. He'd managed to miss the media feeding frenzy that had enveloped Gabe and Macy on their returns to the UK. A small silver lining, but at this point James would take what he could get.

He ran up the path, head down against the rain, and was about to knock when Macy opened the door and pulled him inside.

'You're drowned.'

James stood dripping in the hallway. 'I'm OK.'

'I'll get you a towel.'

She ran to the bathroom, returning with a large white bath towel. As she handed it to him, James noticed how pale she was, and how thin. It was nearly a month since he'd seen her in the flesh and she must have lost a stone in that time, far too much on such a tiny frame.

He frowned. 'You're not eating.'

Macy shrugged. 'Stress.'

'You need to eat.'

He followed her into the sitting room. The fire was lit and crackling cheerfully, but nothing could banish the sadness as they sank onto the sofa together.

'I still love you,' said James. This wasn't the time for small talk, and he was crap at it anyway. 'I still want to get married.'

Macy looked down miserably at her hands, twisting her engagement ring round and round.

'I can't.' Her voice was barely a whisper. 'I can't marry you.'

James took a deep breath. 'Why not?'

He already knew the answer, but some masochistic part of him needed to hear her say it.

'Because I'm in love with Gabe.' Macy looked so utterly

devastated when she said this that James found himself instinctively putting his arms around her. His kindness was too much to bear. 'I'm sorry,' Macy sobbed. 'I thought I was over it. I told myself it was just a crush. I wanted to marry you, to make it work. But when I saw him in LA, I knew it was no good.'

'Does he feel the same way?' James forced himself to ask.

Macy gave a short, joyless laugh. 'No. He adores Laura. He's torn to pieces about what happened. He won't even take my calls.'

James winced. He did not want to think about Macy calling Gabe. He did not want to think about anything. He wanted to go home, crawl under the duvet and never, ever come out.

He stood up, forcing himself to let her go.

'I would have been a good husband, you know.'

Macy looked up at him. 'You still will be. For the right woman.'

'You *are* the right woman,' said James, fighting back tears.

'I'm sorry,' Macy said again.

There was nothing left to say. She sat and watched, frozen, as he walked away, closing the front door behind him with a soft click.

Violet Charteris flicked back her mane of perfectly blow-dried, honey-blonde hair and pretended to type the minister's letter. Out of the corner of her eye, she watched Milo Wellesley, glued to his computer screen as usual, and found herself irritated and attracted in equal measure.

Why wouldn't he notice her?

Violet Charteris was used to being noticed. With her pert figure, high cheekbones, pretty green eyes fringed by long, dark lashes and her wide, sensuous mouth, Violet was extremely beautiful. James Garforth, the Home Secretary, had practically fallen over himself to offer her this internship. The fact that she was reading politics at Balliol and that her father was a Tory peer might have helped matters. But Violet knew that she'd been picked above all the other clever girls because she was sexy, and charming, and because Garforth fantasized about taking her to bed, just like all the other male staff at the Home Office.

Except Milo Wellesley. It was just Violet's luck that the one, properly handsome man in the office, and the only one close to her own age, should also be the only one who didn't fancy her. In fact it was worse than that. She strongly suspected Milo didn't even like her. She'd tried flirting with him. She'd tried ignoring him. She'd played the competitive card (some boys liked that), attempting to score points with the Home Secretary at Milo's expense, staying late and producing beautiful research reports far superior to Milo's efforts. None of it made a shred of difference. The infuriating boy still came to work every day and looked right through Violet as if she were a ghost.

'What are you working on?'

She hated herself for asking, but Milo just kept baiting her with his floppy blond hair and his handsome jaw and his permanently averted eyes.

'Hmm?'

'I said what are you doing?' Violet was irritated. 'There's no need to be so unsociable, you know. I tell you what *I'm* doing.'

Milo shot her a look that clearly expressed how much he wished she wouldn't. Pushing down the lid of his laptop, he stood up. 'I'm going to get a coffee.'

'Mine's a skinny latte,' Violet shouted after him as he left the room, hands thrust deep into his pockets.

Out on Marsham Street, Milo thought again how irksome Violet Charteris was with her constant innuendos and pouting and irrelevant chatter, as if his job were to entertain her. It was March now, over two months since his mother's overdose, but Violet still kept asking him about his family all the time, and 'how things were going'. As if they were friends; or as if it were any of her business. She'd been even more unbearable when the tabloid vultures switched their attention from his mother's insalubrious past to Gabe Baxter's affair with Macy Johanssen.

'Oh, come on. Your father produces *Valley Farm*. You *must* know them,' she goaded him. 'Don't be such a prude! Give us the gossip.'

'I don't know them,' Milo told her stiffly. 'But if I did, I certainly wouldn't gossip about them. Unlike you, I know the harm it can do.'

He knew he sounded preachy and holier-than-thou, but somehow Violet brought it out of him. It was odd to think that, this time last year, he'd probably have fancied a girl like Violet rotten. But now that he knew Magda, everything was different. The scales had fallen from his eyes and Milo could see Violet Charteris now for the vain, spoiled, entitled little madam that she was. *Perhaps*, it occurred to him, *I hate her so much because she reminds me of how I used to be?*

That was an uncomfortable thought. Guiltily, Milo decided to buy Violet a latte. He darted into Starbucks, just as it started to rain again.

Meanwhile, back in the office, Violet found herself alone for once. The minister was in Leeds today, opening a new foundation school. The other two interns, nerdy Mike and dreary Sanjay, had both gone with him; his PA, Helena, was at home with flu.

Seizing the opportunity, Violet hurried over to Milo's desk and gently lifted the lid of his computer. She was hoping to find some porn, or at least some IMs from a girlfriend she could tease him about. Instead, a long, turgid legal paper popped up. 'Illegal Immigration and the Path to Citzenship.' Milo had highlighted a subsection on Poland.

That's odd, thought Violet. *Garforth asked all of us to focus on Inner City Policing this month. What's Milo up to?*

She began to scroll down his browser history.

Curiouser and curiouser.

She was so engrossed, she almost didn't hear the 'ding' of the lift arriving at their floor. She only just had time to re-close the computer and run back to her own desk before Milo walked in, looking handsomer than ever with his hair sleek from the rain, like an otter's.

'I got you a coffee,' he said sheepishly, handing Violet a latte.

She smiled, surprised, and took the cup, deliberately brushing her hand against his.

'Thank you. You're an angel.'

The wettest March in more than a century had transformed the Swell Valley into a muddy, rain-soaked swamp. All along the banks of the Swell, water meadows sank beneath the deluge. In the villages, floodgates and sandbags provided scant protection against the inexorably rising waters, especially along the valley floor.

The new season of *Valley Farm* was due to start filming in April, but the extreme weather was a problem. Quite apart from the frantic rewriting of scripts (viewers didn't want to see relentless rain, so there would have to be far more indoor and village action, and less farm life), Gabe had been sucked back into crisis management mode at Wraggsbottom. Up before dawn every day, and outside in downpours until well after dark, he had no time to focus on anything other than trying to salvage his waterlogged crops, repair damage to the property and keep his sheep from being swept away in the floods. Not that he was complaining. Running the farm was exactly the distraction he needed with Laura and the boys gone – relentless, exhausting, and so physically demanding that his body simply shut down at night and forced him to sleep, whether he wanted to or not. The aches in his muscles, the freezing rain on his face, the cuts and bruises on his hands and arms and legs were all a penance that he wanted and needed, gladly exchanging his emotional torment for the life-affirming sting of physical pain.

Still, at some point the show had to go on. Channel 5 were itching to get started, and with the Fox negotiations still on-going, this season was more important than ever. Scandal-hungry viewers were desperate to see how Gabe and Macy would perform on screen together after the one-night stand that had blown apart both of their relationships. The producers had confirmed that both Gabe and Macy were under contract to present the new series, but beyond that there had been a deafening silence. Would the fallout from Eddie Wellesley's spectacularly imploded political career be a part of this season's storyline? Would Lady Wellesley dare to show her face after the scandal that had gripped the nation and destroyed her reputation? As soap operas go, *Valley Farm* was becoming hard to beat – and they weren't even on the air yet.

At the end of the month, Gabe agreed to meet Eddie for lunch at his London club.

'Ah! There you are. Good to see you, my friend. Good to see you!' Eddie made his way through Brooks's dining room, a man in his element, grinning broadly at Gabe. 'Journey up all right?'

'Fine, thanks.' Gabe followed him to the table, feeling utterly out of place in this stuffy room full of posh ex-bankers and retired brigadiers. Thank God he'd worn a jacket and put corduroys on instead of jeans.

'You look well,' said Eddie.

Gabe raised an eyebrow. 'For a politician you're a terrible liar.'

Eddie guffawed. 'All right then. You look bloody awful. Have you heard from Laura?'

'Of course. I speak to the boys every day. Did you know she's been staying in London, at her godmother's flat in Fulham?'

'I did,' Eddie confirmed. He'd spoken to Laura himself about work a few days ago.

'It's crazy,' said Gabe. 'She's enrolled Hugh at the C of E primary at the end of the road.'

Eddie frowned. That wasn't a good sign.

'Things are no better between you, then?'

'Actually they're worse.' Gabe sighed heavily. 'She filed for divorce this morning.'

Eddie looked horrified. 'No! Oh, Gabe, I'm sorry. I didn't realize it had come to that.'

Poor Gabe looked close to tears. 'Nor did I. One, drunken one-night stand, and she's jacking it all in. After ten years and two kids.' He shook his head. 'Why the hell did I do it, Eddie?'

351

'Because you're human.' Eddie took a deep breath. Now seemed as good a time as any to confide in Gabe about his own indiscretion with Macy in LA, on that very first trip to find a co-presenter. Gabe listened, astonished, as Eddie told him the whole story. 'I was lucky,' Eddie finished. 'Annabel never found out. No one did. In fact, you're the only person who knows, other than Macy and me.'

'Fuck,' said Gabe. 'I'm . . . I can't believe it. I had no idea.'

'Why would you?' said Eddie. 'The point is, you mustn't beat yourself up too terribly. These things happen. They shouldn't, but they do. Have you spoken to Macy since?'

Gabe shook his head. 'I don't think Laura would like that much.'

Eddie gave him a meaningful look. 'Is it Laura's decision?'

'I wouldn't know what to say, anyway,' said Gabe. 'In any case, I've barely left the farm in weeks.'

'Well, that has to change,' Eddie said robustly. 'The show has to go on, Gabriel, now more than ever.'

'Must it?'

'Absolutely. For one thing, you're under contract.'

'Contracts have been broken,' Gabe said darkly.

Eddie shook his head. 'You're still a father to those two boys, aren't you? You're still a provider?'

Gabe shrugged.

'If this American deal turns out to be all we hope for and the show gets syndicated, we all stand to make a lot of money,' said Eddie. 'That's Hugh and Luca's future.'

Gabe hadn't thought of it like that. Somehow, in his mind, it was the show that had caused all the problems. If it weren't for the show, he and Laura wouldn't have rowed, he would never have flown out to LA, never have slept with Macy. Never have *met* Macy. But Eddie was having none of that.

'Dropping the ball now would be like letting the farm go under,' he told Gabe. 'You'd never do that, would you?'

'No,' said Gabe with feeling. 'I wouldn't.'

'Well, then. You and Macy will have to work together, and Laura will have to deal with it.'

They ordered food and talked about other things for a while, mostly Eddie's life. Eddie told Gabe how well Milo was doing at the Home Office and how happy he and Annabel were since the revelations in David Carlyle's book that had nearly destroyed them.

'I would never have given up politics otherwise; never have stepped away from public life and given our marriage the attention it deserved. And Annabel would never have told me. She'd have lived with this awful shadow over her for the rest of her life. But now it's all out in the open, I can't tell you how free we both feel!'

He seemed to mean it. Not for the first time, Gabe marvelled at Eddie's positivity, his resilience. Prison had been 'interesting'. Public humiliation 'a relief'. His wife's attempted suicide: 'the wake-up call we both needed'. Gabe wished he could view life's setbacks with such equanimity. He wondered what it would take to throw Eddie Wellesley off course. An earthquake?

'It explains so much, you know,' Eddie went on. 'Realizing that all this time she was frightened, terrified that the secret would get out. Fear turns us into the very worst versions of ourselves, don't you think?'

'Will you never go back to politics?' Gabe asked.

'Oh, I'm not sure one can ever say "never",' Eddie mused, taking a contemplative sip of his claret. 'If I did, at least I could be fairly sure that my closet was well and truly empty, skeletons-wise.'

The waiter who arrived to clear their plates away couldn't have been a day under eighty. Gabe watched with alarm as he tottered away, balancing china and silverware on his frail arms.

'Should I give him a hand?' he asked Eddie.

'Alfred? Good God, no. He'd be mortified,' Eddie replied.

'But he looks half blind,' Gabe protested.

'Oh, he is! At least half,' Eddie said cheerfully. 'Now listen. You must go and see Macy.'

'OK,' Gabe agreed.

'Between you and me, I spoke to her yesterday and she's also been making noises about breaking her contract and going home,' said Eddie. 'I need you to talk her out of it.'

Gabe's eyes widened. 'The show must go on' was all very well, and Eddie's arguments about Hugh and Luca's futures made sense. But convincing Macy to stay on, after everything that had happened? That was something else. He said as much to Eddie.

'I know it's a lot to ask,' Eddie admitted. 'But I've tried myself and I've failed. I wouldn't ask if I weren't sure that walking out on her contract would be a huge, huge mistake. I'm very fond of Macy,' he added, almost wistfully.

'So am I,' said Gabe. He realized as he said it that it was true. 'OK. I'll do my best.'

Macy woke at five. She'd barely slept, again. If it went on much longer she would have to go and see the doctor and get something to help her get through the nights.

Padding downstairs to the kitchen, she brewed a pot of fresh coffee and stood sipping the bitter, black liquid as she stared out of the window. Cranbourne House's garden was overgrown; a vivid green jungle already, thanks to the heavy rains. Most of the early spring flowers had been battered into submission by the winds, but a few flashes of colour persisted, including red campion and marsh marigolds, along with swathes of chickweed, white stars sparkling against the foliage. Macy could make out little of it at first in the faint dawn light. But gradually the sun's rays began to break through the early morning mist. By the time the sun had fully risen, Macy's coffee was cold. Looking at the kitchen clock she realized she'd been standing there, frozen, for over an hour.

Frozen.

The word summed up her life. Every instinct told her to go home. To pack a bag and catch the next flight back to LA, never to return. It was over with James. She'd made a mess of everything with Gabe. The rumour was that he and Laura were getting divorced. Not so long ago that news would have delighted Macy, but not now. Gabe wasn't going to come running into her arms just because his wife had left him. There would be no silver linings, no happy endings.

Nothing but pain. For all of them.

The thought of going back to work on *Valley Farm* was unbearable, and without work, or a wedding to plan, she had no reason to be here, in this grey, miserable, waterlogged country, where it never stopped raining and the tabloid press had turned her into a pariah.

And yet, she was still here.

Why?

She didn't have the answer herself. Part of it was simply inertia, a profound lack of energy made worse by lack of sleep, a complete loss of appetite and creeping depression.

Part of it was her fear of being sued by Channel 5, or even by a vengeful Laura Baxter, if she walked out on her contract. Eddie, in the nicest possible way, had hinted that this was a real risk. Paul Meyer, Macy's agent, had put it more forcefully. 'Suck it up, kiddo. I know it's hard, but this is business. It's only one more season and this Fox deal is your life raft.'

There was something else keeping her here too. Something emotional, some tie with Fittlescombe and the Swell Valley that Macy couldn't define herself, but which had curled its way around her heart like bindweed, deadly yet unbreakable.

But something had to give. She couldn't stay in this house for ever, walled up like Miss Havisham, doing nothing with her life. If she wasn't going back to work on *Valley Farm*, what *was* she going to do? That was the question.

She showered and dressed and walked into the village for some fresh milk and the morning papers. The *Daily Mail* had written something poisonous about her almost every day since she 'broke James Craven's heart', but Macy couldn't seem to stop herself buying it. Deciding to walk home the long way, past Furlings – it wasn't raining for once, so why not? – she passed Max Bingley and Angela Cranley out walking their dog, the arthritic basset hound, Gringo. They greeted her warmly, and asked a few polite questions about the new series and when filming would start. Macy mumbled something noncommittal in response. She loved Max and Angela, but she wasn't up to small talk.

'You must come over for supper one night,' Angela said kindly, before they walked on. 'Hiding yourself away won't help, you know,' she added, nodding towards the copy of the *Mail* under Macy's arm. 'They'll find someone else to torment soon enough. You'll see.'

It was odd but, instead of lifting her spirits, Angela's compassion seemed to have the opposite effect. By the time Macy unlatched the garden gate at Cranbourne House, she was on the verge of tears again.

I'll go and see a doctor tomorrow, she told herself. *No excuses.*

Pushing open the gate, she stopped dead. Looking very much the farmer, in Barbour, wellies and a flat cap, Gabe was sitting on her doorstep.

'Hullo.' He smiled. 'Any chance of a cup of tea?'

Sitting at Macy's kitchen table ten minutes later, a freshly brewed pot between them, Macy and Gabe looked at each other awkwardly.

'I'd offer you a cookie but I think I'm out,' said Macy.

'They're called biscuits in England,' said Gabe.

Macy smiled. 'What-*ever.*'

It was a relief to get back to their old banter, even if only for a moment.

'I'm sorry about James.' Gabe sipped his tea.

'I'm sorry about Laura.' Macy sipped hers.

'Eddie asked me to come.'

Macy's face fell. 'Oh.'

'I would have come anyway,' Gabe added hastily. 'I mean, I've wanted to. For ages. I should have, I know. I suppose I just . . . chickened out.'

'That's OK,' said Macy. 'You've had a lot to deal with.'

'You know, then? About the divorce?'

Macy shrugged. 'This is Fittlescombe. It's pretty tough to keep a secret around here.'

'Yeah.' Gabe stared into his mug, wondering again how the hell he had come to this point. 'Anyway. We need to make some decisions about the show.'

Macy nodded. 'I know. Are you going to do it?'

'Yes,' said Gabe. 'I am. I wasn't going to, but Eddie talked me into it. Fox will pull out if we do. That's the bottom line. I don't want that to happen.'

'Nor do I,' said Macy. 'I just don't know if we can work together. After all this.'

'I don't see why not,' said Gabe. 'You and Eddie managed it after your one-night stand.'

Macy's jaw almost hit the table. 'He *told* you!'

'Only a few days ago. Don't be angry with him. He was trying to make me feel better. I've been beating myself up so badly about what happened. But he made me realize, everyone makes mistakes.'

Is that what I am to you? Macy thought bleakly. *A mistake?*

But she managed to hide her feelings, just as she had when her father had left and when her mother had died and at countless other turning points in her life.

What the hell? she thought. *If Gabe can do this, so can I.*

'I suppose we *do* make a good team,' she said, raising her eyes over the rim of her mug.

'Yes we do,' Gabe beamed back at her. 'And it's only for one series. Then we can do this deal, you can go home to America and we'll all be rolling in it. What do you say?'

'OK.' Macy raised her mug of tea to Gabe's and they clinked in a toast. 'I'm in if you are, Baxter.'

After Gabe left, Macy sat back down at the table for a long time.

Laura and Gabe were getting a divorce.

She'd been telling herself for days now that this meant nothing. That it didn't spell hope for her and Gabe, as a couple.

But what if she were wrong?

What if it did mean they had a chance?

Some of the old banter, the old camaraderie, was still there between them. She'd felt it just now. Affection, perhaps even flirtation? Not much perhaps. But it was there.

Another season of *Valley Farm* would mean the better part of a year in England. A year in which she and Gabe would see each other every day.

A year was a long time.

Macy allowed herself a small smile.

Where there's life, there's hope,

Her stomach rumbled loudly. All of a sudden she found she was ravenously hungry.

Perhaps she wouldn't need to see the doctor tomorrow after all?

CHAPTER TWENTY-TWO

Laura waved Luca off at St Stephen's Church playgroup on the corner of Sydney Street and headed towards the Kings Road for a late breakfast.

It was early June, and already the wet and miserable winter felt like a distant memory. Chelsea sparkled this morning beneath a bright blue sky. The late-flowering cherry trees erupted with rose-pink blossoms, and the colourful window boxes and pretty front gardens made a cheerful contrast to the ubiquitous white stucco façades, as iconic in West London as red pillar boxes and the Union Jack.

It had been a terrible few months, one of the worst times in Laura's life. But now, at long last, she could see some light at the end of the tunnel. She and Gabe had settled into a civil, even friendly routine as the divorce ground on. On a professional level, they'd both agreed that continuing the show was a financial priority, but that working together day to day was no longer an option. Mike Briarson from Channel 5 had agreed to take over the day-to-day direction of *Valley Farm*'s second season down at Wraggsbottom, with Laura overseeing the writing and editing of scripts and the ongoing negotiations with Fox America from her new base in London. So far the system was working well. Laura trusted Mike, and Gabe and Macy both liked him. It was true that his direction had given a slightly different flavour to the second season, with more unscripted, humorous moments and a bigger focus on village over farm life. But the ratings were fabulous, as big as they had been for last season's finale. Everyone was happy.

Personally, the transition had been harder, at least for Laura. Hugh and Luca, bless them, had adapted brilliantly and all but instantly to their new London life and schools. Laura had moved out of her godmother's mansion flat and into a very pretty, bright yellow cottage on the borders of Chelsea and Fulham, near the football ground (much to both boys' delight). Gabe had the children every other weekend, and regularly popped down during the week to take them to the park after school or out for dinner at Byron Hamburgers, Hugh's new favourite place on earth. A mate of Gabe's had given him a permanent, free option to use the spare room of his flat in Onslow Gardens for these trips, which was within walking distance of Laura's.

'You're the new Chris and Gwynnie,' Laura's friend Kate had teased her, watching Laura give Gabe a friendly goodbye kiss as she waved her sons off for a weekend in Fittlescombe. 'If you can get along that well, I don't see why you're splitting.'

Laura forced herself to laugh. But those sorts of comments hurt terribly. *We're splitting because he broke my heart*, she wanted to scream. *Shattered it into a million pieces. Does nobody remember that?*

Maybe there were people who could survive without trust, who could cope with the constant wondering, the second-guessing, the awful gnawing fear that everything you thought you had together, everything you'd built your life on, was really a mirage. But Laura wasn't one of them. She was about to turn forty-one. It wasn't old, exactly. But it was too old to be living a lie.

She knew Macy and Gabe weren't still seeing each other, that there was nothing going on, despite the constant tabloid hints. Ever since Macy had dumped poor old James Craven, it had felt as though the whole country was busy taking bets on when she and Gabe would get together. They hadn't. But the pain of what had happened in LA, the shock of Gabe's betrayal, still haunted Laura every single day. Just watching Macy and Gabe on *Valley Farm*, kidding around with one another in the easy, flirtatious way that had made the show such a hit, made Laura feel as if someone were slowly dripping acid into her eyes. But she had to watch, and analyse, and edit. That was her job. *I'm a grown-up*, Laura told herself. *Grown-ups do their job, no matter what.*

And things were getting better. They were. Laura still missed Gabe, and their marriage. She missed the Swell Valley, that had been her true home, her happy place, since she was a little girl. She still mourned all that was lost, a life she had truly believed would last for ever.

But she loved her little house in London. She loved being with the boys and seeing more of her old friends. More than anything, she had fallen back in love with her work. Without the irritations and pressures of being on a set that was also her home, she was starting to remember what inspired her about creating television. The prospect of selling the *Valley*

Farm format to America and beyond was wildly exciting. With a Fox show under her belt, Laura would be able to dictate her own terms in British television. Already well regarded, she was on the cusp of joining the industry's true elite. She'd read a lot of articles in women's magazines over the years, assuring her that ambition and a career wouldn't keep her warm at night. But, in a funny way, she discovered now, they did.

'Laura?'

Laura spun round at the familiar voice. John Bingham, her one-time lover and boss, was leaning out of the window of a black cab. She watched in dismay as he asked the driver to pull over, got out and walked towards her.

'How incredible to see you! You look terrific, as ever.'

'Thank you. Er . . . so do you.'

His friendliness was disarming. When Laura had branched out alone and risked it all on *Valley Farm*, John Bingham had barely been able to hide his irritation and resentment, especially once the show shot to the top of the ratings. Yet now he seemed genuinely pleased to see her.

'Do you have time for coffee?'

'Well, I . . . er . . . I'm not sure.' She looked at her watch hesitantly.

'No agenda,' John Bingham assured her. 'I'd just love to catch up. Don't know if you heard, but I'm not in the business any more.'

Laura's eyes widened. She hadn't heard. Then again, she had been rather preoccupied of late.

'I'm working for the dark side now,' John went on. 'Goldman Sachs.' He rubbed his hands together and gave an evil, Ming-the-Merciless laugh. Even Laura had to laugh at that.

'All right,' she said at last. 'One coffee. But I really can't stay long.'

They took a corner table at Patisserie Valerie. John Bingham was no spring chicken these days, but he was handsome in a rugged, patrician, older man sort of way, and still vain enough to dress beautifully: cream shirt, discreet gold cufflinks, perfectly tailored navy-blue trousers in handsome, brushed twill. Laura thought about Gabe's hole-ridden wardrobe and pulled-through-a-hedge-backwards hair and felt almost wistful.

'Congratulations on the show. You must be delighted,' Bingham said smoothly.

'Thank you. Yes, it's going well. We have a loyal audience now and we're still building. It's been a challenge.'

'I'm sure.' Bingham sipped his latte thoughtfully. 'Scandal's a double-edged sword in television, as we both know. Especially with reality formats.'

Laura stiffened.

'It wasn't a dig,' Bingham said hastily. 'I was sorry to hear about you and Gabe.'

'Really?' Laura's eyes narrowed.

'Really.' Again, John *sounded* sincere. 'I know I didn't behave well towards you in the past, Laura, and I'm sorry for that. But I don't like to see you unhappy.'

'Well,' Laura sipped her own coffee and regained her composure. 'I'm not unhappy. Life moves on. Things change. I mean, look at you, taking a City job! At your age, John.'

'Now, now,' Bingham grinned. 'I'll have you know I'm at the peak of my powers and am, in fact, incredibly wise. Speaking of old men, how's Fast Eddie?'

'He's well,' said Laura. 'He's still involved with the show but he takes a back seat now, more of a silent partner.'

'Ha!' said John. 'Eddie Wellesley, silent? I can't imagine that.'

'It's true,' said Laura. 'He's even given up on politics. He spends all his time with Annabel these days. It's quite sweet, actually. Gabe says he sees them in the village, wandering along hand in hand like a pair of teenagers.'

John Bingham looked sceptical. 'Well, *I* saw him at La Famiglia last week having lunch with James Garforth. Very intense conversation,' he added, tantalizingly. 'Now what would someone who's given up politics be doing lunching with the Home Secretary?'

Laura laughed. 'You're such a gossip, John! Eddie's son, Milo's, working for Garforth. I expect they were talking about that. Or old friends.'

'Or the weather?' Bingham teased her. 'Well, you believe what you want to, my dear. But I'll bet you a hundred pounds right now that Wellesley stands in the next election.'

'Done,' said Laura.

They shook hands. For a moment it felt strange, touching the hand of a man who she'd once loved, who'd once had the power to raise her hopes or smash them, to fill her with joy or condemn her to despair. And realizing that now she felt nothing, nothing at all.

Would it ever be like that with Gabe?

She couldn't imagine it.

She would see him tonight. It was a Friday, and his turn to take the boys. The prospect filled her with the same unpleasant mixture of anticipation and despair that it always did, a sort of nauseous churning that reached fever pitch right before Gabe walked through the door.

Outside, John Bingham hugged her goodbye.

'One word of advice,' he said. 'Watch out for David Carlyle.'

Laura looked surprised. She hadn't seen or thought about David in a long time.

'As long as Eddie Wellesley's still attached to *Valley Farm*, silent or not, Carlyle will do all he can to hurt the show.' John told Laura about his lunch with David Carlyle last year, in which the *Echo*'s editor had dangled the carrot of the director-generalship of the BBC to try to get him to discredit Fast Eddie.

'It was all nonsense, of course. Eddie was never in the running for the DG job, any more than I was. Carlyle was playing on my vanity and I paid the price. I ended up looking a complete fool, schmoozing everyone at the Beeb and burning my bridges at ITV. That's why I took the Goldman job, to be perfectly honest. The money was great, but what I really needed was to save face.'

It was an astonishing admission, one that the old John Bingham would never have made to anyone, certainly not to her. Laura was touched.

'Thanks,' she said. 'I haven't heard a peep out of Carlyle in a while. But we'll watch our backs.'

'So.' David Carlyle did up his shirt buttons and sat back down in the doctor's chair. 'What's the verdict?'

Dr Jamie Graham frowned. He'd known David a long time, decades. They weren't friends, exactly, but David was more than just a patient. From the look on his face it was clear he wasn't taking this seriously.

'The verdict is, you had a heart attack. You need to take things easy and you need to *reduce your stress levels.*'

'A mild heart attack,' David corrected him. 'I was barely in pain. The hospital sent me home the same day.'

'Maybe, but it was still a heart attack.' Jamie sounded exasperated. 'That's a big deal at any age, but especially in your late forties and with all the other factors at play.'

David looked out of the window. Jamie had beautiful offices, on the first floor of a classic Georgian building on Harley Street. Outside, wealthy, privileged patients like himself hopped in and out of black cabs, going to or from their expensive doctors. The trees of Cavendish Square glowed green in the bright sunshine. It was a glorious day. He wanted to feel happy but he couldn't, and his heart had nothing to do with it. As usual, it was Eddie Wellesley who'd poured poison into his veins.

Despite everything – despite prison, and public humiliation and the world learning that his wife was a gold-digging, social-climbing home-wrecking fake; despite the party turning its back on him, twice – Eddie was still thriving. His TV show was poised to go global. His marriage, miraculously, seemed to be stronger than ever, with Eddie and Annabel frequently pictured emerging from restaurants hand in hand, like two teenagers on honeymoon. And now, to top it all, rumours had reached David's ears that yet another political comeback might be in the offing. Certainly Eddie's popularity with voters had never been higher. Short of running against Benedict Cumberbatch, he was just about certain to win any seat he stood for if an election were called tomorrow.

A week ago, David's wife, Louise, had shown him a gossip piece in the *Daily Telegraph* about Eddie being seen having lunch in the House of Commons, and David had experienced a strange sensation in his left arm. Four hours later he'd been in A&E.

'Look,' said Jamie, sensing David's darkening mood. 'The results of your stress test were good. Your blood pressure's fine and your general health – cholesterol, etc. – is excellent for your age. But statistically, one cardiac event significantly increases your chances of another. You need to forget about Eddie Wellesley, David. Let the man lead his life, and you lead yours.'

David smiled thinly. 'I couldn't care less about Eddie Wellesley. The man's washed up, a has-been. And I have a national newspaper to run.'

He walked out of Jamie's offices into the sunshine.

Louise stood on the steps like a sentry, her arms folded, blocking his way.

'Lou! What are you doing here?' David asked her. 'I told you you didn't need to come.'

He bent down to kiss her on the cheek but she turned her head away.

'What did he say?' Louise demanded.

'He said I'm fine.'

'Oh, really? So if I went up to his office right now and asked him, that's what he'd say, is it? "David's fine. He can just go back to work and stress himself out and it's *no problem at all*"?'

David laughed. It was adorable, Louise trying to act so tough in her little yellow flowery dress and cardigan.

'I love you.'

'Don't fob me off, David! I mean it. He told you to rest, didn't he? To take it easy?'

'Yes.' David Carlyle snaked his arm around his wife's

waist, despite her protestations. They walked down the street together. 'And I will, Lou. I am. Work doesn't stress me out.'

'We both know what stresses you out,' said Louise, with feeling. 'Or rather *who*.'

'Not any more,' said David, grinning. 'Come on. I'll buy you lunch.'

Gabe stepped off the train at Victoria and looked at his watch. It was still only four thirty, despite the inevitable delay at East Croydon. The announcer had been too embarrassed even to offer a reason this time.

'What're they going to blame it on now?' the man sitting next to Gabe remarked laconically. 'The wrong kind of sunshine?'

Gabe laughed again. He was in a good mood. Filming was done for the week and he was about to spend the whole weekend with his boys. What could be better than that? Plus it was a stunning afternoon and there was still time for him to walk to Laura's rather than take a cab.

As he set off across Buckingham Palace Road and up Eccleston Street, his mind started to wander. It had been a magical few days at the farm. Haymaking started this week – always Gabe's favourite time in the farming year. He'd barely noticed the cameras as he and the men got to work – setting the Krone mower to exactly the right height, so that the forage could regrow afterwards – and made their way methodically through the fields. As Gabe had explained to *Valley Farm* viewers, there was more to haymaking than people thought. It was all about getting the optimal amount of protein and sugar into the finished hay bale. That meant not only making sure you harvested at exactly the right point in the plant's growth cycle, but that you always mowed in the afternoon, to capture as much sunshine as possible and pack in the most energy.

Today, Gabe had spent the morning raking the hay and monitoring the moisture to make sure it was dry enough for baling. It was hot work, and he was aware of Macy watching him as he took off his shirt, his back dripping with sweat alongside the rest of the men.

She'd been watching him a lot lately. Perhaps it had happened before, but he hadn't noticed it. Now, he was aware of every glance, every smile. The hard part was, he liked her. And there was no doubt she was looking great at the moment, sexier than ever. She'd lost a lot of weight in the fallout following their infamous night in LA. For a while she'd been painfully thin. But the shock of seeing herself on film seemed to have jolted her into action and got her eating again. Now she looked slim but perfect. Her boobs were back and she'd started growing out her hair, which she now wore in a choppy, almost shoulder-length style, a vast improvement in Gabe's view.

'I like it,' he told her, when she asked his opinion, something else she was doing a lot more of recently. 'It's less newsreader-y.'

'You thought I looked like a newsreader?'

'A bit,' Gabe admitted. 'A fit one, though. Like Lisa Burke.'

'She's a weather girl!'

'News. Weather.' Gabe shrugged.

'And she has long hair.'

'Exactly!' said Gabe. 'Long hair's better.'

Laura had long hair. Laura had perfect hair, actually, especially when she washed it and left it to dry naturally and it went all curly and wild in glossy black ringlets. *Shaggy sheep*, he used to call it.

Gabe found it amazing how he could miss a person so much, and love them so much and yet at the same time be so furiously angry with them. Or perhaps it was himself he was angry at? At this point, he couldn't tell. All he knew was that for the last six months his life had felt like a particularly vivid, terrible dream, from which he kept expecting to wake up, but never quite could. Were they *really* getting divorced? Was he *really* never going to be with Laura again? Never live under the same roof as his children?

He and Laura were getting along well. They were being terribly polite and respectful and all the rest of it – not just in front of the boys, but all the time. Everybody told him this was a good thing. And yet Gabe couldn't quite shake the feeling that all the politeness was actually the death knell for the marriage. That every smile and every kind, restrained word were nails being hammered into the coffin of his old life. Which wouldn't be so bad, of course. If only the love were dead.

He suddenly found himself turning onto Laura's street. The little yellow house was only a mile and a half from Victoria, but even so the walk seemed to have taken no time at all. Children, still in their smart school uniforms, were playing in the road, scooting perilously close to the parked Mercedes and Porsche SUVs. It struck Gabe how posh they all looked – little Tarquins and Sebastians and Arabellas. Then again, this was Chelsea. He and Laura used to argue about class all the time before they were married. Back then, Gabe thought she was a stuck-up cow, and Laura accused him of being a champagne socialist, which infuriated him, not least because he worried it might be true. Now he found himself wondering whether Hugh would be considered posh. He had a posh name, but did that matter? Back in Fittlescombe it didn't seem to. Everyone went to the same school and the village kids all mucked in together. But here in London, in the real world, the lines felt sharper, more danger-ous somehow. In some undefined way, it made Gabe feel depressed. As if he were losing his sons even more.

He rang the doorbell. As soon as Laura answered, the polite smile that Gabe had come to hate himself for spread across his face. 'Hi!'

'Hi!' Laura returned the smile, feeling equally bleak. 'The boys are just getting changed. Come in.'

Gabe followed her into the kitchen. Already the place looked like a home, with the boys' artwork plastered all over the fridge and a cork pin-board covered with party invitations and lesson timetables from their new school and nursery. In the playroom opposite he could see the Thomas table already set up and tracks and trains everywhere. It was the first thing Laura had bought when she'd moved out, before beds, so Hugh and Luca could have their beloved trains in London as well as at Wraggsbottom. The children's priorities, at least, hadn't changed.

'Cup of tea?'

The brightness in her voice was painful.

'Thanks.'

'I think I've got some Jaffa Cakes somewhere.'

Gabe watched as she flitted around the room, getting out plates and mugs and shoving tea bags into a new, Emma Bridgewater teapot. She was wearing a yellow cotton sundress and flip-flops and her hair was still damp, as if she'd recently had a shower. Suddenly he felt a surge of longing so strong he had to grip the kitchen table for support.

'Laura.'

'Mmm-hm?' She was pouring milk into a jug and didn't look up at first. But when Gabe didn't speak again she looked at him. Instantly she felt her own knees give way. His face! She would never forget it. The sadness. The sorrow. The utter desolation.

'Laura.' His voice cracked when he said her name again.

'Don't, Gabe. Please.' Laura started to panic. If she let the maelstrom of emotions inside her come out now, she'd be drowned in the flood. All her hard-won equilibrium would be swept away, like so many straw houses on a storm-tossed beach.

'This is madness.' Gabe moved towards her.

Laura honestly thought she might faint.

'Hugh'll be down any minute,' she said desperately, looking anywhere but into Gabe's eyes.

'I don't care,' said Gabe angrily.

'Yes, you do.'

'Daddy!' Hugh raced into the kitchen and launched himself into Gabe's arms like an Exocet. Behind him toddled Luca, impossibly sweet in his favourite dinosaur T-shirt and a pair of striped shorts pulled on backwards.

'Going country?' he beamed up at Gabe. 'Going farm?'

'We certainly are!' Gabe painted the smile back on his face. His jaw was set so tightly he felt like he had rictus. He no longer had the strength to look at Laura. 'Have you got your stuff?'

Both boys pointed proudly to their new pull-along suit-cases standing in the hallway. Luca's was a ladybird and Hugh's a spider.

'Right then. Let's give Mummy a kiss and we'll see her on Sunday.'

*   *   *

373

After they left, Laura walked straight to the drinks cupboard and poured herself an enormous gin. The tonic was flat and there was no ice, but she gulped it down anyway like medicine, waiting for the tears to come.

They didn't.

Apparently she didn't have any more left.

CHAPTER TWENTY-THREE

'And, cut!' Mike Briarson's distinctive Brummie accent rang out through the barn. 'That was lovely, everyone. Well done. Let's break for lunch.'

Jennifer Lee wiped the sweat off her forehead with her T-shirt and took a swig from her bottle of water. De-horning the spring-born calves was a backbreaking job. She'd done it last year at Wraggsbottom, and the year before on the Yorkshire hill farm where she'd done her placement at veterinary college. But the animals' distress still bothered her. Combined with the unseasonal heat and the pressure of having cameras following your every move, it made for an unpleasant and exhausting morning.

Walking off towards the orchard, so she could eat her sandwiches in peace, Jen caught a snatch of Gabe and Macy's conversation as she passed.

'What time are you meeting him?' Gabe's question was casual, but there was an edge to his tone.

'He's picking me up at seven.' Macy was almost gloating. *Trying to make him jealous?*

Jen walked on. She'd grown fond of just about everyone she worked with on *Valley Farm*, but sometimes the personal dramas could get draining. Jen felt bad for Laura, but even so she'd been relieved when Laura and the boys had moved to London and Mike Briarson had taken over as director. Compared to Laura's increasingly strained, dictatorial style, Mike's gentle, cheerful presence had made a huge difference to the atmosphere on set. Mike was the calm after the storms of last winter's scandals. But, even now, it occurred to Jennifer that just about everybody on *Valley Farm* was involved in some sort of romantic drama except for her. While Macy's and Gabe's and Eddie's sex lives had been splashed all over the tabloids in the past year, her own had remained pathetically non-existent. So much for TV stardom getting you laid.

It was depressing, watching Gabe and Macy dance around one another on set like a pair of nervously courting birds of paradise. There was obviously an attraction there, but Gabe remained firmly in denial about the reality of his divorce. Macy, tired of waiting, had a date with a rich banker tonight and had made sure the whole world (but especially Gabe) knew about it. Meanwhile, Jen was looking at another night at home in her cottage in Brockhurst, watching reruns of *The Big Bang Theory* and eating more Haribos washed down with red wine than was probably medically advisable.

Just as she was indulging in this little moment of self-pity, she caught sight of Bill Clempson running down the lane. Jen hadn't seen Fittlescombe's vicar since last Christmas, when she'd presented him with her peace offering bottle of sloe gin. They'd talked about getting together in the New Year, but it had never happened. Now that the local protests against *Valley Farm* had faded to a whimper, there was no reason for their paths to cross. Unless Jen were to suddenly become a churchgoer, and things hadn't got that desperate – yet.

Looking at Bill now, it was hard not to laugh. To say he was not naturally athletic would be an understatement. Watching him run reminded Jen sharply of Sheldon from *The Big Bang Theory* attempting the same feat. The way his knees turned in and his arms flapped about gave him the look of a particularly camp penguin.

'Hello!' She waved. 'You look like you're in a hurry.'

Bill stopped and walked over to the hedge, panting, but clearly thrilled to see her.

'Jennifer!' His face was a deep, crimson red. Jen couldn't tell if this was pure exertion, or whether he was blushing. 'How are you? You never came for that drink.'

'No.' Jen looked down. 'Sorry.'

Now *she* was blushing. It was odd. He really wasn't attractive. And yet, standing still at least, there was something very endearing about him. Possibly it was the way he looked at her as if she were Angelina Jolie on an especially good hair day, and didn't seem to notice her filthy T-shirt, the spot on her forehead or the sweat patches under her arms.

'Maybe we could try again,' Bill said shyly.

'Do you still have any left?' asked Jen.

The vicar looked confused.

'The sloe gin.'

'Ah! Er, no. I drank it all ages ago, I'm afraid. It was delicious. But I've got plenty of other things I can offer you.'

Jen raised an eyebrow teasingly.

'Oh, no! Oh dear, I didn't mean . . .' Poor Bill looked as if he wanted the earth to open up and swallow him. 'Actually,' he composed himself, 'I'm glad I ran into you. I was hoping to pick your brains about something work-related.'

Now it was Jen's turn to look confused. *Work-related?* Wasn't his work being a vicar? She wasn't sure how much she could contribute in terms of baptizing babies or hearing confessions or whatever else it was that Bill did.

'I'll explain when I see you. How about Saturday?' He looked at his watch, in a hurry again suddenly. 'I'm sorry to rush, but Brett Cranley's in the village, you've probably heard.'

Jen hadn't.

'He's staying up at Furlings. I'm hoping to catch him before he leaves for London, to see if I can't wangle a donation for St Hilda's benevolent fund.'

'Is Brett Cranley terribly benevolent?' Jen asked sceptically.

'Probably not!' Bill said cheerfully. 'But the Lord helps those who help themselves. I'm hoping if I turn up there in person and ask him in front of Angela and Max, he'll be shamed into giving something.'

Jen laughed. 'That's not very ethical!'

'Nor's dumping silage all over somebody's car,' said the vicar with a wink. 'Let she who is without sin, and all that . . . See you Saturday, I hope.'

He flapped off.

Jen watched him go, feeling suddenly, stupidly happy.

Not a rich banker, perhaps. But it was nice to have a little romantic drama of her own for a change.

Macy swept taupe shadow over her eyelids and brushed a single coat of true black mascara through her long lashes.

It felt odd, going through the motions of getting dolled

up for a date. Truth be told, she had about as much interest in Warren Hansen, the über-wealthy banker taking her out tonight, as she did in beginning a course on bee-keeping. Possibly less, as bees at least produced honey and didn't expect you to waste an evening making small talk or to wash and blow-dry your hair when you could be watching E! news on your computer or fantasizing about Gabe.

On the other hand, Macy knew she was spending too much time fantasizing about Gabe. If things were ever going to move forward between them, she needed to jolt him out of his complacency, to make him jealous – hence her acceptance of Warren's dinner invitation. And if they weren't going to move forward, then she needed to start meeting new men.

Of course the problem was that she didn't fancy anyone. She and James had had a great sex life, but even that had been tainted by the shadow of Gabe. The only other man Macy could remember being attracted to since she'd met Gabe was Austin Jamet, her father's lawyer back in LA. Her dinner date with Austin had ended on a tense note, but things had improved between them since then, and over the past few months they'd become friends of a sort over email.

Since she'd forbidden Austin to contact her about her father, he'd taken to sending her funny snippets about LA life or gossip or current affairs instead. Macy responded in kind, and their on-line banter had become one of the highlights of her day. She liked the way they competed with one another. It was similar to the on-screen relationship she had with Gabe, except that this was private, and real, not for any audience. There was also something American about her relationship with Austin, something that made her feel at home in a way that Gabe never quite could. Not that Macy was remotely in love with Austin Jamet. She'd only met the man once, and besides, Gabe Baxter was the love of her life.

Thinking about Austin reminded her. She owed him a response to his last email, which had made her laugh out loud last night.

Pulling on a red cocktail dress that would send Warren all the right signals, none of which Macy had any intention of following through on, and spritzing herself with Chanel No. 19, she pulled out her phone and read Austin's latest note again. God, he was funny. It was lovely to have a fellow American to share a laugh with every now and then.

Warren's American, Macy reminded herself, as she tapped out a suitably pithy one-line response to Austin's note and hit send. Perhaps she should give Warren a chance?

Gabe peeled back the clingfilm on the bowl of leftover lasagne and wrinkled his nose. It looked like something the dog had thrown up. In fairness, it hadn't been particularly appetizing the first time around. Like everything else Gabe had eaten since Laura left, it had come out of a Tesco box. If there were an Olympic team for 'piercing the film lid several times', Gabe would have been a shoo-in. Not that the standard of cuisine had been much to write home about when Laura had lived here, he reminded himself ruefully. Thrusting the lasagne into the microwave, he heated it up anyway and opened a cheap bottle of wine. It was either the dog-sick lasagne or a bowl of Frosties, and he'd had Frosties for breakfast. *I really must sign up for an Ocado delivery*, he thought for the millionth time.

Laying the kitchen table for one, he wondered idly what

Macy would be having tonight with this tosser from Morgan Stanley. Oysters and osso buco, probably. *Warren Hansen.* What the fuck kind of a name was that?

Gabe didn't want to be with Macy. But it still irked him to think of her throwing herself away on someone so obviously unworthy of her. He imagined Warren as a typical lantern-jawed, white-toothed American wearing an expensive suit and too much aftershave, boring on about Harvard Business School.

On balance, a night on his own eating dog-sick lasagne seemed preferable.

Actually, once he'd smothered it in ketchup and washed it down with plonk, the lasagne wasn't that bad. Flipping through *Horse & Hound* as he ate, Gabe was actually starting to enjoy his evening when a lawyer's letter fluttered out from between the magazine's pages. Norma, the current cleaner, must have slipped it in there by mistake when she was tidying up the kitchen table.

'Leigh & Graylings, Solicitors.'

How Gabe had come to hate that letterhead! A date had been set for the divorce hearing. Gabe's lawyers had done all they could to delay things. But with Gabe's unwillingness to fight with Laura over either custody or finances, he hadn't left them much wiggle room.

In a few weeks, they'd be in court. In a few months at most, the divorce would be finalized. No going back.

It still didn't feel real. But it was. The letter in front of him spelled out that fact in ugly black letters.

The ringing phone jolted him momentarily out of his dark mood. As always when the phone rang, a part of him hoped it might be Laura. But saying what? That she'd changed her mind? *It's not going to happen, you moron*, Gabe scolded himself.

'Hello?'

'Gabe. It's Brett.'

Brett Cranley's deep, gravelly Australian voice boomed out of the receiver, as punchily confident as ever.

'Brett! I heard you were in town. How are you?'

'Oh, you know. Better than you, I guess. Sorry to hear about Laura.'

Gabe liked the easy way Brett talked, as if the two of them spoke all the time. In fact, Gabe hadn't heard from Brett in well over a year.

'Look, mate, are you busy?'

'Busy?' Gabe looked down at his sorry supper and the lawyer's letter. 'No. Not remotely. You?'

'I'm going stir-crazy up at Furlings,' Brett confided. 'I've only been here a day and already I feel like the walls are closing in. I need to escape. You don't fancy a pint, do you?'

In the bar at The Fox ten minutes later, Gabe and Brett sat nursing pints of Guinness and sharing a side of chips.

Brett looked older than Gabe remembered him. The grey that had once dusted his temples had now spread every-where, and the fan of lines around his eyes had become deep grooves. Then again, he *was* older. Gabe calculated that he must be in his early to mid-sixties. But he still had that incredible dynamism; that raw, masculine energy that was part ambition, part testosterone and that had always drawn women to him like waves to the shore.

'How's Tati?' Gabe asked. 'Is she here?'

'No, not this time, thank God.'

Gabe raised an eyebrow. 'Are things not good with you two?'

Brett took a long, deep draught of his beer. 'Things are

fine. You know us. We still fight like two cats in a bag.' He grinned. 'But I love her.'

It struck Gabe that the old Brett Cranley would never have made such an admission openly, despite its obvious truth. Tatiana Flint-Hamilton had tamed him. Or perhaps age had done that?

'I just hate bringing her back to Furlings,' Brett went on. 'It's the same every time: "You stole my house." "If you loved me, you'd get Furlings back."' He rolled his eyes. 'The truth is, Tati's really happy in the States. But she'd rather die than admit it.'

'And what brings you back this time?' asked Gabe.

'The usual. Work,' said Brett, greedily stuffing chips into his mouth. The Fox's chips were the best in the world, bar none: salty and fatty and perfect. 'And some family stuff. Jason and George are adopting another kid.'

'That's great,' said Gabe. Then, seeing Brett's frown added, 'Isn't it?'

'I don't know,' said Brett.

Brett had had a tough time when his son came out as gay, and an even tougher one when Jason got married. Perhaps he was still struggling with it?

'It's not about them being nancies,' said Brett, reading Gabe's thoughts. 'I just think George is too old. Tati still talks about us adopting, but at my age I think it's crazy. Still. Jason's a good father. A thousand times better than I was.'

Brett noticed that Gabe had turned away slightly, lost in his own thoughts.

'How are your boys?' he asked.

'They're good.' Gabe forced a smile. 'They're in London with Laura during the week. I get them weekends and holidays. But I think they're happy.'

'And you?'

'I'm OK.'

Brett gave him a look that clearly said he wasn't buying it.

Gabe sighed deeply and ran his hands through his hair. 'All right then. I'm shit. Life is shit. And, the worst part is, it's all my fault.'

He poured out the whole story to Brett. How he and Laura had been arguing for months. How Laura felt that *Valley Farm*'s success and Gabe's small taste of fame had turned his head.

'And had they?' asked Brett.

Gabe shrugged. 'I suppose so. I could be a bit of a knob.'

Brett laughed.

'But then, you know, I was a bit of a knob when she married me. It seems harsh to suddenly start using it against me now.'

Brett laughed again. 'And Macy Johanssen? Gorgeous girl, by the way.'

'Macy was there,' said Gabe. 'I know it sounds awful to say it like that, but it's the truth. We were in LA, we were pissed as farts, Laura and I had had another barney on the phone. It happened.'

'So you don't have any feelings for her? For Macy?'

Gabe stared into his Guinness, as if the swirling black liquid might hold the answer to Brett's question. 'I didn't say that,' he said softly.

And then he started to talk to Brett about Macy. Thoughts and feelings he didn't know he had until he started saying them out loud. How she'd been a great friend through a terrible time. How he always had so much fun in her company, while he and Laura always seemed to be at odds.

How attractive she was. And how he was pretty sure she was in love with him.

'How was the sex?' Brett asked bluntly.

'It was great,' Gabe replied, equally bluntly.

'Have you done it again?'

'No,' said Gabe. The 'Not yet' hung heavily in the air between them. 'The thing is, I still love Laura. I don't know how to stop loving her. I don't think I want to stop.'

'You don't have to stop,' said Brett. 'And you won't. I still love Ange.'

'Really?' Gabe sounded astonished.

'Of course. She's the mother of my children. We were married for twenty years – twenty good years. She's family. Even if she weren't, she's the loveliest woman on earth. Always has been.'

'So why did you get divorced?'

'Well, firstly, she divorced me. A bit like you and Laura. I fought it in the beginning. I was miserable. I didn't want to lose my family – nobody does. I was scared shitless, if you want the truth.'

'But you loved Tatiana?'

Brett nodded. 'I did, yes. But if you think that takes away the pain, you're wrong.'

'What does take away the pain?' Gabe asked despairingly.

'Time,' said Brett, with reassuring confidence. 'I'm staying up at Furlings now, under my ex-roof, with my ex-wife and her fella. And it's fine. I'm happy, she's happy, everybody's happy. Life moves on, and it *should* move on. My marriage with Ange was a wonderful chapter in my life and a long one. But being with Tatiana is a new chapter, and that's great too. Do you want my advice?'

'Not really,' said Gabe. 'I want my life back.'

'Well you can't have it,' said Brett. 'Not your old life, anyway. Let it go, and give things a shot with Macy.'

Gabe shook his head. Hearing Brett say it out loud like that was shocking.

'I can't. I'm still in love with my wife.'

Brett looked him in the eye. 'I'm saying this as a friend, mate. But she's not coming back. The sooner you accept that, the sooner you can all get on with your lives.'

They ordered more drinks, and Brett dragged the conversation back to less emotive topics. He quizzed him in detail on the ongoing negotiations with Fox, and the complicated finances of syndication. After that they got back to Swell Valley gossip. Before long Gabe had Brett laughing again, filling him in on all the salacious *Valley Farm* rumours, the latest with the Wellesley family soap opera, and hilarious stories about the vicar, 'Call-me-Bill' Clempson.

'I think Jen, the young vet on our show, fancies him,' Gabe told Brett, through tears of laughter. 'Can you imagine? If I sleep with anyone it really ought to be her. Purely as an act of public service. She clearly needs saving from herself.'

'*I* need saving!' said Brett. 'The vicar was round at Furlings today, hitting me up for money before I'd got my suitcase upstairs! I don't even bloody live here any more.'

'Yeah, well. I'm not sleeping with you.' Gabe downed the last of his drink.

'I'll drink to that,' said Brett.

The bell rang for last orders.

'One more for the road?' said Gabe. He was already happily drunk and saw no reason to stop now.

'Nah,' said Brett, getting to his feet. 'Hell hath no fury like an ex-wife woken up by her drunk former husband. Good to see you, though, mate. And good luck.'

Weaving his way home along the dark lane ten minutes later, Gabe thought about everything Brett had said. His deep, gravelly voice drifted back to Gabe now, ringing in his ears in the stillness.

You can be happy again. And you will.

All you have to do is let go . . .

CHAPTER TWENTY-FOUR

Bill Clempson pedalled harder up Wincombe Hill, sweating profusely. It was almost noon on a hot, windless day in the valley, and the sights and smells of summer were everywhere. To the vicar's left and right, hedgerows erupted with honeysuckle and overblown Queen Anne's lace, with bright red poppies and blue cornflowers injecting a welcome pop of colour. Sparrows twittered and swallows swooped low over the fields, like miniature, feathered kamikaze pilots bombing the hay bales.

Rounding the top of the hill, Bill stopped to catch his breath and admire the view of Fittlescombe village, spread out below him like a child's toy town. How beautiful it was here! How easy to believe in God, and goodness and a divine order. Of course recently village life – Bill's life anyway – had been given an added *frisson* by the possibility of running into the lovely Jennifer Lee. Last week, *Valley Farm*'s vet-in-residence had finally taken the vicar up on his offer of a drink. Although the evening had ended with a platonic, even reverend kiss on the cheek, Bill flattered himself that there was something there. A spark, for want of a better word. Just knowing that he might run into Jennifer – outside Wraggsbottom Farm or in the village stores – injected a little kick of excitement and happiness into Bill's days.

It was much needed, to be honest. Having given his all to the campaign against the reality show cameras, Bill felt lost now that local interest in the protest had tailed off. Worse, by continuing to take a moral stand on the issue, frequently referencing the importance of community and of privacy in his Sunday sermons, he feared he might have alienated many of the Fittlescombe flock. And yet, wasn't it a vicar's job to be principled? To stick by what was right, even after it had ceased to be popular?

He felt particularly betrayed by David Carlyle, whose newspaper, the *Echo*, had dropped the anti-*Valley Farm* campaign like a stone the moment it acquired juicier stories about Eddie Wellesley and Gabriel Baxter. The *Echo*'s mean-spirited smear campaigns against both families had left Fittlescombe's vicar looking tainted by association, and had seriously undermined the credibility of the 'Save Our Village' message. To add insult to injury, David had long since stopped returning Bill Clempson's calls, and almost never showed his face in the valley any more, preferring to spend all his time up in London, no doubt plotting more dastardly acts against Fast Eddie Wellesley. It's never pleasant to realize that one has been used. Bill's challenge now was not just to forgive, but to find a new path forward, as Fittlescombe's spiritual leader. *Not easy.*

Pushing off, Bill whizzed down the other side of the hill, sticking his legs out on either side of him like a little boy and grinning as the wind swept his hair back off his face and the meadows and woods flew by. It was so exhilarating, he quite forgot how fast he was going until he turned the corner at the bottom of the High Street and almost knocked a man flying.

'Oh my goodness! I am so sorry.'

Screeching to an ignominious halt, he propped his bike against the wall and rushed over to the man, only to find it was none other than Eddie Wellesley himself.

'Sir Edward!' Bill dusted himself down. 'I do apologize. I was going far too fast, I'm afraid. Are you all right?'

'I'm fine, Vicar. In the pink, in fact!' He was smiling so broadly, he looked as though his face might split in two. 'Another assassination attempt avoided and it's not even lunchtime. That was a joke,' he added, watching Bill's face drain of colour. 'You really should learn to relax a bit, Vicar, if you don't mind my saying so.'

'Er, no. I mean, I don't mind. Ha, ha!' Bill laughed weakly. 'How, er . . . how are things? How's Lady Wellesley?'

'Lady Wellesley is marvellous, thank you,' said Eddie. Even by his own standards, he was unusually chirpy this morning. 'As it happens I've just this second had some rather wonderful news.' He waved his mobile phone vaguely in Bill's direction. 'Piers Renton-Chambers has just resigned his seat.'

'Oh!' said Bill.

Renton-Chambers' resignation had been on the cards for a while. Deeply unpopular locally (even by Tory standards he was seen as wildly out of touch, and lazy with it, with one of the worst voting records in the south of England), he'd been expected to make way for Eddie Wellesley quietly in the New Year. But then had come the bombshell of David Carlyle's book and Lady Wellesley's scandalous past, and the idea had been discreetly dropped. Of course, since then, Fast

Eddie's public popularity had peaked to record highs, and even his wife was getting far higher approval ratings than she had done in her former snob/ice-queen/dignified-victim persona. Rumours had been swirling for months about a return to politics, but Eddie had denied them all. No more, apparently.

'There'll be a by-election in due course,' he explained cheerfully. 'The local chairman just called me to say they want me as the new Tory candidate. Isn't that marvellous?'

Bill Clempson blinked, like a mole emerging into the sunshine. Was it marvellous? He wasn't sure. Around here, Tory candidate meant Tory MP. Chichester and Swell Valley was about as unassailable a Conservative stronghold as you could hope to find in England.

So the rumours were true. Fast Eddie was going to be their new representative in Parliament. Whether that was a good thing, for Eddie or for Fittlescombe, remained to be seen. If nothing else it meant that there was no chance of an exit from the public spotlight any time soon. If Eddie was going back into politics, he wasn't going to be content as a lowly MP. He'd be a minister before you could say 'knife', with the newspapers dissecting his every move.

'Aren't you going to congratulate me?' said Eddie.

'Of course,' the vicar smiled dutifully. 'Congratulations.'

He wondered how Lady Wellesley was going to take the news? Or David Carlyle, for that matter.

Armed with this new, explosive piece of gossip, he pedalled on.

Magda plumped up the pillows in the blue guest bedroom. Throwing open the windows, she let a blast of warm summer air into the room and sighed happily, closing her eyes as the smell of newly mown grass mingled with jasmine joyously assailed her senses.

Life was good now. Better than good. This time last year, she'd wondered if she could face working for Lady Wellesley indefinitely. As much as she loved the Swell Valley and her little cottage and Wilf, and as much as she valued having a steady job that meant she would never have to go back to Poland again, back then everything she did seemed to be wrong. But, ever since her overdose, Lady Wellesley had been a changed person. Happier, kinder, infinitely more relaxed. She still had her moments, of course. Snobbery, in particular, was proving a hard habit to break and Magda still overheard bitchy asides about 'naff' neighbours or 'ghastly little men', whose only crime appeared to be that they wore white socks or used the word 'toilet'. But the old, mean-spirited, toxic, permanently aggrieved Lady Wellesley appeared to have gone for good. More than that, she and Sir Edward seemed madly in love. That was nice to be around. Yesterday Lady Wellesley had even gone out of her way to praise Magda's work, complimenting her on the gleaming silverware.

'I don't think I've seen it shine like that since Eddie's mother had it. Magda, you're a miracle worker!'

Tucking in the bedspreads, Magda smiled. It was amazing how far a few positive words could go. She did get lonely sometimes, with only the Wellesleys and Wilf for company. Milo came down from time to time, and his visits were always highlights. There was something about his energy and sense of humour that never failed to lift Magda's spirits, a bit like having a rambunctious puppy in the house. Milo was always laughing. He made Magda realize that she didn't laugh enough.

The sound of a car engine made her look up. Sir Edward brought his Bentley screeching to a halt in a spray of gravel, hopping out of the car in high excitement.

A few minutes later, Magda heard animated voices coming from the library. Lady Wellesley let out a little scream. *Not more bad news, surely?* Magda panicked. She couldn't take it if things went back to the way they were before. But before she could indulge her dark imaginings any further, the library door burst open and both her employers emerged, hugging one another and smiling broadly.

'Magda!' Sir Edward walked towards her. 'We need champagne! What do we have in the house?'

'And you must join us for a toast,' Lady Wellesley added.

Me? Join you? This *must* be good news.

Magda scurried into the kitchen and opened the fridge. There were two bottles of champagne wedged on the top shelf. A bottle of Tesco's finest rosé, which her bosses drank like water, and a bottle of Pol Roger Brut 1998. Whatever the occasion was, it seemed to warrant the latter. Tentatively setting it on a tray with three glasses, she walked back into the drawing room. Eddie was reclining on the red brocade sofa with his long legs outstretched and his arm around his wife's shoulders. Lady Wellesley had her legs tucked up under her. She looked awfully young, Magda thought, and was leaning into her husband in a manner that was almost doting.

'Is this all right?'

She set the tray down on the vintage naval chest that served as a coffee table.

'Perfect,' said Eddie, who was already de-corking.

'What are you celebrating?' Magda asked.

'*We*,' Eddie corrected her, 'are celebrating my return to politics. There's going to be a by-election.'

'And Sir Edward's going to stand and he's going to walk it,' Lady Wellesley announced proudly. 'There are no more skeletons left in the Wellesley cupboard. Nothing left to hide. It's time to reclaim our lives.'

'Of course, it does mean the house'll get busy again,' said Eddie, handing Magda a glass of ice-cold champagne. 'Lots more entertaining, I'm afraid.'

'And you'll probably have to get used to the press sniffing around again too, making nuisances of themselves,' added Annabel. 'We'll get you some more help if you need it,' she added, misinterpreting Magda's pained expression.

'Oh, that's all right,' Magda said automatically. 'I'm sure I can manage.'

Privately she thought: *No more skeletons in the Wellesley closet. Are you sure about that?*

'Cheers!' Eddie raised his glass to hers.

'Cheers,' said Magda.

She was filled with a deep sense of foreboding.

David Carlyle stood on the platform at Victoria looking impatiently at his watch. It was hot, he was late, and he'd promised Louise he'd be home in time to change before her bloody bridge club dinner tonight. A bunch of old Swell Valley biddies, gossiping about village tittle-tattle like so many twittering birds was not David's idea of a fun night out. But Louise had taken him to task last week for spending so little time down in the country, and he'd promised to make more of an effort.

'I barely see you any more,' his wife complained. 'You're always in London, always working. We're becoming strangers.'

'Of course we're not,' David said brusquely. 'I've just been busy, that's all. It happens.'

But part of him feared she was right. Ever since Fast Eddie had emerged yet again, phoenix-like, from what ought to have been the ruined ashes of his marriage and career, David had thrown himself into his work, desperate to fill the void. Staff at the *Echo* had never known him to be around so much, breathing down their necks, obsessing about every little detail of every day's copy.

So lost was he in his own, irritated thoughts, at first David didn't catch the conversation going on next to him. But as soon as he heard Wellesley's name, his ears pricked up.

'Weren't there any other names in the running?' a fat, middle-aged man with a plummy accent asked his friend.

'No one that could outrun Fast Eddie,' the friend replied. 'He's the party golden boy again. You should see the way Sheila Shand-Smith looks at him. Like a teenager at a One Direction concert.'

Both men laughed. Sheila Shand-Smith, the local Conservative Party chairwoman and head of the selection committee for Chichester and Swell Valley, was a large-bosomed, tweed-clad matron with a whiskery chin and domineering manner. David knew her well and loathed her. The feeling was entirely mutual.

'Anyway, it's official,' the second man continued. 'Renton-Chambers is out and Wellesley is in. There should be a by-election any day now.'

David loosened his tie. All of a sudden he was finding it difficult to breathe. The men's words drifted in and out of his head like clouds across a troubled sky.

By-election.

Wellesley's in.

The odd thing was, he'd known it was coming. Whispers at Westminster had been building to a dull roar in recent weeks: Eddie was an asset to the party. Voters loved him and they needed him back. Even so, hearing his worst fears confirmed now came as a profound shock to David.

The platform started to sway beneath his feet.

'Are you all right, mate?'

A man on David's other side looked at him with concern. David tried to answer but the words 'I'm fine' stuck in his throat and no sound came out. That was when it hit him: an excruciating, indescribable pain in the chest, like a freight train smashing through his ribs. He was dimly aware of voices – 'someone call an ambulance!' – and of his legs sliding out from under him.

Then another crushing spasm, and everything went black.

Within a few days, Sir Eddie Wellesley's political comeback had become the talk of Westminster. As with everything Fast Eddie did, press interest was high. People were particularly curious to see what role Lady Wellesley would play in her husband's campaign and return to public life, and how she would handle the inevitable questions about her past life.

The answer was: directly. On clear advice from Eddie's political agent, Kevin Unger, Eddie and Annabel agreed to appear together on all the morning and daytime talk shows.

'The message is, you're in love with each other, you've learned from your mistakes, and you're both survivors.'

'That's true,' said Annabel.

Kevin Unger smiled. 'That's why it's a good message. You haven't let this break you. Now you want to focus on the good of the country and public service and the *future*. Say that a lot. Future, future, future. You're not interested in dredging up the past, blah, blah, blah.'

And so Milo had woken up on Tuesday morning to see his mother and father sitting hand in hand on Susanna Reid's sofa in the *Good Morning Britain* studio, deftly deflecting questions about Annabel's misspent youth.

'People make mistakes,' Annabel said confidently, 'especially when they're young. But I'm not here to dwell on the past. My husband cares passionately about Britain's future, and I'm here to support him.'

In a pale pink, knee-length dress and cream cardigan, with subtle make-up and her hair loose, his mother looked feminine and *soft*, Milo noticed. Clearly the stylists and image-makers were already at work.

'As you know, David Carlyle suffered a major heart attack earlier this week and is still critically ill in hospital. How do you feel towards David, after all the personal attacks against you in his book?' Susanna Reid asked archly.

Annabel didn't miss a beat. 'As I said, I don't dwell on the past.'

'But he tried his utmost to destroy you, didn't he?' the host pressed.

'We both wish David a speedy recovery,' Eddie chipped in. 'Don't we, darling?'

'Naturally,' said Annabel. 'My heart goes out to his wife. I honestly don't know how I'd cope if Eddie . . .' Her eyes misted up as she let the sentence tail off.

Milo switched off at that point. It was too early in the morning for quite so much saccharine. He still couldn't quite get used to his parents' newfound lovey-doveyness. The political posturing and rampant insincerity were more familiar. *My heart goes out to his wife* indeed! Both his parents despised the Carlyles, as well they might. The fakery used to embarrass Milo when he was younger, but now he understood this was an accepted part of the game. No one spoke unguardedly in politics, not if they wanted to succeed. If anything, he'd become rather defensive, especially of his father. The morning after Carlyle's heart attack, that silly cow Violet from the office had made a snide remark about it being good news for Eddie, and Milo had just about ripped her head off.

'My dad isn't *pleased* when somebody has a heart attack,' he snapped. 'Not everyone's as mean-spirited as you are.'

Violet had pouted and welled up and insisted it was only a joke. Once again Milo had found himself apologizing to her, and overcompensating for the rest of the day at work. Whatever qualities he might have inherited from his father, a cool, unruffled approach to the slings and arrows of politics was not one of them. Every unkind comment hurt. Every whispered innuendo stung. Working at the Home Office didn't help. Now that his father was back in politics, Milo began to wonder whether it wasn't time for him to change careers. Although with a patchy school record and no university degree, the world wasn't exactly his oyster.

A week after Eddie and Annabel's *Good Morning Britain* appearance, and ten days since David Carlyle's near-fatal heart attack, Laura was at home in Chelsea playing Frustration with Hugh when the doorbell rang.

'What on earth are you doing here?' she asked, as a sweating Eddie Wellesley, weighed down with Hamleys bags, loomed in her doorway.

'Is that Baxter shorthand for "How lovely to see you, Eddie, do come in, can I get you a cup of tea"?'

'Of course it is!' laughed Laura, wishing that she'd bothered to put on make-up that morning, or at least to change out of her dirty T-shirt after Luca splattered ketchup all over it earlier.

'You look like you've been in a massacre. Or perhaps you've committed one?' Eddie joked, eyeing up said T-shirt while Laura hustled the boys onto the computer to play Moshi Monsters so that she and Eddie could talk in peace.

'I haven't yet, but I might,' she said, pulling pretty china mugs out of the cupboard, 'if Fox's legal team don't pull their fucking finger out. Honestly, I've never known a deal to take as long as this one. You'd think they were writing the Declaration of Independence, not a simple contract for the US rights to a TV show.'

Eddie nodded sympathetically. 'That's lawyers for you. Paid by the hour.'

'I know, but I'm worried there's something really wrong. This degree of foot-dragging's not normal, is it? I mean Gabe and Macy were out there six months ago. We've had verbal agreement for half a *year*, but still no deal.'

'I know it feels like a long time,' said Eddie, accepting a proferred KitKat while the kettle boiled. 'But from what I understand this is fairly standard, especially with American companies.'

Laura sighed. It *did* feel like a long time. Probably because the Fox agreement had been made the same day that Gabe cheated on her with Macy. In one single, fateful day, Laura's private life had collapsed while her professional life had taken a huge leap forward. Signing the Fox deal and putting it to bed was not only about business. It would mean the end of a painful chapter in her life and the start of something new. Emotionally, Laura couldn't move on until the contracts were signed. Apart from anything else, her and Gabe's respective financial interests in *Valley Farm* made up a big piece of their divorce settlement. Wraggsbottom Farm was Gabe's, but the show was primarily Laura's. Nothing could be finalized, financially, until they knew how much money Fox was paying, when and for what.

'Everyone misses you, you know,' said Eddie. 'On set.'

'That's an outright lie!' Laura laughed. 'But thank you for saying it anyway.'

'Well, I miss you.' Eddie reached out and touched her arm affectionately. 'So much has been going on. I've missed having you to talk to.'

'It sounds as if you've done just fine without me,' said Laura lightly. Seeing him again, here in her kitchen, chatting away like old times, she realized with a sharp pang how much she missed him too. 'Congratulations on your selection. You must be terribly excited.'

'I am,' Eddie admitted, his face lighting up as it always did when he thought about politics. 'I tried to walk away. But there's something about Westminster, I honestly can't describe it. It's like a drug. Luckily for me, Annabel felt the same way. I'd have turned the seat down if she'd said she couldn't face it, but she was all guns blazing from the start.'

'You really love her, don't you?' Laura heard herself saying.

Eddie shrugged. 'I haven't been a model husband. But I've always loved her. We've been together our whole adult lives, more or less. And, you know, almost losing her, after Carlyle's vile book came out . . .' He stiffened visibly. The pain of what David Carlyle had done to his wife was clearly still raw.

'You must hate him,' said Laura.

'I try not to hate anyone,' said Eddie. 'But he's not top of my Christmas card list. Apparently he's going to recover from this heart attack. More's the pity. He's probably propped up in bed now, hatching his latest plot to end my days. Sylvester to my Tweety Pie,' he added mischievously.

Laura laughed. 'Have you seen Gabe lately?' she asked, as casually as she could.

'Not much,' said Eddie. 'I run into him and Macy every now and then in the village, but I'm not on set much these days, and won't be there at all once the campaign gets under way.'

Him and Macy. Was Eddie running into Gabe and Macy together? If so, were they together as friends and colleagues, or was it more than that? Laura was too proud to ask, but even the hint of something going on between them was enough to twist her heart like wet rag.

'Brett Cranley was back in the village recently. I gather he and Gabe were spending time together.'

'Oh,' said Laura. This wasn't comforting news either. Brett Cranley was not what one would call a good influence. *Why do I care anyway?* she asked herself miserably. *We're not together any more.*

'He does seem happier,' Eddie said thoughtfully. 'More at peace with the situation. As do you, my dear,' he added brightly, looking approvingly around the cheerful, homely kitchen. 'I must say it's wonderful how well you've managed to move on, to make a new life for yourself and the boys. You should be proud.'

Laura smiled ruefully. 'I'm not sure that's the word I'd use. But thanks. I do think the children are happy.'

Right on cue, Hugh and Luca burst into giggles in the next room, their laughter blowing away Laura's sadness for a moment.

After Eddie left, she cleared away the tea things and tried

to talk herself out of her creeping depression. It was a good thing that Gabe was moving on. Accepting things. They both had to. Soon the show would sell, the divorce would be finalized and they could all look to the future. The children were happy. She should be proud.

Sinking down onto a kitchen stool, she put her head in her hands and cried.

CHAPTER TWENTY-FIVE

Annabel dashed through Riverside Hall like a whirling dervish, frantically plumping up cushions and checking the champagne glasses for smears. Tonight was the wrap party for *Valley Farm*'s second season and in a fit of generosity and *joie de vivre*, Eddie had offered to host this year.

'It'll be fun, darling, I promise. Magda can oversee everything on the ground and we'll get Atom Events to do the staff and catering and whatnot. Tom Freud's a genius. All you have to do is look fabulous and enjoy yourself.'

Annabel had been sceptical. But the party planners really *had* been excellent, and Magda seemed to be on top of everything. It actually felt rather odd, having nothing to do.

Wandering out into the garden, she let out a little sigh of happiness. In under an hour, the lawn had been transformed into a stunning Titania's fairy kingdom. Tables dressed in crisp white linen sported mismatched vases groaning with apple blossom and peonies and scented stocks. Tea lights hung from the trees in miniature hurricane lamps, and in the rose garden a harpist was practising, her magically soothing

403

melodies wafting through the warm summer's air like a fairy spell. It was understated, beautiful and utterly enchanting. Atom's army of public school staff raced around bearing armfuls of china or staggering under the weight of enormous jugs of Pimm's.

'You see?' Eddie said triumphantly, sneaking up on her from behind and wrapping his arms lovingly around her waist. 'It's all going to work perfectly. People will start arriving in an hour.' He kissed her neck. 'Why don't we go to bed?'

Annabel blushed scarlet. 'Eddie! What *has* got into you? It's five o'clock in the afternoon.'

'So?'

'The house is full of people.'

Eddie shrugged. 'I'll hang a "Do Not Disturb" sign on the door.'

'You're perfectly ridiculous,' Annabel laughed. She looked so beautiful when she laughed. 'Now stop manhandling me and let me go and get changed.'

'Well, what am I supposed to do?' Eddie pouted.

'Have a drink,' said Annabel. 'Relax. Enjoy yourself. It's going to be a simply marvellous party.'

Gabe was late. A ewe had broken one of the fences in the lower field at five o'clock and all the hands had gone home early to get ready for tonight's party, so Gabe had had to fix it himself. Hot, sweaty and in a foul mood, he'd made matters worse by hitting his thumb painfully with a hammer, requiring him to trek all the way back to the house for a bandage and some ice before he could finish the job. Even now, driving over to the Wellesleys more than an hour later, his hand throbbed painfully, despite the four Nurofen he'd taken before he left the house.

Normally Gabe loved parties, but he wasn't looking forward to tonight's event at all. After he'd worked himself up into a frenzy of excitement-slash-nerves about seeing Laura at a formal event, she'd announced last night out of the blue that she wasn't coming.

'I think it could be awkward,' she said. 'And I don't want to steal Mike Briarson's thunder. Or yours.'

'But everyone's expecting you,' said Gabe. 'Eddie, the crew.' It frightened him how crushed with disappointment he felt.

'I called Eddie earlier,' said Laura. 'I think he was relieved. You know Annabel can't stand me anyway.' She tried to laugh but it sounded horribly forced. 'And the crew will all be too pissed to notice. You go, have a good time. It's really your wrap party, not mine.'

Not only was Laura not coming, but Macy, who was coming, was bringing Warren, the obnoxious banker, with her. He'd turned up on set last week, unannounced, and all the girls had fallen into a swoon for him, much to Gabe's annoyance, promptly re-christening him Warren Beatty. Gabe couldn't understand it at all. The guy looked like a fucking newsreader, and he had ridiculous, glowing American teeth. Don Draper, minus the charm.

Worse, things appeared to be hotting up between him and Macy. Gabe had overheard Macy today telling Jen Lee that she was bringing her 'boyfriend' to the wrap party. A couple of weeks ago she'd willingly allowed paparazzi to take her photograph with Warren, walking out of Daphne's together after a romantic dinner in London.

Gabe knew he had no right to be jealous. But that only made him more annoyed. Ever since his drink with Brett Cranley, he'd been thinking more about Macy, trying to

405

imagine what life might be like if they were together. But just as he had moved towards her, she'd pulled away. With his divorce delayed now until the Fox contracts were signed, probably some time in the autumn, he felt as if his entire life were in limbo.

'I'm afraid you can't park here, sir.' A posh child accosted Gabe as he pulled his filthy Land Rover up in front of Riverside Hall. 'Parking for the party's on Church Lane, or in the Vicarage paddocks if there's no more room.'

'Thanks, Rupert,' said Gabe arrogantly, locking the car and marching off towards the garden without a backward glance. 'But I'm in no mood to go for a tour of Brockhurst.'

Stepping through the gate onto the lawn, he scanned the sea of bodies, looking for the bar.

'Champagne, sir?' Another underage Tarquin appeared bearing a tray of drinks. Where did Eddie find all these posh teens? Was there a farm somewhere, breeding them to order? *I'll have a dozen Sebastians and a quarter of a pound of Arabellas, please.* Gabe downed one flute of champagne immediately, then grabbed another, bracing himself to brave the throng.

'Gabe!'

Penny de la Cruz floated across the lawn towards him in some sort of tie-dyed chiffon concoction. She always dressed like a complete dog's breakfast, yet somehow her natural beauty and her kindness shone through. For the first time all afternoon, Gabe smiled.

'Penny! You look lovely. I haven't seen you for ages.'

'I know,' Penny frowned. 'You've become much too famous for the likes of Santiago and me.'

'Hardly,' said Gabe. 'Where is your worse half?'

'God knows,' Penny said cheerfully. 'Chatting up women

somewhere, I expect. I don't think I've ever known a worse flirt. Apart from you.'

'I heard that.'

Santiago had weaved his way through a gaggle of Channel 5 minions to join them. In a white linen suit that only he could have got away with, and a pale green shirt unbuttoned at the neck, he looked as if he'd just stepped off the set of an aftershave commercial. Gabe wasn't naturally vain, but standing next to Santiago he suddenly felt very much the ugly duckling in his too-tight jacket with stains on the cuffs and 'smart' green corduroys, already wearing thin at the knees. His overall look was definitely more old-as-the-hills than Beverly Hills. Then again, this was Brockhurst, not Miami.

'You look like shit,' Santiago observed affably, grabbing a passing waitress and deftly exchanging Gabe's empty glass for a full one.

'Thanks,' said Gabe. 'You look like a pimp. Or an extra from *Miami Vice*.'

'Your co-presenter looks good, though,' said Santiago, ignoring him.

Gabe looked across the lawn at Macy. In a long, backless, emerald-green dress, with diamonds sparkling at her wrists and ears, she'd evidently pulled out all the stops tonight. Everything about her glowed, from her bronzed skin, to her sleek bobbed hair, to her blue eyes that seemed almost luminous sea green in that dress. Standing next to her banker beau, she was talking animatedly to Harry Lister, Channel 5's head of Programming and to Megan Kramer, TV critic-cum-gossip peddler at the *Daily Mail* and one of the most important journalists in the business.

'Who's the guy with her?' Santiago asked.

'Which one?'

TILLY BAGSHAWE

'The good-looking one,' said Santiago, earning himself a scowl from Gabe.

'Investment wanker,' said Gabe. 'His name's Warren Hansen.'

'What's he like?' asked Penny.

'Rich. American. Dull as shit,' summarized Gabe. 'She should have stuck with James Craven.'

'Yes, well, you rather put paid to that,' Santiago reminded him.

'How is James?' Gabe asked guiltily.

'He'll survive,' said Santiago. 'What do we think about love's young dream over there, getting back into politics?' He gestured towards Eddie and Annabel, who were laughing with friends in a quiet corner of the garden. 'They've been glued together all night.'

'I think Eddie's a good MP,' said Gabe. 'And, you know, why shouldn't he stand again? He's done his time, paid the price. They both have. I say good luck to 'em.'

'But don't you think it's rather a risk?' said Penny. 'After all they've been through. What if something else comes out?'

'According to Gabe, David Carlyle's already exhumed all the Wellesley skeletons.'

Santiago raised a sceptical eyebrow. 'Let's hope so. I tell you what, he can't be a worse MP than Piers Renton-Chambers. Did you know the little shit used to fancy Penny? He was all over her like a rash when I came along. Tried to warn you off me, didn't he, darling?'

'If only I'd listened,' Penny joked. 'Laura's not here tonight?' she asked innocently. One look at Gabe's face made her instantly wish she hadn't.

'No.' He downed the rest of his drink. 'I think I'd better go and mingle. Excuse me.'

Penny and Santiago watched as he walked dejectedly away.

'He looks so unhappy,' sighed Penny, leaning into Santiago and entwining her fingers in his.

'I know,' said Santiago, squeezing her hand. 'It's a mess.'

Inside, Bill Clempson sat on a capacious wine-red Knole sofa in the library, sipping Pimm's and listening intently to the woman from Sky.

'We're revamping our reality programming,' the executive was telling him. 'It's an area we've shied away from historically. We never wanted to go too lowbrow.'

The vicar nodded understandingly.

'Channel 5's always had a – shall we say – more "populist" approach than we have.' The woman from Sky smiled ingratiatingly and leaned in closer, affording the vicar an excellent view of her ample cleavage.

Bill cleared his throat nervously. Pushy women unnerved him, especially ones with breasts like . . . was it Lucinda? Oh dear, he'd forgotten already. 'Well, as you know, I've always objected to the intrusion of cameras in the village.'

'Yes,' the woman said archly. 'I heard you were part of the *Echo*'s campaign.'

'Ah, now, no, that's not quite accurate. The *Echo* picked up on our local protest group and offered their support. I was nothing to do with the smear campaign against certain individuals that came later.'

'Still, given your views on the show, I'm surprised you came tonight.'

Bill sipped his Pimm's and put on his forgiving, man-of-the-cloth face, entirely missing the irony. 'I was invited. And, as vicar here, I do think forgiveness is terribly important. Right or wrong, we're all part of one community. And, of course, we're all members of God's family.'

'But you still oppose the filming?' the Sky woman asked.

'I do, yes,' Bill said firmly. 'I think *Valley Farm*'s done a lot more harm than good. Just look at the wrecked marriages, never mind the hordes of tourists clogging up the High Street every weekend.'

'Pity.' The Sky woman looked wistful. 'Because we've been looking to centre a show around a rural vicar. Something that would make the Church more accessible. More real to ordinary people. But given how you feel . . .'

'Ah, well, now, I didn't say I'm against *all* filming,' Bill spluttered. 'Clearly television plays an important part in modern life. I'm all for getting the Church's message across.'

'So you *would* be open to your own show? We were thinking, *A Swell Valley Vicar*. Or perhaps just *Valley Vicar*.'

'If it were the right format, I suppose,' he blustered. His heart was beating so fast he could barely get the words out. 'I mean, it all depends . . . I wouldn't want to be hasty and rule anything out . . .'

'Lovely.' The Sky woman reached into her evening bag and whipped out a pen and paper. 'What's your number, Vicar? And an email address would be great. I'll have one of our producers get in touch.'

Ten minutes later, an already tipsy Jen Lee found Bill still sitting on the sofa, staring into space like a stunned mullet.

'Are you all right?' She sat down next to him.

'Fine,' he said. 'I think Sky have just offered me my own TV show.'

Jen burst out laughing. 'Oh my God, that's priceless. How hilarious! I can't wait to tell Gabe.'

Bill bristled. 'What's so funny about it?'

'Are you serious?' Jen frowned.

'This wouldn't be anything like *Valley Farm*,' Bill said crossly. 'It'd be a chance to spread the Lord's word, not some two-bit, trashy nonsense that glamorizes adultery and makes rural life into a cheap soap opera.'

Now it was Jen's turn to bristle. 'You hypocrite! All your ranting and railing and moralizing about TV cameras in the village. But when it's your *own* show, bring it on.' She stood up, disgusted.

'I told you,' said Bill, 'it's not like that.'

'It's exactly like that,' said Jen furiously. 'You'll be a laughing stock, you know. They're only interested because *Valley Farm*'s been such a huge hit. What are they calling it, *Valley Vicar*?'

Bill blushed and looked down.

'Oh my *God*,' Jen said again. 'It's a spin-off!'

'It is *not* a spin-off. And if it turns out to be, I wouldn't do it. For heaven's sake, I only said they'd approached me. I didn't say I'd . . . Jennifer. Jen!'

But the vet had already stormed off, her long hair flying behind her like an angry comet's tail.

The party roared on drunkenly and in most cases happily. After a delicious buffet supper of cold poached salmon, local potato salad and asparagus, followed by apple and blackberry crumble and an eye-watering array of cheeses, guests took to the floor and attempted drunken versions of the Charleston to the accompaniment of a 1920s band.

Milo, who'd stupidly allowed himself to be talked into bringing Violet Charteris from work (they'd buried the hatchet for the umpteenth time the other day and he'd agreed to take her along to the party in a fit of guilt), had been hoping to catch Magda in a 'quiet moment' all evening, but so far there hadn't been any. Sustaining himself on brief smiles as she flitted from the kitchens to the tables like a distracted moth, he'd been forced to spend most of the night entertaining V, who would insist on clinging to him like a limpet.

'I thought you wanted to meet Gabe Baxter,' said Milo, pouring himself a sparkling water at one of the tables after yet another exhausting round of dancing. 'He's over there, on his own. Go over and introduce yourself.'

'I couldn't do that,' said Violet. 'I'd be embarrassed.'

'I'll introduce you if you like,' said Milo.

She shook her head vehemently. 'It'd still be too obvious. By the way, I was chatting to your mother earlier.'

'Why?' Milo stiffened.

'Oh, you now, just this and that.' Violet tossed back her hair flirtatiously. In a very short gold dress and sixties-style white boots, she looked a knockout this evening, even Milo had to admit. He just couldn't understand why she'd gone to so much effort and then failed to chat up any of the famous, eligible men she'd claimed to be so keen to meet.

'She wanted to know how you were doing at the Home Office,' Violet went on, sitting down uninvited on Milo's lap. 'I told her you were James Garforth's golden boy.'

'What did you say that for?' Milo could feel his temper building.

'Because it's true. And because she's your mother,' Violet answered honestly. 'It always pays to be nice to mothers. In any case, she kindly offered me a bed for tonight, if I wanted to stay over. Wasn't that sweet of her?'

Milo gritted his teeth. He knew his mother was desperate for him to get together with Violet. The Charterises were exactly the 'right kind of family' in Annabel's book. The problem was that Milo wouldn't be sleeping with Violet's family. He'd be sleeping with Violet, who was possibly the most irritating female on earth, after his mother. Those two really deserved each other.

Just at that moment, Magda came past, carrying a tray of used champagne glasses.

'Hold on!' Violet beckoned her over imperiously, draining her glass and adding it to the tray. She looked through Magda as if she were completely invisible.

Mortified, Milo touched Magda's arm. 'Can I help you with those?'

'I'm fine,' Magda mumbled. She didn't want to talk to Milo now, with his stunning girlfriend draped all over him like a long-legged limpet. She knew it was preposterous to feel jealous. The very idea of her and Milo together was laughable, a fact she'd made clear to him on numerous occasions. But actually seeing him with Violet stung more than she'd imagined possible.

'Please. Let me help.' Milo stood up, unceremoniously turfing Violet off his lap. Unfortunately he caught the edge of Magda's tray as he did so, causing it to sway perilously as the glasses clinked together.

'I said I'm *fine*.' Magda glared at him, miraculously righting the tray and hurrying off to the kitchen before anything else could go wrong.

'What a rude maid.' Violet frowned disapprovingly. 'My family would sack anyone who spoke to them like that.'

Milo gave her a look of naked contempt.

'Thank God I'm not in your family.'

He walked away.

*   *   *

Macy leaned back against a mulberry tree while Warren went to fetch their coats.

It had been a lovely evening. Warren had been attentive and looked handsomer than ever in his bespoke business suit. Everyone had been complimentary about the show and her work this series. Even Santiago had come up and congratulated her. For the first time since her fling with Gabe and the breaking off of her engagement to James, she felt as if the village had forgiven her. The thought of moving home to LA, once the Fox deal was done, was bitter-sweet. Macy would miss the Swell Valley.

She also knew she'd looked terrific tonight. She wasn't particularly vain, but every girl had moments when they felt properly sexy, when everything had gone right. This evening's party had been one of those moments for Macy. The mermaid-green dress, the way her hair fell across her face, the glow of her skin, glistening faintly with scented oil. She'd been aware of men looking at her all night – one man in particular. But Gabe had made no attempt to come over and talk to her, or even to catch her eye. If anything, Macy got the distinct impression he'd been avoiding her.

Emboldened by numerous glasses of champagne, and the realization that it was now or never, she walked over to where he was sitting in a quiet corner of the garden, slumped in one of Eddie's deck chairs.

'I haven't seen you all night.' She smiled down at him, trying hard to look unconcerned. 'Did you enjoy the party?'

Gabe looked up at her, swaying above him like a green goddess. Or perhaps she wasn't really swaying? He'd had far too much to drink.

'Not really. I see that you did, though. You and lover

boy were joined at the hip. Where is he, anyway? Upstairs polishing his teeth?'

'He's getting our coats,' Macy said stiffly.

An awkward silence fell.

'You don't make this easy, you know,' Macy said at last.

'Make what easy?'

'Is it because Laura isn't here?' Macy snapped. 'Is that why you're in such a sulk? Because your soon-to-be-ex-wife had something better to do?'

'Laura's got nothing to do with it,' grumbled Gabe, unconvincingly.

'Well, you can wear a hair shirt for the rest of your life if you want to and sit about tearing your hair out and moaning like your life is some ancient Greek tragedy,' said Macy angrily. 'But stop bitching at me for trying to move on.'

'I'm sorry.' For once Gabe sounded it. 'You're right. I'm being a dick.'

He reached up and took Macy's hand. 'Forgive me?'

Macy felt as if a million hot needles had suddenly passed through her body. She entwined his fingers in hers, her lips instinctively parted and her pupils were dilated with desire.

'It doesn't have to be this way,' she heard herself saying. 'You know it's not Warren I want. Not really. Just say the word—'

'Macy.' Gabe cut her off. His voice was gruff with desire too, as he stroked her wrist with his thumb. But there was something else there as well. Sadness. Resignation. Macy couldn't bear to hear it.

'Don't.' She snatched her hand away.

'I want to. I just can't.' Gabe looked close to tears. 'I don't know how to flick the switch and stop loving her. How do people do that?'

'I wish I knew,' said Macy with feeling. 'If you figure it out, be sure to let me know. Ah, there you are!'

Warren arrived. She turned to him with a bright smile as he helped her into her coat. *She's wasted as presenter*, thought Gabe. *She should be an actress.*

'Can we give you a lift home?' Warren asked Gabe politely. 'It's on our way.'

Gabe wished he would stop saying 'we' and 'our'.

'Thanks, but I'll make my own way,' said Gabe. 'Goodnight.'

Watching them walk away, he felt the last vestiges of hope leak out of him, like water through a rusty sieve.

Fuck.

Fuck. Fuck. Fuck.

CHAPTER TWENTY-SIX

No sooner had summer arrived in the Swell Valley than it was over. Magda woke up one September morning to see the beech leaves around Riverside Hall already tinged with copper. When she opened her bedroom window, a cool, distinctly autumnal breeze wafted in, waking her as effectively as a splash of cold water on the face.

Only the day before she'd been walking past Wraggsbottom Farm and noticed that the camera crews were back. Could it really be that the third series was starting filming already?

There seemed to be more of them this time: lots of Americans called Ryan and Justin and Brittany running around the village with clipboards and iPads sounding harried and important. Magda had overheard Eddie on the phone telling people that the Fox deal had now been agreed and the Americans were working closely with the British producers to 'streamline' the *Valley Farm* format – whatever that meant. Macy Johanssen had returned from Ibiza looking thin and bronzed and deliriously happy with her new beau, Warren Hansen. Gabe Baxter looked well too. He'd taken the boys to Provence in August, his first holiday with them as a single parent. Despite dreading it before they left, they'd evidently all had a marvellous time, thanks in large part to Davina, the new über-efficient holiday nanny. Gabe had returned looking rested and fit. A rumour was going around the village that he'd also come back sober. Apparently he hadn't touched a drop since the evening of the wrap party.

Magda thought about Gabe Baxter as she pulled on her clothes and whistled for Wilf. One of her duties was walking into the village for the morning papers, and the old border terrier enjoyed these early trips to the Preedys' shop. Pulling her grey cashmere cardigan more tightly around her against the wind (a cast-off from Annabel, the cardigan was a bit bobbly but wonderfully warm), Magda set off with the dog trotting excitedly at her heels.

She'd lived with the Wellesleys for a year and a half now and had come to adore the Swell Valley, And yet, as much as she felt at home here, Magda was aware that she remained very much an observer. An outsider looking in.

She knew who Gabe Baxter was, and what was going on in his life. But even though he smiled at her whenever they met, Gabe knew nothing about her. To him, to everyone in the village, Magda was just a cleaner.

I'm invisible, she thought. She wasn't being self-pitying. She was simply observing a fact.

She could perfectly well have made more of an effort: joined the amateur dramatics society, or the bridge club, or started going to church. There were plenty of ways to meet people locally, to get involved. But she hadn't. Part of her wondered why. Was it because she was Polish that she felt so removed from it all? Or was she simply too afraid of the ghosts of her past, her unhappy family life, to reach out to others? She felt safer on her own, alone in her little cottage. Most of the time she was content. But occasionally the loneliness got to her. Milo was the only person who really knew her, who noticed her at all. And knowing Milo was turning out to be something of a mixed blessing: lovely when she saw him, increasingly hard when she didn't, and painful all the time because, whatever feelings she might have for him, she had no option but to ruthlessly stamp on then.

I'm the cleaner. He's my bosses' only son. This isn't Cinderella.

Whenever she found herself tempted to reply to one of Milo's hilarious emails, or to flirt back when he caught her eye or touched her hand on one of his rare trips home, she forced herself to remember the stunning girl sitting on his lap at the *Valley Farm* wrap party. Intelligent, beautiful and aristocratic, *that* girl was Milo Wellesley's future. Not a young Polish cleaner too frightened of her own shadow even to get out of the house. As for Milo's feelings for *her*, Magda knew that they were no more than a passing crush, the sort of whimsical notion that young boys got into their heads from time to time.

He'll get over it. He only wants me because he can't have me.

Magda bought the paper and headed home. As she turned the corner into Swan Lane, two police cars sped past her so fast she had to yank Wilf up onto the verge to prevent him being flattened. A third car followed a few seconds later.

Their speed was odd, but not their presence. Ever since Sir Edward had been triumphantly returned to Parliament as the local MP in a by-election that attracted unprecedented national coverage, the police had been regular visitors to his Riverside Hall surgeries, along with various local magistrates, county court judges and councillors. But when two more unmarked Mercedes came gliding along the lane, sinister shadows with blacked-out windows and quiet engines, like two cats about to pounce, Magda began to feel nervous.

This wasn't normal. Something was up.

Her suspicions were confirmed back at the house. A veritable army of police and other official-looking vehicles were parked on the gravel drive, as if a messy child had got bored of his game of cops and robbers and left his toy cars scattered about everywhere. Wilf, sensing a drama brewing and not wanting to miss out, began barking frantically and straining at his lead. Unthinkingly, Magda reached down and unhooked the border terrier's collar, sending him careering off towards the house like a fluffy brown missile.

Inside, Eddie was so angry it was a wonder flames hadn't started shooting out of his nostrils.

Pacing in front of the library fireplace, he shouted at a policeman. A very senior policeman, if the rows of gold stripes on the shoulders of his jacket were anything to go by.

'I've told you,' he roared, 'this is a mistake. All right? A mistake. Now I'd like you to leave.'

'I'm afraid we can't do that, sir,' the policeman responded, with commendable politeness. 'As I explained, according to our information—'

'False information!' Eddie seethed. 'Where did you get it, I wonder? Could your "source" be David Carlyle, by any chance?'

The policeman said nothing.

'This is a witch hunt!' Annabel spat. 'That's what it is. The whole world knows that man's on a mission to destroy Eddie. And now you, the police, the very people who are supposed to protect us, are bloody well *colluding* in it. Worse, you're involving an innocent young woman.'

'Lady Wellesley, no one's colluding in anything,' the policeman said calmly. 'This has nothing to do with either David Carlyle or your husband.'

'Like hell it doesn't!' spat Eddie, picking up the phone. 'I'm calling my lawyer. This is harassment.'

'Neither of you is under arrest, or even under suspicion. At this stage,' the policeman added ominously, while Eddie dialled. 'Our information comes directly from the Home Office. We came as early as we could this morning, to minimize disruption to the family. But the fact that the young lady appears to have absconded doesn't bode well . . .'

'No one has absconded, you ridiculous man,' said Eddie. 'I told you. Magda's taken the dog for a walk, like she does every morning.'

With impeccable timing, Wilf sauntered into the library.

The policeman raised a laconic eyebrow.

'This dog?' Bending down he patted Wilf. 'Because this dog does seem to be very much *here*. Wouldn't you agree, Sir Edward? Whereas Miss Bartosz is very much *not* here.'

A scream, sudden and shrill, caught them all by surprise. Eddie dropped his phone and rushed into the hallway.

'What the blazes do you think you're playing at?'

Magda, wide-eyed and plainly terrified, had been pounced on by two burly officers. She looked desperately to Eddie for help as they dragged her back towards the front door.

'Let go of her!' Eddie shouted. 'She's an unarmed woman, for heaven's sake. She's not a suicide bomber.'

The two officers glanced at their boss, who nodded for them to continue. Ignoring Eddie, they dragged the still screaming Magda outside.

'I'm sorry, sir. This is standard procedure in deportation cases.'

421

'Well it shouldn't be,' said Eddie. 'She's a cleaner, not Osama bloody Bin Laden. In any case, Magda's not here illegally. I've said it before and I'll say it again. This is a mistake. You have no idea how much egg you guys are going to have on your faces tomorrow, Chief Inspector. Then again, you wouldn't be the first idiots to be taken in by David Carlyle's spin.'

The policeman put his hat back on. 'I'm sorry, Sir Edward.'

'You will be,' said Eddie, rushing back into the library to retrieve his phone.

Carlyle had gone too far this time. Trumping up ridiculous charges against a perfectly innocent cleaner, all in a last-ditch attempt to smear Eddie's name.

To Eddie's immense relief, his lawyer picked up immediately. 'Simon. Thank God. It's Eddie. Now listen, we've got a real situation here.'

Outside, Milo pulled up in his black VW Golf just in time to see Magda being bundled into the back of an unmarked police car. Tears streamed down her face. She looked like an absolutely terrified calf being led to the slaughterhouse.

'What the fuck!' He raced over. 'What's happening? Get your hands off her!'

He tried to pull one of the policemen back by his shoulder but the officer shrugged him off easily, like a shire horse flicking away a fly. Milo tried again. This time it was Magda who stopped him.

'It's all right.'

'It's not all right. What's happening?'

'I . . . I think they're going to deport me. I can't go back there, Milo. I can't!' The tears welled up again.

Before he could say anything else, Magda was pulled inside the car and the door slammed shut. Milo watched in mute horror as she was driven away. Within seconds the other cars all followed. Nothing was left but a cloud of dust.

'Did you know about this?'

Eddie's voice, accusing, jolted Milo out of his stupor. He turned round to find his father standing right behind him.

'Know about what?'

'That she was here illegally. That she didn't have papers.'

'No.' Milo looked down at his shoes. 'I didn't know. But after a while maybe I . . . I suspected.'

'You *suspected?* And you didn't think to *tell me*?'

'I wanted to handle it myself. I was trying to help her.'

'I think you'd better come inside,' Eddie said furiously. His voice was almost a whisper but his lips were trembling and his fists clenched. That's when Milo knew he was in deep trouble.

Back in the library, his mother twisted her diamond and sapphire engagement ring around and around and looked at him intently.

'You were trying to help her?'

'Yes,' said Milo.

'Even though you knew she'd lied to us? That she'd put your father's career at risk? It was *Magda* you were concerned about?'

'Yes!' Milo defended himself. 'You don't know her, Mum. Neither of you does. She had a terrible childhood. Her dad was a drunk, abusive. All she ever wanted was a normal life, away from Poland. A fresh start. She works hard. Isn't she the sort of person we should *want* to come to Britain?'

Eddie sighed deeply. It was a titanic effort to keep his temper.

'You're missing the point. I'm an MP, Milo. I can't employ

an illegal immigrant. The fact that I have, unwittingly or not . . . it's a disaster. It's the end. And *you* could have prevented it!'

'By getting Magda sacked?'

'She's a charwoman!' Annabel exploded. 'What on earth is *wrong* with you?'

Milo looked at his mother with naked contempt. 'Being a cleaner is Magda's job. It's not who she is. She's an incredible woman.'

'God give me strength . . .' muttered Eddie.

'I love her,' Milo said baldly. 'I'm in love with her.'

Annabel burst into laughter.

'Laugh all you want,' Milo said furiously. 'But I'm going to marry her. I'd have thought you of all people would understand.'

'Understand what?' said Annabel.

'What it's like to fall in love with someone from a completely different world.'

Milo glared at his mother defiantly. It was an unspoken rule, since Annabel's overdose, that the past, *her* past, was never mentioned or even alluded to. But her hypocrisy was too much for Milo to bear.

To his surprise, however, she reacted calmly.

'You're right,' she said. 'I do know what it's like. And I can tell you it is damned hard. *Damned* hard. You have no idea what you're signing up for, Milo.'

He turned to go but she called after him, her voice rising and ringing with emotion.

'I'll tell you something else, Milo. When *I* made those sacrifices, I made them in pursuit of a better life, not a worse one. Your father *was* from a different world, but it was a better world than the one I crawled out from. It was a world worth striving for, a life worth striving for! I wanted a better life for myself then, just like I want a better life for you now. So if you think I'm going to sit back and watch my only child crawl back into the bloody abyss that I've spent my life escaping, by marrying a penniless, immigrant *char*, you can think again!'

'I don't know what to tell you,' said Milo, 'except you're wrong. I'm leaving now.'

He stormed out.

'Hold on.' Eddie ran after him. 'Where are you going?'

'What do you care?' snapped Milo. He didn't want to admit how much the exchange with his mother had shaken him. He knew that in her own, warped way, she was trying to show him love. But she was wrong about Magda, so wrong he didn't know where to start.

'Don't be childish,' said Eddie. 'Of course I care. We both do.'

'If you really want to know,' Milo said grimly, 'I'm going to see the person who turned Magda in.'

The colour drained from Eddie's face.

'For God's sake, don't! The damage is done, Milo. Magda will be deported and I'll have to resign. If you try to confront Carlyle, he'll have you done for harassment, or assault. Do you want to go to jail? Milo? Milo!'

The black Golf was already tearing off down the drive.

Louise Carlyle was making a pot of tea when the phone rang.

'This is Eddie Wellesley.'

'Oh! Er . . . hello.'

'Is David home?'

Louise hesitated. David was home, watching the golf in

the family room. But he'd been so much better recently, so much calmer and happier. She didn't think she could bear it if the feud between him and Eddie Wellesley started up again.

'I know you must be worried about him.' Eddie's voice sounded calm and kind. 'But it really is important that I speak to him. It'll only take a couple of minutes.'

Reluctantly, Louise took the phone through to David.

'Eddie Wellesley, my arse. Who is this?' David barked.

When he realized it really was Eddie, he was too shocked to do anything but listen.

'I had nothing to do with it,' he said, once Eddie finally stopped talking.

'Oh, come *on*, Carlyle. We're both too long in the tooth for these games.'

'I mean it,' said David. 'I know nothing about your cleaner, Wellesley. If it *had* been me, don't you think I'd be shouting it from the rooftops?'

This was a good point. Even so, Eddie wasn't sure whether he believed him.

'My son, Milo, is on his way to you,' he said. 'Milo's very fond of Magda and his blood's up. I suggest you keep your gates firmly closed.'

'Are you threatening me?' David's voice took on a harder edge.

'Of course not. I'm warning you, you fool,' said Eddie. 'Perhaps I shouldn't have bothered.'

He hung up.

'What was all that about?' asked Louise, returning with two mugs of tea.

David looked at her blankly. 'I have absolutely no idea. But I *think* Eddie Wellesley might be about to resign.'

'But . . . he was only just re-elected.'

'I know.' David broke into a grin. 'Marvellous, isn't it?'

Magda was silent as the female guard led her down a long, windowless corridor. The staff at the detention centre had actually been kind, but the place itself was awful. Peeling paint on the walls, too-bright strip lights that buzzed like dying flies above one's head and the smell of burned hopes in the air.

Magda was led into a room full of women and children. Part dormitory, part living room, it had metal bunks stacked against the walls and a television blaring in one corner that no one was watching. Nobody so much as glanced up at Magda.

'This is your bunk.'

The stripped bed in the corner of the room had a blanket, sheet and tiny pillow wrapped in Cellophane at the end of it, the sort you get on a plane.

'You'll be interviewed in the morning. The Home Office will send someone down to talk to you. Supper's at six, lights out at nine, toilets are through that door. Any questions?'

Magda shook her head.

Too numb to speak, she was still in shock. Somewhere on the long drive east to Folkestone, all the fight had drained out of her.

Deep down she'd always known this day would come eventually. As soon as Sir Edward Wellesley had decided he was going back into politics, she'd known it would only be a matter of time before someone found out. And yet she'd dared to hope, to believe, that if she kept her head down and herself to herself, that perhaps the storm would pass over her this time. That she'd be safe.

She'd thought about leaving many times. She *should* have left, for Sir Edward's sake, if not her own. But she couldn't do it. She realized with shame that Milo was the reason. Somewhere along the line, as ridiculous as it was, Magda had fallen in love with him. His laugh, his smile, his occasional kind words, tossed casually in her direction. In her loneliness, she'd allowed those things to mean too much. She'd allowed them to mean everything.

And now it was all over. Not just the fantasy, but her entire life in England, the life she'd worked so hard to build for so long.

She was being sent back to Poland. Back to hell.

Milo would never speak to her again.

I brought all this on myself.

Too tired even to cry, Magda lay back on the bunk and stared at the bed above her.

Violet Charteris was just heading out for lunch in Belgravia when Milo turned up at her flat.

'Darling!' She flung open the door and smiled, tossing back her newly washed blonde hair. 'What a lovely surprise.'

In a sexy, dark green dress that brought out the colour of her eyes, and knee-high suede boots, Violet knew she looked good. Milo, however, was clearly in no mood to be charmed.

'It was you, wasn't it?'

'What was me?' Violet asked innocently. Leading him into the drawing room of her stunning flat, she sank down onto the antique Knole sofa and invited Milo to do the same.

'You told immigration about Magda.'

'Oh. That.' Violet rolled her eyes. 'I might have said something.'

'You *did* say something, you stupid bitch!' Milo shouted at her. 'Why?'

'Why not?' Violet shouted back. 'She was breaking the law, Milo. I guessed something was up when I saw you snooping around about Poland at work.'

'You went on my computer?'

'It's not *your* computer. It's the office computer. And you were the one doing something shady, not me. In case you hadn't noticed, we work for the Home Secretary, Milo. We can't go around protecting illegal immigrants just because you happen to have the hots for your parents' cleaning lady!'

Milo stepped forward, looming over Violet like a giant oak tree about to fall. Looking down at her pretty, spiteful, doll-like face, he felt an overwhelming urge to smash his fist into it.

'You have no idea what you've done,' he hissed at her.

'Actually, I do. I've done the right thing.' Violet stuck out her chin defiantly. 'And I've done you a favour. I love you, Milo. I want to be with you. This ridiculous obsession had to end some time.'

Bending down, Milo put his face very close to Violet's. It took a supreme effort of will not to hit her.

'I wouldn't sleep with you now if you were the last woman on earth,' he said venomously. 'You make me physically sick.'

Turning on his heel, he stormed out of her flat.

CHAPTER TWENTY-SEVEN

Eddie stared out of the window of his first-class carriage as the train rattled through the wintry Sussex countryside. Last November had been nothing but rain, but this year the cold was back with a vengeance, plunging Southern England into a deep, almost Nordic frost. Bare trees shivered in the bitter wind, while stiffened blades of grass made the fields look oddly static, sparkling grey-white beneath an ice-blue sky.

Usually Eddie loved this sort of crisp winter weather. But today he was too worried to enjoy it properly. Neither he nor Annabel had heard from Milo in almost a month. Magda had been deported back to Poland in October. The next day Milo had resigned from the Home Office in disgust, precipitating a fairly spectacular row with his mother. Eddie had given things a few days to calm down before dropping in at Milo's London flat. But Milo wasn't in – not then or on any of the subsequent occasions Eddie called. His mobile phone went straight to message, and a few worried phone calls established that none of his old friends had heard from him either.

Panicked, Annabel had insisted on calling the police. But as Milo was an adult and there was no reason to believe he was in any immediate danger, there was little they could do.

'He wouldn't be the first young man to get a bee in his bonnet after a row with mum and dad and go off on his own for a bit,' the policeman told Annabel. 'He'll turn up. Probably when he wants some money,' he joked. But Annabel wasn't in the mood for joking.

Eddie was worried about her, too. He'd resigned his seat back in September, as soon as it had become clear that the case against Magda was watertight.

'She's illegal. We employed her. That's that,' he said stoically. 'Ignorance is no defence under the law, and even less of a defence in politics. It's over.'

He waited for the feelings of anger and disappointment and loss to hit him, but oddly they never did. Perhaps because of all the ups and downs of the last few years, Eddie found he was strangely detached about this latest blow. But Annabel took it badly. Eddie watched with alarm as she began to lose weight and withdraw again socially. He'd come so close to losing her last time, the prospect of it happening again filled him with utter dread. He found himself becoming furious with Milo, for disappearing in a melodramatic sulk just when his mother needed him the most.

Ironically, as so often in Eddie's life, while one area of his life was imploding, another had begun to blossom. He had barely given *Valley Farm* a thought for months, but now the lawyers had finally thrashed out a deal with Fox. Eddie was on his way to London now to sign papers that would make him a considerably richer man. Macy would move back to the States in January to front the new US show, and the search was already under way for a replacement UK presenter. If the American version was a success, plans were already afoot to roll out the format in other territories across Europe and Asia. There was so much to look forward to. If only Eddie could convince Annabel to look forward instead of back and to embrace their new future.

Outside the train window, grimy Victorian terraces had replaced the frosted fields. They were already in London, and Eddie hadn't even noticed. Time seemed to race by so quickly these days. Blink, and everything had changed.

An unusually melancholy Eddie got off at Victoria and hailed a cab to Fox's Shepherd's Bush offices.

'Didn't you used to be Eddie Wellesley?' the cabbie asked guilelessly.

Eddie grinned. He'd got into a frightful habit of taking life seriously. Hopefully seeing the lovely Laura Baxter again would snap him out of it.

Laura felt her stomach flip over with nerves and regretted not eating breakfast this morning. She'd been in a rush to get the boys off to school – every Monday morning was the same mad panic of missing shoes, lost reading books and Marmite-stained ties – but she was also too stressed to eat. Which was weird, as today's meeting at Fox was a formality and a celebration more than anything. It had taken the best part of a year, but all the tough negotiating had been done. All Laura, Gabe and Eddie had to do today was sign their contracts and raise a glass to the next glorious chapter in the *Valley Farm* story.

Except that for Laura and Gabe, it meant more than that. Once they signed the Fox deal, their divorce could finally go through. Again, this was a good thing. This was closure, something they both needed. But, annoyingly, Laura's body stubbornly refused to celebrate. In the lift at Fox's offices, her palms were sweating as she pressed the button for the fifth floor. Her stomach was making awful noises, her heart was pounding and she had a horrible feeling that blood was rushing unattractively to her cheeks.

'May I help you?'

The girl at the fifth-floor reception smiled politely as Laura approached the desk.

'Laura Baxter. I'm here for a meeting with Steve Levenson.'

'Oh, yes. If you'd like to come through? Your colleagues are here already. Steve's on his way.'

Laura's 'colleagues', Gabe and Eddie, both smiled broadly when she walked into the meeting room. For the first time all morning, she found herself relaxing a little.

'Laura!' Eddie hugged her first. 'You look divine, as ever. I can't quite believe this day has come, can you?'

'No.' She hugged him back. 'Where's the fat lady? And the singing?'

'I'll sing if you like,' said Gabe, kissing her on the cheek. 'The hills are alive, with the sound of mon-eee!'

In a dark wool suit with a navy-blue shirt and striped silk tie, he looked unusually formal and disarmingly handsome. Laura wondered slightly desperately if she would ever stop fancying him.

'When Levenson gets here, let's play a game. The first one of us to get the word "discombobulate" into a sentence has to buy the other two lunch at the Connaught afterwards. With very, very expensive wine.'

He seems so happy, Laura thought. The mischievous twinkle in his eye was back, the one she hadn't seen since the old days, before *Valley Farm*, before the cameras and the fame and Macy Johanssen, before it all went wrong.

'No games,' she said sternly. 'And no discombobulating the Americans. Let's for God's sake just sign the papers, take our cheques and get out of here. Before they change their minds!'

'Hear, hear,' said Eddie.

'Spoilsport,' said Gabe. 'You do look lovely,' he added, throwing Laura completely and making her blush crimson at the very moment that the Fox executives walked in.

'Hello everybody.'

Steve Levenson, a humourless individual at the best of times, looked even more po-faced than usual this morning. Wearing an ugly, double-breasted suit and smelling far too strongly of cologne, he was followed into the room by a string of lawyers, like so many bald ants silently following their leader. Laura noticed that no one was carrying any papers.

'I'm sorry to have kept you waiting.'

'Not a problem,' Eddie said smoothly.

'We've waited a year,' Gabe said drily. 'A few more minutes isn't going to discombobulate us.'

Laura shot him a dirty look.

'I'm afraid I have disappointing news.' Steve Levenson looked at each of them unblinkingly. 'We no longer feel the show is right for us.'

A stunned silence descended.

Gabe was the first to break it. 'This is bullshit. We had a deal.'

'We were in the advanced stages of negotiations, which we entered into in good faith,' Levenson replied carefully. 'But in the final analysis we don't feel that this format is quite what we're looking for.'

'It was what you were looking for last week,' said Eddie. 'What's changed?'

The lawyers exchanged uncomfortable glances.

'You're doing your own show,' Laura said quietly. 'You're ripping off our format, giving it a new name and cutting us out of the deal. All those "consultants" on set this season, taking notes . . . all the legal delays . . . You never had any intention of signing with us, did you?'

'That's a ridiculous accusation,' said Levenson, blushing furiously.

'*Do* you have another show?' Eddie asked bluntly.

'We have a number of scripted reality projects in the works,' one of the lawyers piped up. 'Some of them may appear to bear some superficial resemblance to *Valley Farm*. But that's purely coincidental.'

Gabe stood up. 'This is bloody fraud, that's what it is! You've strung us along for a year, a year in which we could have found other partners, made other deals. And now you think you can steal our format from under our noses?'

'No one's stealing anything, Mr Baxter.'

'Oh, yeah? Well, a court will be the judge of that. If you think we're letting this lie, you've got another think coming, you prick.'

'There's no need for name calling,' the American said primly. 'I can assure you, we're as disappointed as you are that this didn't work out. We've devoted considerable resources—'

But Gabe wasn't listening. Pushing back his chair in disgust, he walked out of the room. Laura and Eddie followed him.

The three of them took the lift down to the reception

area in stony silence. Outside on the street, the cold November air hit them like a slap in the face.

'Fuckers,' Gabe brooded. 'They won't get away with this.'

'They will,' Eddie said quietly. 'Intellectual property rights are notoriously difficult to defend in court. And their pockets are a lot deeper than ours. A protracted legal battle could ruin us.'

'They've already ruined us!'

'Nonsense,' Eddie said robustly. 'There are plenty of other places we can take the format. We just need to be more canny about it next time. And in the meantime our domestic ratings are good. Channel 5 are keen to keep going.'

'I agree with Gabe,' said Laura, belting her black cashmere coat more tightly around her. 'We can't just bend over and let them shaft us like this. It's a matter of principle.'

Gabe put an arm around Laura's shoulder and pulled her in to him. For the first time in a very long time, they felt like a team. Laura's arm slipped around his waist. She squeezed him back.

'You can't afford principles I'm afraid,' said Eddie firmly. 'I'm as pissed off as you are, believe me. But I'm not pouring good money after bad and I strongly advise you both not to do so. We'll all recover. The person who this *really* affects is Macy.'

Macy's name cut the bond between Laura and Gabe like a scimitar through silk. Nothing was said, but they stepped away from each other, the moment of closeness gone.

'She was all geared up to move back to the States with what's-his-face,' Eddie continued, oblivious.

'Warren,' said Gabe.

'God knows what she'll do now.'

'I'll call her,' said Gabe. 'Break the news.'

'No. I'll do it.' Eddie's tone made it clear he would brook no argument. 'I'm the one who got her involved in *Valley Farm* in the first place. I'll tell her. But I'd like to do it in person.' He looked at his watch. If he hurried, he could still catch the 2.02pm back down to the Swell Valley. 'Will you two be all right if I make a dash for it?'

Laura and Gabe watched as he jumped into a cab.

Even now, after this awful, unexpected news, there was something ludicrously chipper about him, a relentlessly positive spring to his step.

Laura looked at Gabe. Part of her wanted desperately to ask him to lunch. To hold on to that brief, lovely moment of togetherness they'd felt, united in outrage against Fox. But the moment was gone, and Laura's courage with it.

'I'll see you on Saturday then?' she said miserably.

'Yep.' Gabe looked at his shoes. 'And at some point we need to talk about next steps. With us, I mean. The decree nisi.'

'Of course,' said Laura. The divorce had been put on ice for this deal that never was. Now there was no reason not to go ahead with it. 'I'll call my lawyers today. You should do the same.'

Gabe hugged her goodbye but it was a perfunctory gesture, back to business as usual. Watching him walk towards the Tube, Laura felt every atom of happiness leave her body, like dust being sucked into an invisible vacuum cleaner.

How had it all gone so terribly wrong?

Back in the Swell Valley, Macy was also having a difficult day. She'd woken up at five with terrible period cramps – never a great start – then gone downstairs to check her emails. Seeing one from Austin Jamet at the top of her inbox, she opened it eagerly, hoping for his usual amusing banter. Instead she read a short but strongly worded paragraph informing her that her father was in his last days, perhaps hours, and was 'literally begging' to see her before he passed away.

Macy slammed the computer shut and began pacing the house. How dare her father try to emotionally blackmail her like this? And how dare Austin agree to do his dirty work for him? For a lawyer he certainly seemed more than usually concerned about his client's personal affairs. She wanted to go for a run to work out her frustrations, but icy cold sleet was pounding down outside and she'd be soaked to the bone. Today was supposed to be signing day with Fox, a celebration. But of course Per Johanssen had to spoil that, the way he spoiled everything good in Macy's life.

By the time Warren called at ten, she'd written four drafts of an email to Austin and deleted them all, before finally sending a two-word note – 'Not Coming.'

'You should go if you want to,' Warren told her, inadvisably.

'I *don't* want to!' Macy was borderline hysterical.

'You could see some houses while you're out there. That Colonial in the Beverly Hills Flats looked great.'

'Is that all you can think about? House-hunting?' Macy snapped.

She knew she was being unkind and unfair. Warren was giving up a lot to move back to California with her. His bank had agreed to transfer him to their LA office, but he'd be earning a fraction of what he made in London and would have to rebuild his practice from scratch. Meanwhile, Macy blew hot and cold. One day she was excited about the move and nagging him to look at listings with her. But the next she shut him down completely. As if not talking about leaving England would somehow prevent it from happening.

A knock at the kitchen window made her jump out of her skin.

'Only me!' Eddie shouted through the glass. He had a thick winter coat but no hat or umbrella, and his wet hair clung to his head like an otter's pelt.

Macy rushed to the door. Behind Eddie, pellets of ice were bouncing off the ground like ricocheting bullets as the sleet turned to full-on hail. 'My God, come in! You look half drowned.'

Eddie stepped inside, shaking the water off his coat and hair like a dog. 'Bloody miserable out there,' he smiled. 'It's like a war zone.'

Macy smiled back. 'Well, it's good to see you.' Passing him a towel from the warm rail by the Aga, she pulled down two champagne glasses from the cupboard. 'How did it go up in London? I assume you came over to celebrate?'

Eddie hung up his wet coat on the back of the door and sat down heavily at the kitchen table. 'Actually, no.'

He told her the whole story. How Fox had refused to sign the deal. How it looked as if they'd been stringing them along from the start. At some point during his spiel, Macy sat down too, her legs weak beneath her.

How could this happen? *Why* had this happened? She knew it was completely irrational, but she blamed her father. Per Johanssen had poisoned things somehow. Like deadly ivy, he'd extended his tendrils of misery across the Atlantic and into Macy's life and choked all of the good things out of it.

She had a plan. She and Warren, together, back in the States. Her career would take off again. Everything would be just like it was before. Before she came to England and met Gabe Baxter and lost herself.

'Macy?'

She hadn't realized that Eddie had stopped talking until he reached across the table and took her hand.

'I know it's bad news. But it's not the end of the world, you know.'

She looked at him blankly.

'You could still move back to America if that's what you want. Begin again over there. Or you could stay on here. Channel 5 are still keen to do a third series of *Valley Farm*. I'm certain they'd take you back as co-presenter if you asked them. You and Gabe could—'

'No.'

The word shot out, like an accidentally fired bullet.

'I can't. I can't go back, Eddie. I can't work with him.'

Eddie frowned. 'But I thought . . .'

'I love him.' Macy stared down at the table, tracing random lines of grain on the wood with her finger. 'I wish I didn't. I've tried not to.'

'I see.' Eddie said quietly. 'And what about this chap of yours? Warren?'

Macy shook her head. 'It's no use. Life would be so easy if we fell in love with the right people, wouldn't it?'

'Yes,' Eddie smiled at her kindly. 'It would.'

He stood up to leave. 'Don't make any rushed decisions, my dear. Try to think of what's best for *you*. Forget about Gabe and Warren, forget about other people's expectations. What do you, Macy Johanssen, really want?'

Macy showed him out and sat back down at the table.
What do I really want?
What do I, Macy Johanssen, really *want?*
If only she knew.

CHAPTER TWENTY-EIGHT

Two weeks before Christmas, a thick blanket of snow fell over the Swell Valley and normal life ground to an abrupt halt. So many teachers couldn't get into work that St Hilda's Primary School closed its doors, leaving the delighted village children with an entire extra week of holiday in which to build snowmen, go sledging and generally get into the Christmas spirit.

At Wraggsbottom Farm the usual December root and vegetable picking was impossible. Instead Gabe and his team spent long days digging sheep out of drifts and repairing walls, fences and outbuildings damaged by the severe weather. The cameras captured some of this for the upcoming '*Valley Farm* Christmas Special'. But they missed a lot too, and Gabe found he was glad of the time alone. Waking at five to give the livestock their first feed, pulling on his wellies and crunching out through a deep white crust towards the barns, Gabe felt as if he were living in a Christmas card, like a Nativity-scene shepherd tending his sheep. Above him, the stars still shone in an ink-black sky. Around him all was beauty and peace. There was a magic to Wraggsbottom at moments like this that couldn't be captured by a camera lens. He loved these moments, although he missed Laura and the children terribly.

Over at Riverside Hall, Annabel Wellesley went through the motions of preparing for the festive season. In the kitchen, she soaked the sloe berries in gin and prepared the Christmas pudding. In the grand hall, she got the gardeners to put up the twelve-foot Norway spruce, and dutifully trimmed the tree with lights and baubles. In the library, she lit fires and put out Eddie's favourite Diptyque Myrrhe candles, the ones that made the entire house smell like a medieval church. But she felt like a ghost in her own house, a stranger in her own body. While the snow on the lawn muffled the sounds of nature, the wind and birdsong, and wrapped everything in a numbing white quilt, so Annabel felt as if all her senses were somehow numb and muffled. As if she were in some odd sense removed from herself, and from reality.

She knew she was depressed. She just didn't know how not to be. What should have been the merriest of Christmases, full of old Westminster friends and jolly political parties, was now set to be a dull, village affair. Even the much-talked-about sale of *Valley Farm* in America had come to nothing. Macy Johanssen was returning to America after Christmas. And though according to Eddie the show would go on, it felt to Annabel very much as if its moment had passed. Gabriel Baxter was no longer the happy-go-lucky family man he had been when it started. The Reverend Clempson and his hardy band of protestors had long since disbanded, and the presence of cameras no longer roused any emotion in the village, either anger or excitement.

Things were no better on the family front. Ever since the

Fox deal went wrong, Eddie had been spending more and more time up in London; supposedly on business, although Annabel couldn't stop herself worrying he might have an ulterior motive. Not that she could blame him if he *were* playing away. He was probably tired of being met with vacant stares at home and climbing into bed next to a zombie. In her current, depleted state, Annabel could no more have sex with her husband than fly to the moon. As for Milo, he had apparently disappeared off the face of the earth, more concerned about the life problems of the family cleaner than his own mother or father and the misery that Magda's 'secrets' – aka lies – had caused.

One Tuesday afternoon, having finished hanging holly garlands all the way up the grand staircase, Annabel sat down in the drawing room with a cup of tea and *The Times*. Eddie had left for London yesterday and wasn't due back till tomorrow. Alone as usual, Annabel had polished the silver, walked Wilf, and continued the thankless task of decorating a house that no one but she spent any time in. Gazing out of the window, wondering listlessly how she might spend the remaining hours before bedtime, she was astonished to see a car coming down the drive. And not just any car. Milo's black VW Golf – filthy dirty and so overloaded with suitcases strapped to its roof that it looked as if it might be about to sink into the ground, was hurtling towards the house at inadvisably breakneck speed.

Dropping her newspaper, Annabel ran to the front door. She hadn't realized till that moment quite how worried she'd been about her son. But as the car came to a halt, the sensation of relief was so overwhelming she found she had to lean against the wall for support.

'Hello, Mum.'

Unfolding his long legs, Milo climbed out of the driver's seat, smiling at Annabel as if nothing had happened. She waited for him to come up the steps and fall into her arms. But instead he walked round the car and opened the passenger door. To Annabel's horror, Magda Bartosz emerged.

'Lady Wellesley. I'm so sorry . . .' she began.

Milo put a protective arm around her shoulders. 'You must call her Annabel.'

'She most certainly must *not*,' Annabel spluttered. She turned to Milo, her relief already replaced with outrage. 'What on earth is *she* doing here? I thought they sent her back to Poland.'

'They did.' Milo was still smiling, an almost beatific look of happiness on his face. 'It took me a hell of a time to track her down, too. But I did it. I found her, and I asked her to marry me, and I'm delighted to say she accepted.'

Annabel gripped the wall more tightly.

'You're engaged?'

'Nope. We're married!' Milo looked adoringly at Magda. 'We didn't think we'd get Magda's papers through in time for Christmas. There's such a backlog at this time of year. But James Garforth kindly pulled some strings and here we are. We've been driving for four days straight, but,' he threw his arms wide, 'we made it.'

Eddie held the phone away from his ear to prevent himself being deafened.

'All right, darling. Calm down.'

'Calm *down? CALM DOWN?* They are *married*, Eddie. *Married*. That conniving little witch has married our son!'

'Yes. I got that part,' Eddie said calmly. 'Where are they now?'

'At The Fox. I told Milo in no uncertain terms that that *woman* wasn't welcome in our house.'

Eddie sighed heavily.

'Well, *is* she?' Annabel demanded. It upset her that Eddie wasn't with her on this. Was she really the only person who could see that Milo was going to get hurt, perhaps irreparably? It was true that she and Eddie had overcome tremendous hurdles in their own marriage of opposites. But Annabel didn't want their son's life to become a similar trial by fire. Milo and Magda had nothing in common, not a single thing. Even if one overlooked the woman's blatant duplicity, surely it was obvious that the union was doomed?

'Magda clearly used Milo to get papers,' Annabel explained wearily. 'Next stop, British citizenship. We have to do something, Eddie.'

'I'm not sure what it is exactly that you think we can do. If they really are legally married, then the deed is done.'

'Well *un*-do it!' Annabel screeched hysterically. 'You still have some influence, don't you? Get it annulled.'

'Darling, be reasonable.'

'I am being reasonable. Has the whole world gone mad? Milo's married a Polish scrubber – a woman who, do I need to remind you, hammered the final nail in the coffin of your career – and you're acting as if it's no big deal!'

'I didn't say that. I'm worried about him too. I . . .'

Eddie broke off. Standing in the hallway at Riverside Hall, Annabel froze. She distinctly heard a woman's voice in the background.

'Where are you?'

'I'm in London,' Eddie answered, just a little too quickly.

'Where in London?'

'At the flat.'

'Who's with you?'

'Annabel, for God's sake, you're being ridiculous,' said Eddie. 'No one's with me.'

'Is it Laura? It is, isn't it? It's Laura Baxter.'

'I have to go.'

'I know she's there, Eddie! I heard her voice. Put her on!'

'I'll call you later,' said Eddie, and hung up.

Walking up behind him, Laura put a hand on Eddie's shoulder. 'Problems?'

'There are always problems,' Eddie muttered.

'Not my fault, I hope?'

'No.'

He turned around to face her. In a wine-red sweater, dark jeans and boots, Laura looked, to him, quite beautiful. She gave him a quizzical look.

'What are you thinking?'

'I'm thinking,' said Eddie, 'that we all need to start looking forward, rather than back. Life isn't infinite. When your time's up you can't flip the egg timer over and start again. It's now that matters. Right now. Today. Are we where we want to be? Are we with who we want to be with?'

Reaching up, Laura touched his cheek. 'It isn't always that simple, though, is it?'

'Actually,' said Eddie, covering her hand with his. 'It is. It really is.'

CHAPTER TWENTY-NINE

Wedged between Penny and Santiago in a cramped pew at the back of St Hilda's Church, Macy wondered again how on earth she'd been talked into this.

'I hate carols,' she'd grumbled, as Santiago practically frog-marched her into the back of the car.

'Nobody hates carols,' said Penny. 'It's Christmas Eve, it's snowing and it's a village tradition. You'll love it.'

'I won't love it,' said Macy, as a woolly hat was unceremoniously plonked onto her head by Santiago and a coat thrust over her shoulders. 'Honestly, I'm not a Christmas person. I have too much packing to do. I can't even sing.'

'Nobody cares!' said Santiago cheerfully, and truthfully. 'This time next week you'll be in sunny California and you will miss this place like hell. You're coming to the carol service and that's that.'

He was right. Macy would miss this place. The house, the village, the people. Warren had been ridiculously nice about it when she told him she *was* going to California, but she was going alone.

'I knew the writing was on the wall. I guess I just didn't wanna read it. I'm a stubborn bastard.'

'You're a lovely stubborn bastard,' said Macy. 'I wouldn't have survived this year without you.'

It was true. Without Warren, she couldn't have got through the days, working with Gabe. Being *this* close to him, day after day, but knowing she could never quite reach him, never occupy the place in his heart that he filled, utterly, in hers.

Gabe was bound to be at tonight's carols, another excellent reason for Macy not to go. But, as usual, Penny and Santiago had refused to take no for an answer. And so here she was, wedged between the two of them like one more sardine in a giant, festive tin. But she had to admit it *was* festive. Reverend Clempson and his redoubtable team of WI battle-axes had done a stupendous job with the church flowers. Red roses, green ivy and plump white mistletoe berries hung from the altar, the deep stone windowsills and the ends of the beautifully carved oak pews. At the back of the church, between the font and the belfry, a simple Christmas tree decked only in white lights bathed everything around it in a magical glow. Clove-stuffed oranges and hand-tied bundles of cinnamon, like miniature fire logs, had been placed in gleaming silver bowls at the foot of the altar, beside the chipped but charming wooden Nativity scene. It was the same one they'd been using in the church since before Gabe was born, and it had to be said that there was a certain seventies vibe to the shepherds' orange and brown striped robes. In one of his rare mischievous moments, Max Bingley had been overheard observing that the figure of St Joseph had a 'rather *Joy of Sex* beard', a comment that had since become part of Fittlescombe village lore. The spices mingled with the smell of burning candles and incense, the combined aroma as deliciously Christmassy as a batch of freshly baked mince pies.

Macy watched the vicar flitting happily up and down the nave, eagerly greeting his parishioners. The church hadn't been so full since Logan Cranley's wedding, but back then the bad feelings over *Valley Farm* had been running high. Now all was peace and goodwill.

'Oh my *God*,' Penny whispered in Macy's ear, nudging her hard in the ribs. 'That's your friend, isn't it? The vet. What's her name?'

'Jenny. Yes, it is,' said Macy, equally astonished to see Jenny Lee and the vicar holding hands in what could only be interpreted as a very couply gesture.

'Are they an item?' asked Penny. 'I thought she hated him.'

'I guess things change,' Macy giggled. 'Maybe Call-me-Bill has hidden talents underneath that cassock?'

'Oh, God, don't. What a horrible thought,' Penny shuddered. 'Speaking of unexpected couplings . . .'

Milo Wellesley and his new wife had just walked in. Milo's shock shotgun nuptials to the Polish cleaner who had done what David Carlyle had spent a lifetime trying and failing to do – ending Eddie Wellesley's political career – was the hottest piece of village gossip since Gabe and Macy's fling. Apparently Eddie was on board with it – he'd been heard in the pub telling friends he'd always liked Magda, despite everything – but by all accounts Annabel had gone into a full-on Victorian-style 'decline' at the news, barely getting out of bed since Milo and Magda's return. Things between her and Eddie were apparently at an all-time low.

'She's terribly pretty, isn't she?' said Penny, as Magda

glided past in a bubble of newlywed happiness, hand in hand with Milo, and joined Eddie in one of the front pews. 'I can't believe I never noticed her before.'

'I don't think I ever *saw* her before,' said Macy. 'Talk about a dark horse.'

The organist began playing the first strains of 'Once in royal David's city'. Moments later a very small boy stepped up to the front of the church and began singing the opening lines in a voice so thin and breathless and pure it brought the whole church to a quivering standstill. But then the congregation joined in for the second verse. Santiago began belting out the words with a gusto and confidence that utterly belied his lack of talent.

'It's the same every year.' Penny rolled her eyes. 'He thinks he's Pavarotti.'

Santiago's singing was so loud and so tuneless that a number of people turned round to see where the awful noise was coming from. Some were scowling, like the furious Mrs Wincup. But others were plainly amused, including Gabe, who smiled even more broadly and waved when he saw Macy standing sheepishly at Santiago's side.

Macy's stomach gave its usual, familiar flip. *If only I'd never met him.*

After the service, Gabe made a beeline for her outside. The snow had stopped falling, but there was still plenty underfoot, as well as treacherous slicks of ice, completely invisible in the darkness. It was only six o'clock, but the sky was pitch-black and the air so cold that it hurt to breathe in.

'I'm so glad you came,' Gabe told Macy, hopping from foot to foot and hugging himself against the cold. In navy-blue corduroy trousers that had seen better days, and at least three tatty sweaters pulled one on top of the other under his Barbour, he looked his usual hot mess. 'I wasn't sure I'd see you again before you left.'

'I'd have come to say goodbye.' Macy belted her chic Max Mara coat more tightly around her tiny waist.

'Would you?'

'Maybe not,' she admitted sheepishly. 'You'll be busy, anyway, preparing for the new series. Have they settled on my replacement yet?'

'Actually,' said Gabe, 'it's not happening.'

Macy did a double take. 'What?'

'I changed my mind.' He shrugged. 'Took a leaf out of your book. I need a new start. Or rather, I need my old start back.'

'So . . . you're not presenting the show?'

'There is no show. I told Channel 5 I want the farm back. My old life, my old rhythms. That's who I am, really. They were pretty good about it, actually. I think they were relieved. It wouldn't have been the same without the two of us anyway.' He nudged her affectionately in the ribs.

'What about Eddie?'

'He doesn't care. I think he's got enough shit to deal with on the home front. Did you notice Lady Wellesley didn't make it tonight?'

They both looked over to where Eddie was climbing into his car, with Magda and Milo in the back. He seemed unhappily lost in thought. 'He's aged ten years in the last month,' said Gabe. 'Like it's all caught up with him at once.'

'What about Laura?' Macy couldn't help herself asking. 'Didn't she mind you cancelling the show?'

'Not really. She still owns the format. She could do the show somewhere else if she wanted. Or sell it abroad. It's none of my business now, anyway. Laura got my share of the production company as part of the divorce.'

'Your divorce went through?'

Gabe looked surprised. 'Yeah. Decree nisi came through two days ago. I thought you knew.'

'Why would I know?'

'I dunno. Village gossip? I had a few in The Fox that night.' He thrust his hands deep in his pockets. 'Anyway, it's done.'

'How do you feel?' Macy asked cautiously.

'Relieved.' Gabe stared at the ground. 'Sad, but you know. Like I say, it's done. The boys and Laura are driving up tomorrow morning,' he added, his face instantly brightening. 'We decided to do Christmas Day together this year. Show the kids that we're still a family and all that. Come to think of it, I'd better go home and wrap the damn presents.'

'Thomas the Tank Engine?' Macy asked, grinning. She remembered Hugh and Luca's obsession.

'No!' said Gabe. 'Would you believe they are totally over trains?'

'Never.'

'I know! Two years bankrupting us with those bloody toys, and now it's all over.'

Macy smiled. They looked at each other and realized there was nothing left to say.

'Good luck, Macy.' Leaning forward, Gabe kissed her on the cheek.

'Thanks.' She kissed him back. 'You too.'

She watched him walk away in the direction of the farm. For all his bravado about his children and new starts, he cut a lonely figure in the dark.

'Gabe!' she called after him.

He turned round.

'Merry Christmas!'

He waved, and was gone.

Penny and Santiago tried to get her to come over to Woodside Hall for mulled wine and sausage rolls, but this time Macy was firm.

'I have to go home and pack. And have a bath, and watch *Ray Donovan . . . on my own,*' she insisted. Penny and Santiago dropped her off at Cranbourne House. It was a relief to watch the two of them drive away and to unlatch the garden gate by herself. Walking gingerly along the garden path – ice and lichen were a lethal combination – she was just thinking how charming the garden looked in winter with its lit-up holly bushes and frosted topiary, when something in the house made her stop dead.

A movement. A shadow, flitting past the drawing-room window. Was it real or imagined? She'd been so rushed when Penny and Santiago hustled her out of the house earlier. Had she forgotten to lock up?

No. The front door was locked. Slipping her key inside, Macy opened it and stepped into the hallway. Everything was quiet and as it should be.

I'm being silly, she scolded herself. *No one breaks in on Christmas Eve. Especially not in a sleepy country village like this one.*

The drawing room was empty too, and unchanged except for the dying embers in the fireplace. Walking over to throw on some more logs, Macy felt a heavy male hand on her shoulder and gave a scream worthy of a Hitchcock heroine. Grabbing the poker, she swung round at the intruder.

A startled Austin Jamet caught hold of the iron rod seconds before it would have slammed into his face.

'Macy! It's me! It's only me. Jesus!'

It was such a shock to see him here, in her house, holding her poker, for a few seconds Macy was too stunned to say anything. When at last she found her voice, she wasn't happy. 'What is it with you and breaking and entering? You can't just walk into people's property. You have to knock. And wait.'

'I'd have died of hypothermia. Do you know how cold it is out there?'

'You could have telephoned.'

'I tried. You never answer.'

'So leave a message.'

'Would you have called me back?'

'No.' Macy stood up and dusted the soot off her hands. 'I wouldn't. Because I don't want to speak to you. Or my father. I thought I made that perfectly clear in my email.'

'Ah, yes. The email. That's the other reason I came in person. That email didn't sound like you.'

'Well, it was me,' said Macy defiantly. 'Angry me.'

'I read it more like sad you,' said Austin. 'Very, very sad you. It wasn't the Macy Johanssen I know.'

'Well maybe you don't know me as well as you think you do,' snapped Macy.

Austin had made himself at home on Macy's sofa, stretching out his long legs in front of him and spreading his arms wide, as if this were a club and an accommodating butler were about to bring him a cigar and a glass of Laphroaig. Apart from Gabe, Macy didn't think she'd ever met a man with such natural arrogance. It was both attractive and deeply annoying.

Austin suddenly leaned forward and said seriously: 'Macy, there's something I need to tell you. Your father's dead. He passed away three days ago in Palm Desert.'

455

Macy did her best to look nonchalant. 'So? I knew he was dying. Now he's dead. So what?'

Austin sighed. 'So a lot, actually.'

'Look, Austin, I don't know what he told you, or what bullshit lines you've been swallowing. But all Per Johanssen ever wanted from me was money. A slice of my fame and fortune, such as they are. Or were,' she added, a touch bitterly.

'You're wrong,' said Austin. 'Do you know how I first met your dad, Macy?'

Macy looked at him suspiciously. 'When he walked into your office and pulled out his cheque book?'

'Nope.' Austin sipped his drink. 'I met Per when I was sixteen. He changed my life.'

Now he had Macy's attention. She'd always suspected there was more to Austin's dealings with her father than the usual lawyer/client obligations. At long last, it seemed, she was about to find out what. Sitting down again in the chair opposite him, she said, 'Go on.'

'I was kind of a hopeless kid back then,' Austin began. 'Venice was rough, like I told you. My home life sucked. At sixteen I was busy getting thrown out of school, shoplifting and generally doing my level best to rob myself of any decent future. Anyway, your father had been invited by the careers department to give a talk at my high school.'

'The school where the math teacher got shot?' Macy remembered.

'Exactly. I can't even remember what Per's talk was about.'

'How to be a deadbeat dad?' Macy quipped.

Austin grinned. 'Nah. We knew all about that already. I think it was entrepreneurship or something. Anyway, I missed most of it. I was outside in the parking lot trying to steal your dad's car. He came out earlier than I expected and caught me red-handed.'

'What happened?' Macy asked.

'Well, that's just it. I was waiting for him to call the cops, or at least to report me to the school administration. But he didn't. Instead he gave me his business card and asked me to come to his offices the next day.'

Macy listened, rapt.

'So I show up at his real-estate offices, this angry, barely educated black kid. And your dad gave me a choice. Either I start working there for free every Saturday and after school, or he tells the school what happened. And that was the start of it.'

'The start of what?'

'Everything. My new life. Those offices became like a second home to me. A first home, really. I learned to type, to file, to show up on time. I made friends. I started believing I could have a future. Your dad became kind of like my unofficial godfather. He paid for my entire college education, Macy. And law school. He was amazing.'

'Yeah, well,' Macy said bitterly. 'Good for you. I guess it's a shame he was such a grade-one asshole to his own kid. He drove my mother to her grave, you do know that, right?'

Despite her angry tone, there were tears in her eyes. Austin leaned forward and took her hand. He knew she might hate him for what he had to say next, but he owed it to Per.

'I didn't know him back then. I'll admit that. But Per told me a very different story about the end of his marriage.'

'I'll bet he did,' scoffed Macy.

'Your mother had a long history of alcoholism, from way before they met.'

'That's not true!' Macy said hotly. 'That bastard drove her to it.'

'She got clean briefly while she was pregnant with you,' Austin said calmly. 'But soon after she relapsed. After that it was chaos. She would disappear for weeks at a time, often with other men she'd met while out on a bender. Your father cared for you almost entirely alone until the age of three.'

'That is a flat-out lie!' Macy shouted. Her mouth had gone dry and her head had started to hurt. Why was Austin saying these awful things?

'It's not a lie,' he said quietly. 'I have medical and court records to prove it. Per kept copies of everything. In case, in future, you ever reconciled.'

For a moment Macy sat in silence, overwhelmed by the raging torrent of emotions coursing through her. She didn't believe what Austin was saying. Couldn't believe it. And yet there were huge chunks of her childhood memories that were missing . . .

Turning on Austin accusingly she said, 'If that were the case, if my mom was the bad guy and Per was some sort of saint, why did he leave me with her? Why did he disappear and never come back?'

'Because your mother threatened to kill herself if he took you,' said Austin. 'She'd gotten clean again by then, but she was still sleeping around.'

Macy shook her head. 'This is baloney.'

'Look, he wasn't a saint,' said Austin. 'Far from it. He divorced your mother because he couldn't take it any more. That was selfish. He was thinking of himself, not of you. He got a job in New York, and he started a new life. I think seeing you or keeping in contact was too painful. But it was the biggest regret of his life.'

'As it fucking should have been!' said Macy. She started to cry.

'Macy, listen to me,' Austin squeezed her hands in his. 'I'm not saying Per's version is the truth. I never knew your mother. And in my experience, when families break down, there's never only one truth anyway. In any case, nothing excuses what he did. But he *did* love you. And he *was* sorry. And he changed. He changed. The man I knew was a good man. Deeply kind. Like I say, I owe him pretty much everything.'

Macy stood up and walked around. This was a lot to take in. Too much. But in the end she wasn't sure if it changed anything. It explained more about Austin than it did about her father. Perhaps Per *had* changed. But if he had, the fact remained it was too late. He was dead. Both her parents were dead. Macy was on her own.

'There's something else,' said Austin.

Macy sighed heavily. 'Do I want to hear this?'

'Fifteen years ago, your father got into the alternative energy business,' said Austin, all business again suddenly. 'Wind farms.'

'He always was full of hot air,' Macy giggled nervously. 'Sorry. Bad joke.'

'He sold his business eighteen months ago.'

She gave him a 'so what' look.

'For a hundred and eighty million dollars.'

For a moment Macy froze. Then she burst out laughing. 'Bullshit!'

'I have all the paperwork with me if you'd like to take a

look. You should, at some point,' Austin said casually. 'Seeing as how you're his sole beneficiary.'

'I don't want it,' blurted Macy. Austin noticed that her hands were shaking. 'I won't touch a penny of it. He abandoned me. Mom and me. This isn't . . . No.'

Standing up, Austin put his arms around her. For a moment Macy stiffened, taken aback. But then she softened, leaning into him, eyes closed, letting his strength soothe and calm her.

'I understand,' he said. 'I do. But you don't have to keep it for yourself. You could give it away. Start a foundation. Do something amazing. With that much money, Macy, you can change the world.'

Macy looked up at him. Without thinking she found herself clasping her hands around his neck, standing on tiptoes and planting a kiss on his lips.

'What was that for?' Austin's eyes widened.

'I don't know,' said Macy. 'I think I'm still in shock.'

Austin broke into a grin. 'I like shock. Can I shock you some more?'

'I doubt it!' said Macy. 'I think you've done enough for one evening. Did Per really leave me a hundred and eighty million?'

'He did. Which leaves me in something of a quandary.'

'Oh?' Macy raised an eyebrow. 'How so?'

'The thing is, Macy . . . I like you.'

For the first time since Macy had met him, Austin sounded nervous. It was really quite endearing.

'Do you?'

'I do. A lot,' he went on. 'I like you a lot. But if I ask you to have dinner with me now, it's going to look as if . . .'

'Ah, I see. As if you're after my money?' Macy finished the sentence for him.

'Exactly.'

'But I already told you. I don't want it.'

'You say that now,' said Austin.

'I mean it.'

Looking at Macy's proud, defiant, beautiful face, he could almost believe that she did.

'I wanted you from the moment I saw you, you know,' he said, grabbing hold of her again.

This time Macy pulled away. 'I can't.' She looked down at the carpet, biting her lip.

Austin looked crestfallen. 'Why not?'

'It's nothing to do with the money,' Macy said quickly. 'I know you're not like that.'

'Well, what then?'

'The thing is I . . . I'm still in love with someone else,' Macy stammered.

'Gabriel Baxter, you mean? No you're not,' Austin said confidently.

Macy frowned. 'Yes I am. I just told you I am.'

'Nope.' Austin shook his head. 'You just think you are. You don't want to be a farmer's wife.'

'Oh, no?' Macy looked at him archly 'What do I want then, according to you?'

'This.' Austin kissed her hard on the mouth. Macy tried to remember why she ought to resist, but suddenly found that she couldn't. When he slipped a hand under her sweater, expertly unclipping her bra, and began caressing her left breast, she knew the battle was lost.

'I'm a terrible girlfriend,' she whispered through gasps of pleasure.

'Mmm-hm.' Austin's hand moved lower.

'I mean it. I'm always unfaithful. I can't commit!'

'That,' said Austin, kissing her neck, 'is because you've never been with the right man.'

In that crazy, joyous moment, Macy believed him.

Eddie's heart lifted when he walked into the bedroom. He'd expected to find Annabel slumped under the covers after the carol service, staring at the same page in her novel that she'd had open since this morning. But instead the bed was made, the clothes tidied away and he could hear the shower running in the master bathroom.

'Darling! You're up.' A cloud of steam enveloped him as he walked into the bathroom. Annabel turned off the shower and stepped out. He handed her a towel. 'You look better. Are you up to joining us for supper? I've carved the ham and Magda's made a rather fancy-looking cauliflower cheese.'

'I won't be here for supper.' Annabel looked at him coldly. 'I'm leaving. Tonight.'

Eddie looked perplexed. 'What do you mean, leaving?'

'I mean leaving.' Pushing past him, Annabel opened the bedroom wardrobes and began to dress. 'Leaving this house. Leaving you. Leaving.' Two packed suitcases sat at the bottom of the cupboard, side by side like squat black bodyguards. Eddie felt his stomach lurch.

'But why? This is madness.' He tried to touch her arm but she shrugged him away. 'I know you don't approve of Milo and Magda. But it *is* their life, and what's done is done.'

Annabel spun round furiously. 'Milo and Magda? You think this is about Milo and Magda?'

'Well, isn't it?' Eddie's frown deepened.

'No, you bastard!' To Eddie's astonishment, she hit him in the chest, hammering both fists against his ribcage as hard as she could. 'It's about you! You and Laura fucking Baxter! Did you really think I was going to sit back here passively, the good little wife, while you had another affair right under my nose?'

'Annabel—'

'Well, you know what? A few years ago, I would have. I did, for heaven's sake! Twice! But no more. Not after this year. I've been to hell and back, Eddie, and I've survived. I'm not going to let you destroy me again. I'm not going to live with any more lies. Not one. Not ONE!'

'Annabel.' He grabbed hold of her more forcefully by the shoulders.

Letting out a scream like a banshee, she kicked out at him wildly, her arms and legs flailing, scratching at his face like a woman demented. 'Let go of me!' she yelled. 'Let *go!*'

'I will not.' Wrapping his arms tightly around her entire body, like a human strait-jacket, he waited for the struggling to stop. Eventually it did. Panting with exhaustion, Annabel slumped in his arms. 'Listen to me,' said Eddie. 'I am not having an affair with Laura Baxter.'

'Liar!' Annabel turned her head away in disgust. 'She was in the flat that day. I heard her, Eddie.'

'OK, yes,' Eddie admitted. 'She was. But not because we were having an affair.'

'What then? Business?' Annabel scoffed. 'You don't *have* any business with her, Eddie. Not any more. I checked with our lawyers. *Valley Farm*'s been cancelled. Something else you lied to me about.'

'I didn't lie,' said Eddie. 'I just didn't tell you. You've been so fragile lately, I was worried . . . I didn't want to push you over the edge.'

'Well, you lied about Laura,' Annabel shot back. 'And you're still lying now!'

Being careful not to release her completely – he was still scared she might bolt – Eddie turned Annabel round to face him.

'I lied to you about her being in the flat. I'm sorry. But I asked her there to talk about her husband.'

Annabel's eyes narrowed suspiciously. 'Gabriel? Why?'

'Because those two still love each other. It's as plain as the nose on both their faces. And because I'm fond of them, I didn't want them to go through with a divorce that I knew they would both regret.'

Annabel digested this information. She wanted to believe him so badly. But she didn't quite dare.

'They are divorced, though, aren't they? The news was all round the village.'

'Yes,' Eddie said sadly. 'Unfortunately, I couldn't convince Laura.'

'But why?' Annabel asked. 'Why do you care so much about somebody else's marriage? Ever since you met that woman you've been obsessed with her. I know you, Eddie. I can see it in your eyes.'

'Then look at my eyes.' Reaching under her chin, he tilted her head up to look at him. 'I'm in love with you, Annabel. I'm obsessed with you. I swear to you, on Milo's life, on my mother's grave: I have never slept with Laura Baxter. Do you believe me?'

Annabel Wellesley looked up at her husband. The thought of trusting him again was terrifying. She looked at her packed bags and the life of calm and peace and loneliness that they promised.

Milo knocked on the bedroom door. 'Sorry to interrupt,' he said sheepishly. 'But we're laying places for dinner. Just wondered if we're going to be three or four?'

Eddie looked questioningly at Annabel, who returned his gaze. When it was just the two of them away from politics, away from the media and the spotlight, they were happy together. Why was it that those peaceful moments never seemed to last? The truth was: marriage to Eddie had always been a rollercoaster, and it probably always would be. On the other hand, it was the only life Annabel really knew. And she did love him.

'Four,' she told Milo.

Eddie's face crumpled with relief.

'But do try to encourage your wife not to burn the cheese crust. If there's one thing I can't abide, it's overcooked cauliflower cheese.'

Gabe didn't realize he was drunk until he took a sip of his fifth mug of mulled wine and realized he'd stirred two teaspoons of salt into it. Tipping it down the sink, he poured himself a whisky instead, grabbed a large handful of Quality Street from the bowl on the table and returned to the mountain of half-wrapped presents on the drawing-room floor.

He'd enjoyed the carols and seeing Macy. In a funny way he felt as if they'd really made peace. But afterwards, back at the farm, a deep gloom had descended almost immediately. Just looking at the boys' toys brought a tear to his eye. Tomorrow they would play at being happy families, and Gabe would give it his all. But that's what it would be: an act. Tonight, wrapping presents alone, he felt the full weight of their loss, like a millstone on his chest, crushing the breath out of his body.

Determined not to wallow, he'd opted for the three-pronged cure of Marks & Spencer's ready-made mulled wine (two bottles), an entire packet of Mr Kipling's mince pies, and Jeremy Clarkson on the telly.

It worked for a bit. But now Gabe's head hurt, the present mountain was both unfinished and moving, and the *Top Gear Christmas Special* was still on Live Pause, because Gabe had put the Sky remote down somewhere earlier and now couldn't find it. He'd have to do some serious tidying up before Laura and the kids arrived tomorrow. They weren't due till ten, though, thank God. If he got to work right after the first feeding at five, he should have the place sparkling in good time.

He ignored the first knock on the door, assuming it was something falling off a hook in the kitchen. Whatever it was, he would fix it tomorrow. After a lot of Alka-Seltzer. But the second knock was more insistent.

Who on earth would be coming round at nearly ten o'clock at night on Christmas Eve? He prayed it wasn't Macy. In his current, drunken state, his powers of resistance were not at their peak, and that was one can of worms he really didn't want to reopen.

Weaving his way to the door, he opened it and was immediately knocked flying by two small, human missiles. Hugh and Luca, both in pyjamas with duffel coats and woolly hats pulled on over the top, tackled him to the ground, squealing with excitement as they clambered on top of him like a pack of hyenas bringing down an elephant.

'Daddy!'

'Has he come yet?'

'He hasn't come yet, has he?'

'Who?' said Gabe, pulling one son to each side of his body so he could breathe.

Hugh gave him a withering look. 'Father Christmas, of course!'

'Oh! Of course. Er, no. He hasn't. Not yet.'

Laura stood in the doorway behind them. In a camel wool coat and boots, with chic leather gloves and her skin glowing from the cold, she looked as beautiful as Gabe had ever seen her. She was swaying a bit, and every now and then there were two of her. But that only made her twice as lovely.

Setting down her suitcase, she pulled two hand-knitted stockings out from an outside, zip-up pocket and handed one to each of the boys.

'You see. I told you. Why don't you run upstairs and hang them on your beds right now? Then you can clean your teeth and get into bed quick sticks. Dad and I'll be up in a minute.'

Gabe stood up and rubbed his head as the boys shot up the stairs, still in their coats and heavy boots, which made a terrific clomping noise as they disappeared to their old bedroom.

'I thought you were at your parents?,' he said to Laura. 'I wasn't expecting you till the morning.'

'I know,' said Laura. 'I changed my mind. Is that all right? I know it's rather at the last minute.'

'It's amazing!' said Gabe. 'I'm so happy you're here.'

Too drunk to hide his emotions, he glowed with happiness like a human lamp. Laura glowed back.

'So am I.'

The two of them stood there, beaming silently at one another like a couple of mute teenagers.

'I had lunch with Eddie the other day,' Laura told him. 'He gave me a bit of a talking-to.'

'Oh?' Gabe tried in vain to stop the hope from flickering to life inside him.

'Yes,' said Laura. 'He said you were still in love with me.'

Gabe's mouth went dry. 'You know I am.'

'And he said I was still in love with you. And that we only have one life, and really I should stop being such a dick and call off the divorce and move back in.'

A terrible silence fell. Gabe cleared his throat.

'He said "dick"?'

Laura smiled. 'He said "dick".'

'I think I was the dick,' said Gabe.

'You were,' agreed Laura. 'That's what I told Eddie. But the thing is . . .' She bit her lip and looked at the ground. Gabe thought he might faint waiting for her to go on. 'He's right. I've tried to do this without you. And it just doesn't work.'

Gabe walked over to her. Tentatively, he reached out and placed a hand on her cheek. It was ice cold beneath his warm fingers, but so soft and round and perfect he could have collapsed with longing.

'What doesn't work?' he asked gruffly.

Laura looked up, blushing furiously. 'Erm . . . life. Everything. Sleeping. Breathing. That sort of thing. I thought . . .'

She broke off again.

'Yes?' Gabe said impatiently. Didn't she know she was killing him?

'I thought we might try again?'

Gabe grabbed her face and kissed her so hard she staggered backwards against the door. It wasn't so much a kiss
as an invasion. His face ground against hers, the stubble
scraping at her skin. His mouth, hot and soft and tasting
of wine and cinnamon and cloves, pressed into hers until
they were one body, one being. Laura responded in kind,
running her hands over his body like a blind woman,
drinking in every inch of him, delirious with longing and
relief.

Finally pulling away, Gabe grabbed her hand and pulled
her into the drawing room. Despite his neglect, a fire was
still burning in the grate. He began rummaging through the
stacks of paper scattered on the coffee table.

'This place is a tip!' said Laura.

'Shhh,' said Gabe, still rummaging.

'And can we please turn off James May? What have you
done with the controller?'

'Shut *up*!' said Gabe. 'Ah. Here it is.'

Pulling out the decree nisi, he passed it to Laura, keeping
hold of one end of the paper himself. 'Let's do it together,
shall we?'

Laura smiled. 'Yes. Let's.'

Walking over to the fire, they held the document over
the flames.

'One. Two.'

'Three,' said Laura.

They watched together as it fluttered down onto the
burning logs, curled up and blackened at the corners, then
exploded all at once into a bright, white flame.

'What are you *doing*?' Hugh and Luca appeared behind
them, hopping up and down in their pirate pyjamas. 'You
said you'd come up. He could be here *any minute*!'

'Sorry,' said Gabe, clasping Laura's hand. 'Mummy and I got a bit distracted.'

'We're coming now,' said Laura.

Following their children up the stairs, hand in hand, Laura and Gabe looked at each other and realized there was nothing left to wish for.

Christmas had already come.

If you've enjoyed

THE
SHOW...

Find out where
it all began . . .

The Swell Valley short stories

Available to buy now

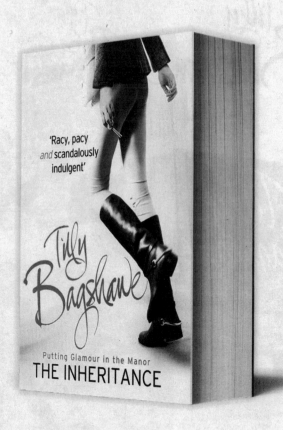

Read more from

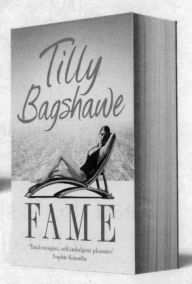

Tracy Whitney – Sidney Sheldon's
most popular and enduring heroine –
is back again in the sensational and
gripping follow-up to

CHASING TOMORROW

Sidney Sheldon's
Reckless

by

TILLY BAGSHAWE

Coming October 2015

Master storyteller Sidney
through

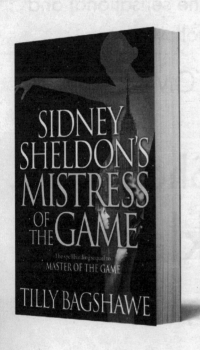

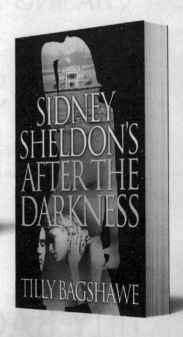

Sheldon's legacy continues
Tilly Bagshawe

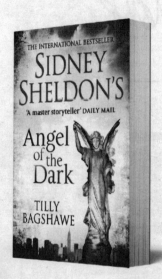

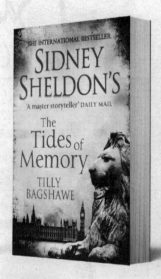

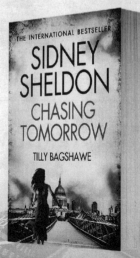

Keep up to date with

www.tillybagshawe.com